Of course the first person she ran into was Daniel.

As she approached, they glared at each other. He didn't like her any more than she liked him. He seemed to think she was a spoiled rich girl who'd never struggled a day in her life. She didn't have much use for doctors per se, especially good-looking ones, after her experience with Nick, but if he was going to have the credentials, she thought it was self-indulgent, even selfish, of him not to use those talents. Egotism, either way.

Then, at the same time, they both started to say, "I had a dream . . ."

She slapped a hand over her mouth with horror at her inadvertent admission.

"Oh, crap!" he said. "We had dreams about each other, didn't we? The same dream."

"I don't know what you're talking about."

He snorted his disbelief.

"Bite me!"

"Seems I already did."

THE
CAJUN
DOCTOR

A Cajun Novel

SANDRA
HILL

AVONBOOKS

An Imprint of HarperCollinsPublishers

HarperCollins
PUBLISHERS
Since 1817

Excerpt from *Cajun Crazy* copyright © 2017 by Sandra Hill.

THE CAJUN DOCTOR. Copyright © 2017 by Sandra Hill. All rights reserved. Printed in the United States of America. No part of this book may be used or reproduced in any manner whatsoever without written permission except in the case of brief quotations embodied in critical articles and reviews. For information, address HarperCollins Publishers, 195 Broadway, New York, NY 10007.

First Avon Books mass market printing: June 2017

ISBN 978-0-06-256636-2

17 18 19 20 21   QGM   10 9 8 7 6 5 4 3 2 1

This book is dedicated to my good friend and critique partner, Cindy Harding, who was a godsend in the writing of this book.

In the course of my twenty-year novel writing career, I had two critique partners who died, way too young, and other critique partners, who have come and gone. Relocations. Bad fits. Work commitments. But always, Cindy has been there.

A most remarkable woman, Cindy is an extremely talented writer, of course. Look for her books in the future. She writes wonderful women's fiction. But more than that, she has a knowledge and expertise in so many things that flesh out her own books and add to the color and details of mine.

Most important, she is a wife and mother of five children. She lives on and runs a farm. Yes, she is up at the crack of dawn to take care of cows (many, many cows), and, yes, she has birthed more than a few calves, and yes, she sometimes has to cancel critique for "haying," or mowing fifty acres (an exaggeration, but not by much), but then she does so much more.

- She maintains the tradition of all the generations of women in her family by visiting all the family graves on Memorial Day where they discuss the history of each individual and lay flowers. Oral history, so to speak.
- She occasionally makes personality-specific floral wreaths for coffins. I know, weird. But interesting.
- She paints landscapes and then paints walls, as well, in the 200-year-old farmhouse she re-

stored. Only Cindy would know about a designer paint that probably cost about a thousand dollars and went on the consistency of oatmeal. Did I mention she ran a kitchen redecorating business for awhile?

- She knows all about weapons and teaches a course on "Women and Guns."
- She has a son who does rodeo, so she therefore can tell you anything about the rodeo circuit.
- She owns a beautiful fawn-colored Belgian draft horse and can tell you more than you ever wanted to know about horses in general.
- She recently arranged an elegant "Afternoon Tea on the Farm," for a friend's wedding shower, complete with china and fine tablecloths, and then she provided the floral arrangements for the wedding reception tables from her own flower garden.
- She is an avid antiquer, like me, accompanying me to many an estate auction, and regaling me with all her incidental knowledge on so many subjects. Who else would consider buying a $700 poster of a cow?
- She has a love of purebred bulldogs.
- She has lived among the Amish and often hires them. There isn't anything she doesn't know about the Plain People.

No wonder her husband Jeff surprised her with a BMW convertible for their last anniversary. He knows the treasure he has.

So, if I ever write an artist heroine who likes elegant teas and antique china, but can stick her arm up a cow's butt to help with a breech delivery, and shoot a target with a rifle at fifty paces, who falls in love with a cowboy who can ride rodeo as well as a tractor, when he isn't riding his Belgian draft horse around his farm or a BMW up the lane where a bulldog is barking . . . well, you can be sure I got the details just right.

Thanks for all your help and humor over the years, Cindy.

Chapter One

The Big C strikes again . . .

The first time Dr. Daniel LeDeux met ten-year-old Deke Watson, Deke asked him what it felt like to have sex. The second time they met, Deke asked what it felt like to die.

Lying back in one of a dozen leather reclining chairs at the Juneau, Alaska Pediatric Medical Center, with a first dose of chemo blasting into his IV, Deke looked like any other pre-adolescent kid, iPod blaring in his ear, baseball cap turned backward on his head, freckles dotting his pug nose, a wide mischievous grin on his face. He was a little on the thin side, having been feeling lousy for a long time and only recently diagnosed with Chronic Myelogenous Leukemia. CML.

"Seriously, if I'm gonna die from this crud, I'd like ta

know what it's like ta boink a girl." He batted his stubby eyelashes at Daniel with fake innocence.

Boink?

Deke was joking, of course. At this stage, he was full of hope for a complete remission, as he should be. No time, or need, for fearing death. As a pediatric oncologist, Daniel had seen hundreds of cases, many of which defied the odds for survival. No need for a miracle here. Unless Deke's CML morphed into AML, Acute Myelogenous Leukemia, his chances were good. Deke's question was a blatant guilt trip ploy to get some info Daniel might not otherwise be inclined to share.

While Daniel checked his patient's pulse and heart rate, he said, "I think those kinds of questions should be put to your dad, don't you?"

"Sure. If I had one!"

Daniel arched his brows.

"He skipped out when I was five. Cokehead."

Daniel nodded. Not an unusual story. He recalled now that Deke's mother, Bethany Watson, a special ed teacher, had been raising him single-handedly for a long time. Dealing with childhood cancer was a kick in the gut for a couple; it was a body blow for one parent to handle alone. He had to admire her bravery.

"If you don't wanna give me the goodies . . ."

"Goodies?"

"The details about sex," Deke explained. "You could always just give me a *Playboy* magazine . . . you know, if you're too shy to talk about sex. One of the old magazines, not one of the new PG versions." More batting of eyelashes.

Daniel laughed. "Nice try, kiddo."

"My buddy Chuck says it feels like every hair on your body is doin' the hula, and your cock is like a train racing to the finish line."

Cock? A ten-year-old using that word? Daniel shouldn't be surprised. Kids today knew things that would have been shocking twenty years ago. Still, he stopped checking the latest white cell count on Deke's chart to stare at him. "Chuck has had a lot of sex, huh?" Now, that *would* shock him.

Deke ducked his head sheepishly. "Nah! He's only ten, too, but he *has* seen a *Playboy* magazine. *Three* of them. The good ones, too. He has older brothers."

"Wow! A man of experience!" Daniel could remember the time his identical twin, Aaron, now a pilot, had shown him a stash of *Playboy* magazines he'd hidden under his mattress . . . a cool trade scored with AJ Coddington for five Snicker bars and a Big Blaster water pistol. Come to think of it, they'd been about ten, too . . . more than twenty years ago.

That evening he went to his mother Dr. Claire Doucet's house for dinner. Already he could hear Barry Manilow crooning through the sound system he and Aaron had given her for a Christmas gift last year. Big mistake, that. Now they got to hear Barry in every room of the house and outdoors on the patio. Their mother and Melanie Yutu, her longtime significant other, best known to them as Aunt Mel, had attended dozens of the crooner's concerts . . . thought nothing of flying cross-country, one end of the United States to the other, to hear him in person.

Sad to say, he and Aaron knew the words to every Barry Manilow song ever written, and there were lots of them.

But tonight he had something else on his mind. After he sat down at the dining room table, he asked Aaron, who'd also been invited for dinner, "Do you remember those ratty old *Playboy* magazines you used to hide under your mattress?"

Aaron grinned at him. "No, I don't think I do. Unless

you mean . . . oh, let me see . . . um, Karin Mantrose, May 1992. Turn-ons: Being naked on a fur in front of the fireplace. 36–20–34. Which had nothing whatsoever to do with that Sherpa bath mat I bought from Walmart with my paperboy money. Uh-uh."

Daniel grinned. "Or DeLane Velasquez, June 1991," Daniel reminded him.

"Turn-ons: Bubble baths for two," they both said at the same time, then gave each other high fives.

"How about Patti Ann Jones? Remember that one," Daniel said.

"How could I forget? Her ideal date was with a brown-eyed, curly-haired male."

"And our hair was curly in those days. We were sure she was just waiting for us to grow up." It was amazing what stuck in a young boy's head, Daniel thought. Hell, a man's head, too.

"You two are idiots," his mother said as she placed the big tureen of jambalaya on the table. "Thirty-something adolescents!"

Coming up beside her, Aunt Mel scoffed, "Any gal with a twenty-inch waist beyond the age of twelve is anorexic or wearing a corset."

"Could someone please turn down the volume on that music? I can barely hear myself think," Daniel said.

"Barry is best at full volume," his mother asserted, although she did go over and turn a knob so that "At the Copa" was only a distant backdrop.

"What brought up the skin mags? You're not usually a memory lane kinda guy." Aaron leaned back in his chair and studied him in a way he knew would annoy Daniel. "Oh, don't tell me. You met a centerfold today at the medical center. You have all the luck!"

"I wish! No, it was a young kid, a new cancer patient, who wanted me to buy him a *Playboy*."

"Don't you dare," his mother said. "With all the malpractice suits today, you could be sued. Somehow they'd find a way to prove that pornography causes cancer." His mother was a GP in a small medical group that struggled under the burden of monumental malpractice insurance premiums.

He noticed his mother's hand shaking as she sat down next to him and placed a napkin on her lap. Reaching over, he took her hand in his. "Mom? What's up?"

She and Aunt Mel exchanged odd glances.

Oh, this is not good.

"Tell them," Aunt Mel prodded, her eyes welling unexpectedly with tears.

Definitely not good. Aunt Mel was not a crier.

Squeezing Daniel's hand, which she still held, his mother took a deep breath and said, "I have cancer."

He and Aaron said the same foul word under their breaths. To show how serious the situation was, neither woman reamed them out, as they would normally.

For a moment, Daniel felt faint with shock, but then he choked out, "What kind of cancer?" Being an oncologist, that was the most important question he had to ask.

"Uterine."

The most deadly. "What stage?"

"Two. It's already spread to my lymph nodes."

Oh, shit!

"And that's all I'm going to say on the subject tonight," she declared. "I'll show you all the records tomorrow, and you can start interfering in my medical care then. For tonight, I just want to have a nice family dinner."

He and Aaron, who was equally stunned, looked at each other. They didn't have to be twins to read each other's minds this time. Their mother was in big, big trouble.

"I knew it!" Aaron stood angrily. "Mom, I even asked you last month if you were sick when I noticed how much weight you'd lost, and then I caught you at home in the middle of the day, puking your guts out. You said it was the flu."

His mother shrugged. "I didn't want anyone to know yet. I was waiting for the right time."

"There's a right time to discuss cancer? Coulda fooled me, and I've been dealing with it for ten years. How long have you known?" Daniel narrowed his eyes when his mother squirmed in her seat.

"Three months, and don't take that tone with me, Daniel. I have a right to handle this any way I want."

Daniel stood now and shoved Aaron in the chest. He had to have some way to vent his fury, and, yes, fear. "You knew something was wrong and didn't tell me? I'm a doctor, lamebrain!"

"Mom's a doctor, too, in case you hadn't noticed." Aaron shoved him back.

"Yeah, but she's a GP, not a specialist."

"Whatever!"

"Both of you, sit the hell down and listen," Aunt Mel yelled.

Duly chastened, they sank back into their chairs and watched with disbelief as their mother calmly served up the jambalaya and salad, then passed slices of warm bread to each of them. Aunt Mel poured iced tea into four glasses.

They expect us to eat? Now?

"And don't be such sad sacks," Aunt Mel added. "Things aren't hopeless. Your mother and I are still going to Hawaii this summer." They had been planning that two-week vacation for years. Icing on the cake was the fact that good ol' Barry would be performing there at the same time for a few days.

Four months away, Daniel thought. *Please, God, let her get a chance to wear that lei. Help her and I'll lobby*

for Barry Manilow songs, rather than Muzak, in the hos-
pital elevators . . . a penance for all my past sins . . . and
any forthcoming ones, too.

Nine months later . . . prayers are answered, but not
always the way we expect . . .

Daniel's eyes burned, and he blinked back tears as he approached the little house on Arctic Lane.

His mother had died two days ago at the far-too-young
age of fifty-three, after what had turned into a painful
battle with cancer, despite several trips to the Mayo
Clinic, and some experimental treatments outside the
U.S. Cliché though it was, death had been a blessing.
Didn't make the loss any easier, though.

And now here he was, asking for another dose of
heartache. He should have developed thicker skin by
now, considering his specialty, but instead he felt like he
was at the end of his rope. He had no business coming to
this particular house over which the heavy cloud of hospice care hovered. His work as a pediatric oncologist had
ended when Deke left the medical center last week, for
good. In-home nurses had taken over.

The hospital lawyers would deem it unwise, from a
legal standpoint, for a physician to involve himself personally with a patient. Especially off-premises.

Lawyers! They couldn't know, or care, how close
Daniel had gotten to the kid over these past nine months,
even with all the time he'd taken off for his mother. There
was just something about Deke that touched him, deeply.

He was dragging with him the most pitiful example of
mankind. Jamie Lee Watson, once a promising Marine
lifer, now a thirty-five-year-old thin-as-a-skeleton, nose-
bleeding cocaine addict. Apparently, the man had seen

things in Iraq that only drugs helped him forget. Daniel had found the whereabouts of Deke's father last week, but it had taken him all that time, when he wasn't at his mother's bedside, trying to get the man halfway lucid, showered, and dressed in clean clothes. The new, barely improved Jamie Lee was not a happy camper.

"This is a train wreck about to happen," Jamie Lee complained.

"Not if I can help it."

"My kid . . ." His words trailed off as he choked up, fully aware of Deke's rapidly deteriorating condition. "My kid doesn't need a loser like me."

"He needs you, all right."

"Why?"

"Because you're his father. Simple as that. He doesn't care if you're the President of the United States or a circus clown."

"Bethany is gonna have a fit."

"She's the one who asked me to find you."

Jamie Lee stared at him with the most incredible hope in his bleary eyes before he masked the emotion by rubbing his hands over his face, a face which Daniel had personally shaved for him, removing a year-old beard. Jamie Lee would have probably slit his own throat.

Before Daniel had a chance to knock, the door flew open and Bethany smiled . . . a smile that did not reach her bloodshot eyes. "You came."

It wasn't clear if she was referring to Daniel or her long-absent husband.

Daniel stepped aside and shoved Jamie Lee forward. "Go for it, buddy."

"I am so sorry, Bethany," Jamie Lee said. That apology covered a whole lot of ground, Daniel suspected.

She nodded, seemed to hesitate, then opened her arms to give Jamie Lee a comforting hug. Almost immediately, she stepped back, putting space between them.

"Deke's been in and out of a coma for days, but he asks for his daddy when he wakes up." She laughed, but there was no mirth, just an odd tone of near-hysteria.

With a squeeze to her shoulder, Jamie Lee walked into the dining room which had been converted into a sickroom with a hospital bed and medical equipment. The oxygen machine whooshed away while an obscene number of tubes ran from the child's frail body, no attempt to hide his bald head under its usual baseball cap. A nurse moved away from the bed to give the stranger room. Daniel and Bethany stood in the open doorway, watching.

It was odd the things you noticed in times of crisis. Birds chirping outside the open window. A Disneyland souvenir glass on the sideboard. A framed photo showing a much younger Deke with his mother and a guy in a buzz cut and military uniform, all of them smiling.

"Hey, slugger," Jamie Lee said, clearly uncertain what to do, where to put his hands. But then he leaned over and kissed his boy's cheek. "That's what I always called him. Slugger," Jamie Lee nervously told Daniel.

Miraculously, considering his sedation, Deke's eyes fluttered open. "Dad?"

"Yeah, it's me," Jamie Lee choked out.

"I prayed . . . that . . . that you . . . would come," Deke finally got out. Talking was difficult at this stage.

"That's me . . . the answer to a little boy's prayer," Jamie Lee muttered.

"Am I dead yet?" His little hand clung to his father's. "Are you an angel?"

Jamie Lee started to weep then. Hell, they all had tears in their eyes.

"No, I'm hardly an angel, son. Just your daddy."

"I'm afraid. Will you stay with me?"

"As long as you want, slugger."

And he did stay with him for the next five hours, never

moving from the seat the nurse had pushed behind him, never releasing his son's grip on his hand, until Deke slipped away. The death was almost an anticlimax.

Daniel had gone back to his office for several hours and returned just in time. As he left for the last time, he wondered how many more of these cancer deaths he could handle without going insane.

A dog is a dog, no matter the breed . . .

Samantha Starr walked down the corridor of the French Quarter courthouse with her new lawyer, Lucien LeDeux, at her side. They were headed toward a conference room where they would meet with her horndog ex-husband Dr. Nicholas Coltrane (aka Nick the Prick), his shark lawyer Jessie John Daltry, and an associate judge for the Fourth Circuit Court of Appeals, District of New Orleans.

"Don't say anything," Luc warned her. "You know the good doc will try ta rile you into a hissy fit, which won't sit well with the judge. Just let me do all the talking."

"I'll try."

"Not good enough. I've studied the records, *chère*. You're paying Coltrane as much alimony as you do because of your outburst last time."

She stiffened and raised her chin haughtily. "Or because the judge was a female influenced by my ex's dubious charms. Nick commented on my lack of sex appeal as an excuse for his adultery, and the judge didn't even reprimand him."

"Huh? No way! You are as hot as a goat's behind in a pepper patch."

"Charming."

"Oops. That's my Tante Lulu's favorite Cajun saying. Hang around her long enough and she wears off on you."

Samantha knew and even worked on occasion with Louise Rivard, better known as Tante Lulu to everyone, and she was outrageous in appearance, actions, and general reputation. Not the role model Samantha would set for herself.

Luc grinned. "Anyhow, don't let the asshole put you down."

"Oh, please! I am what I am." Samantha was five-foot-ten in her bare feet. When she wore heels, she was taller than Nick's five-eleven frame, which had annoyed him to no end. If that wasn't bad enough, her body was covered with freckles from forehead to toes, and not the attractive kind. Once, in a drunken rage, Nick had likened her freckles to tobacco juice spit on her by a redneck farmer. Orange spittle. As for her bright red hair . . . no more! She paid a fortune to her hairstylist to keep it a more subdued auburn.

Samantha hated that she'd taken so much care with her appearance today . . . white, long-sleeved, Chanel pantsuit with a fitted peplum jacket, matching stiletto pumps, and tailored, jade-green, collarless, silk blouse . . . to match her green eyes, her only feature that she really liked. Her auburn hair was swept off her face in a neat chignon. Emerald drop earrings in a platinum setting and her great-grandmother's emerald-and-diamond filigree ring were her only jewelry. Unfortunately, there was no way to cover the freckles on her hands, face and neck. She hadn't dressed to impress Nick, but for her own self-esteem which always tanked in his presence. "I don't need phony compliments."

"The dickhead has done a job on you, darlin'. Talk about!" Luc just shook his head. "We can discuss that later. Maybe you should have stayed home and let me handle this."

"No. I am not going to let him continue to bleed me.

Did I tell you that a friend of mine saw him in the South of France? He was on the freakin' French Riviera for a month. A month!"

Luc sighed. "Yes, you told me. His lawyer says it was a medical conference."

"For a month? What kind of medical conference lasts a month? SDU? Slimy Doctors United?"

Samantha had been married to Nick for five years and divorced for another five, but she was still paying for that mistake. And not just with the continuing humiliation of his serial adultery, or the very public, acrimonious divorce. Nope, the jerk had demanded alimony, that on top of her having paid his way through medical school. And he kept wanting more and more.

It wasn't just that Nick knew the salary and benefits she drew from her family business, not to mention stock she owned in the company and a sizeable savings account. But he was aware of the gold coins and bullion, worth anywhere from a million and a half to two million dollars, depending on the market, stored in her bank safety deposit box. It started out as a million dollars in gold, a gift her grandfather gave on the birth of each of his grandchildren. In her case, it had almost doubled in value. Being of conservative Scottish stock, her grandfather preferred hard, cold metal, over stocks and bonds. Portable wealth. Since that gold wasn't "earned" during their marriage, the courts had denied Nick access to it, over and over. But he kept trying.

During the course of her relationship with Nick, she'd met many of his physician friends, and they all seemed to be focused on their net worth and what expensive toy they could buy next. Very few were in the profession for the good they could do. And most had been divorced at least once, or were blatant adulterers. And talk about the conversations when Nick and his gynecologist buddies got together! If she heard the joke "I've seen more pussy than Hugh Hefner," one time, she'd heard it a hundred.

Thus, her bias against doctors. It was an unreasonable bias, to lump all male doctors into one assumption. She realized that, but perhaps it was understandable.

"SDU? Sounds like a sexual disease. But see, that's the kind of remark that will get you in trouble." Even as he chastised her, Luc had to smile. "All we need is time. Wish you had contacted me earlier, but not to worry. I've got investigators checking into his activities. We're gonna nail his sorry ass to the wall, one way or the other."

"I wish I'd hired you sooner, too. My old lawyer, Charles Broussard, was a lovely man . . . a friend of my grandfather . . . but not the sharpest knife in the drawer, not a barracuda like Daltry."

"I eat big fish for breakfast," Luc bragged.

He probably did. That, or fried gator kidneys if his crazy aunt had any say.

Samantha put one of her recently manicured finger-nails to her mouth and began to gnaw nervously.

Luc slapped her hand away. "Enough of that! You have to walk in there as if you own the world. Fearless!"

"Pfff! How do I do that with a man who looks like some kind of Norse God in Armani? And a lawyer who sharpens his teeth on people like me?"

"No, no, no! Daltry is a shark, guar-an-teed, but, darlin', you hired yourself an even badder shark. A Cajun shark. The best kind." He waggled his eyebrows at her. "Here's a clue on how not ta be intimidated. When I'm in court, if it's a man tryin' ta disconcert me, I just picture him naked, walkin' down Bourbon Street with a string of Carnival beads looped around his . . . um, family jewels. If it's a woman, I picture her, naked, too, but with a behind the size of a bayou barge, doin' a Cajun shimmy snake dance. In both cases, people are laughin' their asses off at them."

Samantha's jaw dropped open before she burst out with a giggle.

And that was how her ex-husband and his lawyer saw her as she and Luc entered the auxiliary courtroom. And, to her surprise, Nick was the one who looked disconcerted.

"Game on, Samantha?" Luc whispered in her ear.

"Game on," she agreed, leaning in to his ear.

As Nick and his lawyer stood, Nick's eyes widened with surprise at what must seem an intimate interplay between her and her lawyer. Luc might be fifty years old, give or take, and married with kids, but he was still handsome and successful, the type of man Nick had always intimated would never be interested in her.

The two lawyers exchanged cool greetings while Nick pulled his charm mask on and smiled at her. "Samantha, it's good to see you again."

Liar!

Giving her an insulting head-to-toe survey, he winked at her and drawled, "Lookin' good, babe."

Another lie. Among other things, Nick had more than once suggested she get breast implants. And skin bleaching to reduce the freckling. Like Dolly Parton and Michael Jackson, for heaven's sake! The image still made her blood curdle.

Her upper lip curled with disgust at Nick's continuing swarmy smile. Was there ever a time when she'd thought him attractive? Aliens must have invaded her brain.

"Oy-yay! Oy-yay! Judge Bernadette Pitre presiding in the case of Coltrane vs Starr," the bailiff called out through an inner door which had just opened. The judge was followed by a court reporter with her portable steno machine.

"Oh, no! Another female judge!" Samantha complained to Luc.

Seemingly undismayed, he patted her arm and murmured something that sounded like, "Thank you, St. Jude."

"Your honor, Jessie John Daltry representing Dr. Nicholas Coltrane." The judge nodded at Daltry, but then frowned when Nick, in an impeccable gray suit with lavender shirt and purple striped tie, his blond hair perfectly groomed, and reeking of Bleu de Chanel, said with a teeth-showing, I-can-get-any-woman-I-want smile plastered on his sun-tanned face, "It is such a pleasure to meet you, Ms. Pitre. I have heard so much about you. Congratulations on your recent—"

"Are you tryin' ta influence me, young man?" the judge asked with steel in her deep Creole voice. At fortysomething she was not that much older than Nick's thirtyfour, but she was a big-boned, mocha-skinned Amazon of a woman who clearly handled her courtroom in a nononsense fashion. She looked a little bit like Queen Latifah in a judge's gown.

Samantha had to grin at a female stonewalling Nick's charm tactics.

Then the judge turned to her and Luc, and groaned aloud. Samantha could swear she said under her breath, "Oh, crap!"

Not a good sign.

"Lucien LeDeux! What're you doin' here, *cher*? Shouldn't you be down the bayou chasin' ambulances or somethin'?"

Instead of being insulted, Luc just grinned. "How's yer Mama, Bernie?"

"Jist fine. And that old bird, Tante Lulu?"

"Still causin' trouble. Thanks fer askin'."

Samantha did a mental Snoopy dance as they all sat down, Nick and Daltry looking as if they'd swallowed bad crawfish. It would appear that Tante Lulu's outrageousness had unexpected benefits.

"I've read the history on this case. It appears that Ms. Starr is requesting a termination of alimony payments . . . very substantial alimony, I see here . . . to her ex-husband Dr. Nicholas Coltrane. How come a doctor needs alimony?" the judge asked right off the bat.

"Because Doctor Coltrane deserves to live the lifestyle he shared with Samantha Starr while they were married. The same would be true if the genders were reversed, and a woman wanted alimony from her husband." Daltry then cited some statute which supposedly supported his position.

"Don't y'all be tryin' ta teach me the law, Mistah Daltry."

"My apologies, your honor," a red-faced Daltry said.

Judge Pitre nodded. "For how long? It's been five years. How long before Dr. Coltrane *earns* an income to match his former lifestyle?"

There was a telling silence which pretty much said, "Forever."

Then Daltry said, "Records show how expensive the medical equipment is in the facility Dr. Coltrane had to purchase for his practice after moving out of a Starr family building. That on top of rising office salaries, insurance, etc. Little is left for even a minimal standard of living."

The judge raised her eyebrows skeptically.

"Your honor? If I may speak?" Luc stood and picked up a folder, which he opened on the table.

The judge nodded.

"There are new circumstances that warrant the termination of alimony payments to Dr. Coltrane."

"I object," Daltry said, standing abruptly. "What are those documents? We're entitled to discovery."

"Don't be an ass, Mistah Daltry. This isn't some highfalutin', on-TV, criminal trial," Judge Pitre exclaimed.

Daltry flushed again and plopped back down into his chair.

Nick raised his hand in the air like a little kid asking his teacher for permission to go to the bathroom. At Judge Pitre's surprised nod of acceptance, he smiled his lopsided smile, the one that meant he was playing the ain't-I-adorable card. "I never wanted a divorce. It was Samantha who rejected my affections."

"You were screwing the neighbor's babysitter, you prick!"

"Samantha!" Luc hissed. "Remember. Carnival beads."

"So not true! Your honor, Samantha is very insecure," he confided in a whisper as if they couldn't all hear. "She was always looking for infidelity in our marriage."

"And you were looking for size double-D's." And, yeah, taking Luc's advice, Samantha had to admit that Nick did look silly in her mind picture, bare-assed naked, with an erection standing out like a bird's roost, holding strands of colored beads. She couldn't help but grin.

"Atta girl," Luc said, guessing what she was thinking.

Nick snarled at her seeming amusement at his expense, then told the judge meekly, "I even suggested we take ballroom dancing classes together, not just to heal our marriage, but because, I have to tell you, Samantha has no sense of rhythm at all."

Samantha returned the snarl. "And you have no sense at all, period."

The judge put her face in her hands, then shouted, "Enough! Does anyone have anything to present today that is remotely sane? Otherwise, I'm going down to Arnaud's where I plan to order a Hurricane . . . or five."

"Your honor," Luc said with exaggerated meekness, "I submit credit card statements for Doctor Coltrane which indicate he is living a lifestyle that far exceeds his supposed medical debts, despite his claims of near poverty."

"There are privacy laws, LeDeux. You have no right to those records," Daltry sputtered.

"Shut up!" the judge said, then turned to Luc. "Continue."

Shoving one sheet of paper after another toward the judge, Luc explained, "In the past six months, designer suits worth ten thousand dollars, restaurant expenses totaling twenty thousand dollars, jewelry, fifty thousand dollars, and purchase of a condo during his recent one-month stay in the Cote d'Azur."

Judge Pitre's jaw dropped with each sheet. Daltry looked a bit shocked, as well.

But Luc was on a roll. "I would like the court's permission ta subpoena Cerise Barclay, Antoinette Gaudet, and Pussy Gate."

"Your honor!" Daltry protested.

"You bitch!" Nick seethed at Samantha. "You're just jealous because you're such a dog no man would want you."

"You're the dog, Nick," she snapped back, leaning across the table.

Luc tugged on her arm, pulling her back. "Shhh. He's baiting you. Naked. Carnival beads. Naked. Carnival beads."

"You didn't think I was a dog at one time," Nick went on. "In fact, we'd still be together if I hadn't had a vasectomy . . ."

"Without telling me," she pointed out, sitting now, but with her arms folded over her chest in anger.

Nick shrugged. "Just because you drooled over kids didn't mean I wanted to propagate the likes of you."

The judge was pounding on the conference table. "Silence! Everyone!"

When they'd all quieted, though everyone was simmering, Judge Pitre addressed Luc. "Subpoenas, Luc? What do you think this is, *Law and Order*?"

"No, but the women will never come testify unless you order them to."

"Who are they?"

"Coltrane's mistresses."

The judge raised a silencing hand when Nick and Daltry prepared to protest again. "And the one with the funny name . . . Pussy-something?"

"Pussy Gate. A stripper," Luc said succinctly, not even breaking into a grin, even though he probably wanted to.

Nick flashed her a venomous look. Hey, she hadn't even known about the stripper. She'd thought his tastes ran higher class than pole dancers.

"This case is postponed until . . ." the judge consulted her calendar, "two months from now. September 15. At which time I expect documentation, supporting case law, and decorum. From both sides. Do I make myself clear?"

"I'll be ready to leave in a few minutes," Luc said, motioning toward the clerk who'd stayed behind while the judge left the chamber.

Samantha went into the corridor ladies' room while she waited for Luc to complete some court paperwork. Although everything seemed to have gone well today, she felt drained . . . and frustrated that the case would be continued for another two months.

Nick was waiting for her when she came out.

She tried to step around him, but he blocked her way, then grabbed her with a pincer-hold on her upper arm, dragging her into a side corridor leading to a maintenance closet. The hatred on his face turned his normally perfect features into something scary.

"Have you lost your mind?" she asking, slapping at him. Her handbag dropped in the process, and her carefully-styled hair came undone.

Shoving her up against the wall, he spat out at her, "You stupid cunt! Do you honestly think I'm going to let you get away with this?"

"Let me go!" She tried to squirm away from him, but his arms now bracketed her against the wall.

"You're not getting away with this, *Sammie*." He used that nickname deliberately because he knew she hated it.

"Wanna bet, *Nickie*? The cash cow is about to shut down for business."

"Don't count on it." He made an obscene milking gesture with a hand on one of her breasts, then returned the hand to the wall beside her head.

Unable to squirm out of his extended arms, she tried to calm herself down. "Isn't it time you earned your own way, Nick?"

"You owe me, Sammie," he said, spittle settling at the edges of his lips.

"For what?" Samantha knew she should scream for help, but she didn't want to appear frightened. It was just Nick, after all. All flash and no bang, as her grandfather used to say.

"For five years of torture living with you."

She should shut up, but she had to ask, "So you never loved me?"

"Get real!" He gave her another of those insulting once-overs. "As if! Now, you're going to go inside that courtroom and drop this complaint for termination of alimony, or—"

"Or what?"

He shook her until her teeth practically rattled. "I know where you live, Sammie. Remember that."

"What? Are you threatening me?"

Nick had been a heartache during their marriage and an expensive pain in the ass since then, but he'd never threatened violence before. This was something new, and, truthfully, a little scary.

"I'm not afraid of you," she lied. "You are the biggest mistake of my life, and I'm done paying for it."

As voices came closer, he released her and turned on his heels, but, before he stormed away, he said, "You'll be done, all right, unless you back down."

She decided not to tell Luc about Nick's actions. Not just yet. She didn't want to get involved in filing a complaint with the police, which is what Luc would surely demand. Not just yet. And truth to tell, she was a bit rattled.

Samantha was an educated woman. And a wealthy one. Her family owned Starr Foods, a chain of supermarkets throughout the South. Her grandfather, Stanley Starr, a Yankee carpetbagger from Boston whose family had emigrated from Scotland, founded Starr Foods with a little French Quarter grocery store after World War II. There were now more than a hundred stores. Thus, she was guaranteed a healthy income for life. Not that she didn't work for it, both in the accounting department and as director of the Hope Foundation, the umbrella organization for Starr Wishes and Jude's Angels, the latter being Tante Lulu's brainchild.

To outsiders, Samantha appeared independent and confident. And she *was* good-looking, dammit, no matter what Nick said. Not beautiful, but attractive.

Despite all that, by the time she returned to her Garden District home that evening, she felt shattered. Forget about physical threats, her ex-husband wounded her with words, every single time.

What she needed was a Prince Charming to rescue her. Nah.

She would settle for a suit of armor, or thicker skin.

Chapter Two

What's your theme, baby? . . .

One week after his mother's death, a still reeling Daniel LeDeux stood in her backyard.

Don Ho was belting out "Tiny Bubbles" from the loudspeakers. A pig was roasting on a monster rental spit in the backyard, which was decorated with sand and fake palm trees. Among the fifty or so guests were men wearing garish, floral, Hawaiian shirts and women dazzling in sarongs or skimpy, fake grass skirt outfits, all accented by artificial leis. Luckily, the weather had cooperated. While normally the July temps in Alaska didn't go above the sixties, it was in the low eighties today. Everyone sipped at drinks adorned with pineapple slices and little umbrellas. Macadamia nuts were heaped in one bowl, and a questionable grayish purple poi of three different consistencies was available for one, two, or three-finger dipping. Those who had already overimbibed on the coladas were dancing in a wacky hula-style conga line that skirted all four sides of the house.

It was the best luau Juneau, Alaska had ever seen.

At the same time, it was the wackiest funeral Daniel and Aaron had ever attended. Unfortunately, the guest of honor was their mother, whose body, donated to science, had already winged its way to the Johns Hopkins research facility in Baltimore more than seven days ago.

"I feel a little guilty," Aaron confessed to him. "Like we should be howling with grief, instead of partying."

Daniel shook his head. "No need. She was in so much pain. Even morphine didn't cut it near the end."

As a single parent, their mother had struggled to bring twins into the world, care for them while attending college and medical school, and provide a loving home for thirty-odd years. Her death was a monumental loss to both of them. But, really, they'd said their good-byes to her months ago, when she'd still been able to put two coherent sentences together.

He squeezed his brother's arm.

"Cancer is a bitch," Aaron said.

You're telling me! Try watching a ten-year-old kid wither away to nothing.

"You boys havin' a good time?" Aunt Mel asked, giving each of them a hug.

"Just super!" Daniel remarked.

Smiles twitched at their lips as they viewed her attire. She was a native Aleut, except for some Russian blood contributed by an anonymous grandfather, thus her height of five-foot-eight. Despite a huge appetite, Mel had always been skinny. Now, she had her almost nonexistent hips tucked into a grass skirt riding way too low on her butt. Halved coconuts looked like torpedoes covering her breasts, which were also practically nonexistent. A circle of lavender orchids lay atop her permed, bottle blond hair. On a chain about her neck hung a half of a silver heart pendant to match the one their mother had always worn. Although Mel had a smile on her mouth, her eyes were red-rimmed from crying.

"Just wait 'til the singing starts," she said. "Father Sylvester is gonna lead us in hymns."

"Yippee!" Aaron said under his breath.

"At least it's not Barry Manilow songs," Daniel murmured back, with a hand over his mouth.

"Gag me at the Copa," Aaron quipped.

Despite their whispered remarks, neither of them would ever deliberately hurt Aunt Mel, who had been with them since they were toddlers. In fact, she had given Aaron his first flying lesson when he was twelve years old and later welcomed him as half owner of her air shipping company.

"I know it's cornball, having a theme funeral, but your mother and I never made it to Hawaii. Fate intervened." Tears welled in her eyes and dripped down her flat, round face onto her lei. "Do you think it's crazy? Or disrespectful?" She spread her arms out to indicate the whole shebang.

"No, it's wonderful." *My nose is probably growing.*

"This is just what I want when I die," Aaron added. "A theme funeral."

Daniel gave his brother a sideways glare of warning.

"Except mine would be held in a strip club, or a Playmate Mansion kinda place. Clothing optional. And there would be a wet T-shirt competition, and lap dancing, and Victoria's Secret models, and—"

"Oh, you!" Aunt Mel punched Aaron playfully on the arm. At least the tears were gone, which had probably been his intention.

"Mellie!" State Representative Rogers stepped up and gave her a sympathetic hug. "Come with me. There's someone I want you to meet." Before they walked off, Aunt Mel told the two of them, "We need to talk later. I have something important to discuss with you."

She probably referred to their mother's will, which surely left everything to her, as it should. "There's no need, Aunt Mel. We can talk later this week."

Aunt Mel shook her head. "No. I promised your mother."

On that puzzling note, she strolled off with the politician, whose wife had been a longtime MS patient of their mother's.

They were silent then as they sipped at their drinks, then grimaced at the sickening sweetness.

"I keep thinking Mom will step out of the house and push her famous gumbo on us," Daniel remarked. *Or talk to me about medicine. She understood what it was like to lose a patient. Lots of patients.*

Aaron looked at him with concern.

Oh, great! I probably have tears in my eyes, too.

"If that hula dancer over there in the grass skirt decides to give me a lap dance, I won't complain." Aaron was clearly trying to cheer him up, like he had Aunt Mel.

"Yeah, right. That's Kirima Kulowiyi, a nurse from Mom's practice," he told Aaron. "She's married to a roughneck who does hard manual labor out on the oil rigs. That's him over there by the barbecue . . . the guy who looks like he could bench press a polar bear."

"Okaaaay," Aaron said with a laugh. Then, blinking rapidly to hide his own tears, he put down his fruity drink and took a beer out of a cooler and handed a second one to him.

Raising the bottle, as if in a toast, Daniel took a long draw before wiping his mouth with the back of his hand. "I quit my job today," he announced out of the blue.

"Job? Being a doctor isn't a job. Do you mean that you won't be working at the pediatric medical center anymore?"

"No, I mean that I'm quitting medicine."

"No way, Dan! You love being a doctor."

"Correction. I used to love being a doctor." Daniel didn't elaborate. It went without saying that working day in and day out with terminally ill kids ate away at a man's spirit. Losing his mother was the last straw. *Did I mention that Deke Watson died on Tuesday . . . just two days after Mom? Ten years old, and he weighed fifty pounds. Amy Lewis lost two of her baby teeth on Wednesday . . . and all her hair. Lionel Harris got his tenth spinal tap yesterday. Shiiiit!*

Just then, Father Sylvester and Aunt Mel could be seen wheeling a portable organ into the backyard. Aaron and Daniel looked at each other, put their empty beer bottles on a picnic table, and headed toward the front yard and their cars parked in the driveway. They'd already said their goodbyes to their mother.

"Whoever said that funerals are for the living, not the dead, knew what they were talking about," Aaron remarked, as if reading his mind.

"Yep. Singing 'Amazing Grace' isn't going to help Mom now."

And it might just push me over the edge.

Aaron summed up the situation very well. "Time to do what comes natural. Let's go get blitzed."

Who knew they had a "Daddy Dearest?" . . .

"Your roots are in Louisiana. Cajun country," Aunt Mel told them the next morning. For the third time. Daniel and Aaron were having trouble understanding the news.

"Oh, my God! We're rednecks," Daniel finally exclaimed to Aaron.

Aaron just grimaced with fake horror at Aunt Mel's announcement.

Aunt Mel put down a tray of coffees, then smacked them on their respective shoulders before sitting down behind the desk in her small home office. Daniel and Aaron sat in chairs before the desk, their long legs extended and crossed at the ankles. *Like twins, for crying out loud!* Daniel cringed at his use of the expression "for crying out loud," even in his head; it had been a favorite of his mother's.

"Idjits!" Aunt Mel had just told them about their mother's last wishes, that they know their family history. Like they cared at this late date!

"Just 'cause you have Cajun blood doesn't make you rednecks," Aunt Mel explained patiently, like they were little boys who didn't know any better.

The two brothers hadn't returned to their mother and Aunt Mel's house until this morning, having exceeded their goal of getting blitzed last night. They'd both ended up knee-walking drunk. *My head feels the size of a basketball. Which isn't helped by the fact that good ol' Barry is belting out "Mandy" for about the thousandth time. Don't CDs ever wear out?*

Their mother's death was hitting them hard today. This house, without her in it, felt empty and sad. Any minute now he expected her to come into the room and ruffle his hair or kiss his cheek.

I miss her, too, he heard in his head, and it wasn't him thinking those words. Glancing over to Aaron, he realized that it was his brother whose word-thoughts he'd read. Twins did that a lot. He could feel Aaron's silent pain, literally. They nodded at each other with understanding.

Aunt Mel, fulfilling their mother's wishes, was telling them about their father, Valcour LeDeux. A father whose surname their mother had given them, and nothing else over the years. And about their mother's family, the Doucets. There were apparently a lot of Doucets in Louisiana. This was a rogue branch of the Bayou Black Doucets. Like he gave a damn about any family branches!

"I thought our father was dead," Daniel said, scanning once again the documents and newspaper clippings spread across the desk.

"I thought Mom was from France." Aaron's brow furrowed with puzzlement. "Hell, that's how she always explained her accent. I should have known better. It was the strangest French I've ever heard. I mean, what born and bred French woman says, 'Holy crawfish!'?"

"Like you know French!" Daniel remarked.

"Hey, I dated that French model."

"For what? A week?"

"What's your point?"

"The point," Aunt Mel interrupted them, "is that your mother was pure one hundred proof Cajun, same as your father, which makes you two morons Cajun, too."

Cajun? I don't even know what that means.

Picking up on his mind cue, Aaron teased Aunt Mel, "Cajun . . . does that mean I have to chew tobacco and wrestle alligators?"

"Don't you dare!"

"Or talk like Dennis Quaid in that old movie, *The Big Easy*?" Daniel added.

Aaron glanced at him with surprise.

"Hey, I have a sense of humor when I want one."

Aunt Mel sighed. "I like Dennis Quaid. He can put his slippers under my bed any ol' time."

Which was ridiculous, and they all knew it. Aunt Mel was as gay as . . . well, their mother. The two women had been together longer than many married heterosexual couples.

"I don't understand why Mom wanted us to know about this now. Why, after all these years of keeping us in the dark?" Aaron asked.

"She wanted you to know that, even though she's gone, you still have family."

"You're family. That's enough for us," Aaron said.

"Ah, honey," Aunt Mel said, getting up from her chair behind the desk and giving Aaron a big hug. "I know that, but it's not the same." She dabbed at her eyes with the tissue she always had tucked in her bra strap under her blouse, and sat back down.

"Your mother wants you to go there and meet your relatives."

Daniel choked on his coffee. Whoa! Learning about his family history was one thing. Going all huggy face with a bunch of strangers was something else. "I beg your pardon?"

"Why in God's name should we go there?" Aaron asked.

"Closure."

"Whose? Ours? I could care less," Daniel said.

"You're gonna do it for your mother's sake. Yeah, that horndog loser treated her like dirt. Yeah, he never told her he was married. Yeah, he suggested she get an abortion, said he had too many brats already. And, yeah, her own family, the Doucets, put her out like so much garbage, without a penny. They were ashamed of her being pregnant and not married."

"All the more reason for us to stay put," Daniel concluded.

"In Valcour's defense, though not much," Aunt Mel went on, as if he hadn't even spoken, "Valcour did give your mother a sizeable payoff that enabled her to go to college and med school. No skin off his teeth, of course, him being filthy rich from oil drilling. And he gave her you two precious boys. You have to go back, for your mother's sake."

"Like hell! I'm not going to Louisiana to meet some no-good man who did my mother wrong or a family that kicked my mother to the street . . . uh, bayou. I don't care if he's a tycoon or a ditch digger, he means nothing to me." Daniel poured himself more coffee to calm down his temper.

"Looks Like We Made It," Barry warbled.

"I wish!" Daniel and Aaron said at the same time. Sometimes, that twin thing in their heads was a pain in the ass.

"That's all I need in my present mood . . . a trip to the Southland. I just gave up medicine. I want to wallow for a while. Maybe I'll sit myself down on a glacier and push out to sea."

Aunt Mel cast a blistering glance his way, which he ignored.

"I don't know, bro." Aaron tapped his closed lips thoughtfully. "It might be fun to kick some Cajun butt."

"I'm going to make sure I have a bottle of booze and a good book on that iceberg."

"How about a woman?" Aaron asked.

"Nope. I'm considering celibacy. Women are too much trouble."

"Hah! When did you turn into Mister Grumpy?" Aaron asked him.

"I like being grumpy. People stay out of my way."

"Would you two shut the hell up and listen to me? You have half sisters and half brothers you should meet," Aunt Mel insisted. "Aunts, uncles, cousins."

Daniel put his face in his hands.

"Some of them . . . most of them . . . are good people,

despite that blasted Valcour. Lucien LeDeux is a lawyer, married to a chemist. Remy is a pilot, like you, Aaron; he's married to a Feng Shui decorator. René was an environmental lobbyist and musician; he now teaches and is married to a lawyer. He still plays in a band, The Swamp Rats. Tee-John is a cop, about to marry a newspaper journalist. Charmaine owns a bunch of beauty salons and is married to a cowboy. One of the nephews is a New Orleans Saints football player."

Holy hell! Since when had Aunt Mel become a Le-Deux genealogist?

"Andy LeDeux? He's one of our kinfolk?" Aaron asked. "Wow!"

"Kinfolk? You're already sounding like a frickin' Cajun." Daniel flashed his brother a frown.

"I didn't know they had cowboys in Louisiana. But never mind. I can't leave the air shipping business, even if I wanted to," Aaron said.

"Yes, you can. We have an offer to sell the whole kit and caboodle . . . the air shipping business, the warehouse, both planes, everything. We would make a tidy profit."

"We do?" Aaron looked surprised, and pleased.

"And I could retire to Florida. Buy a condo. I'm sick of the cold."

This was the first Daniel had heard of his aunt wanting to move.

"Looks like we both might be unemployed," Aaron commented to him. "Synchronicity, that's what it is." Aaron looped an arm over his shoulder. "Here you are, in need of fun to cure your grumpiness, just when we're both out of work."

"Listen, Aunt Mel, if our father, Valcour LeDeux, wanted nothing to do with Mom, why should we want to know him? Or vice versa. As for the Doucets . . . they wouldn't help a pregnant girl. If those are family ties, I don't want them," Daniel seethed.

As Barry segued into "Blue Velvet," Aaron tried to lighten the mood. "Now that we're Cajuns, we probably shouldn't listen to any more cornball Barry Manilow songs."

"Oh, you!" Aunt Mel laughed. Their opinion of Barry Manilow was a longtime joke in the family.

"In fact, we should probably adopt Cajun music," Daniel added.

"You're right. I'm gonna buy me some rowdy Cajun music right after we leave here. The kind that makes people have to stomp their feet." Aaron glanced down at his low-heeled, urban cowboy boots, as if checking to see if they were stomp worthy. Actually, he would probably fit in perfectly, as he never had in Alaska where the normal attire was fur-lined parkas, flannel shirts, and clunky Timberland boots.

"The Cajuns use accordions and washboards, don't they?" Daniel asked Aaron, continuing the jest.

Aaron nodded. "Yep, and they yell yee-haw a lot."

"Would you two stop?"

"Who's the midget in this picture?" Aaron asked, holding up one of the newspaper clippings. It carried the headline Oil Tycoon Hit by Cajun Traiteur.

"Aaron! People don't say midget anymore. They say 'little person'." Aunt Mel smacked Aaron on the knuckles with the will.

Aaron rolled his eyes. "Who's the *little person* rapping our dear ol' dad with a folded umbrella? And what the hell's a *traiteur*?"

"That's Louise Rivard, honey. Tante Lulu, she's called. A LeDeux family matriarch of some sort. Not a midget . . . um, little person, I don't think. Just short."

"What's a *traiteur*?" Daniel asked.

"A folk healer," Aunt Mel answered. "Some of these letters are from her."

"Oh, that is just peachy. We're not just swamp trailer park trash, we have voodoo in our genes." Daniel shook his head, more with indifference than amusement or revulsion.

"In fact, as soon as your mother died, I notified her and told her to spread the word. She got back to me right away with condolences, but, most important, she has something to give you two. 'Something important.' You need to go there to pick it up, as soon as possible," Aunt Mel told them.

"What does she want to give us?" Aaron asked. "Maybe it's some kind of family inheritance."

"Why can't she just mail it to us?" Daniel wanted to know. "And isn't it convenient that she waited until Mom was gone before offering it to us?" He, for one, had no desire to travel below the Mason-frickin'-Dixon line, on the whim of some old lady.

"Maybe it's a plantation. Maybe we inherited a bleepin' Tara," Aaron teased.

"Frankly, I don't give a damn," Daniel said.

"Or it could be a trunk load of gold, too expensive to mail. Yeah, that's it, pirate gold."

"Pirates in Louisiana?" Daniel raised his brow with skepticism.

"Sure. Didn't you ever hear of that pirate Lafitte? He had digs in Louisiana, didn't he? Maybe we have pirate blood, too. That would be cool."

"You two are demented," Aunt Mel concluded. "The bottom line is, you have relatives in Louisiana. Your mother wanted you to know them. And one of them has 'something important' to give you."

"It's a Miracle," Barry announced, jarring them all.

It would be a miracle if Daniel survived this Aunt Mel

session without his head exploding. He counted off on his fingers. "So we're Cajuns." One finger. "Our maternal grandparents were bastards." Two fingers. "We're bastards." Three fingers. "Our father was a bastard, for sure." Four fingers. "An honorary aunt has a secret something for us." Five fingers. "Big deal!" Six fingers. Daniel was not all that upset. He was never going to meet these people. What did it matter?

Aunt Mel slapped a hand on the desk. "You're going! If you don't go, how will your mother ever rest in peace?"

How could they refuse now?

Barry was thankfully silent.

Chapter Three

(TWO MONTHS LATER)

*M ore LeDeux men? Hallelujah! The South will rise
again! . . .*

Daniel agreed to go to Louisiana with Aaron, provided
they only stay long enough to get the mysterious "gift"
Louise Rivard had for them. Then, they were off to the
Bahamas for a week of bonefishing.

To everyone's surprise, Daniel really had resigned
from his medical practice. It had taken two months to tie
up all the red tape. And Aunt Mel really was entertaining
an offer for the air shipping business.

Now he and Aaron had decisions to make about the
rest of their lives. Where better than out on a boat with a
fishing rod in one hand, a cold beer in the other, basking
in the warm sun?

Better that than the cold glacier he had been contemplating.

They boarded an Alaska Airlines flight headed for Louis Armstrong New Orleans International Airport, and almost immediately began running into people who knew their Southern kinfolks. Especially the apparently notorious Louise Rivard, known to one and all as Tante Lulu, even though *tante* translated to "aunt" in Cajun.

Kinfolks? Did I say . . . uh, think kinfolks? See, already I'm talking like a redneck. Next I'll be saying y'all and darlin' and "pass me the grits."

"I remember the time Tante Lulu entered a belly dancing contest when she was eighty years old. And won," a Delta Airline attendant told Aaron at a stopover in Seattle. Aaron had been flirting nonstop with Vanessa between her hostessing duties while Daniel tried to sleep.

"My PawPaw swears by Tante Lulu's rheumatiz potions," Frank Guidry, the pilot, who was "born on the bayou," confided to Daniel. "The old lady is a first class *traiteur*, y'know. A folk healer."

Daniel knew, and barely restrained himself from rolling his eyes.

"If you ever need a lawyer, check out Lucien LeDeux," a fellow passenger, a gray-haired businesswoman from Baton Rouge, advised from across the aisle. She had a silver pin that said "Proud to Be a Cajun" on the lapel of a neat, rose-colored suit. "He's known as the Swamp Solicitor. Slicker than spit on a doorknob, he is. In a good way," she'd added at the apparent expression of distaste on Daniel's face.

Okaaay.

The desk clerk, Linda Jo Dupuis, at the Bourbon Orleans Hotel where they stayed that night, had taken one look at the register as they'd signed in and exclaimed, "LeDeuxs! I dint think there were any more of you stud muffins left. Are you two as wild as the rest of the Le-Deux men?"

"Yes," Aaron answered before Daniel could react.

No filters! People below the Mason-Dixon line appeared to have no filters on their mouths. And his brother was no better!

Linda Jo was six-foot tall. Although she wore a conservative black, belted dress, it was sleeveless, exposing the biceps of a linebacker and tattoos up one side and down the other of her muscular frame. She looked as if she could handle any old wild thing that came her way, man or animal.

Good thing I decided to quit medicine. I'd never be able to hang my shingle here, unless I want to be known as the Stud Muffin Doctor. Holy crap!

"Are you here fer the weddin'?"

"What wedding?" Aaron asked.

"Are you kiddin'? Half the wimmin in Dixie are cryin' the blues, as we speak. Everyone knows that Tee-John Le-Deux is gettin' hitched t'morrow. He was the wildest of the LeDeux bunch, guar-an-teed. Unless . . ." Beulah eyed him and Aaron speculatively.

Daniel answered before Aaron could this time. "No! We'll leave that distinction to our . . . um . . . to John Le-Deux." Daniel still couldn't believe he had half brothers, let alone say it out loud. Including, presumably, this John person. And at least three others, besides! And those were only the "legitimate" ones.

The porter, who carried their luggage to the room, having overheard the conversation at the reception desk, surmised, out loud, that Valcour LeDeux might have fathered up to a dozen children in all. Once again, Daniel mused that people here in the South seemed to have no reservations about discussing personal matters, even with strangers.

But, really, hadn't their father ever heard of condoms?

They drove their rental car into Houma late the next morning and got directions to Tante Lulu's home at a beauty salon owned by their half sister Charmaine Le-Deux Lanier. They'd tried calling Tante Lulu last night and this morning, but all they'd gotten so far was her answering machine: "Hi, y'all. This is Tante Lulu, as if ya dint know. Tee-hee-hee. Leave a message or call me back. Iffen this is an emergency, and ya need some herbs quick like, jist come on by and get 'em from mah pantry. Buh-bye!"

That is just great! Drive-by prescriptions!

Charmaine wasn't in her shop, but a huge framed photograph of her hung in the foyer, taken a long time ago when she'd been Miss Louisiana. A good-looking woman, Daniel had to admit, especially in that skimpy white bathing suit, and despite all the big fluffy black hair, which must have been the style back then, at least for Southern belles. "Why did they wear high heels with bathing suits in competitions back then?" he asked Aaron as they returned to the rental car. "I mean, how many women do you see walking around the pool in high heels?"

"Because high heels make a woman's butt stick out and her boobs arch up, kind of perky like," Aaron answered with a grin. Aaron knew lots of interesting crap like that.

The drive down a two-lane road that ran parallel to a bayou was like a trip back in time to the 1950s. The only station they were able to get clearly on the radio played a weird kind of French music. Cajun, they presumed, with its unique twang. "*Jolie Blon*" or some such thing.

Old wooden signs planted in the ground must have been repainted over the years, otherwise they would have been rotted away. The jingle on these particular ones read:

"HIS CHEEK"
"WAS ROUGH"
"HIS CHICK VAMOOSED"
"AND NOW SHE WON'T"
"COME HOME TO ROOST"
"BURMA-SHAVE."

There were old trailers with disabled appliances in the front yards, but bigass satellite dishes on the roofs and shiny new, expensive pickup trucks in the driveways. Here and there a general store advertised a mixed bag of goods and services, such as fresh okra, squirrel meat, haircuts, and live bait, all in one place. A taxidermist, who was also an undertaker, had a stuffed alligator hanging from a sign in front. But then there were quaint homes on stilts at the edge of the water, and the occasional old plantation, some restored to their former beauty, others falling prey to the encroaching jungle-like vegetation.

Because their rental car had a faulty air-conditioning system, they'd been driving with the windows open. Heat shimmered over the slow-moving, dark bayou waters. The high humidity seemed to magnify the vibrant colors of lush foliage and caused the white clouds overhead to writhe and swirl constantly, a phenomenon explained by Aaron who was somewhat of a weather authority, being a pilot. When Daniel got back to Alaska, he was never going to complain about the cold again.

Seen from the air yesterday, the Southern Louisiana bayou country had looked like one of Aunt Mel's lace tablecloths. Better yet, like an illustration of the vascular system of the human body, veins and arteries going this way and that, except that here it was hundreds, maybe thousands, of different streams twisting and turning through the land. Up close, the landscape was even better. The scenery was an amazing assault on the senses, both visual and otherwise. Swarms of insects. Butterflies of every color and size imaginable. That fishy mud smell in the streams, along with decaying vegetation, offset by the almost overwhelmingly sweet aromas coming from flowers the size of saucers. A great blue egret stood, one-legged, on a partially submerged cypress log, its long neck and bill extended, waiting for its next meal to appear. A deceptive calm enveloped the area, deceptive because the area was teeming with all kinds of dangerous animals. The creepy live oak trees dripping gray moss helped to paint a picture of both peace and peril.

Daniel had to admit to being enthralled. He hadn't expected to like the bayou country. He still wasn't sure that he did. But a sense of coming home filled him the deeper they got into Cajun land. And Aaron felt it, too. He could tell by the way Aaron's hands tightened on the steering wheel and the rapt look Aaron kept darting his way as if to say, "Can you believe this?" Maybe there was something to that genetic memory crap some folks claimed to exist.

They found Tante Lulu's home on Bayou Black a short time later, and Daniel was pleasantly surprised as they pulled onto the crushed shell driveway. Instead of the trailer on concrete blocks he'd been halfway expecting (yeah, he was guilty of a little cultural bigotry, or maybe it was low expectations because of the way his mother had been treated), there was a trim little cottage covered with climbing roses, a penned-in vegetable garden, and a life-size statue of a saint standing in a circle of pansies. And a ten-foot, armor-plated alligator sunning itself in the backyard!

"Holy frickin' Dixie!" Daniel exclaimed as they both rolled up their automatic windows, which immediately turned the inside of the car into a sauna. "What the hell is that?"

"An alligator," Aaron answered.

"I know it's an alligator. What's it doing here?"

"Well, the bayou is only a hop, skip and a gator jump down the lawn," Aaron pointed out.

"Don't be a wiseass. What are we gonna do?"

Aaron laid on the horn. "We'll see if Louise Rivard is home, first of all."

"And let her come out and handle the alligator?" Daniel asked.

"You have a better idea?"

He didn't.

Aaron laid on the horn a few more times, but there was no movement from within the house. Even though it was only eleven a.m., the old lady must already be at the wedding.

"Guess we should have asked at the beauty salon where this wedding was going to be held," Aaron said.

"Or we could just go back to the hotel, relax by the pool, and come back tomorrow," Daniel contributed.

"Nah. Since we're already here . . ." Aaron pressed on the horn and didn't let up for a couple of seconds. Aaron knew very well that he probably wouldn't be able to talk Daniel into returning on this fool's errand again, if they left now.

Meanwhile, they both watched with fascination as the huge reptile raised itself on short stubby legs and started ambling their way, faster than you would expect a creature of a thousand pounds, give or take, to move. When it got closer, it opened its mouth, displaying enormous piano-key size teeth, and let loose with a mighty bellow which caused them both to jump in their seats. By now, sweat was rolling down their foreheads and necks, and not just because of the humidity.

"Oh, shit! That gator roar was probably a broadcast to all his fellow gators up and down the bayou, 'Hey, everyone, check out these two idiots in a metal coffin'," Daniel pointed out.

"Don't be such a killjoy. This is fun."

"Are you nuts? Let's get out of here." Aaron had turned off the engine when they'd stopped because the vents were just blowing hot air. Did gators eat metal? This one looked as if it could devour a bus, let alone a little Camry.

Just then, there was a knock on the passenger window which about caused Daniel to have a heart attack. He turned, halfway expecting to see a herd of alligators, but instead saw an old man wearing denim overalls, the kind with shoulder straps, and no shirt, but heavy work boots, trying to get his attention. He had a garden rake in one hand and a cigarette with a long ash in the other.

Daniel rolled his window down halfway. "Hurry up and get in the backseat before that alligator gets any closer."

"Huh? Why would I do that? Thass jist Useless." The guy sure was brave with only a yard tool for a weapon. You'd think he was carrying a rifle or something. Daniel would, if he lived here, which, God forbid, he ever would.

"It won't seem useless when that creature gobbles you up," Daniel said.

The old codger looked at him as if he was crazy, then cackled at some hidden joke. Hidden to Daniel, anyhow. He didn't see anything funny in this situation.

The old guy took a long draw on his cigarette, blew out a smoke ring, then dropped the butt to the driveway, stomping it out with his boot. "Useless is the gator's name. All he wants is some Cheez Doodles."

Daniel and Aaron's jaws dropped as the man went over to a metal garbage can beside the house, took out a handful of the cheese snack and tossed them toward the backyard. The gator immediately turned and trotted away, eating a row of the orange crunchies on its way.

"Have we landed in Wonderland yet, Alice?" Daniel asked his brother.

"I think so."

"I get first dibs on being the Mad Hatter."

"No kidding. You're already a little bit mad."

"And getting madder by the minute. This ranks up there with one of your top ten crazy-ass ideas, Aaron. Even worse than the time you talked me into zip-lining off that cliff during a hailstorm."

"It wasn't hailing when we started."

"Honestly, let's get out of Dodge. We came, the old lady wasn't here, no reason why we should hang around. Let's forget this whole thing."

"And you think Aunt Mel will be satisfied with that explanation?" Aaron asked him.

They both knew the answer to that.

The gator, having had its treats and presumably not considering the two scaredy-cats in the car to be tasty, went for a swim. The danger gone for the moment, Aaron and Daniel got out of the car.

The old guy returned and extended a hand. "I'm Jackson Dufrene, Tante Lulu's neighbor. Kin I help you fellas?"

They introduced themselves and shook the man's hand.

"Well, Tante Lulu's off ta the weddin', of course. She's been gone since dawn, had ta have a finger in all the doin's, lak always. Over ta the bride's house, first off, no doubt, then over ta Our Lady of the Bayou Church fer the services. The reception's bein' held up yonder at the Ter-rebonne Country Club. Ya kin find her there, guar-an-teed. Guardin' the Peachy Praline Cobbler Cake she made special fer the weddin'. Five tiers!"

Way too much information! "Oh, we wouldn't intrude on a private event like that," Daniel said. "We'll just go back to our hotel and—"

"Pooh! They's prob'ly five hundred people gonna be there. Folks comin' ta see that rascal Tee-John get hitched from all over the world. Even New Jersey. One or two more won't make no difference. Besides, you two are fam'ly. Where'd ya say you two was from?"

"Alaska," Aaron said with a wink at Daniel. They had a pretty good idea what was coming next.

"Alaska! Well, doan that beat all? Doan suppose ya live in igloos up thataways anymore?"

"Not lately," Aaron said with a straight face.

"How do you know we're family?" Daniel asked.

"'Cause ya said yer last name was LeDeux. And ya look jist lak yer papa, thass how. Valcour LeDeux, the no-count, good-fer-nothin' bastard, 'scuse my French, breeds good-lookin' chillen with like features. Wild as kudzu in a garden patch, all of 'em, but I ain't got no more young girls at home to warn offa y'all."

Daniel should have been affronted by the man's words, but what could he say when Aaron just chuckled like a moron.

Thus it was that Daniel found himself, an hour later, with his brother Aaron, about to gatecrash the tail end of a Cajun wedding reception. In hotter than frickin' hell Louisiana. Where the bridegroom was none other than their supposed half brother John LeDeux. And the hostess of this shindig was none other than the notorious Tante Lulu, whom Aunt Mel had told them about.

They had to park about a half mile away in an overflow lot. Old Jackson might be right about how many people were invited to this reception. Daniel had attended big weddings in the past, but he'd never heard of anything this big. You'd think the bride and groom were royalty or something. Cajun royalty. The William and Kate of the bayou.

Shiiit!

One saving grace was that, from this distance at least, it appeared that the bridal party was the only one in tuxes and gowns. Others were dressed in everything from semi-formal wear to what Aunt Mel would have called church clothes. He and Aaron wouldn't stand out too much . . . him in a button-down shirt, khakis, and loafers, and Aaron in his usual denim and boots, with a T-shirt that said, "Alaska Air Shipping." Okay, maybe Aaron would look like a hick, but he wouldn't.

The crowd filled a huge reception hall, its various side rooms, and spilled out onto several patios that overlooked a golf course. Tents had been erected in the back where it looked as if food would be served buffet style. There was a drink tent, as well, which is where he and Aaron headed. Drink of the day was oyster shooters, which he and Aaron declined in favor of longneck bottles of cold beer. Manna in this heat! Strangely, no one else seemed to mind the high temperatures. At least, they weren't sweating like pigs, like he and Aaron.

"Let's go inside, find some air-conditioning," he suggested, though with this many bodies, he doubted there would be much relief.

The closer they got, the louder the band. More of that twangy Cajun music like they'd heard on the radio. Once inside, they made their way toward the dance floor where a dark-haired man in a tux walked around a wide circle, holding hands with a dark-haired woman in an old-fashioned lace wedding gown. The bride and groom.

"What is it?" Daniel asked an elderly woman next to him.

"*La Fleur de la Jeunesse.* The Flower of Youth." The woman sighed. "They doan hardly sing the old songs like this anymore, but Tante Lulu insisted, and that was that."

Tante Lulu again! That woman sure gets around!

The five-piece band was situated up on a dais at the

far end of the massive room. The band's singer, who wore some kind of washboard contraption over his chest, wailed out the seemingly sad lyrics in Cajun French, followed by an English translation.

"J'avais promis dans ma jeunesse."
"I promised in my youth."
"Que je m'aurais jamais marier . . ."
"That I would never marry . . ."
"C'est aujourd'hui qye na tete est couronnée."
"But today my head is crowned."
"Et mon Coeur est omé d'un bouquet."
"And my heart is crowned with flowers."
"Adieu la fleur de la jeunesse."
"Goodbye to the flower of youth . . ."

Meanwhile, the bride and groom, still walking the wide circle, were joined by others from the bridal party, then their guests. A long snake of couples circling the room.

But then the band morphed into a different song, this one more upbeat, and the bridal couple began to slow dance in the middle of the dance floor, she with her arms looped around his neck, he with his hands on her hips, almost cradling her butt. They smiled at each other as they swayed to the music. Occasionally, when the crowd clapped, they kissed. They were good dancers. Soon the dance floor was filled. Much laughter and a rebel yell here and there. These were people who enjoyed a good time.

"This really isn't the right time for us to be connecting with family," Daniel said.

"You're right," Aaron conceded. "Let's get out of here."

They set their empty bottles on a table and were about to wend their way back through the crowd when, in a break between songs, they heard a high-pitched female voice exclaim behind them, "Oh, my God!"

They turned as one to see an old woman, no more than five feet tall, in a calf-length red gown, rushing toward them on what appeared to be red orthopedic shoes. A cap of gray curls covered her head, and dangly diamond earrings flashed in her little ears. She wore fake eyelashes. A smear of bright red covered her thin lips, which suddenly spread into a wide smile. She was eighty, if she was a day. Or more.

It had to be the notorious Tante Lulu.

Coming closer, she spread her arms wide in welcome. *What? Are we supposed to hug her, or something?*

Yes, Daniel soon realized as the little person, whose head came only to his chest, took his face in both hands and tugged him downward so that she could kiss him on one cheek, then the other.

Daniel would have bolted if he could have.

Actually, she smelled good. Like vanilla and peaches. And he found himself returning the hug.

"Welcome, welcome," she said.

She did the same to Aaron, who exchanged a puzzled look with him over her shoulders. *Who does she think we are?*

"Doan even try ta deny yer more of that Valcour's chillen. And twins! Oh, Lordy, what am I thinkin'? Ya mus' be the boys from up Alaska way? I'm so sorry 'bout yer mother." She hugged them again.

Daniel was feeling really uncomfortable, especially since people around them were starting to stare with curiosity. "Uh, I know this isn't really the right time, but I understand you have something for us. Maybe you could just tell us where it is, and we'll be on our way."

"We kin take care of that later."

Daniel narrowed his eyes at her. "I thought it was something important."

"It is important. Doan rush me."

Taking each of them in hand, she began to lead them

through the crowd. "Come, come," she said, "we will go talk, private like, in the sittin' room."

"Is our father here?" Daniel asked right off.

"Pfff! That Valcour, he's off on a cruise with his wife Jolie. Prob'ly afeared he'd be asked ta pay fer the weddin'. Not that the ol' buzzard don't have more money than he deserves. I gotta warn ya right now, yer papa is so crooked he could swallow nails and spit out corkscrews. The man's been down in the sewers so long he knows the rats by name. But he ain't nothin' but a fart in a windstorm when ya get right down to it."

Enough with the metaphors. We get the picture.

"Doan ya be worryin' none 'bout that."

I wasn't. To tell the truth, Daniel was having trouble following her train of thought. And talk about TMI.

"You got other fam'ly here, boys." She squeezed their hands, as if they'd been worried about lack of family. He had no time to correct that impression, though, because she was motioning for them to sit on one of the couches in the small room, and she sat on the other couch.

"You mus' be Daniel, the doctor," she said to him, "and you mus' be Aaron, the pilot. Yer Aunt Mel tol' me 'bout you boys. Ya kin call me Tante Lulu, like everyone does."

He wondered idly what Aunt Mel had said that would allow Tante Lulu to identify them so easily.

"I kin tell by yer sad eyes the troubles ya seen lately," she told Daniel. "Yer aunt sez ya been depressed and are gonna quit medicine."

It appeared Aunt Mel had a bigger mouth than he'd realized.

"Ya do know that depression is a no-confidence vote in God, dontcha?" She gave him a stern look, then reached forward and patted his knee. "I prayed ta St. Jude fer ya, and here ya are. Hallelujah! You jist watch now. Happiness has a way of sneakin' in through a door ya dint know ya left open."

She smiled then.

Daniel had no idea what he was supposed to say to that. And Aaron wasn't helping at all by commenting to the old lady, "Amen!"

Just then, the door opened and a woman peeked in. "Sorry to interrupt, Tante Lulu, but the caterer has a question about the crawfish." The woman was stunning. Tall, even taller with strappy black high heels, a long mane of auburn hair, and a killer body in a form-fitting green halter dress, that ended just above the knees. She must be at least five-ten in her bare feet, judging by his own six-foot-two. The freckles that covered much of her body only seemed to add to her allure.

Tante Lulu stood and said, "Boys, this is Samantha Starr, a friend of the fam'ly. Samantha, this is Aaron LeDeux. He's an airplane pilot. And this is Daniel LeDeux. He's a doctor, retired at the moment."

Samantha nodded at Aaron, but she frowned at Daniel. Because he was a doctor, or because he was retired, he wasn't sure. In any case, she'd already turned, giving Daniel a full-blown view of her backside, which was amazing. A slim waist and wider hips, giving her buttocks sort of a heart shape. And it moved when she walked away. Up, down, up, down.

Tante Lulu stood, about to follow, but the old bird noticed the direction of his stare, and remarked, "Thass what I call a hot cha-cha hiney."

Aaron burst out laughing, and Daniel found himself blushing.

Tante Lulu asked the oddest thing then. "Ya got a hope chest yet, Daniel?"

And thus began their new life in the South.

Chapter Four

A dog, a cat, and birds, oh, my! . . .

"He's stalking me," Samantha told Lucien LeDeux when he came to her house the Monday following the wedding.

"That's what you said on the phone."

"Should I buy a gun?"

"Uh. Maybe not yet."

"Tante Lulu says she can lend me hers."

"*Mon Dieu!* Is she still packing a pistol in her purse? She must have bought another one. I buried the last one in her okra patch."

"I think it was a shotgun she mentioned. Pump action. Twelve gauge."

He rolled his eyes. "Let's talk first."

Samantha hadn't really been serious about a gun. Though her ex-husband *was* beginning to creep her out.

Luc took one of the two mugs of strong Creole coffee she'd just made and followed her from the kitchen into the atrium which she'd converted into a sunny library-lounge. Floor-to-ceiling bookcases on the house side with French doors leading out onto a wraparound patio from the three other sides. Her grandfather's old partner's desk sat in the middle, and two low couches gave the sunny room an inviting atmosphere. A great place to take care of Starr or foundation business when at home, to read a good book (she was hooked on biographies), or to chat with friends (who were few and far between since the divorce).

It was one of her favorite rooms in the two-hundred-year-old Garden District home. Nick had hated it, wanting instead to raise prize orchids there or some such thing. Not because he knew a bleepin' thing about orchids, but he'd read in *Architectural Digest* that it was a hobby of old-rich families (as compared to new-rich, like himself, thanks to the Starr family well he kept dipping in). Truth to tell, Nick had never been overly fond of the house as a whole, which was small by Garden District standards, being a converted carriage house.

In fact, Nick never could fathom why a woman with such financial assets would choose to live in such an understated manner, and not just in her housing choices. She liked designer clothing, but she had no qualms about keeping the quality, often timeless items for years and mixing and matching outfits for maximum use. In fact, the Chanel pantsuit she'd worn to court was more than ten years old, purchased on her honeymoon to Paris. As for jewelry, she had several good pieces, but nothing flashy or overly expensive. Unlike Nick, who had two Rolex fifteen-thousand-dollar watches and a Bvlgari chronograph that did everything but fly a plane.

And speaking of planes . . . at one point, Nick had wanted her to buy a Piper Aztec plane. When she'd argued the lack of need for such an extravagant purchase, he'd said it would only be a small plane. Still, a plane!

"Why not buy a yacht while you're at it?" she'd asked.

"Now that you mention it, think about the kind of networking we could do among my medical colleagues," Nick had remarked, giving her the coaxing smile he'd perfected over the years.

She now knew what kind of networking he'd had in mind.

Thank God that part of her life was over. And thank God there had been no airplane or yacht to deal with during their divorce.

Samantha sank down onto one couch and Luc onto the other. He took a sip of his strong coffee and made a humming noise of appreciation. She placed hers on the coffee table between them, a huge crosscut slab of an ancient cypress tree in the shape of an elongated egg. Its patina and whorls of age rings spoke to Samantha. Truly a work of art, by both nature and the craftsman.

Luc put his mug down, too, and ran a finger over the top of the table. "A Jacque Vermain?"

She nodded, surprised that Luc would recognize the work of the backwoods craftsman. His pieces weren't sold in any shop. You had to know someone who knew him, and even then the old codger might not let you come out to his bayou workshop to view his pieces.

"My sister-in-law Rachel . . . you've met her, haven't you?"

"Remy's wife?"

"Uh-huh. Anyhow, Rachel is an interior decorator," Luc said. "She fell in love with Vermain's furniture and talked him into making her a massive dining room table fer their big family. They've adopted a pigload of kids, y'know. And my wife has one of his salad bowls, which we're not allowed ta eat out of. Go figure."

"It probably cost as much as the down payment on your Beemer."

"Really?" Luc pretended shock but wasn't really all that concerned. He could afford a thousand-dollar salad bowl, or two. "Anyhow, Tante Lulu wants him to carve her a statue of St. Jude, but thus far he's declined. Not his thing."

"Hey, I heard he was just commissioned by some Jewish congregation in Biloxi to make a carved, arched double door for its synagogue." She'd read about it in the style section of the Sunday paper. Which was becoming a rarity in itself . . . print newspapers, that was. To her, lolling about on a Sunday morning with a computer version of the *New York Times* wasn't nearly as satisfying as a print edition spread all over the place. Another thing Nick hadn't been able to stand. "So, St. Jude might not be far behind," she concluded.

Luc smiled. They both knew how persistent the old lady could be when she wanted something.

"The wedding was wonderful," Samantha commented then, which wasn't really a change of subject. Everyone knew that Tante Lulu was largely responsible for the wedding celebration, and, Good Lord, they must have invited half of the South.

"Yeah, it was great, wasn't it? Did you see Charmaine dirty dancing around her husband Rusty, like he was a friggin' stripper pole?"

"No, I must have left by then."

"She was three sheets to the wind, although it doesn't take much of a breeze for Charmaine to show off her assets." He grinned and added, "Never thought I'd see the day my brother Tee-John would settle down, though."

Actually, Luc, Remy, and René were brothers, while John and Charmaine were half brother and half sister, having different mothers. Or something like that.

"Way I hear it, all you LeDeux men were . . . are . . . wild."

"True enough," he said, making a little bow, as if she'd paid him a compliment, "but all in the past, once we married." He winked at her to show he hadn't tamed down all that much. "Anyhow, none of us were ever as bad . . . or good . . . as Tee-John. I was certainly never a stripper, even if Tee-John only ever did it for a week or so on a bet until Tante Lulu dragged him home by the ear from Atlantic City. That boy probably taught Charmaine some of the moves she demonstrated at the wedding, or maybe it was the other way around." He grinned at Samantha, and she could see why the LeDeuxs had a reputation for charm.

"Well, Tee-John might be the king of cool, but the Cajun Men Revue your family puts on occasionally comes a close second. I saw you out at Angola Prison a few years ago." And they had been really good, doing a bayou version of that old Village People act. Even Luc in his conservative business suit. Macho Man, for sure.

"Don't remind me. I swear, my aunt could talk a bear into doing the hula." He shook his head as if to rid it of a distasteful memory.

The LeDeux clan was notorious throughout the South, especially with their leader, the outrageous Tante Lulu, calling all the shots. But, really, the Starr family was no better, Samantha had to admit. And there was an amazing thirty-some of them floating around, most of them involved with the family business, others just reaping the profits. Can anyone say alimony? Or freeloader? But all of them a little bit weird.

Stanley Starr, her grandfather who founded the grocery store chain, walked around in white plantation suits, under which he wore suspenders and arm garters. With his white hair and goatee, he resembled the late Colonel Sanders of chicken fame. Grandfather had a thing for Elvis and would allow no Muzak in his one hundred stores, only old Elvis songs. Coming from Scottish immigrants, Stanley instilled in his children . . . or at least some of them . . . a love of all things Scottish.

Then there was her father Bruce Starr who was currently on his fifth wife, Florence, a former women's prison warden. Well, actually a superintendent of women's prisons for the state of Alabama, a political appointment. Bruce cherished his Scottish heritage, too, and was often seen in a kilt, knee socks, and sporran. In Louisiana! They'd even had haggis for Thanksgiving one time. Eew!

Samantha's mother Colette Starr, the first wife, lived on the Cote d'Azur when she wasn't skipping from one society hot spot to another. You'd never know that her mother had been born in a Baton Rouge trailer park and her real name was Colleen.

Aunt Dot, a fifty-something, butch lesbian to the max and proud of it, ran the marketing section of Starr Foods like a general. She was responsible for Starr Foods being a gay pride sponsor for one of the Mardi Gras floats last year.

Her uncle Douglas (which he insisted be pronounced Doog-lass in a Scots dialect) was an overaged Casanova who hit on every woman he met. He, too, was often seen in a kilt and liked to use words like "bonnie" and "braw" and "Wheesht!" and "lassie" and "Dinna fash yerself!"

Her half brother Wallace was responsible for Starr Foods owning a thoroughbred racing farm in Kentucky. They'd yet to have a winner, but it was a great write-off in taxes, or so Wallace claimed. All of his racers had names related to Scotland, such as "Highlander," "Braw Laddie," "Loch Lassie," "Bagpiper," "Tartan," "Heather Now," and "Whiskey Girl."

Aunt Maire had an obsession with pink, the color, not

the singer. Everything she wore had to be pink, even her hair, lipstick, and nail enamel. Her house in the French Quarter was painted pink (which gave the historical preservationists a fit), and the interior was enough to give a person a Pepto-Bismol headache.

Angus Starr, her stepbrother by marriage or some such thing (yes, Angus, like the cow), was never seen without a laptop or the latest electronic gismo. Angus, ten or so years younger than Samantha, was the son by a previous marriage of Darla, her father's third wife. Angus, when he wasn't attending one college or another (*Can anyone say professional student?*) was supposedly working on a computer project for Starr Foods that would revolutionize their distribution, but he rarely showed up for work, it being too boring for his superior brain.

"I heard you met the newest additions to the LeDeux clan. At the wedding," Luc said, jarring her from her reverie.

"News travels fast on the bayou. You mean the Alaska twins?"

"Yep. Tante Lulu's already got her matchmaking wheels whirring."

"Not in my direction, I hope."

"Would that be so bad?"

"Puh-leeze. I have enough of a man problem with Nick. Besides, what I don't need is another egotistical, arrogant, two-timing doctor."

"You paint all the medical profession with one brushstroke?"

"Believe me, I've seen enough with Nick and all his colleagues to write a book. Sleazebag doctors and the women they screw. You know the difference between God and doctors? God doesn't think he's a doctor."

"Whoa," Luc said with a laugh. "Anyhow, only one of the twins is a doctor. Daniel. The other one is a pilot. In fact, Aaron has already talked to Remy about possibly flying copters with his company."

"Oh." Funny, but the only one she'd noticed was Daniel. He'd been so compellingly attractive to her that she hadn't even noticed the brother Aaron. "Well, that's neither here nor there. I'm not in the market for another man in my life, doctor or otherwise."

"Okay. Tell me what Nick's been up to." Luc took a small notebook and a pen out of the inside breast pocket of his suit jacket.

"I told you about his threats after the hearing."

"That was two weeks ago. Are you regretting not filing a complaint like I suggested?"

She shrugged. "He showed up last Friday. I came home from work to find him here, inside the house."

That got Luc's attention. He sat up straighter. "Trespass."

She shrugged again. "I'm not sure it could be classified that way. He was supposed to turn in his house keys before the divorce, but he claimed he just found the duplicate."

"Which you made him turn over, right?"

"Right. And I had a locksmith here to change all the locks the next day."

"What did he want?"

"He apologized for his behavior in the hallway after the hearing. He said he wanted to try for a reconciliation."

Luc made a snorting sound of disbelief, which Samantha found rather insulting. "More like another shot at the money tree. No reflection on you, darlin', but Nick is a world-class leech. I hope you told him to get lost."

"I told him I wasn't interested, but he didn't believe me. In fact, he tried to . . ."

"Please tell me, he didn't . . . you didn't?"

She was rather insulted, again, this time that he thought

she could be so gullible. "Of course not." But then, she had to admit, "My grandfather showed up. I'd invited him for dinner. Nick is so clueless, he actually tried to stay for dinner."

Luc shook his head with disgust.

"Every day since then, he's been sending flowers or showing up at my house or my office. Nothing threatening exactly, just persistent."

"I suspect his lawyer has told him that he's going to lose his bid for more alimony. In fact, he might be cut off completely."

"From your mouth to God's ears!" Their new hearing date wasn't until next month, but maybe Luc had heard something.

He shook his head in answer to her silent question. "Nothing from the court, but rumors are flying about Nick's building project. Apparently, he lost a malpractice suit last year, and his rates are now through the roof. Then he hired that hotshot architect from Boston who drives around town in a hot damn silver Rolls Royce that cost more than most folks' homes. That on top of a shitty economy and new, restrictive bank loan regulations . . . well, he's getting desperate."

Samantha knew exactly who Luc referred to. Nick had read about Frank Fenton-Lewis in *Architectural Digest* (*Where else!*) a long time ago and swore he would use his services someday.

It's not that Samantha couldn't afford the alimony. She just hated that so much of her cash was going to the bum. And, frankly, if she'd still been with Nick, she wouldn't have blinked at giving him the capital for his little Taj Mahal which was pretentious in design, to say the least. Skylights? And Italian marble floors? Really?

"Desperation . . . that's exactly what I'm sensing about him," Samantha said. "Barely controlled anger under a façade of pseudo charm. Okay, I admit it, he scares me a little."

"Do you want me to file for a restraining order?"

"Do I have grounds?"

"Probably not. Yet. But we could file anyhow. He wouldn't like the publicity, even if we didn't get a court order. It might deter him."

"Or it might provoke him into doing more."

He nodded, acknowledging her point. "Okay, here's what we're going to do. What kind of security system do you have here?"

"Just a keyed entry and motion detectors."

"I'm going to send a security expert over tomorrow to check out your whole property. It's a good idea for a single woman to do that anyhow."

"No gun?" she asked with a laugh.

"Do you have a gun permit? Do you know how to use a weapon?"

"No and no." And she didn't want to, either. Not even to wipe out her evil ex-husband.

"How about a dog?"

"Huh? You mean, like a pit bull or something."

"Not necessarily. Dogs bark and intimidate intruders. Even little ones can be a deterrent."

"I've never had a dog. My parents got divorced when I was a kid, and it never worked out with our living arrangements. And Nick is allergic to pet dander."

"See. Even better."

"I don't know. I wouldn't know the first thing about finding a guard dog."

"I have a friend with a pet rescue farm outside the city, up near Charmaine and Rusty's ranch. Mick Andreas. C'mon. I'll go with you."

"Now?" She wasn't sure she was ready to make a decision, right now.

"Sure. Mick is a client, as well as a friend. I have some papers to deliver to him. C'mon. It'll be fun. We can stop at my place along the way and pick up my girls. They love going out to Mick's place. Last time, they talked me into adopting a chicken, Miss Cluck-Cluck."

She raised her brows, not sure if he was serious or not.

"The truth," he said, making the sign of the cross over his chest. "We had fresh eggs every morning until Tante Lulu decided Miss Cluck-Cluck would make a good Sunday dinner."

Now, she knew he was kidding.

"Actually, the neighbors were starting to complain."

Maybe.

Thus, it was that by seven p.m. that evening, Samantha was the proud (stunned would be a better word) mommy to:

— Axel, an older German Shepherd who had been abused, resulting in a limp, half an ear gone, and bald spots.
— a Savannah cat with a mean attitude named Madeline who had the size and appearance of a small cheetah, including the typical black spots against a cinnamon background. The exotic animal had already turned up her nose at cat food, but apparently leftover fresh salmon at twenty dollars a pound would suffice. (Good thing her family owned a chain of supermarkets.)
— a cockatoo that could speak three languages.
— the two peacocks out in her backyard, here only for temporary fostering, but they kept pooping on the patio and pecking at the glass windows of the atrium, wanting to come inside. Samantha was pretty sure the fostering was only going to last until tomorrow, once her neighbors heard the noise or got a whiff of the turds. The only reason

she'd taken them at all was because they had been returned five times to the rescue farm so far, and there was a hint that they might have to be "put down."

And then the phone rang.

It was Nick. On her new private number! "Hey, sweetheart," he said.

"Are you kidding me? Sweetheart?"

"Now, sweetheart."

"What do you want?"

"I just wanted to say, let's get together. Just you and me. No lawyers. What do you say?"

Not a chance! She was about to end the call without saying anything more . . . it was best not to engage in any interaction with the creep . . . but then Nick asked, "What's that noise in the background?"

There was the screeching noise of the peacocks, the barking of the dog, the hissing of the cat, and the bird squawking, *"Merde! Merde! Merde!"*

"It's my bodyguards," she replied. With inordinate pleasure!

Chapter Five

I'll have my mint julep out on the verandah, Scarlett . . .

Daniel was driving out to the far end of Terrebonne Parish where he was meeting his brother Aaron. He kept checking his GPS to make sure he followed the directions his brother had given him. Aaron wanted him to see a property he was considering buying.

Hard to believe that they had been in Louisiana for two years now, he mused. Harder, still, to believe that their mother had been gone for so long.

Times flies when you're having fun. Or not. Having fun, that is.

Daniel lived here in the South, only intermittently, but Aaron was here for the long haul. His brother flew copters for Remy LeDeux's company and rented Remy's houseboat for living quarters, but that might change if he bought this place he wanted to show him. Daniel already knew he was going to tell Aaron it was too far out. If Aaron wasn't careful, he would be considered a hermit, like his brother. On the other hand, no chance of that! Aaron was the social butterfly of the family.

Aunt Mel had sold the air freight company, but was still in Alaska trying to get rid of her home in a down real estate market. What she would do then, he had no idea. Maybe move to Florida like she'd once said. Take a cruise. Go on a world tour.

Daniel traveled back to Alaska occasionally to help her out, but mostly because he had nothing better to do. Sometimes, he just got in his car, which he'd brought down to Louisiana, and drove. To Florida. To Texas. As far north as Kentucky. A regular bleepin' tourist.

Searching. Always searching. For something. His soul, maybe.

While Aaron had settled comfortably into the Cajun culture, Daniel was still restless and unhappy since he'd given up medicine. Oh, he served on one of Tante Lulu's charitable foundation boards, and had even tried a return to medicine by donating his services to fight Ebola in Africa for six months, but he was more depressed and aimless than ever. "No wonder! Why dint ya jist dunk yer head in a barrel of vinegar and expect ta come up smellin' of honey," Tante Lulu had commented at the time.

Mostly, he just hung out in the fishing camp he rented on a remote bayou. No TV, but he read a lot. Mostly thrillers, by writers like Grisham, Clancy, or Thor, but the occasional medical journal, too. And he was becoming a fan of classic rock music, the louder the better. No, not Barry Frickin' Manilow. Songs like "Glory Days," "Another Brick in the Wall," "Barracuda," "Roxanne," "Paint It Black," "Dream On," and the like. No one to complain about the noise, except the gators and the snakes, and they weren't talking. Most people probably thought he lay around listening to boring classical music. Okay, he did like Mozart and Beethoven in the right circumstances, but he had a wild side, too. Really.

"Fishing camp" was the term given to cabins on stilts out in the swamps. His was nicer than some, but still, it was temporary, and, in fact, he'd have to move soon since the owner wanted to sell. Would he look for another fishing camp to rent, or something else? And would it be here in Louisiana, or somewhere else? Decisions, decisions, and all he wanted to do was go fish, which he was becoming quite good at, by the way.

Aaron and Tante Lulu never gave up on trying to shake him out of his self-imposed "prison." Really, he just wanted to be left alone. He would emerge from his cocoon when he was ready. And he didn't need any psychiatrist to tell him that, either. Or Aaron who took that "brother's keeper" Biblical quote way too seriously. Or Tante Lulu who had an opinion on everything in the world.

When he complained about their interference, Aaron usually answered, "Sue me!" and Tante Lulu advised, "Get over yerself!"

They still didn't know what it was that Tante Lulu had to give them since she'd misplaced it and hadn't been able to find it. Hah! Daniel wondered sometimes if there ever had been an actual "something important" she needed to give them. In fact, one time he'd told the interfering busybody just that and was rewarded with a thwap to the side of his head with a folded fan.

Supposedly, it was something from their deceased maternal grandmother in a small sealed box that rattled around like it might be a key, or an heirloom ring, or a voodoo medallion, according to Tante Lulu. "But then,

Dolly Doucet was in a nursin' home, at the time, with the Alls-hammer, crazy as a loon. Soz, it might jist be her false teeth.''

There were times Daniel barely restrained himself from throttling the old lady. Like yesterday, when he'd grumbled, "It couldn't be too important if you lost it."

"I dint lose it! I put it somewhere safe where I wouldn't forget it. It'll come ta me any day now."

"Since it was originally intended for our mother, and she's dead now, we might be dead by then, too."

"An' I might jist be the one ta do it, fool! Where'd ya put that hope chest I had made fer you?"

That had shut him up. Tante Lulu had made hope chests for both him and Aaron, as she did for all the men in her family. Good Lord! What was Daniel going to do with hand crocheted doilies and embroidered pillow-cases, a cast iron skillet, and six different St. Jude statues? St. Jude was the patron saint of hopeless cases and a favorite of Tante Lulu.

Daniel saw Aaron leaning against his pickup which was parked along the berm of the road ahead. He pulled up behind him, turned off the engine, parked, and got out.

Daniel's jaw dropped at what he saw before him. "You're kidding, right?"

"Nope. This is going to be our new house."

"Our?"

"Of course. Do you think I'd exclude you from such a sweetheart deal?"

Daniel was faced with the most outrageous thing his brother had done yet. Interference didn't begin to describe it. "This isn't a house. It's a mansion. A frickin' *Gone with the Wind*, Where-the-hell's-Rhett, Tara plantation!"

"I've been worried about you, Dan. To say you've been morose would be a world class understatement."

"Morose? You been reading the dictionary again?"

"Wallowing, then."

"You've been talking to Tante Lulu."

Aaron shrugged, as if that was a given.

"It's not your problem, Aaron. *I'm* not your problem. Or your project."

"I beg to differ. Does 'my brother's keeper' ring any bells?"

"That brother's keeper bullshit was old the first time you said it. By now, it stinks like a loaded diaper."

"You're depressed."

"So the hell what?"

"Ever since you quit medicine and Mom died . . . hell, ever since we came to Louisiana two years ago, you've become more and more withdrawn," Aaron went on, ignoring Daniel's comment. "And that's despite the warm welcome extended to us by all the LeDeux family."

"Except for our slimy no-good father." To say Valcour LeDeux hadn't laid out the welcome mat was a vast understatement. He was more worried that they might want something from him, like money.

"Daddy Dearest doesn't count." Aaron wasn't about to let him divert his attention as he continued on his tirade. "Those years spent with sick and dying kids killed something inside you, Dan. All that on top of losing Mom."

"So now you've become Dr. Phil of the Bayou?"

"Whatever works. Anyhow, look around you. Bayou Rose Plantation is a gem just waiting to be polished."

"More like sandblasted." His brain snagged on something Aaron had said. "You bought a house with a name? Bayou Rose Plantation? A better name would be Weed Jungle."

"Tsk-tsk! It hasn't been an operating sugar plantation for well over a hundred years. This stretch of the bayou was wider back then and deep enough for flatboats."

"Crap! Now you're gonna give me a history lecture."
Daniel raised his eyes heavenward, as if for assistance.

"I prefer to call it a mini-mansion with commercial development prospects."

"Now you're a Dixie entrepreneur, as well as a historian. Have you lost your mind?"

"No more than usual. C'mon. Hop in. I'll give you the tour."

He got in the passenger side of the truck, and Aaron turned the motor on, moving slowly up the horseshoe-shaped driveway to the front steps, which were located more than two hundred yards from Bayou Black, via a sloping overgrown lawn, through a canopied alleé of live oaks dripping moss. After parking, Aaron sat quietly for a moment, for dramatic effect, no doubt, taking in the ambience—*Can anyone say creepy?*—then grinned. "Actually, I didn't buy a mansion, Danny boy. *We* bought a mansion."

Daniel turned slowly, inch by inch, to stare at him. It was the stare he'd perfected to make nurses and interns cower.

Pilots were immune, apparently, because Aaron just grinned. Some more.

"You didn't!" Daniel ripped out.

"I did," he said cheerily. Reaching over to open the glove compartment, he handed him the official sales agreement with the bank loan document attached. Both of their names were on them.

"You forged my name."

"Yep."

"Why?"

"You have a better credit rating than I do."

"Son. Of. A. Bitch! How did you manage it?"

"Combed my hair like a nerd, wore sunglasses and dorky clothes." Aaron tended to wear jeans and T-shirts most of the time while Daniel preferred Dockers and golf shirts. "Oh, and I perfected your frowny face."

Daniel frowned at him. "There's no way you could have gotten away with that. Don't all parties have to be present at a closing?"

"Not when you have Tante Lulu on your side with her friends in high places."

That explained it. The old lady seemed to be able to get around all kinds of regulations and red tape with her network of friends and politicians.

"We're not nine years old anymore, Aaron. You can't keep pulling this crap."

"I know," Aaron said, with not an ounce of regret. "By the way, you owe me twenty-five thousand dollars for your half of the down payment."

"Don't hold your breath."

"Don't tell me you're short of cash."

"Hey, I'm not the one who sold half of an air shipping company for a bundle."

"No, you're the one who made a killing in IT stocks before they crashed."

A stalemate.

They both got out of the pickup truck and stood, scanning the building and grounds. Daniel idly kicked a black snake out of the way. They'd both become accustomed to the reptiles after living in this semitropical climate. There must be a thousand varieties here, and they bred like sex machines. Snake heaven!

Taking center stage was a once-stately, raised-style plantation house, three stories above an open loggia, or verandah, or porch, or whatever the hell you called it. Massive wood columns, at least fifty feet high, stretched from the ground to the top of roofed galleries that encircled all sides of the mansion's second and third stories. A wide staircase rose majestically to the middle of the second floor, which was obviously the main living quarters, the norm here in bayou land where you only had to dig a foot to reach water.

"It's a Creole building in the Greek Revival Style, in case you aren't familiar with historical architecture in the Southland."

Daniel looked at his brother as if he'd grown two heads and remarked, "Bite me!"

"Tsk-tsk-tsk. It's not as run-down as it looks," Aaron said.

Daniel raised his brows skeptically.

"Okay, so it needs a little work."

"Like new plumbing, electricity, a roof, landscaping, and paint?"

"Yeah, but other than that it has great potential. Besides, we can both work on restoring the place in our spare time." Spare time being the key words here. While Aaron worked as a pilot for Remy LeDeux, Daniel did pretty much nothing, in Aaron's opinion. Therefore, the not-so-hidden message here was that Aaron thought it was time for Daniel to stop licking his wounds and get a life. Although why Aaron would think turning him into a carpenter was a step toward getting a life defied understanding.

"Aaron, what makes you think that you or I have the talent for restoration?"

"How hard can it be to sand wood and pound nails? Don't you ever watch *Home and Garden* on TV? Oops, I forgot. You don't have a TV. It'll be our DIY project. That's code for Do It Yourself. What we need is a trip to Home Depot."

"What we need is brain transplants if we take this on."

"Do they transplant brains now? Golly, gee, ain't science amazing!"

"Aaarrgh!"

"C'mon, Dan. We can do it. Remember that time in wood shop when we made those little cars for the Pinewood Derby?"

"You idiot! We were cub scouts. And my car looked like a brick with wheels. Yours was lopsided and wouldn't roll, even down the inclined plane."

"We can learn."

Daniel leaned against one of the columns and his elbow broke through. They both went wide-eyed at how rotten the wood was.

"Seems the termites have been kissing the oak," Aaron remarked with dry humor.

"Who are you kidding? The termites have fucked that wood to dust."

"Guess they should have used cypress. That's more resistant to pests, according to Tante Lulu. That's what we'll use in restoration. She knows someone that can give us a truckload cheap."

"That is just great. Why don't you just make the old lady building supervisor and be done with it."

"Good idea," Aaron said as he checked the sturdiness of the steps with his boot, then sat down, elbows on knees, chin braced in his palms.

"You better be kidding." Daniel sank down beside him. "Why did you do this? And why involve me?"

"First of all, I think we've both decided not to go back to Alaska. There's nothing for us there anymore. A few friends, and Aunt Mel . . . that's about it. And I for one prefer the warm weather."

"Go on," Daniel prodded. "This ought to be good."

"Second, there's a lot of acreage. I'm thinking about putting a mini runway in here, buying a small plane, and opening my own business. Aerial swamp tours, transport, that kind of thing. Same as I had in Alaska, but here in Louisiana."

"An investment, then?"

"Could be. We don't have to decide right away."

Draping an arm over his brother's shoulder, Daniel said, "Show me around this dump, and tell me what you have in mind."

Aaron walked Daniel through the house, praising all the highlights, or potential highlights, skimming over the problems. "The electricity and plumbing are antiquated, but they work. So, at least we can move in while the renovation goes on."

"Together? You and I are going to live together again? Next we'll be having sleepovers."

"Only if they involve women. Hey, we can divide the house into apartments if that'll make you feel better, but it would mean more expenses and delays." Aaron widened his eyes and stared at him with innocence.

Which Daniel wasn't buying. He knew a con job when he heard it. "I'll probably regret this . . . in fact, I'm already regretting it . . . but I'll give it a try."

They bumped fists.

"Truthfully, I've got to move out of that fishing cabin. And I haven't been able to exert myself enough to find my own apartment."

"See, it was meant to be."

"I wouldn't go that far. Maybe it will help me get away from Tante Lulu and all her machinations. She claims St. Jude has his eyes on me for some love bolt thing."

"He's the patron saint of hopeless cases," Aaron informed him, as if he didn't already know that.

"Which is Tante Lulu's unsubtle way of saying I'm hopeless, I guess. But I have no idea what that has to do with thunderbolts."

"Thunderbolt of love, baby," Aaron explained.

"Pff! She keeps telling everyone we meet that I'm not gay. As if that were even in question. Just because I don't have a woman in my life, just because I won't let her set me up on dates," Daniel complained. "I don't look gay, do I?" He turned to face Aaron.

"Well . . ."

Daniel swatted his brother on the arm for his teasing.

"Hey, she's got me in her crosshairs, too," Aaron said. "Except in your case she has a specific woman in mind. Samantha Starr."

"What? Is that old biddy nuts? Not gonna happen." Samantha Starr had become the bane of his life since he'd first met her at his half brother John LeDeux's wedding. For some reason, she'd taken an instant dislike to him, just because he was a doctor and her ex-husband had been a doctor. Of course, it didn't help that he baited her every chance he got. It didn't help, either, that he seemed to run into her everywhere, probably Tante Lulu's doing. At the foundation board meetings. At LeDeux family gatherings. Even the fish and bait store where she'd been buying a fifty-pound bag of dog kibbles. She was irritating, sarcastic, condescending, and for some inexplicable reason, sexy as hell. Inexplicable because she was not his type of woman. An erotic splinter, that's what she was to him, and it was lodged smack dab where it would hurt most. Down yonder, as Tante Lulu would say.

Not that the old lady would remark on his down yonder.

On the other hand, maybe she would.

"Samantha is a good-looking woman," Aaron said.

"If you like full-body freckles."

"I suspect you do."

"She hates my guts."

"I don't know about that."

"I do. She told me so. More than once."

"That's like Suzi Benton telling me that I stink like frog spit before she kissed me. On the mouth. Yeeew!"

"Aaron! You were eight years old."

"I'm just sayin'." Aaron grinned at him, then went serious. "But . . . um, about Tante Lulu—"

"Yoo hoo!"

Both of their heads snapped up at the same time. Then they stood, walked to the end of the gallery, and peered around the side of the house. The old lady was approaching from the backyard. *Do they call the back area of a plantation a yard?* Daniel wondered with what had to be hysterical irrelevance.

"Holy hell, Aaron!" he said then, just noticing all the outbuildings surrounded by metal fences. "What in God's name are they?"

"The former slave quarters made into kennels. The previous owner, who died thirty years ago, was a dog breeder. Showed Redbone Coonhounds all over the world. Blue ribbons out the wazoo. The property was fallin' down even back then."

Tante Lulu was huffing and puffing closer.

"What the hell is *she* doing here?" Daniel asked him.

"Uh."

"Oh, no! Don't tell me you invited her here today?"

"Uh."

Daniel smacked him on the arm, again, then walked back, and stepped doggedly down the rickety steps. Aaron rushed to catch up, probably hoping, with futility, to do a bit of damage control before Tante Lulu barreled in.

The petite Cajun lady was outrageous as ever in a glittery red T-shirt with the logo, "There's Still Plenty of Zippedy in the Old Doo-Dah," tucked into child-size capri pants. Her hair was bright curly red today, matching her lip gloss. Typical Tante Lulu. "Hey, y'all. My niece Charmaine dropped me off a bit ago soz I could have a look around. Ain't this nice?"

Without waiting for an answer, the old lady reached up to give Aaron a hug. When she turned to do the same to him, his glower stopped her short. But only for a moment. She yanked him down by the ears and gave a big smack on the cheek.

"Are ya sure ya ain't gay, Daniel?" Tante Lulu smiled with a wicked gleam in her eyes.

Daniel growled, and Aaron stepped between the two of them.

Tante Lulu craned her little neck around Aaron and addressed Daniel. "Congratulations, boy. I guess Aaron tol' ya 'bout all the plans fer Bayou Rose Plantation."

Daniel turned slowly to look at Aaron. "All what plans?"

"The animal rescue operation," Tante Lulu informed him gleefully. "Lordy, Lordy! My charity's been concentratin' on orphans and poor families startin' back after Hurrycane Katrina, but no one's lookin' after all the animals left behind. So many of them got loose and were never rounded up. They been begettin' and begettin' ever since, lak the Bible. Lots of them need homes, and some of them need doctorin'. Good thing—"

"Whoa, whoa, whoa!" Daniel knew about Jude's Angels, Tante Lulu's charity that operated under the umbrella of the Hope Foundation. Hell, he served on its board. He ought to know. But this was the first he'd heard about animals. "What animal rescue operation?" Just then, the fenced-in buildings out back were making sense. "You can't possibly think that I'm going to work with animals."

Tante Lulu waved a hand airily, like she was the queen, and they were her minions. "Jist 'til ya get back ta reg'lar doctorin', honey."

"I'm a physician . . . not a veterinarian."

"Same thing. But not ta worry. It's jist a blip of an idea

fer now. Mebbe sometime in the future. Mebbe you'll have a better idea."

Daniel didn't trust the old lady's blips. Not one bit. As for other ideas, he couldn't say out loud what ideas were in his head at the moment. "I thought you were going to build a flight operation here," Daniel accused Aaron.

"Can't I do both? That's the great thing about twins. We multitask."

Daniel told him what he could do with his multitasking.

Ignoring them, Tante Lulu was on a tear. "—and the doctor's office in the *garconniére*?"

"The garden-what?"

"Not garden. Gar-son . . . *garconniére*." She waved her hand toward an odd-shaped building off to the side of the house. Sort of hexagonal in shape. It wasn't very big. There couldn't be more than one or two rooms on each of the three stories. "Bachelor quarters. These kinda buildings were fer the planter's sons once they were growed up but not yet married."

"Sort of a nineteenth century bachelor pad," Aaron elaborated.

"Lots of hanky panky went on in them, I understan'."

"Sex on the Bayou, for sure," Aaron commented.

He was going to whack Aaron a good one when they were alone. "That's where I'll stay then," Daniel decided.

"Not on the bottom floor, though. Thass fer yer doctor's office."

"Whaaat?"

Tante Lulu walked over to a straggly plant and was examining it. Being a *traiteur*, she was always picking up new herbs or seeds and putting them in little plastic zipper bags in her gigantic purse.

"Don't ignore me, old lady." Daniel put his hands on his hips and glared alternately at Aaron and Tante Lulu.

"You think I'm going to treat cancer patients out here in the boonies, when I'm not out rounding up mutts?"

"It won't jist be dogs. There'll be dogs, cats, birds, and other things."

It was the "other things" that worried Daniel. He gritted his teeth and counted to ten in silence.

"As fer cancer patients . . . not ta worry! Yer gonna try yer hand at being a GP. A GP is a general practitioner." She was still yanking up plants while she spoke. Bending over, she gave them a good view of her tiny little ass. Not a pretty sight.

"I know what a GP is." He pulled at his own hair with frustration.

"It'll be a first step back ta yer callin'." Tante Lulu closed her purse and walked back toward them.

Daniel, hands still on his hips, glared some more. "You have no right to interfere in my life."

It was Tante Lulu who now put her hands on her hips and glared up at him. "Thass what family does, boy."

"You aren't my—"

Tante Lulu put up a halting hand. "Doan you dare say that we're not family. We are. And we care about ya, even though ya make it sore hard sometimes, bless yer Yankee heart."

Daniel put his face in his hands, then raised his head and said, "Sorry."

Tante Lulu nodded.

"But I still say I'm not Yankee. I'm from Alaska."

"Cain't get any farther north than that."

"I need to get out of here." Daniel looked at Aaron, pleadingly.

"You take Samantha out on a date yet?" the old lady inquired of Daniel.

"No, and I don't intend—"

"Best ya hurry up. I read in *Cosmo* that men reach their sexual peak at thirty."

Daniel didn't know what was more outrageous. That Tante Lulu, who had to be ninety if she was a day, read *Cosmo*, or that she was discussing his virility, or lack thereof.

But her brain had already veered in another direction. "You can leave, Daniel."

As if I need her permission!

"Aaron will stay with me."

Aaron's face took on an expression of alarm.

Good!

"Aaron kin come back ta town with me when Charmaine comes ta pick me up. I gots ta introduce him ta his neighbor first."

"You do?" Aaron asked.

And wasn't it odd that she needed to introduce just Aaron, not the two of them? Not that he wanted to be included in any of her plans.

"Yep. Del Dugas. A farmer about a half mile away. Old man Dugas bought the farm back fifty years or so, but he died five years ago leavin' the place ta Del." She was grinning at Aaron as she spoke.

Aaron looked as if he was about to puke. "You think I would be interested in a farmer? I'm not gay."

Tante Lulu chuckled. "Ever'one this side of the Mason-Dixon line knows that. Yer brother, on the other hand . . . Ooooh, I forgot. I brought you boys a housewarmin' gift." She pointed to the far end of the ground level verandah where a dismantled St. Jude birdbath sat in the shadows. He knew it was St. Jude because everyone who ever met Tante Lulu found out within minutes that he was her favorite saint. A regular fan club she had going. The statue would probably be six feet tall. "Charmaine helped me unload it. I figger ya kin put it in the rose garden."

"What rose garden?" he and Aaron both asked.

"The one over there," she said, pointing to a jungle on

the east side of the house, opposite from the *garconniére*. "Also, before ya start, mebbe ya should hire Jem Hawkins, the snake catcher."

It would seem Tante Lulu had her finger in a lot of restoration pies. Surprise, surprise. And was it a coincidence that the folks she talked into restoring these old dumps . . . uh, plantations . . . were usually dumb Yankees? No surprise there, either.

"Jem's nickname is Stinky 'cause he allus smells like swamp water, bless his heart," Tante Lulu continued. "Stinky sez ya got twelve different species of snake colonies here."

Oh, that was just what Daniel needed to hear! Aaron wasn't too thrilled, either. "We have *colonies*?" he choked out.

Then Tante Lulu, whose brain skittered from one subject to another like popcorn over an open fire, turned to Aaron again. "Mebbe ya oughta go comb yer hair and tuck in yer shirt afore we go over ta the Dugas farm. If ya wanna ask fer a date, ya gotta be spiffied up a bit. But not all freaky neat lak Daniel. Ya gotta be laid-back cool. Lak that Matthew McConaughey fellow in the car ads, or Richard Simmons, of course."

McConaughey, Daniel could see, but the other? It boggled the mind, but Tante Lulu considered the reclusive exercise guru to be a "real hottie." She'd told them so on more than one occasion.

"I can get my own dates, thank you very much," Aaron said.

"Did I fergit ta tell ya . . . Del is short fer Delilah?"

Daniel couldn't believe how much he was enjoying his brother's discomfort, even if the old bat had called him "freaky."

"Delilah?" Aaron frowned. "No, you didn't mention that the farmer was a lady. But I'm still not—"

"Oh, and it's not the usual kind of farm."

He and Aaron exchanged glances, knowing there was bound to be a zinger to come.

"Okay, I'll bite. What does the sweet Delilah raise on her farm?" Aaron asked with a sigh of resignation.

"Alligators."

ZING!

"Ya ever seen a lady wrestle an alligator?"

DOUBLE ZING!

Daniel had to see this! No way was he heading back to his bayou fishing camp now. He got his jollies any way he could these days (translated: not very often), and watching Tante Lulu pull off a love connection for his brother promised to be amusing, especially when her Cajun cupid's dart involved a female alligator wrestler. Oh, boy! This was almost as good as the time Aaron had a blind date with a mortician.

Aaron, who was usually game for anything new, was muttering, "Not a chance!" Daniel wasn't at all surprised to hear his brother claim a sudden emergency and hightail it off the plantation.

Leaving Daniel with the cagey matchmaker from hell.

Chapter Six

W̶ho says busybody is a bad word? . . .

    Louise Rivard's niece Charmaine was driving her home to her cottage on Bayou Black after visiting the "boys" at Bayou Rose. Watching the passing scenery through her open car window, Louise mused that she must have traveled this way ten thousand times, maybe fifty thousand, her humble home having been in the Rivard family for generations. It was a ride Louise always enjoyed.

    The memories . . . ah, the memories this road evoked! Many of them involved her fiancé Phillipe Prudhomme and warm summer days in his old Triumph sports car, the radio blaring out "Chattanooga Choo-Choo." That was 1942, of course, after Phillipe got drafted into the war. The Big War. Phillipe, bless his soul, died on D-Day.

Enough of that! Otherwise, she would be weeping. Even after all these years.

The landscape along the two-lane road which ran parallel to her beloved bayou was like a step back in time. Old peeling billboards and painted wood Burma Shave signs that had been restored by some misguided parish historical society member. Really, there had to be more important relics of the past.

She sighed and continued to watch the passing scenery in silence. Cajun style houses, including some on stilts, and the occasional rice plantation from another era. A few shanties and run-down trailers. Boudreaux's General Store, the fish and bait shop whose owner also sold Avon beauty products, a landscape company that had a special running on crushed oyster shells and mulch, some small, blue-collar cottages, like hers, that had been built a long time ago by men and women involved in the fishing industry, whether in the swamp or out on the Gulf.

The best thing of all about living here in Southern Louisiana was the lush flowers and trees that grew in the sub-tropical climate. Magnolias the size of dinner plates, picturesque live oak trees dripping gray Spanish moss. Fruits and vegetables that grew so well that a person didn't hardly need to go to the grocery store. And of course there was the ageless, coffee-colored bayou stream.

"You're awful quiet today, auntie," Charmaine said suddenly.

"I was just thinkin'. Nothin' important," Louise said. "But there is somethin' I wanna discuss with you. Charmaine, honey, we gotta have us a powwow."

"Lawdy! A powwow?"

Ignoring Charmaine's question, Louise mused, again, on another subject now. *I must be in a musin' kind of mood today.* "Funny, ain't it, how over the years so many people come ta refer ta me as Tante Lulu, or Aunt Lulu, that I think of mahself in the same way?"

"That, and busybody, bless yer heart, auntie."

"Yep. An' they say it lak it's a bad thing. 'You old busybody!' Frankly, I'm more pee-owed at bein' called old."

Charmaine arched her brows at her. No one could do a good eyebrow arching better than Charmaine. Hers were "artificially enhanced."

"Doan ya get me started on the age bizness. Yer only as old as ya feel, and I'm feelin' 'bout forty and frisky."

Charmaine arched her brows again, but the girl knew enough not to say anything.

Anyone under fifty was a girl to Louise.

Charmaine was probably thinking "Lawdy!" That used to be Louise's favorite expression before Charmaine took it over. Let her! She'd be taking over a lot more than that before long, if Louise had her way. But she wasn't about to say that out loud . . . yet. Instead, she said, "I know I got a few years under mah girdle, but I doan let that get me down, lak some folks with puffy lips and foreheads so tight they cain't hardly blink."

"Don't look at me. I haven't had any work done."

"I was thinkin' 'bout Flora Mae Benoit. When I saw her goin' ta communion at Our Lady of the Bayou Church, I almost fell off mah pew. Fish lips! Thass all I'm gonna say on the subject. And didja watch them Academy Awards las' time? Half the actresses, and even some of the actors, looked lak their skin was pulled off their faces and tied in the back with a rubber band. One clip, and there'd be skin flyin' everywhere. The idjits are allus lookin' fer the fountain of youth, when they's already drownin' in the fountain of dumb."

Charmaine blinked at Louise's long tirade, then asked, "Auntie, yer so skinny. Why would ya be wearin' a girdle?"

As if that's the most important thing I just said! Didn't the girl listen?

"Ta hold up mah folds, silly. When ya get old, yer skin kinda sags inta folds, dontcha know? Not that I'm old, mind you. Jist ripe."

"Lak a peach?" Charmaine giggled.

"Zackly!"

"A peach with folds?"

"Well, mebbe more lak an orange. All those dimples. Some folks sez cellulite is jist butt dimples, what spread to yer thighs."

Charmaine grinned and shook her head, as if Louise were hopeless.

She wasn't. There was method in her madness. Always had been.

How did they get on the subject of age, anyhow? Well, she couldn't blame Charmaine. Not really. For some reason, Louise's mind seemed to bounce from one subject to another these days, like fleas on a mangy dog, and she needed to speak what popped up at the moment, lest she forget. Usually, she then forgot her original thought. Oh, right. Now, she remembered. "Back ta our powwow . . ."

"A powwow? Lawdy!" Charmaine said, and she didn't mean it in a nice way.

Lawdy was a strange kind of word. Louise realized that she missed it. The word could mean, "Lawdy, that is such a good idea!" Or "Lawdy! Are you crazy?"

"Are we gonna enter a belly dancin' contest again?" Charmaine asked. "We haven't done that in ages, but I don't think I'm in shape for that anymore."

Hah! Who is she kidding?

Charmaine had been Miss Louisiana at one time, and even now, in her forties, she looked darned good . . . and knew it. Today, she wore a red halter top that stopped just above her belly button where a little diamond stud sparkled, like a blinking neon sign saying, "Look at me! Look at me!" Her white capri pants might have been painted on, they was so tight. There were no panty lines, for sure, and no shadow at the crotch. She must be wearing a thong, or maybe she got one of them Brazil thingees that were offered by one of the five beauty salons and the ranch spa that Charmaine owned.

Louise was thinking about trying one herself (*the Brazil thingee, not the thong. Thongs jist got caught up in her crack*). But she had this odd reservation about being hairless down there. Some folks made sure they always wore clean underwear in case they had to make a sudden trip to the emergency room. She, on the other hand, didn't want to arrive at the Pearly Gates and have to explain to St. Peter why she . . . (*Well, you get the picture.*) Better yet, how would she explain it to Phillipe? The only Brazil they knew about back then had been the country . . . and Carmen Miranda. In those days, women just sprinkled on a bit of talcum powder . . . snow on the forest, so to speak . . . and that was that. In any case, she didn't have much left down there anyhow.

Back to Charmaine. Her dark brown, almost black, curls were piled on top of her head (*The higher the hair, the closer to God, dontcha know?*) in a deliberately sexy mess, and she had a bunch of gold chains with dangly pearls hanging from her ears like chandeliers. Her white wedgie sandals, on top of all that hair, made her about six feet tall. A self-proclaimed bimbo with class, that's what Charmaine always said. That, and bimbo with a brain. Same thing.

Daniel LeDeux about went bug-eyed when Charmaine had first stepped out of her car back at the plantation. Charmaine had that effect on men, all men, but especially her husband Rusty. That would be Raoul Lanier, who had to be the best-looking man in Louisiana. Whooboy! Louise even got a tickle down yonder looking at him. When he walked down the street in those tight jeans and scuffed boots and cowboy hat, the ladies about swooned. Not that he noticed. The boy . . . who was on his way to fifty now, too . . . had eyes only for Charmaine, which was as it should be. While Charmaine's favorite expression was "Lawdy!", Rusty's was "Mercy!" and he was usually saying it when he saw his wife in one of her get-ups.

"No, we are not entering any more belly dancing contests," Louise said. "Not that I couldn't. The last time we did any belly dancin', you decided ta become a 'born again virgin.' And ya married fer the fifth time."

"I only had four husbands, Rusty being mah first and last," Charmaine said indignantly. Her many marriages were a sore point with Charmaine. "And the other three didn't count since it turned out mah first divorce from Rusty was never valid."

"Don't be pitchin' a hissy fit. I was just teasin'."

"Are we gonna put a voodoo curse on someone, then? Powwow sounds sort of hoo-dooey."

Louise gave her the stink eye. Charmaine knew better than that. Being a devout Catholic and even devouter follower of St. Jude, Louise didn't believe in none of that voodoo-hoodoo.

Louise swatted her on the arm with a bunch of cattails she'd picked down by the bayou at Bayou Rose just before they'd left. Cattails were good for just about anything in her *traiteur* business . . . a natural antiseptic, pain reliever, blood coagulant, and so on, but they also made good eating, her favorite being the roots sliced raw into salads.

There wasn't much that Louise didn't know about bayou plants and how they could feed and heal the human body. She'd learned at the knees of her mother and grandmother, who had been folk healers, too.

"Sorry," Charmaine said, even though she didn't mean it, not one bit. Else, she wouldn't be grinning her way like a drunk possum. "But, ya gotta admit, auntie, Native American powwows do usually involve singin' and dancin' jist lak voodoo rituals."

"Powwow also means a planning session. I do declare, Charmaine, cain't ya jist listen?"

"I'm listenin'. And stop shakin' those cattails around. Yer gonna make a mess in mah car."

Hah! The inside of Charmaine's ess-you-vee was messy enough as it was with her makeup case and a Charmaine's Health Spa carry bag on the console between them, and odds and ends of beauty salon pamphlets and samples and such lying on the floor and backseat, even clipped to the sun visor and in a cup holder. Despite those scented products, the vehicle smelled a bit like cow poop which was understandable, considering that Charmaine lived on a ranch. In fact, the car doors on both sides had the logo "Triple L Ranch" imprinted on them.

"Time fer some matchmakin'," Louise declared. "Thass what we're gonna powwow about. I been hearin' thunderbolts in mah dreams, which is a sure sign love is on the horizon. Plus, I'm bored."

Charmaine pulled into the crushed shell driveway of Louise's cottage, which originally was built in the old Cajun style . . . an exterior of half logs with a chinking of *bousillage*, or fuzzy mud, a mixture of clay, Spanish moss, and crushed clam shells. Later, the structure had been stuccoed over. Then last year, she'd painted it a pretty yellow color with green shutters and a green metal roof. The colors made her happy.

Rock-edged flower beds surrounded the house, and a wire-mesh fence enclosed neat rows of her vegetable and herb gardens. And then there was a stretch of lawn that led down to the water's edge, centered by a St. Jude birdbath and a spreading fig tree heavy with ripe fruit that would soon have to be picked. She saw many fig dishes on her horizon: roasted figs with shallots, fig jams and preserves, and her MawMaw's fig cake topped with caramel icing and chopped pecans. She even liked figs in her salads, along with the slivers of cattail roots. Yum!

This place had been a refuge for Louise after Phillipe's death, but also to all those who'd come under her maternal wing in the decades since.

Useless came shuffling up the lawn, seeming to sniff the air.

"Doan be givin' the critter no Cheez Doodles t'day. He's gettin' fat."

"A fat alligator?"

"Uh-huh! I need ta find that boy a girlfriend, and it ain't gonna do no good if he's got a big ol' gut. René thinks Useless is a young fella of about thirty. Gators live ta be fifty or so, y'know. Mebbe even a hundred. Of course, that was before that *Swamp People* show on TV what makes all Cajuns seem lak dumb rednecks. They's gonna make gators as extinct as dinosaurs."

Charmaine rolled her eyes and grabbed for Louise's carry bag. "Lawdy!" she exclaimed as they both exited the car, Louise using her cattails to shush away the gator. "What have you got in this bag? It's so heavy."

"Nothin' special. Mah makeup. Mah herbs. Mah wallet. Mah cell phone. Mah revolver."

"Whaaat? I thought Luc confiscated that weapon."

"He did. I bought another one. A gal cain't be too careful with all the druggies around t'day. Besides, it came in handy las' week when I had ta shoot a water moccasin in mah shower. By the by, kin Rusty come by one day and repair a broken tile fer me?"

"Sure. But why didn't ya just whack it with a shovel, lak ya taught us ta do?"

"'Cause it was bigger than mah shovel. I wasn't takin' no chances. What if it weren't totally dead from mah whackin' and I tripped over mah St. Jude doorstop and then it bit me? I could be deader'n a swamp stump before anyone came and found me."

"Tante Lulu! That's dangerous. I worry about you being here all alone."

Louise admitted, "It might not have been a water moccasin. It was prob'ly a water snake. But it *was* big."

Charmaine's mouth was gaping open. But then she snapped it shut and asked, "Who's your matchmaking target this time . . . I mean, who needs matchmaking? Daniel, or Aaron? Or is it Simone LeDeux, that cop we met at Tee-John's wedding before she went off to Chicago. I heard she's back in town."

"And ain't that somethin'? Every time I think we tagged all of that horndog Valcour LeDeux's chillen, another one shows up. Wish I could get that man out of mah mind. He's lak a booger what can't be thumped off. Oops, sorry fer sayin' bad things 'bout yer daddy."

"Hah! Daddy has never been much of a daddy to me. Or to Luc, Remy, René, Tee-John, Daniel, Aaron, or now this Simone, and God only knows who else. Let's not talk about him anymore. I just get depressed."

Ain't that the truth? Louise unlocked the door and went through the small living room and directly into her kitchen.

Charmaine followed and immediately opened the fridge and took out a pitcher of cold sweet tea, pouring a glass for each of them.

Louise took a couple beignets out of the bread drawer and set them on a plate in the center of the table. "I got some leftover shrimp and grits with andouille sausage, if yer hungry," she said.

"No, this will be enough. Rusty is makin' barbecue fer dinner."

Louise sat down wearily and looked around. Her

kitchen was a charming room, if she did say so herself, with red-and-white checkered curtains and a matching tablecloth over an old 1940s red-and-white speckled porcelain enamel table on metal legs with four red leatherette chairs.

Off the kitchen was a pantry holding all of Louise's *traiteur* remedies. There was only a single window, but it provided enough light for her to handle her herbs and potions with mortar and pestle on the butcher block table in its center without going squinty-eyed. Even out here in the kitchen, she could smell the pungent dried herbs that hung from the pantry ceiling. Glass containers with handwritten labels were arranged on the floor-to-ceiling shelves, containing all the medicinal remedies she'd gathered from old and new recipes, some of them decades, even centuries old. The grandchildren always got a kick out of looking at jars holding the novel items, like alligator hearts, or possum tails, or frog tongues.

Enough with the reminiscing! "Back ta our matchmaking mission," Louise said, sitting down at the table across from Charmaine who'd just taken a bite of her beignet and sighed with pleasure. "I doan know fer sure, but I'm thinkin' Daniel is in most need of lovin'. He's got the blue devils badder'n I've ever seen. Well, no wonder! That boy has had a lot of rain in his life, bein' a children's cancer doctor. What he needs is some rainbows, of course."

"Of course." Charmaine was probably being sarcastic. She licked the sugar off her fingers, then wiped them on a St. Jude napkin. "And we're gonna bring him rainbows? With a love match?"

"Exactly."

"I'm afraid ta ask. Do ya have anyone in mind fer him."

"Samantha Starr."

"Lawdy!" Charmaine said. "Those two don't even like each other."

"Charmaine! How ya ever gonna take over fer me, if ya doan learn nothin'?"

"Huh? Take over what?" Charmaine narrowed her eyes with suspicion.

"Mah jobs."

Charmaine's suspicion turned quickly to alarm. "Tante Lulu! Is something wrong? Did you go to the doctor? Is it your heart?"

"I'm fine. But I won't allus be around, and someone's gotta be willin' ta step inta mah shoes."

Charmaine exhaled with relief, as if she'd been holding her breath. "I have enough to do with mah beauty salons without becoming a folk healer, too."

"I'm not talkin' 'bout mah *traiteur* bizness. I got plenty of folks willin' ta take that over, includin' Grace Sabato. She knows almost as much about herbs as I do. And I got it in mah will that Luc takes over mah charities . . . Jude's Angels, fer instance. Tee-John already tends mah garden, even if he does say some bad words when he gots ta hoe around the okra. I better not look down from heaven one day and see my garden gone ta seed. And I'm gonna bequeath Useless ta Remy."

"I thought it was Remy who pushed that gator off on you in the first place."

"I'm pushin' back. Oh, not right away. Doan go gettin' that scaredy-cat look in yer eyes again. But eventually."

"Okay, Grace, the folk healing; Luc, the charities; Tee-John, gardening; Remy, the gator. What about René?"

"Oh, he's gonna take over the Cajun Village People acts in the future."

Charmaine grinned. Probably with relief that she'd escaped that one.

Years ago, the LeDeux family started putting on music and dance revues modeled on the old Village People acts. Usually they were done in conjunction with one of Louise's matchmaking ventures.

"How about Daniel, Aaron, and Simone?"

"I'll think of something fer them later."

"Okay. I'll bite. What do you have in mind for me? Keep in mind I have a chain of beauty salons to run, and my daughter is a teenager now. Mary Lou is a handful."

"Pfff! Those beauty parlors practic'ly run themselves now. And Mary Lou is the best behaved teenager I ever met. Spends all her spare time with her daddy runnin' the ranch. You should be thankin' yer stars fer all yer blessings. I know all about wild teenagers, believe me. I pretty much raised Tee-John, dint I?"

Louise could see her pondering the words. "You're right. I am blessed. So, again I ask, what do ya have in mind?"

"Sort of a family matriarch."

"Huh? What? Like *Dynasty*, or *Dallas*, or *Downton Abbey*?"

"Like me. Oh, doan go all scary eyed again. I'm not plannin' on kickin' the bucket anytime soon. It's a role ya gotta ease into."

Charmaine rolled her eyes.

Folks did that a lot around Louise. As if she wouldn't notice!

"Tante Lulu! I'm not even a blood relative."

"Bite yer tongue, girl. Yer as much mah family as the boys."

"I know, I know," Charmaine said, with tears in her eyes. "Your adopted niece then."

"Hmpfh! Mah niece Adele was married ta Valcour LeDeux, and I stepped in ta take care of her chillen when Adele died . . . Luc, Remy and René, which would make them mah grand-nephews, I s'pose. Or great-nephews. Whatever. Then that Valcour married Jolie and had Tee-John, who also was in need of mah help. So, technically, Tee-John's not mah blood kin, either, but I'll go ta mah grave callin' him mah nephew. So, it doan matter if yer mama got involved with Valcour, too, and no Rivard blood was passed on. When ya came ta me fer help, did I say, no, 'cause yer not mah blood kin?"

Charmaine leaned down and hugged Louise, clearly realizing how much she'd riled her up. Louise had tears in her eyes, too, probably had mascara running down her cheeks.

"So, it's settled. Yer mah 'niece,' blood or not."

"Okay."

"So, are ya agreein' ta be the family matriarch, too?"

"Oh, I doan know. Aren't I a little young to be a matriarch?"

"I been a matriarch since I was yer age. What are ya implyin' here?"

Charmaine put up her hands in surrender. "What exactly does a matriarch do?"

"A matriarch is the go-to person fer anyone in trouble. But ya gotta sniff out trouble, too. Lak a detective. And matchmakin', of course."

"In other words, a busybody."

"Zackly!"

"Lawdy!"

"One more thing," Louise said. "I'm worried about Richard."

"Richard who?"

"Fer shame, girl! There's only one Richard fer me. Richard Simmons." She sighed. For many years, Louise had been a fan of the exercise guru. What a hottie!

"Why are you worried about Richard Simmons?"

"I haven't seen him on TV lately. Mebbe he's sick. Mebbe he got fat and doesn't want anyone ta see him. Mebbe terrorists are holdin' him fer ransom. Mebbe aliens have come down and kidnapped him. Mebbe we should go to Hollywood and check it out."

"No! Absolutely not! This is where I draw the line.

No Richard Simmons. No Hollywood. No whacko road trips."

"Whatever ya say, Charmaine," Louise agreed.

"Yeah, right." Charmaine sighed. "You got any bourbon fer this tea?"

Chapter Seven

There was no escaping him anywhere . . .

When Samantha's alarm went off that morning, she realized that she'd been in the midst of yet another of the alarming sex dreams that had been plaguing her lately. Nightmares, really, because they starred that irritating, full-of-himself, condescending Daniel LeDeux, of all people.

Ever since she'd met the twins at John LeDeux's wedding a few years back, she intermittently ran into the evil twin, Daniel. Hard to avoid anyone named LeDeux here in the South, but especially hard for Samantha, who had so many personal connections with Luc and with Tante Lulu through their joint efforts in the Hope Foundation.

Daniel wasn't really evil, of course, but he was irritating to the point of madness. Usually, Samantha would

avoid someone so toxic to her well-being, but she couldn't avoid running into the man every couple months as he bee-bopped in and out of Louisiana . . . when he wasn't holed up in that old fishing camp like a self-absorbed hermit. When it came to brooding, he gave Heathcliff a bad name.

Just being a doctor was bad enough in her book, of course, because of her experience with Nick and his buddies who obsessed over material things . . . biggest boat, most expensive car, higher income. Yes, she knew it was unfair to lump all physicians together. She couldn't help herself, though.

As for Daniel, she hadn't seen any evidence of greed . . . so far. But each time they met, like at the periodic meetings of the Hope Foundation board on which they both served, thanks to Tante Lulu's bulldozer persuasion methods, he said or did something to annoy her, deliberately.

So why would she be having erotic dreams about such a man?

It was a puzzle.

Freud would have a field day analyzing the whys and wherefores of her apparently hidden attraction to the man.

The more likely scenario was that the meddling maniac of the bayou, Tante Lulu, had probably put some kind of curse on her. Not that Samantha believed in curses, or voodoo, or even the old lady's faith in St. Jude miracles.

She was over thirty years old. No longer a slave to her hormones like she'd been when she'd gone brain dead and married Nick more than ten years ago while he'd still been in medical school. Hard to believe the gall of the jerk to demand alimony at their divorce trial seven years ago, but she'd thought that was all over two years ago when Judge Pitre, bless her heart, had denied his request

for additional alimony and issued a temporary restraining order because of his harassment. Now, it was starting
all over again. The man never gave up!

Last week he'd reached new lows by filing yet another
court petition, this time a lawsuit, claiming she'd lied in
initial hearings regarding her financial statements and
demanding a million dollars in punitive damages.

"That guy must have balls the size of soccer balls,"
Luc had remarked on relaying that latest news.

To which she had responded, "Yeah, but an itty bitty
penis."

"We should put that in an amended reply." Luc had
been half serious.

"Can we?" she'd asked.

"Unfortunately, no." Luc had grinned at her. "But
maybe you could accidentally blurt it out at our next
hearing."

She should have known better than to marry Nick. Really. What man with movie star good looks and enough
charm to peel a grape would look twice at an overly tall,
auburn-haired woman with splotchy freckles all over her
body? He'd pointed out her shortcomings ad nauseam,
but only after the wedding certificates had been signed,
and then only in the slyest manner. Like, "Do you really
think you should wear that red dress, darlin'? It makes
your freckles look like zits." Or, "Have you gained
weight, honey?" Or, "A woman as big . . . um, as tall as
you . . . really should avoid heels."

So, why was she dreaming about another too good-
looking man who clearly did not like her any more than
she liked him? Shaking her head with disgust, she sat up
and turned off the still shrilling alarm.

But then, cued by the alarm clock, her family began to
awaken and come to say "hello."

"Woof, woof!" said Axel, her German Shepherd the

size of a pony, who'd been ancient when she adopted him two years ago and was even more ancient now. He would have jumped up onto the bed beside her if he was able. Axel had recovered from his broken hip; German Shepherds were genetically predisposed to hip problems anyway, but the wise ol' guy knew his limitations and avoided jumping wherever possible. His bald patches had filled in. And she no longer noticed that half of one ear was gone. Despite being in better health, he would not be winning the Westminster dog show anytime soon.

"Yip, yip, yip, yip, yip!" Five orphaned, thankfully crate-trained, three-month-old puppies of indeterminate breed announced their presence from their downstairs cage. Adoptions had already been arranged for the cuties. So many abused and abandoned animals to be rescued! Her fostering efforts had started two years ago as a security measure, but she had discovered she was a soft touch for animals about to be put down for lack of adoptive owners. Who was she kidding? It probably fed some maternal yearning of hers for children.

Axel would miss this particular bunch of puppies. He'd taken over their care from the beginning, almost like a mother dog with its litter, which was a miracle considering Axel was a castrated male.

"Meow!" Sleeping at the foot of the bed, but now yawning awake, was Madeline, her gorgeous Savannah cat. Maddie, also one of her initial adoptees, had been a hard animal to adopt out, despite her beauty, because she resembled a small cheetah and scared families with children. Savannahs were hybrid cats with both domestic and wild blood. Although Savannahs could be sweet and affectionate, Maddie had been mistreated, causing her to have trust issues. Samantha liked to think she and Maddie, now a permanent member of her "family," were soul sisters.

There were three other cats, Garfield, Felix, and Max, rambling around her large home, tough-as-nails, indoor/outdoor critters. They were a Maine coon breed, who came in when they chose, not when she directed. These were recent entries into her home which she'd thought would have been adopted by now. She wondered idly, the blasted dream still lingering in her mind, whether the LeDeux brothers might not need mousers at their new home on Bayou Black. A bleepin' plantation, for heaven's sake! Hadn't Tante Lulu mentioned the possibility of the twins sheltering animals in some of their outbuildings?

Maybe, she thought with a grin, she ought to put bows on them, and take them for a housewarming gift to the brooding Daniel. He needed something to lighten him up.

Or maybe she ought to take others from her menagerie. A good choice would be Clarence, the foul-mouthed cockatoo whose lone vocabulary was "Holy shit!" usually said at the most inappropriate times. Or Emily, the small potbellied pig with a serious case of depression due to a broken heart. (*Yes, a depressed pig. And small only compared to other pigs. Emily weighed in at about sixty pounds.*) Or how about the goat? Oh, Lord, would she like to unload Grumpy! And, yes, he and Doctor Grumpy would get along just great. There were also a few ducks, one goose, and an honest-to-God miniature llama in the middle of the Big Easy. Thankfully, she'd been able to get rid of the two peacocks she'd gotten originally from the rescue farm. Her neighbors had complained, with good reason, about the peacocks' screeching cries. She expected the same fate for the llama, ducks, goose, and goat, and she'd warned the rescue center, "No more outdoor animals!"

Over the past two years, she'd probably fostered two hundred different animals in her home. The worst had been a monkey named Eli. He'd thrown food and feces at her or anyone who got near his cage, and masturbated constantly. Eew! Never again! She'd also drawn the line at snakes and rodents.

Her family thought she was crazy and said she was compensating for lack of a real family.

Well, yeah!

The daughter of wealthy divorced parents, she'd never really had a normal family life, just boarding schools. Her father was on his fifth wife . . . six if you counted the brief five-day marriage to that Bourbon Street stripper. Her mother, a quintessential jet-setter, lived in the South of France, and supported one boy toy after another.

Neither parent had ever had much time for her. As a result, Samantha had always yearned for a large family of her own. A man who loved her, with at least three, maybe five children. And that's exactly what Nick had promised her. Turns out, he'd never wanted children, despite his promises before their marriage. In fact, he'd had a vasectomy without telling her.

She could only imagine what Daniel would say if he knew her pathetic life story, or if he saw her current "family." His sarcasm would be unavoidable.

Ah, well, Samantha thought, as she got out of bed and padded down the stairs and out to the kitchen where she opened the door for Axel to go out and do his business. She put on the coffeepot, and began the lengthy process of feeding her own personal zoo. It was a Sunday; so, she wouldn't be going into the office, but she planned to do some work as the director of the Hope Foundation, a growing operation founded by Starr Foods after that horrible hurricane devastated her town, and which expanded a few years ago to take the LeDeux family's Jude's Angels under its umbrella, mostly at the instigation of Tante Lulu.

To her annoyance, the erotic dream stayed with her for a long time. While she drank her coffee. While she fed the animals. While she studied her budget and put together an agenda for the next board meeting. While she took a shower and dressed for the day.

Good thing she was the only one who knew about it.

It was her dirty little secret.

The Awakening, non-Kate Chopin style . . .

Daniel awakened in his *garconniére* bedroom, sunlight streaming through the open windows, more contented than he'd felt in years.

Hell! Who wouldn't be contented after the wet dream of the century? And with stone-cold Samantha Starr, of all people, who wouldn't touch his cock with a ten-foot pole. Man, he thought with a smile, wouldn't he enjoy telling her about the dream? She'd probably faint with disgust.

With a wide yawn, he went into the bathroom up here on the third floor. In the past month, he, Aaron, and a small team of high-priced contractors, plumbers, and electricians . . . who knew plumbers earned more than doctors? . . . had done some basic restoration work. New plumbing and electricity in the big house and the *garconniére*, as well as replastering and painting one bedroom and one sitting room in each structure for Aaron and Daniel, and rudimentary kitchen appliances, like a coffeemaker. Just enough for them to live on-site.

This morning Daniel was going to paint the walls on the first floor, which very well might be a medical office at some point in the future. Oh, not an office open to the public. More a place he could set up his medical library and supplies. Do research. Maybe even ease back into part-time practice at some Louisiana facility. George La-roche had been begging him to join the staff of his oncol-ogy center in Houma, even promising him his own pediatric unit.

It was just something Daniel was thinking about at this point. He hadn't even discussed it with Aaron. Face it, Daniel had been burned out by medicine, big-time. Working with terminally ill children did that to a body. But he could feel himself healing. Maybe he was ready to take back his life again. Maybe.

He'd begun the process of applying for a Louisiana medical license. Not because he had any immediate plans, but Tante Lulu kept nagging him about it, for some strange reason, probably because she wanted him "to get off his lazy ass." There was no such thing as a national medical license. In the U.S., it was state by state, which sometimes posed a problem for physicians who practiced in multiple states. Although, after Hurricane Katrina in 2005, when there was such a dire need for trained medi-cal personnel, the legislature had passed a law allowing doctors from other states to write prescriptions and order tests for treatment.

So, he'd filled out the cumbersome forms, just to shut her up, and soon he would take the exam. The question was what to do with the license once he obtained it . . . or whether he wanted to do anything with it.

For now, he would content himself with work around the plantation. After painting, he planned to go help Aaron with some sanding, of which there was enough work for an army. A landscaping firm would arrive this afternoon to begin clearing away more of the jungle.

A half hour later he walked down the narrow steps to the first floor, cup of coffee in hand, when he glanced out the window, then did a double take. There was a line of about fifteen people sitting on the ground outside the *garconniére*, as if they were waiting for something. Or someone.

He frowned. *Me?*

Setting his coffee cup down on a windowsill, he opened the door and said, "Can I help you?"

"Are you Doctor LeDeux?" a woman in front of the line, holding an infant, asked.

"Yeeees," he answered hesitantly.

"We're here to see you."

And all the others piped in:

"My Sally has the whoopin' cough."

"I cut mah hand on a friggin' chain saw an' it won't stop bleedin'."

"The runs are runnin' me ragged. Too much Cajun Lightning, I 'spect."

"I need ta renew mah birth control prescription. Quick-like. Mah hubby Jack is horny as a jack rabbit these days. Ha, ha, ha."

"Kin I get some of that viiii-ag-rah?"

"We heard the clinic was openin' t'day."

Clinic? Oh, my . . . ! Daniel put his face in his hands and counted to ten. He would bet his left nut that Tante Lulu had something to do with this.

In this day and age, people didn't do this country doctor bullshit. Did they? Was he expected to be some kind of Little House on the Bayou kind of physician?

"Uh. The clinic isn't open yet."

Tante Lulu must have heard he'd received the provisional documents—*God bless the bayou grapevine!*—and figured he was open for business. In fact, the speed with which his application had been processed was amazing, now that he thought about it; more than a few steps must have been skipped. The interfering busybody!

"Cain't ya help us?" the woman with the baby asked worriedly. The skin on her baby was yellow with jaundice, and the cough was alarming.

"There must be some other doctor or medical center where you can go."

They shook their heads, one after the other. One man revealed, "My family, we doan take no charity. Tante Lulu sez yer cheaper than the average doctor. Plus, yer willin' ta barter fer services."

Tante Lulu is surely the Mouth of the South.

"I kin fix cars."

Would that include Beemers?

"My Dora makes the best jambalaya and lazy bread this side of Nawleans."

Is that my stomach growling?

"I got a bushel of tomatoes here, and baskets of cucumbers, potatoes, melons, and okra."

Okra? What the hell would I do with okra? I hate the stuff.

"I'd like to have the baskets back, if ya doan mind."

"During deer season, I kin send ya some venison."

Bambi . . . they expect me to cook a dead Bambi? Well, Aaron knows more about that than I do. Or Aunt Mel, when . . . if . . . she ever moves here.

"Do ya like squirrel?"

"For a pet?"

The old guy cackled. "Hell, no. Ta eat, doc."

To eat? Yeech!

"In a few weeks, I kin bring raspberries, huckleberries, and peaches."

Okay, fruit, I like.

"I'm a plumber. Laid off since March."

Glory days!

"I do electrical work."

Glory, glory days!

So it was that Daniel helped most of the people, using a card table, several folding chairs, his basic medical kit, and a prescription pad. Others he referred to a doctor that he knew took on an occasional indigent patient.

And it felt damn good, to his surprise.

Even so, he put a sign outside proclaiming that the clinic would not be open for another month. Actually, never. If he was going back to medicine, it would be in the field he'd once flourished in. And he for damn sure wasn't going into private practice requiring a gazillion dollars in malpractice insurance. As it was, he could be in big trouble just for the little bit of medicine he'd engaged in today. Even dispensing aspirin could result in him losing the license he didn't really have yet.

Oddly, he caught himself whistling as he painted later that morning. And it wasn't just due to the instant gratification of hard labor. He felt as if he was awakening from a deep painful sleep.

Of course, it helped that he had awakened this morning with another kind of instant gratification.

Bewitched, Bothered and Doggone Bewildered . . .

Samantha approached Bayou Rose Plantation that afternoon with trepidation. After her embarrassing dream, she didn't want to be within a mile of Doctor Dreamy, but she'd promised Tante Lulu she would come to discuss some ideas for abandoned animals to be relocated here, assuming Daniel and Aaron were on board. Of course it would be a long time before they would be in a position to offer any services on a large scale; work would be needed on the facilities to meet health code specs and zoning regulations for the kennels. If, in fact, that would be the ultimate use made of the plantation. So, plenty of time for convincing. On Tante Lulu's part, not hers.

As she drove up, she saw that the arched entry sign for Bayou Rose had been repaired and repainted. Farther on, she could see that the old lady had turned this into a party, as usual. The landscaping people were already hard at work, clearing away the jungle, with the help of every LeDeux in the world, it seemed. Dozens of them, of all ages. And was that . . . yes, it was that notorious snake catcher Stinky Hawkins. *The Times-Picayune* ran feature articles on him every other year.

Of course the first person she ran into was Daniel. As she approached, they glared at each other. He didn't like her any more than she liked him. He seemed to think she was a spoiled rich girl who'd never struggled a day in her life. She didn't have much use for doctors per se, especially good-looking ones, after her experience with Nick, but if he was going to have the credentials, she thought it was self-indulgent, even selfish, of him not to use those talents. Egotism, either way.

Then, at the same time, they both started to say, "I had a dream . . ."

She slapped a hand over her mouth with horror at her inadvertent admission.

"Oh, crap!" he said. "We had dreams about each other, didn't we? The same dream."

"I don't know what you're talking about."

He snorted his disbelief.

"Bite me!"

"Seems I already did."

"Did you do something to plant those . . . those perverted ideas in my head?"

"You thought they were perverted? Even the suck and tuck move?"

She ignored his question and continued, "You're supposedly a doctor. Bet you slipped me a pill or something." It's the kind of thing Nick would have done in a heartbeat, if he'd thought of it. But probably not with her. He'd want to play out his fantasies with one of his many mistresses.

"No *supposed* about it. I *am* a doctor, even if I don't practice anymore. What you're suggesting is criminal behavior, which I would never participate in. Nor would I need to." He raised his chin defiantly.

"Oh, jeez. No need to get bent out of shape. I didn't really think you gave me anything."

He visibly tamped down his temper. "Let's return to that 'perversions' discussion—"

"Please don't."

"I've never heard about that new erogenous zone . . . you know, the one you showed me in the dream. They certainly never taught *that* in medical school. I figured it was some *Cosmo* kind of thing."

"I don't read *Cosmo*. It wasn't me who . . . never mind."

His lips twitched with humor.

Samantha was embarrassed. Every single time she met Daniel their conversations seemed to spiral out of control. They threw sparks off each other, and she was at least partly to blame, she knew that.

Time to change the subject. Samantha inhaled and exhaled. Once again, Daniel had managed to bring out this bitchy side of her personality. Yeah, he was a doctor, but she should be able to judge people on their own merits, not by their professions. It was Nick's fault, she decided. That was her story, and she was sticking to it. For now.

"I brought you a housewarming gift," she said, in a forced tone of politeness.

He grinned, sensing how hard it was for her to be nice to him.

"This is Max. A kitty just for you."

He stopped grinning.

Out shot a golden-haired Maine Coon cat with a lop-sided red bow tied around its neck. The cat immediately went over to Daniel and hissed up at him.

"That's not a kitty. It's a pony. How much do you feed this animal? Do they have Weight Watchers for cats?"

"Max likes to snack on mice."

"Eeew! I hate cats."

"I think Max likes you." The cat was clawing at his pant leg with one paw. "Oh, isn't that cute? Max wants a hug."

Carefully, he lifted the animal as if it might attack at any minute. Which it might. "I hate cats," he repeated.

Max licked his face, and he cringed, then hid a smile. Samantha could tell that he didn't hate cats as much as he claimed. Bored with licking, Max jumped down and rushed over to sniff at the snake barrel.

"Max could probably catch snakes, too. In addition to mice."

"Oh, that's just wonderful."

Just then Tante Lulu noticed them from over at the buffet table set out on the ground floor verandah. "Yoo hoo! Over here."

Chapter Eight

Matchmaker, folk healer, and tour guide, too . . .

She and Daniel glanced at each other, remembered the dream, and stomped toward the old lady for a confrontation.

"Did you put a spell on us?" Samantha demanded to know.

"Huh?"

"I thought you didn't believe in that voodoo junk," Daniel added.

"Huh?"

"Don't play the innocent with me, you meddling dingbat. I know what you're capable of." Daniel looked as if he'd like to throttle Tante Lulu.

The old lady narrowed her eyes at him. "I doan like yer tone, boy. If yer not careful, I'm gonna toss ya in one of Stinky's snake barrels." Then she turned to Samantha with a smile. "Did I tell ya Daniel ain't gay?"

Daniel stiffened.

Samantha had to laugh. The old lady sure knew which buttons to push on Daniel. She was always telling people that he wasn't gay. She wasn't sure if it was because he rarely dated, or because of his appearance, which didn't look gay to her, or something else.

But Daniel was learning not to rise to her jibes every time. He just walked away.

"Looks like they're making a lot of progress outside," Samantha remarked then. The wide area between the alleé, or alley, of live oaks . . . now the horseshoe-shaped driveway, its open side facing the bayou . . . had been denuded and new grass sown. The branches with hanging moss on the two-hundred-year-old trees on either side of the road had grown together into a canopy of sorts. Right now a sprinkler system was in operation to get the lawn going, although it rained so often in this semitropical climate that it probably wasn't necessary. Workers were tackling the garden on one side of the house and putting paving stones around the *garconniére* on the other side.

Tante Lulu nodded. "Helps when ya got family ta pitch in."

"And money to pay an army of workers." Samantha had heard the two brothers were fairly well off, but she knew from friends' experiences with old house renovations that money wells could soon become money pits.

"That, too." Tante Lulu was in a gardening outfit today. Straw hat, coveralls, and sneakers. Her hair appeared to be purple, or maybe it was a wig. Little dangly earrings in the shape of shovels and rakes hung from her ears. Gardener chic? "C'mon. I'll show ya 'round, 'specially the area where I think they could house some animals, if we kin convince Aaron and Daniel."

Samantha didn't like the sound of that *we*.

"Show me, too," Daniel said, coming up behind them.

Samantha glanced his way with chagrin.

"What? I'd like to know what the old bird's plans are, too, especially since I own half the place. I still don't understand how we could house a bunch of animals here. Who's gonna take care of them? I mean, there would have to be a manager or vet on hand, wouldn't there?" He noticed Tante Lulu grinning at him. "Oh, no! I'm not qualified—"

"A doctor's a doctor, I allus say."

"Forget about it!"

"Whatever you say," Tante Lulu said with a meekness suspicious to say the least.

"And where do you expect me and Aaron to be when this is going on?"

"It's all in St. Jude's hands, honey."

Samantha could tell he was restraining himself from saying something nasty, even sacrilegious.

"Besides, I have the perfect person in mind fer manager," Tante Lulu added.

"Who?" Daniel demanded to know.

"I'll tell ya when the time is right."

"By the way, Daniel"—Samantha had an idea—"do you know what you need to keep your lawn nice and tidy?"

"Does Hummer make lawn mowers?"

"Very funny. A goat."

"A what? No, no, no! A monster cat, I can accept." Said cat was lying on the grass, munching on something. He hoped it was catnip. "But no goats. No way! And what the hell are you doing with a goat anyway?"

"Thass a great idea," Tante Lulu said to Samantha. To Daniel, she explained, "Samantha rescues animals in her spare time. Bet she's got a goat or two. Sheep would be good, too. Bet she could give ya some dogs, too. Or wouldja prefer pigs and rats."

Daniel turned to stare at Samantha with surprise. "You have pigs and rats?"

"Well, I have one pig. Only one. A potbellied pig. Not the kind you raise for meat. But no rats; Tante Lulu is referring to gerbils. And, actually, I got rid of . . . I mean, I found a home for . . . the goat this morning. One goat, not two," she said pointedly, glancing toward Tante Lulu. "A farmer from Alabama, in town for the Holstein convention, heard about my goat. And he also took the llama, the goose, and all the ducks. He would have taken Emily, the pig, but she's a pet breed, not a farm porker, and besides that, Emily is depressed, which is off-putting to some people. My neighbors are probably celebrating as we speak. There had been talk about goose liver pate and Peking duck. Oh, and I forgot. I have a cockatoo named Clarence I'd love to get rid of."

"Samantha!" Tante Lulu said with shock.

"What?"

"Ladies doan mention a man's private parts."

"Huh?"

"You mentioned yer boyfriend Clarence's wiener."

"Oh, good Lord! Clarence is a bird."

"Well, it ain't ladylike ta mention a bird's privates, either."

Samantha threw her hands in the air, a gesture of surrender.

Daniel's jaw dropped with amazement, whether at her array of pets, or her as their caretaker, or Tante Lulu's mistaking her cockatoo for a penis, she wasn't sure. But then, his quick survey of her attire ended with, "Been shopping at Walmart, have you?"

Okay, so he'd decided on a change of subject. And he had a point there. Samantha did like designer clothing, some of which might not be animal friendly, as in a magnet for pet hair or other animal unmentionables. Today, she wore a Pucci, silk, one-shoulder blouse in a shell and seagull motif with artful knots at the shoulder and hemline, over stretch cotton crop pants, Rebecca Minkoff ankle cuff sandals, a floppy straw sun hat, and Kate Spade retro sunglasses.

His sarcasm deserved no response. She could have countered with an argument that quality merchandise lasted forever and never went out of style. Or she could have countered with a comment about his khakis and loafers as inappropriate for the outdoor work to be done here today. Instead, she continued her earlier conversation about rescue animals. "Not to worry about missing out on the goat, though, Daniel. I have lots of other animals left. Puppies and cats, in particular." Samantha batted her eyelashes at Daniel, hoping to have a customer. As much as she'd come to care for her rescued pets, it would be nice to have an empty house for a change. Not that she'd ever be totally empty. No way would she give away her German Shepherd Axel, or her cat, Maddie.

"I do not want any more animals." He enunciated each word for emphasis. "And don't be giving me those come-hither eyes unless you're ready to hither."

The image of their shared dream shimmered in the air between them.

Samantha could feel herself blush.

Daniel just grinned.

"Holy Sac-au-lait! Doan get yerself in a snit," Tante Lulu said to Daniel. To Samantha, she whispered, "Mebbe ya should ask Aaron instead. He ain't so persnickety."

"I am not persnickety, whatever the hell that is," Daniel protested. "By the way, old lady, I don't appreciate your setting up a medical practice for me, either."

"Oh, did all them poor sick folks come t'day?" Tante Lulu inquired with the innocence of a cobra.

"Where's Aaron?" Samantha asked, trying to defuse the situation, although she had no idea what they were talking about. Another of Tante Lulu's machinations, she was sure. Although, if it had anything to do with Daniel being a doctor, she could understand.

"He was here all morning. Not sure where he disappeared to," Daniel said, frowning, as if he'd just realized his brother was missing.

Tante Lulu, who had started to climb the steep steps in front of them, had the answer. "He's over at the Dugas gator farm, tryin' ta sweet-talk Del."

"That's just great," Daniel remarked. "He'll be back soon, or I'll go drag him back. He's not leaving me here alone to handle this mess."

Samantha homed in on only one thing. "Gator farm?"

"Don't ask," Daniel warned.

Off Tante Lulu went then, talking away, irregardless of whether anyone was listening.

Turns out, the old lady was an excellent tour guide, Samantha had to give her that, as Tante Lulu interspersed her descriptions of the various rooms with a bit of the history of the house and the property that she knew so well. In fact, old sepia photographs of the house as it had looked in the mid and late 1800s were tacked on the wall of the entry hall.

Still other photos showed the exterior and interior of the house as it had been during more prosperous days. Unfortunately, all the furniture, fine Aubusson and Tabriz carpets, and paintings were missing, even the lighting fixtures, but the painted-over woodwork, ornate crown molding, and ceiling medallions on the fifteen-foot ceilings remained, along with the wide, carved stairway that ran up the center of the main floor's hallway, and the eleven-foot-high sliding pocket doors, a Victorian-era addition, separating the rooms. Although they were scuffed and ingrained with decades of dirt, the random-plank cypress floors would be magnificent when refinished. And the tall, floor-to-ceiling windows remained intact, albeit with wavy glass.

Rooms on each of the three floors were separated by a twelve-foot corridor . . . wasted space in today's house designs. On the main floor, there were two parlors, a dining room, library, and office. Six bedrooms on the second floor and four on the third floor, along with a nursery or schoolroom, and servant quarters. There were a total of four full and three half bathrooms, which had been installed at the turn of the last century . . . as in clawfoot tubs and pedestal sinks and shaving mirrors . . . on these three floors, along with the ground level where the kitchen, pantries, laundry, and other storage rooms were located. Only two of the bathrooms were functioning, and one of them had recently been modernized by Aaron with luxury improvements, including a rain forest shower, not at all in keeping with the historic nature of the building, but the kind of thing a bachelor would consider essential. There was no basement because of the high water table here in Southern Louisiana.

"Did you know the original owners?" Daniel asked.

"Idjit!" Tante Lulu jabbed him with an elbow. "How old ya think I am?"

"I meant the last owners," Daniel amended.

"Oh, okay, then. Yep, the Gaudette fam'ly lived here when I was growin' up. Left suddenly 'bout thirty years ago. Rumor was there was some kinda hanky panky takin' place with Missy DuBois and them dogs."

Samantha wouldn't touch that last observation with a telephone pole.

Daniel made a sound that was halfway between a snort and a chuckle.

Time for another change of subject. "Forget about the kennels. This would make a wonderful family home," Samantha remarked. "I can see all the possibilities for restoration, but also ways to make it a comfortable living space. Children would flourish in this setting." In fact, it was the type of home she'd always dreamed of. Before she'd become disillusioned by Nick and her failed marriage.

Her Garden District home in New Orleans was more than adequate, but not perfect, for kids who needed, or would appreciate, open spaces to run and play, not to mention the bayou for swimming and fishing. If she'd gotten pregnant with Nick (hopefully, three times . . . two girls and one boy), she would have moved. Maybe that was another reason Nick had been unhappy with her. He was definitely a city person.

She glanced up to see Daniel watching her closely before he asked, "Is this the type of home you grew up in?"

"Hardly. We had nice homes, don't get me wrong." In fact, lavish for the most part. "But my father married five times, and changed houses each time. My mother cavorted around Europe, never spending more than a year in any one place. She practically invented the word *cougar* for older women, younger men."

"And you?"

"I spent most of my time in boarding schools since I was eight. Same for my younger half brother Wallace. Plus, we grew up in different homes with different mothers. We were never close." Suddenly, she realized how much she'd revealed and turned away from him.

Luckily, Tante Lulu picked up the conversation. "If yer grandma Sophie hadn't been ill fer so many years before she died, things woulda been different fer you, Samantha. I guarantee it. Yer grandpa Stanley and grandma Sophie were good God-fearin' people, but they let their chillren run wild and neglected the grandchillren whilst

Sophie was ailin' and then when Stanley was grievin' after her passin'."

"I hardly remember her," Samantha said. "I was away at boarding school, like I said, and when I came home, they didn't allow her many visitors." Her grandfather was a good man, and they'd bonded in the last few years, but he hadn't been there for her when she was young, or even in her Nick/marriage period.

"How's yer mama, by the way?"

"Just great. Colette is still living in France." Her mother insisted that her daughter call her by her name, not Mother, or, God forbid, Mama, which would age her, apparently. "Still taking on one gigolo after another. I haven't seen her in two years, at least." And then she'd been living with a twenty-year-old artist who fashioned himself the next Salvador Dali. To Samantha, his paintings resembled nothing more than splotches of color thrown on a canvas.

"A cryin' shame, thass what it is," Tante Lulu said, patting Samantha on the arm. "Family is the most important thing in the world, honey."

Tante Lulu stared at Daniel then, as if with some hidden meaning.

"What? I didn't disagree."

"Then do somethin' about it."

"About what?"

"Makin' a family." On those words she stomped away.

He gasped. "Me? Start a family? Are you crazy?"

Samantha burst out laughing, so comical was the expression of horror on his face.

"Go ahead. Laugh. You do realize that she means that I should start a family with *you*."

It was Samantha's turn to be horrified.

Her and Daniel? A family? No way!

But then a blip of a picture flashed into her mind. Her

and Daniel. In bed. Doing what usually led to making a family. "I need to get out of here," she said.

Daniel's laughter followed after her.

And then the other shoe dropped . . .

Daniel couldn't keep his eyes off Samantha the rest of the afternoon. He tried. Really hard. To no avail.

Her words about a bleak childhood caught him unawares. It was contrary to the impression he'd had of her before. Stone-cold bitch. Raised in a rich family that spoiled her rotten. Everything handed to her on a silver platter.

And of course there was the dream.

He could guess what would be featured in the next ones. Freckles.

The clothing she wore today wasn't exactly sexy, but the clingy, off-one-shoulder blouse, leaving all that exposed skin, was more sexy than if she'd been nude. Well, not really. But it *was* a turn-on. The freckles should have been unattractive . . . there were so many of them, but instead they'd become a turn-on for him. He could picture all kinds of sex games he could play with those freckles. Connect the dots. Where's Waldo? Hide and seek. Etch-a-Sketch. And she was tall, too. Really tall for a woman. Only a few inches shorter than himself. He usually preferred more petite women. Usually. Somehow, suddenly, the idea of sex with a woman almost his height posed lots of interesting ideas.

He'd stuck it out through the extravagant meal, Tante Lulu style. *Can anyone say Peachy Praline Cobbler Cake?* Through the show put on by the snake catcher who'd gathered a scary fifty-seven adult reptiles from the property. Through all the landscaping projects that included clearing a garden which, remarkably, still had some viable rosebushes to be brought back to life. The St. Jude birdbath was already in place, a regular tweety-bird spa.

There would be months . . . hell, years of work yet to be done here. Still, everyone expressed satisfaction with jobs well done. Aaron had been working closely at his side all day. They made a good team, always had, no matter what they were doing.

Some of the younger kids were running around . . . the LeDeux kids and grandkids, a veritable tribe. Playing tag, or hide-and-go-seek. Screeching, laughing. They were just being kids. Normal, healthy kids.

That's when he felt the need to escape. The depression began to weigh him down, the memories overpowering. Would he ever be able to forget those last days on the job in Alaska? The day he'd been forced to surrender one more child to that beast, cancer. Deke.

Doctors were warned not to become attached to their patients. But how could he have resisted Deke?

He headed back to his digs. He figured Aaron could do the honors in saying good-byes and thanks to all their guests.

"I thought I'd find you here," Aaron said, a short time later, coming up the steps to the second floor living room of the *garconniére* where he was lying on the sofa, long-neck Bud Light in one hand, TV remote in the other. Max cuddled at his feet. He should have known Aaron would follow him, sensing his mood.

"Just watching the races," he lied. Nascar had never been a big attraction to him, though it was practically a sacred obsession here in the South.

"Since when do you have a cat? I thought you hated cats."

"I do."

Max looked up and hissed his opinion, then resumed licking his private parts.

Aaron took a beer out of the small fridge, swallowed half the bottle in one long swig, then raised a questioning brow. His brother knew him too well.

"So, where's De-li-lah?" Daniel asked.

"She wouldn't come."

"Shy?"

"Just the opposite. Did I tell you she can wrestle a two-hundred-pound alligator?"

"You might have told me a time or twenty."

Aaron made a face at him.

"I take it she isn't shaking the sheets with you yet."

"Hah! I can't even get her near the bed. In fact, she won't even go out on a date with me. Don't tell anyone."

"Meaning Tante Lulu?"

"Got it in one."

"She's already crocheting doilies for you, y'know."

"Don't snicker, bro. She's doin' the same for you."

"She is the most interfering busybody. Her family, too."

"*Our* family," Aaron reminded him.

"Our family," he conceded. "But I gotta tell you, there are times when I feel as if I can't breathe."

"Like today?"

"Near the end, yeah."

"Do you wish we'd stayed in Alaska?"

For a moment Daniel considered the question, then said, "No. This feels like home now."

"Did I push you into this Bayou Rose Plantation business?"

"Hell, yes!"

Aaron, not a bit repentant, sank down into the leather recliner Daniel had just bought, pulled the lever 'til he was almost prone, then clicked on the vibrate button. "Wow!" he laughed and played with the different settings, like a kid with a new toy.

They heard a huffing noise coming up the steps. Then

Tante Lulu emerged into the room. "Ain't this nice?" she said, "but you need a few knickknacks."

Daniel rolled his eyes.

Tante Lulu looked closer at the cat, which was lying on its back now, stretching its big body like some porno stud. "That cat is preggers," she announced.

"What? No! Max is a guy." *Isn't he?*

"Boy, you studyin' ta be a half-wit?"

Daniel leaned down to check, and, yep, a bunch of little nipples. Some kitty! And if pregnant, it was clearly not this cat's first ball game.

"Max? More like Maxine," Tante Lulu chuckled.

Samantha must have known when she gave him this gift that it would keep on giving. "I'll kill her. I swear I will."

Aaron was bent over, laughing.

"I got good news," Tante Lulu announced, sinking down into a chair and cooling herself off with her Richard Simmons fan. Back and forth, Daniel was treated to the exercise nut's smiling face. "I jist got off the phone with Aunt Mel."

He and Aaron sat up straight, then said, "Uh-oh!" Since when did Tante Lulu know Aunt Mel, or know her well enough to call her "Aunt"?

"Aunt Mel is thinkin' 'bout movin' ta Loo-zee-anna."

Well, that wasn't so bad. He and Daniel had known Aunt Mel was lonely since their mother had died and they'd moved here. *Oh, my God!* It just occurred to Daniel that Aunt Mel was the person Tante Lulu was considering to run an animal rescue operation from their house.

"She and I are gonna be best buddies."

Aaron choked on his beer.

"If she comes, she'll bring her Barry Manilow collection. She'll stay in the big house, of course."

Daniel tried to keep a straight face as Aaron went bug-eyed with shock, his lifestyle not being conducive to a chaperone.

"You two are the first to know," she announced, pausing as if hearing a drum roll in her head. "I'm thinkin' 'bout turnin' gay."

Did the old bat even know what a homosexual was? "Gay as in happy, or gay as in . . . ?"

"Gay as in less-bean, idjit."

Chapter Nine

Unexpected company ...

When Samantha returned home that evening, it was barely five p.m., but the motion detector lights were on in the backyard. She pulled into the detached garage at the end of the yard, by the alley, and pulled out her cell phone with the 911 number at the ready.

She wasn't really worried. One of the animals had probably tripped the sensor again. Even though she'd locked them inside, sometimes one of them banged against a window or glass door, which triggered the sensitive security system. Still, it was best to be safe. She picked up the metal bat she kept in the backseat.

If it was Nick, she'd enjoy whopping his lying, two-timing, greedy ass.

As for burglars, the sound of Axel barking like a maniac, as he was now, announcing her arrival, was enough to give any creep second thoughts. If that didn't work, Clarence, her cockatoo, kept squawking "Holy shit!"

When she emerged carefully from the garage, it wasn't her ex-husband or a trespasser she found, though. It was her stepbrother Angus. Well, stepbrother-by-marriage, actually, since Angus was the son of her father's third wife, Darla, by a previous husband. No blood relative. Angus huddled against the building, in the shadows under the overhang, along with a pregnant, young woman sitting on the ground, leaning against him, legs extended. Her feet were bare. A pair of white sneakers sat on the ground beside her. They'd probably been pinching her, by the looks of her swollen feet and ankles.

Samantha hadn't seen Angus in more than a year, and he wasn't looking so good. Even in the shadows, she could see that he was very thin. His blond hair was disheveled, and he wore a rumpled T-shirt and dirty jeans with a pair of old Nikes. Angus had to be at least twenty-five by now, but he looked about fifteen with his boyish features. Growing up, people always said he looked like Opie on that old *Andy Griffith* show. He still did, somewhat. An older Opie.

They'd never been close, because of the age difference and the fact that they'd been raised in different homes. Plus, Angus had been a geek with a superiority complex, even from a young age, considering the rest of mankind subpar to his intellect. Which was probably true when it came to anything electronic. Angus had built his own computer when he was only ten years old, and he bought every techie toy on the market the minute they became available.

Despite his skinny, geeky appearance, Angus had a line of tiny gold rings up the side of both ears, along with an eyebrow piercing, something he'd started doing as a teenager, rebelling against his inner Opie. And his arms were still covered with those old tattoos that had practically given his mother a heart attack. Rebel without a cause, Samantha had always said.

"Jeez, Angus, you should have warned me you were coming. I could have hurt you." She held the bat out for emphasis.

"Sorry, Sam. I didn't know where else to go." He held his side as he stood up and groaned. He must have been sitting for a long time. She noticed that he had a leather laptop bag over his shoulder, with an iPad and several other electronic devices peeking from a side flap. A cell phone was clipped to his belt. Some things never changed.

"What are you doing back here?"

"Are you kidding? Every time I step in your yard, sirens go off, lights flash, and all those animals you have inside bark, and meow, and chirp." He adjusted the bag and dusted off his behind, then resumed pressing a hand to his side. "You got a zoo in there or something?"

Or something. "What's wrong with your side?"

He ignored her question as he helped the girl to her feet. She groaned, too.

"And this is . . . ?" Samantha asked.

He blinked with confusion for just a moment before realizing that Samantha hadn't met his friend yet. "Sorry, Sam, this is Lily Beth Fontenot. From up Lafayette way. Lil, this is my sister Samantha Starr . . . um, stepsister. I mean . . . my mother was married to her father, after he was divorced from her mother, and another woman, and after my mother was divorced from my dad, and . . . whatever!"

"Hi," Lily Beth said with a shy smile. "Samantha Starr sounds lak a movie star name."

Yep. Just call me Julia Roberts. "Nice to meet you," Samantha said, then arched her brows at Angus after glancing meaningfully at the girl's belly.

"Not mine," he told Samantha, holding both hands in the air.

Lily Beth tsk-ed her disgust.

"Lil is a friend who, um, needs some, I mean, my help."

"I wouldn't need yer help if ya didn't get me in this trouble in the first place," Lily Beth snapped, elbowing Angus, which caused him to wince.

Samantha noticed Lily Beth's deep Southern accent, something she'd managed to lose, being educated up north, both at boarding schools and then Columbia. Angus, too, had lost his Southern accent. In his case, he'd gone to lots of colleges, including MIT. Usually, he got bored and tried again somewhere else. She didn't know what university he was associated with now. Maybe none. He was supposed to be working at Starr Foods on some complicated computer system. This, too, was boring to him.

"But what I need right now is ta pee," Lily Beth said. "I swear, mah bladder's 'bout ta explode lak a Mardi Gras water balloon."

"C'mon," Samantha said, pressing the buttons on her remote to turn off the backyard motion sensors. "Be careful where you step. I haven't had a chance to clean up yesterday's poop yet. The goose and duck droppings are especially bad."

"You have geese and ducks?" Angus asked, clearly shocked.

"I did have . . . until this morning. Now, I only have dogs, cats, a bird, a pig, and the occasional goat, and llama."

"Boy, have you changed!" Angus muttered behind Samantha.

"You think?" she muttered back.

Just then, Lily Beth tripped over a dog toy, and Angus half walked her the rest of the way with an arm around the back of her waist. The girl sighed and rested her head on his shoulder.

After keying in the numbers on the security box next to her patio doors, Samantha turned the knob and stepped aside as Axel bolted out to do his business. She opened the dog crate and five yipping puppies, who thankfully hadn't had any accidents inside the crate, tumbled out and rushed after Axel. Her exotic Savannah cat Maddie followed suit, but only at a leisurely amble, giving the three humans a glance of dismissive importance. Two other cats, Garfield and Felix, a Maine coon breed, followed after Maddie. The animals would be secure because of the brick wall that surrounded her property.

Emily, her depressed potbellied pig, who also lived in a kennel crate but was litter trained, chose not to go outdoors; instead, she voiced her displeasure at Samantha's long absence by emitting a long oinking sound. And Clarence, her cockatoo, proclaimed, this time aptly, "Holy shit!"

Angus's glance shot to the bird's cage. She could understand his surprise. Clarence's voice, even when squawking, had a distinctive male sound. "What the fuck are you doing with all these animals?"

"Rescuing them for adoption."

"Cool!" Angus said.

"Bathroom?" Lily Beth asked urgently.

"Down the hall, first door on the right," Samantha said.

Samantha got her first good look at Angus then, and gasped.

"Holy shit!" Clarence opined.

There were bruises on Angus's cheek and chin. The little finger of one hand looked crooked, and might be broken. The way he was holding his side indicated an injury, maybe his ribs. And she'd noticed a limp when he walked inside. "What happened to you?"

"It's a long story, but the gist of it is that Lil and I have to get out of town. Pronto!" he said. She saw fear in his hazel eyes.

"Holy shit!" Clarence again.

"Is that all that bird can say?" Angus asked.

"Pretty much," she answered.

"Cool!" Angus sank down onto her low sofa, putting his face in his hands for a moment.

She sat down on the sofa, as well, and Emily immediately came over and nudged her leg with her pink snout, making pleading grunts. Understanding her cue, Samantha picked up the pig and placed her between herself and Angus. Potbellied pigs were very affectionate creatures and Emily was especially needy because of her depression.

Angus looked askance at the two of them. "Un-be-lieve-able!" he muttered under his breath.

She understood his surprise. Most people reacted that way to pet pigs. What they didn't realize was that pigs, especially potbellied ones, were very intelligent and clean. Better than many dogs or cats.

"Why aren't you at school, Angus? Last I heard, you took a leave from Starr Foods and were attending Clemson." She stroked Emily's back as she spoke, noting the pig's quivering delight at the caress.

"Clemson was last year. I'm at Tulane now. Or, I was. That's where Lil is . . . was . . . a student . . . a grad student."

This was not good. Not good at all. Another college bites the dust? That had to be at least six or more for Angus, the quintessential professional student. What was happening with him? It's not that he wasn't smart. In fact, his mother had once told Samantha that Angus was in the "Mens for Kids" program when he'd been only six years old. Which had sounded kind of smarmy to Samantha, but it turned out that she'd meant Mensa for Kids. Angus had an I.Q. of more than 145, Samantha had learned later. Lot of good it had done him, she thought, looking at him now.

"Dad would help you, with whatever problem you have. Wouldn't he?" Angus was not a natural child of Samantha's father, but her dad always seemed fond of Angus, having married his mother Darla when the boy was a tween. Even after the divorce and Darla's death, Dad kept a soft spot for the boy.

Emily was fast asleep now, her chin resting on Samantha's knees, snoring softly.

Angus shook his head with a small smile at the two of them. But then he answered her question. "Bruce is at some wholesalers' convention in Los Angeles with Florence. Last I saw him was at Easter when I dropped by the house. He told me he's cutting me off, cold turkey. Just because I asked him for some tuition help. Florence has him on some Tough Love kick." Florence, her father's current wife, *was* a bit of a hard-liner, having been involved with female prisons at one time. Florence was certainly unlike his other wives who fit more in the trophy wife category: a debutante (Samantha's mother), a Las Vegas showgirl (Wallace's mother), a Dallas Cowboys cheerleader (Angus's mother, Darla, who died of a drug overdose), and Lilith, a voodoo priestess.

Well, maybe Lilith hadn't been the usual trophy wife with her turbans and matching dashiki-style gowns. She'd been colorful, though. Too bad Samantha hadn't thought to ask Lilith for a voodoo curse against Nick.

"Your Uncle Wallace has a nice place in Kentucky. The horse farm is pretty this time of year, and—"

Angus waved a hand dismissively. "Too much in the open. People coming and going. Plus, Lil pukes at the smell of horse shit . . . any kind of animal shit, actually. I'm surprised she didn't react to that litter pan over there.

Usually, Lil would be hurling like a drunk at Mardi Gras at just a tiny whiff of poop."

Samantha rolled her eyes with frustration. "Um, how about Callum?" Callum Starr was Angus's natural father. Another Scotsman. In fact, he was Bruce's second cousin. Thus, the same surnames. Talk about complicated, dysfunctional families!

"He moved back to Scotland last year where he raises sheep. He doesn't have two dimes to rub together. I can only imagine how Lil would react to sheep shit."

"Holy shit!" Clarence said suddenly.

Samantha gave the bird a dirty look, then turned back to Angus.

She pounced on the one thing he said. "So, this is about money, after all?"

"Only partly."

She stared at Angus, waiting, but he resisted telling her more.

"In any case, your father would give you and Lily Beth a place to go, wouldn't he? You said you have to get out of town."

"Do you have any idea how much plane fare costs to Scotland?"

Actually, she didn't. But, honestly, money again? He could hem and haw all he wanted, but she would bet her bottom dollar Angus was looking for a cash bailout of some sort.

"Why not go back to work on your project at Starr Foods? Here's an unusual concept. Earn the money."

His face reddened, and he shifted nervously. "That would take too long. We have to skip this town, like yesterday."

"Why?"

"Um . . . it's a long story."

Aaarrgh! She felt like pulling at her own hair. "Bottom line: Are you expecting me to give you the funds? Is that why you're here?"

"No, although I could use some cash. Scotland wouldn't work. That's the first place he . . . they . . . would look for me . . . um, us. Well, second place, actually. First, they would check Bruce's house here in Nawleans. And Uncle Wallace's horse farm would be third. Or maybe that would be your place."

Someone would follow them all the way to Scotland? Oh, boy, I smell trouble. And she didn't even want to think about his reference to her home. What is going on? A thought occurred to her then. "Are you on drugs?"

"Hell, no!"

Samantha should have known better than to suggest drugs. After his mother's untimely death from Oxy, Angus had always had an abhorrence for any kind of drugs. Even something as simple as Tylenol or cough medicine.

If the fool thought she was going to give him money carte blanche, without any explanation, he had another thing coming. She was getting tired of this runaround. "What . . . is . . . it . . . then?" she asked through gritted teeth.

Before he could answer, if he would, Lily Beth walked in and laughed when she saw the pig sleeping between her and Angus. At the same time, she leaned down and petted some of the yipping puppies who encircled her, seeking attention. Then, raising her head, Lily Beth inquired, in a small, embarrassed voice, "Could I take a shower? We've been on the run for two days, and I stink lak a skunk." Still in her bare feet . . . which were not just swollen, but crusted with dirt . . . she wore a high-waisted sundress, white with purple lilacs, exposing thin arms and shoulders, which appeared sunburnt. Her fingers also appeared swollen.

Was that a reason for concern? Samantha wondered. She had been three years old when her father and his second wife Giselle had been pregnant with what ended up being her half brother Wallace. She recalled Giselle complaining, constantly, about edema or something that sounded like that. Her ankles had blown up to the size of her knees, a monumental disaster for Giselle, who'd been fixated on her body, having been a Las Vegas showgirl. But hadn't there been some worry that the swelling was a precursor to something more serious?

Not my problem, Samantha told herself.

"In fact, I would love ta take a bath. Do ya have a tub?" Lily Beth asked. "If I could relax in a warm bath, I'd be so thankful."

Now that she mentioned it, Samantha could see that Lily Beth's blonde hair hung in a limp ponytail, and her thin shoulders slumped with exhaustion. There were dark smudges under her violet eyes. She was rather petite to be carrying such a big belly. It had to be tiring, on top of the stress of whatever problems she and Angus had.

"Sure," Samantha said, giving Angus a look that said loud and clear that their discussion was not over. She led Lily Beth upstairs to the guest bathroom, where there was a soaking tub as well as a shower. Samantha turned on the warm water and poured in some Jessica McClintock crystals, which immediately filled the air with a flowery fragrance.

"Ahhhh," Lily Beth said in appreciation.

"Are you sure you can manage getting in and out of a tub?" Samantha asked.

"I'll be careful."

Samantha nodded and handed her clean towels and pointed to a basket of small, individually wrapped soaps, toothbrushes, disposable razors, and sample sizes of toothpastes, mouthwashes, deodorants, and finger nail files. "I'll find some clean clothes for you to wear. They might be too big for you, but—"

"Hah! A tent wouldn't be too big fer me."

"How far along are you, honey?"

"Seven months, but it feels lak ten."

She looked big, even for seven months, but it was probably just the contrast with her petite body. The swelling didn't help.

Samantha had so many questions, like who was the father? What was Angus's involvement? On the run for two days? Why? Where were Lily Beth's parents? For the moment, though, Samantha just said, "Yell if you need help."

Shortly after, Samantha put a pair of elastic-waisted running shorts and oversized T-shirt with a pair of fuzzy socks on the bathroom sink vanity and picked up the sundress, panties, and bra from the floor. She would toss them in the washing machine. "Come downstairs when you're done," she said to Lily Beth who appeared to be basking in bath heaven, her head propped on the back edge of the tub, her eyes closed. She was using her big toe to let more hot water into the tub, making the room steamy.

"I'll make some soup and sandwiches," Samantha said finally.

There was a pause and then a weepy sounding, "Thank you."

When Samantha got down to the sunroom again, she found Angus asleep on the sofa, one of the puppies spread flat out on his chest and the others nestled at his feet. She'd forgotten to put them back in their crate, something she never did. That's how upset she was by this whole mess. Emily snored away between his ankles, having been bumped by the dogs.

Angus's cell phone was on the floor. He must have been checking email or texting or whatever. She shook him awake, causing the pups to start yip, yip, yipping, Emily to give her a dirty look, and Clarence to squawk "Holy shit!"

"Go up to my bathroom and take a shower," she told the groggy Angus as he sat up. "Here's a pair of sweatpants and a tee that should fit. Bring your dirty clothes down with you afterwards so I can wash them. I'll make something for you guys to eat." Meanwhile she was gathering up the puppies to return them to their comfy crate home.

Angus stood, wincing with pain. "But we need to get out of town. Can't you just—"

"Go!" she ordered. "We'll talk later. And don't think you can soft soap me, either."

"But—"

"You heard me." She put both hands on her hips. "You're too old for this stuff, Angus. When are you going to grow up? Yeah, we have a dysfunctional family, but so does half the world. It's time you stopped dallying around and straightened up. Stay in college, get a degree, or another degree, or get a job and work, for a change. Life is boring sometimes. So the hell what!"

"Holy shit!" Clarence interjected, as if for emphasis.

Angus shuffled off, out of the room, but over his shoulder he remarked, "Nick's right. You can be a bitch."

Chapter Ten

Sometimes a gal just needs a hero . . .

Whoa, whoa, whoa! "What did you say?" She rushed after Angus, forcing him to turn, halfway up the stairs, and face her. "Did you mention Nick?"

"Um." The guilty expression on his face was telling.

"You know my ex-husband?"

"Oh, I know the dude all right."

"Nick the Prick?"

"Definitely."

"Holy shit!" Clarence remarked.

My sentiments exactly. The fine hairs stood up on the back of her neck. As far as she knew, the only time Angus would have met Nick was at their wedding, more than ten years ago, and he had only been about thirteen then. "What the hell is going on?"

"Stop yelling, Sam! If you must know, Nick is the cause of all our troubles. Or most of them."

On that ominous note, Angus continued climbing the stairs, wearily.

Axel approached Samantha then, carrying his food dish in his mouth. A hint if she ever saw one. She fed the animals (her pantry was loaded with various types of pet food) and cleaned the cats' and Emily's litter boxes, the puppy crate, and the birdcage. When she was done, she sprayed the areas with Lysol, and to her nose, at least, her house smelled fresh.

Afterward, she went into the kitchen to open a can of Starr chicken noodle soup and make a few ham and cheese sandwiches on one of Starr's new artisan whole grain breads. The pups and Emily, drowsy now that their stomachs were full, went to their various crates to snooze. Axel, Maddie, and the two other cats sat at her feet waiting for some food to drop. Which it did. She couldn't resist dropping some scraps of thin-sliced ham or strips of Swiss cheese for them. Axel even liked mustard on his, especially the whole seed, wine-infused condiment imported from Ireland. Pub mustard, they called it.

It shouldn't have been a surprise to her when she clicked on the answering machine on the counter and heard Nick's voice. "Sam, is Angus there? Have you heard from him? The minute he contacts you, I expect you to call me. D'hear? It's important. That piece of shit relative of yours . . ." He paused and when he continued, his voice was calmer. "Just tell that stepbrother of yours, or whatever the hell he is, that I'm not angry. He just needs to come back to my office so we can resolve . . . things. He and Lily Beth, both."

Yeah, right. He wasn't angry. More like flaming furious. Samantha could practically hear the phone lines sizzle.

She had a lot to think about.

Finally, Angus and Lily Beth returned, walking into the kitchen together, both looking much better, though worried and exhausted. The white T-shirt, with the Krewe of Rex, Mardi Gras letters in the traditional purple, green, and gold colors, fit Angus perfectly; Samantha had bought it for a sleep shirt last year. He'd pulled his long blond hair off his face with what Samantha recognized as one of her elastic ponytail holders.

Lily Beth's belly strained against the oversized shirt and elastic-waisted running shorts Samantha had given her, but at least they fit. She, too, had pulled her blonde hair back into a ponytail.

They looked so young.

Sitting at the counter, the two ate voraciously, accompanied by all the two percent milk Samantha had in the fridge and then a pitcher of sweet tea. They even devoured the generous slice of Tante Lulu's Peachy Praline Cobbler Cake which Samantha had brought back from the plantation for her bedtime snack.

Samantha had shooed the animals back into the sunroom and set up a child gate so that Angus and Lily Beth could eat in peace.

"So, y'all own the Starr grocery stores?" Lily Beth commented as she licked the last bit of icing off her fork.

Samantha gave Angus a dirty look. Had he been bragging about the family wealth . . . even as he was poor as a church mouse? And was Lily Beth with him because she thought he had hidden assets? "Not us precisely. It's a family enterprise, and we're a big family. We all work in the stores or the main office, or at least some of us do." She gave Angus a meaningful frown at that last.

"I love the fruit tarts they sell in the Starr bakeries. Every birthday, growin' up, I asked mah mother fer a fruit tart, instead of a traditional birthday cake."

Not a gold digger then, Samantha decided. She'd just been making conversation. "I know," she said, "The fruit tarts are my favorite, too. Next to the Chocolate Domes."

"Oh! Yes!"

"Are you still hungry, Lily Beth?" Samantha asked. "I have a frozen pizza in the freezer. Our latest. Sicilian flat bread with garlic pesto."

"I'm always hungry, but, no, if I eat anymore, I'll bust."

An uncomfortable silence followed. Samantha still didn't know why they were here. Or what trouble they were in. "You mentioned your mother. Can't you go home for help?" Samantha knew she sounded like she didn't want to help them. Frankly, she didn't, and she kind of resented being put on the spot by a person or persons who weren't really her responsibility. Not that she would turn them away. Still . . .

Lily Beth shook her head, seeming to be choked up.

"Lil's parents died in a car accident last year," Angus told Samantha.

"I am so sorry," Samantha said, feeling bad now. "Let's go in the living room," she suggested. Because of the brick wall around her property, the interior of the house, from the back, wouldn't really be visible to anyone circling the perimeter or cruising the alley out back. Like Nick. Still, she would feel better away from all these windows. She would tidy the kitchen later. Or in the morning. She planned to take off work tomorrow, except for a foundation board meeting at noon. And she had to deliver some of these animals to new homes. Thank God!

Lily Beth headed right for the sofa and, instead of sitting at one end and making room for Angus, she laid down on her side, head on a throw pillow, and curled up into as much of a fetal position as she could with her belly, and fell immediately asleep.

With a blush, Angus apologized, "She's been through a lot."

Samantha could only imagine. She went over and arranged a soft mohair afghan over the girl's body, then motioned for Angus to sit on one side chair while she sat in the other. The room was chilly from the air conditioner having been left on all day. So, Samantha also clicked on the gas fireplace, which she rarely did in the summer or in the daytime. It wasn't even seven p.m. now. But the fire did give the room a warm glow.

Most of her furniture, aside from what was in the sunroom, was antique, gathered over the years through family hand-me-downs or French Quarter antique shop forays, a mishmash of different eras and fabrics and style which was oddly comfortable, especially with the cozy fireplace. The sofa Lily Beth lay on was a tufted camelback in a gold and green floral pattern. The chairs, passed down from her grandmother, were faded velvet and damask in colors that complemented the sofa. The carpet was a very old Aubusson that was threadbare in places; it once graced a bedroom in the former Orleans Crescent Hotel. One of the hurricane lamps had belonged to a cousin of Robert E. Lee. She cherished the history and provenance of all the pieces.

"Now, give it to me straight, Angus. How did you get involved with Nick? And start from the beginning." She decided not to tell him about Nick's call. Not yet.

Angus gulped, then started to talk. "I met Nick at Harrah's in Lake Charles a year or two ago."

"A casino?" She'd never known Nick to go the casinos, except for the one in Monte Carlo that time when they'd been on vacation. More a touristy kind of thing.

"I have this little problem," Angus said.

Uh-oh!

"Well, it's a big problem. Gambling."

"Oh, Angus!"

"I'm not an addict. But I developed this computer program for beating the odds at Blackjack, all kinds of poker, actually. Not card counting. Something better. Awesome. But so far it hasn't been perfected."

"Oh? Just how far from perfection are you?"

He grimaced and disclosed, "Two hundred thousand."

"Dollars?" she gasped.

"No, doubloons." He immediately regretted his sarcasm and said, "Sorry. Yeah, that's my current balance, but it keeps growing every day, no matter how much I pay them. Interest. I even sold my Jag." Now, that was big. Angus loved the Jaguar that he'd inherited from his mother on his sixteenth birthday. Samantha's father had bought the red Jaguar convertible for Darla as a wedding gift. Angus's present situation had to be serious for him to have given that up.

"Pay them . . . who? Loan sharks? The mafia," she scoffed, then went slack-awed at Angus's nod. "You can't be serious. This isn't New York City, or Sicily, with some Marlon Brando godfatherly character."

"Not that mafia. The Dixie Mafia."

Her slack jaw went slacker. She'd forgotten about those Louisiana lowlifes. "Oh, Angus!" She sighed, then straightened and asked, "How is Nick involved? Is he into gambling now, too?"

Angus shook his head. "Nah. I mean, he would if it worked. He needs money bad, even worse than me. But he's not very good at gambling."

That was like the pot calling the kettle black, but she refrained from pointing that out.

"Again, what is your involvement with Nick?"

"I work with him."

"How? You have no medical experience. You're a tech expert."

"Not his medical business. His other business."

"And that would be . . . ?"

"Selling babies."

"Whaaat?" she practically shrieked, causing Lily Beth to roll onto her back and blink several times before falling back asleep.

"For more than a year now, I've been helping Nick solicit college students willing to let him deliver their babies and then put them up for phony 'adoptions.' Easy peasy, actually. That Nick is one slick dude." Angus actually had the nerve to grin as if the enterprise and Nick were commendable.

Seeing the glower on her face, he got serious and continued with his explanation. "Nick delivers the babies himself to avoid any detection from hospital personnel. He gives the girls ten thousand dollars up front, another ten thou on delivery, I get ten thou, and then Nick sells the babies for up to a hundred thou, mostly to foreign markets."

"Angus! That's illegal."

"I know, I know. But it's not really that immoral. People want babies, and there aren't enough newborns to satisfy the need."

"Splitting hairs," she remarked.

He shrugged.

"What's your involvement?"

"I hack into the files of college medical centers. In particular, I look for pregnant coeds, then cross file that with those seeking counseling, then another cross file for those either getting or applying for financial aid. Also, word of mouth. I know lots of people on lots of campuses. Piece of cake finding chicks in financial trouble, who are pregnant but not wanting to abort."

"Have you lost your mind?"

"We've been very careful, covering our tracks. Not

just one college. Here and there across the South. It's like shooting fish in a barrel. The girls are thankful for our help, usually. Of course, they don't know the babies are being sold."

"Of course," she said, sarcastically. "Just how many are we talking about here?"

"Twenty, this past year."

"WHAT?" she screeched. She did the quick math in her head. Twenty times a hundred thousand dollars equaled two million dollars. Even with the thirty percent to Angus and the girls, that was a huge profit.

"Shhh. You'll wake Lil."

"Getting information from you is like trying to catch dandelion fluff, but I'm beginning to connect the dots between you, Nick, Lily Beth, and the, Holy Cripes, mafia. Spit it out, please. All of it."

"Nick is desperate for money, and—"

"Nothing new there."

Angus scowled at her interrupting him. "Nick is desperate for money, and I'm desperate for money. But now, Nick is furious with me, and with Lil, for reneging on her baby deal. So I can't rely on that income anymore. The mafia wants me to pay them back, like yesterday. If the mob doesn't kill me, Nick will."

"Why is Nick so upset about Lily Beth? Surely, if he's dealt with so many pregnancies, it can't be the first time a girl has changed her mind."

"Yeah, but this is *the* kickass gene pool. A physicist and an athlete. He's got a frickin' bidding war going on for the baby."

"Lily Beth is an athlete?" Somehow, she didn't look the part, but then it was hard to tell with her baby bump.

"No, Lil is a physicist. Well, a doctoral candidate. She's already racked up two hundred G's in student loans, and she lost her fellowship money. She couldn't stop barfing long enough to teach her classes. Some dude in her class had a thing for garlic."

"Really? Lily Beth, a physicist?" Samantha was having trouble fathoming that idea. Talk about making rash judgments about someone! "How can Nick get away with this? What hospital does he use for deliveries?"

"No hospitals. Have you seen that medical building of his? Southern Women's Maternity Center. Talk about luxury. It's like a spa for rich women needing to pop out babies."

"Angus!" Samantha chided.

"Well, it's true. The women can get manicures and pedicures in between labor contractions. One lady had her roots done by a hairstylist just before they wheeled her in for a C-section."

Angus had to be exaggerating. But then, knowing Nick, maybe not.

"In any case," Angus went on, "there are more nooks and crannies, including several specially equipped birthing and operating rooms. He does the 'special' deliveries after hours. Plus, his girlfriend, Misty Beauville, assists him."

"Misty? Is she a doctor? Or nurse?"

"No. An extreme athlete of some kind. She does marathons. But she has EMS training, or something."

Samantha rolled her eyes. "You've got to go to the police."

"No, no, no. We can't."

"Why? Nick has to be stopped."

"He'll kill us. He already showed us his gun collection."

"Nick has a gun collection?"

Angus nodded. "Believe me, there was a motive in his showing us the weapons. And don't forget, I have the Dixie Mafia dogging me, too. Literally. If you think Nick has guns, you've gotta see what Jimmy Guenot has out on his plantation. Dogs. Big wild rabid dogs . . . pit bulls, I think . . . that he starves and then sics on enemies, or those loan sharkees who fail to pay up on time. That's what happened to me when I went there yesterday to try and reason with Jimmy." He lifted his shirt to show bite marks and scratches on his sides and abdomen. None of them appeared to have broken the skin, but just barely. "Good thing I had a tetanus shot last year. Good thing I can run fast. But I think I broke my finger vaulting over the chain link fence."

"Ang-us! Listen, Tante Lulu's nephew, John LeDeux, is a cop, and I think he had a case involving the Dixie Mafia a few years back. Let me call him."

"No!" he said vehemently. "I'm gonna land in jail, or dead, for what I've done for Nick, and what I still owe in gambling debts."

"How about Lucien LeDeux? He's my lawyer, and as good as they come. Let me call him. I bet he'll have good advice."

"No police. No lawyers."

"Well, if nothing else, Lily Beth has to see a doctor."

"No doctors, either. It would get back to Nick."

"What are you going to do then?"

"Hide. Somewhere no one will find us. Just for a while. 'Til we have a chance to think. Regroup."

"Where?"

"Well, Bruce has that condo in Costa Rica. He just bought it last summer; so, Nick probably doesn't know about it. Maybe if we could get there and hide out 'til things cool down."

"Dad would never agree to that."

"He doesn't need to know. I hacked his passwords and was able to contact the caretaker. I told him Bruce was my dad. I can pick up the key anytime. Bruce is so busy, he'll never know."

Angus underestimated her father. "Have you thought this thing through? Do you have money for airfare? What would you live on while you're there? Do you plan to get a job? How about prenatal care for Lily Beth, maybe even delivery? And how long would you need to regroup in Costa-freakin'-Rica?"

Angus just looked at her, and she knew he was banking on her being his personal banker.

"It's not a solution, Angus. You're just postponing the inevitable."

"I know. I've been a world class loser, and I *am* going to get my act together, but right now my responsibility is to Lil. She has no one. Just me." He exhaled whooshily. "I got her into this mess. I have to be the one to get her out."

"So, if I get you plane tickets to Costa Rica and if I loan you some money, do you promise . . ."

"We can't go commercial. We need a private plane to get us there so there's no record."

"Whoa! Not too demanding, are you, Angus?"

"Don't you know anyone who could get us there? Doesn't your friend Tante Lulu have a nephew with an air charter business?"

Samantha didn't know Remy LeDeux that well, but she did know someone else with the credentials. Hmmm.

"Please, Sam. If you help us, I promise to own up to everything. I'll talk to any police or lawyers you want. And I'll pay you back for the money you lend me. Believe me, I've learned my lesson."

"Take Lily Beth upstairs and put her in one of the guest bedrooms. You take the other. I know it's only eight o'clock, but you're both beat, physically and mentally. Get some rest. I'll see what I can do to help you." She put up a halting hand when he started to protest. "I know, time is important. We'll do something first thing in the morning."

Angus woke up the sleeping girl and half walked, half carried her upstairs. When she was alone, Samantha sighed. What a godawful mess! This was worse than anything she'd ever imagined about Nick.

What an immoral, in fact criminal, no-good excuse for a man her ex-husband was! She wouldn't be surprised if he'd involved Angus in his schemes just to get back at her. Oh, she couldn't delude herself. Angus was equally responsible.

Again, what a godawful mess!

First things first. She went into the kitchen and cleaned up the mess. While she discarded trash, put away whatever food hadn't been eaten (not much), and wiped off the counter, she thought, thought, thought about the options. Then she took a shower and put on a comfy sleep outfit, silk pants and a camisole top, and tried to get some rest. It had been a grueling day. Finally, at nine p.m., she admitted that she'd never be able to sleep unless she took some action. So, she picked up her cell phone and scrolled down to find a number she'd just added in this afternoon, a contact she had hoped to leverage finding homes for rescued animals.

"Hello. Aaron LeDeux here. I'm not available at the moment. Leave a message. You know the drill."

"Hey, Aaron, this is Samantha Starr. We talked this afternoon about the possibility of an animal rescue operation at Bayou Rose. But that's not why I'm calling. Aaron, something has come up here. Something very . . . dangerous. Can you call me right away? I need help!" Aaron was a pilot. He had access to planes. And maybe, just maybe, his assistance would be less obvious than using Remy's company.

Samantha clicked off the phone and tucked it in her pocket. It was still early, and she doubted she would sleep tonight, but she should try. Tomorrow promised to be a busy day. She determined that first thing in the morning she was making one particular phone call.

Tante Lulu could recommend a place for her to buy a gun.

Or maybe not.

Chapter Eleven

*S*ometimes being a hero is just too much damn
trouble . . .

Daniel awakened suddenly to the sound of a phone ringing. Upon opening his eyes and feeling the crick in his
neck, he realized that he'd fallen asleep on his sofa. His
new pet cat, Maxine . . . *the apparently pregnant cat,
dammit . . .* didn't even bother to raise its head.

Last he recalled, he and Aaron had been watching a
rerun of one of the late-night talk shows. Jimmy Fallon
and Justin Timberlake doing a funny, surprisingly good,
singing/dance duet about being happy.

Which brought up a pet peeve of Daniel's. Why did
happy people always try to make everyone else happy?

"If life gives you lemons, make lemonade."

"If a door shuts, open a window."

"Life is just a bowl of cherries."

"Miracles do happen."

"Every cloud has a silver lining."

Bullshit! These Pollyannas needed a good dose of reality. Personally, he believed there was a lot to be said for being grumpy. A good shield against the crap side of life.

Forget Jimmy Fallon and Justin Effin' Timberlake and goofball gladness. Now there was an infomercial blasting away on the TV. *No, I do not need a supersonic toilet plunger that doubles as a concrete mixer, thank you very much.*

The phone continued to ring in the middle of his jaw-cracking yawn. A quick check of his watch showed it was only nine o'clock. What a boring life he led, fast asleep when he could be out on the town, like Aaron, or wherever the hell he went when he disappeared every night. *Who would be calling me on a Sunday evening?*

— Aunt Mel? She called whenever the mood hit her, but they'd already talked to her today. When Tante Lulu had dropped her bomb that afternoon about Aunt Mel possibly moving here, Daniel had called Alaska, and Aunt Mel said there was nothing definite, but a Realtor was bringing by a hot prospect. Maybe she'd come for a visit sometime to see if she would like it, before making a commitment to move.

— Speaking . . . rather thinking . . . of Tante Lulu, maybe it was her calling. The old bird had no sense of appropriateness when it came to anything, whether it be time or subject. For example, her constantly telling people that he wasn't gay. As if that were even a possibility! Yep, she could very well be calling for something as simple as asking if he wanted any more okra from her garden. The answer was "Hell, no!"

— An emergency? *Oh, Lord, don't let it be one of those "patients" I served today. I don't care what Tante Lulu says, I am not licensed to practice in Louisiana. Yet. If ever.*

— Or, most likely, it was just a wrong number.

Rising groggily, he followed the sound of the phone. Not his cell phone ringtone, he belatedly recognized, rather Aaron's raucous Zydeco music. Daniel had no idea what time Aaron had left . . . *Didn't Aaron mention a late night date? One of his mysterious bootie calls? But this was early yet. An early bootie call then? As in an extra long bootie call? . . .* but he must have forgotten his phone.

— Maybe it was just Aaron trying to find his phone. If it was, Daniel was going to demand to know where he went on these nightly jaunts. What if something urgent came up, like angry snakes returning in hordes to overtake the plantation house, or a miraculous appearance of St. Jude at his namesake birdbath, or Publishers Clearing House knocking on the door?

I must be losing my mind.

The ringing stopped, finally, and the phone pinged, indicating it was going to voice mail.

Daniel scrambled to dig the device out of the side crease in the recliner and checked the caller ID. To his shock, he saw that it was Samantha Starr. Huh? Without any hesitation, he fumbled around and eventually clicked on "voice mail," hearing a female voice: "Hey, Aaron, this is Samantha Starr. We talked this afternoon about the possibility of an animal rescue operation at Bayou Rose. But that's not why I'm calling. Aaron, something has come up here. Something very . . . dangerous. Can you call me right away? I need help!"

Daniel couldn't help but notice the nervousness, maybe even fear, in Samantha's voice. Was it that loser ex-husband of hers? Daniel had heard rumors about the guy. A slimeball, to say the least. Or maybe she had an intruder.

And, frankly, why would she call Aaron, and not him? That really pissed Daniel off. He wasn't sure why.

Quickly, he hit reply to Samantha's call on Aaron's phone, but got a busy signal. He tried again three more times. Still busy.

Maxine sidled up and rubbed against his leg. "Meow, meow!" Was the cat trying to tell him something? Some hidden message about Samantha? Yeah, right. More like, where's the rest of that canned tuna fish? That's all Daniel had been able to find for a cat in his meager pantry. Samantha had brought along a box filled with kitty litter, but no kitty kibble.

He glanced out the window toward the big house and saw only a dim lantern on the outside wall of the main floor verandah. The mansion itself was dark, indicating no one was home. Aaron left the exterior light on if he was out for the night. Usually. But then, his pickup truck was missing from its usual parking spot, as well.

Daniel hit reply on Aaron's cell phone a few more times, to no avail. Next, he made a visit to the head, then splashed cold water on his face. Looking in the mirror, he saw that he looked like hell. Bed head, day-old whiskers, bleary eyes. With a sigh of resignation, he went into his bedroom and replaced his wrinkled, cat-hair-covered khakis and golf shirt with a pair of faded jeans, a plain gray tee, and ratty athletic shoes. Five minutes later he was on his way to New Orleans.

"Siri, give me an address for Samantha Starr in New Orleans," he said, clicking the Bluetooth button on his steering wheel. Once it gave him an address, he ordered, "Siri, give me directions." Easy peasy, as Tante Lulu would say.

There was very little traffic; so, it took him only half an hour to get to the city. Cruising through the upper-class Garden District neighborhood, he soon found Samantha's home. A brick, two-story dwelling surrounded by a chest-high brick wall. Not much of a front yard, but there was probably more property in the back, which he couldn't see from here.

Getting out of his car, which he parked on the street, he noted there were no other vehicles around. They must be parked in driveways or garages. Not many parties or visitors on a Sunday evening, he guessed. But wait. There was a dark-colored car down the street a ways. He couldn't tell through the tinted windows if there was anyone inside, or not.

He wasn't sure what he'd been expecting . . . maybe an ultra-modern penthouse condo . . . but definitely not this. It was so . . . so . . . traditional.

Expensive, though. Samantha's house was smaller than the antebellum mansions surrounding it, probably an original carriage house, but worth a fortune nonetheless. Daniel didn't know much about real estate, but he would bet his favorite stethoscope that this structure was in the million-dollar range. Which wasn't surprising with Samantha's monied background. Spoiled rich girls did not rent condos in the ninth ward. Which was probably unfair of him, but no more unfair than her sweeping generalization about doctors.

He opened the front gate, which caused motion detector lights to go on . . . *Good for her!* . . . and walked up the short sidewalk to the front door. Since there were lights on inside, he had no qualms about ringing the doorbell. He probably would have even if the lights were out. He took perverse pleasure in needling Samantha all the time. Like some adolescent kid who pulled on a girl's pigtails, or teased her incessantly, in an asinine attempt at seduction. The sort of stunt Deke Watson might have pulled, if he'd lived long enough.

Oh, crap! Where did that thought come from? He did not allow himself to think about the boy, even after all these years. It was pointless, and, frankly, hurt too much.

Even so, he sometimes wondered if Jamie Lee, Deke's father, had stayed clean and stuck around to console his estranged wife, Bethany? And did they have other children? Daniel couldn't imagine taking such a second chance on grief, but that was him. And wasn't it interesting . . . or telling . . . that he remembered their names after more than two years, when he'd dealt with hundreds of parents of sick kids in his career?

He shook his head to clear it of those disturbing memories, which wasn't really necessary since the noise on the other side of the door would have shocked the dullest brain. It appeared that his doorbell ringing had awakened a menagerie. Loud dog barking and cat meowing. And somewhere more distant inside the house, the yip yip yipping of puppies. At least he didn't hear any goats bleating. Samantha had mentioned a goat, and geese or ducks, hadn't she? But, no, she'd claimed to have gotten rid of those other animals earlier in the day. And a pig . . . he seemed to recall something about a depressed pig.

He pressed the doorbell again.

"Oh, damn!" he heard Samantha say on the other side of the door. She'd probably looked through the security hole to see who was there. His assumption proved true when the door swung open suddenly, and Samantha gaped at him. "You! What are you doing here?"

"Thanks for the warm welcome." Before he had a chance to say more, a German Shepherd the size of a small pony limped up to him and barked loudly, practically in his face. He would have been alarmed except the dog's tail was wagging and it had a loopy grin on its face. On the other hand, there was more danger with the long-legged cat with spotted fur that resembled a cheetah, which arched its back and hissed at him, but then it seemed to sniff the air . . . probably smelled Maxine on him . . . and ambled off to do some cat thing. He also heard other dogs barking somewhere else in the house, and two more cats prowled by, scarcely paying him any attention, and was that a pig sitting on a low stool before the window? Yep, the animal was oinking. It didn't look depressed to him, but how did one recognize pig depression?

Holy fricking animal house!

"Seriously, Daniel, what are you doing here?"

"You wound me," he said, clapping a hand over his heart. "I come as Prince Charming to the rescue, and you treat me like the Prince of Frogs."

"Some prince!" She surveyed the area behind him as if expecting someone lurking on the street. Seeing something, she flinched and murmured with dismay, "Still there."

He assumed that she referred to the car with the shaded windows. "Who's still there?" he asked.

Before he could turn around and check the object of her distress, she stepped back, allowing him entrance to her home. In fact, when he hesitated, she grabbed his arm and yanked him in, slamming and locking the door behind them.

Ooookay!

A quick glance around showed the foyer of the house with a central hallway going forward into some kind of windowed great room. A staircase in the hallway led upstairs. To the left was a library/office, and to the right, a living room where a gas fireplace provided the only light. It was to the latter that she led him.

There was a sepia-toned, framed photograph on one wall of a Civil War officer. Robert E. Lee or someone equally important, he guessed. "One of your ancestors?"

"Pfff! My ancestors were running around the highlands in kilts chasing sheep during the American Civil War. What are you doing here, Daniel?"

He didn't like her tone. Not one bit. And decided to ignore her rudeness. "Oh, that's right. I heard about your family's Scottish ancestry. In fact I met your father at one of the Hope Foundation board meetings. He was wearing a kilt. At the time, I thought it was odd, but then I've seen odder in the French Quarter on a Saturday night."

"Hah! You see lots odder just being around Tante Lulu," she remarked.

"You have a point there."

"You still haven't answered my question. What are you doing here?"

"I'm not sure," he admitted.

"You better not be thinking of a bootie call, just because we shared a few dreams."

What the hell? Talk about a hit from the left! "More like sexual fantasies. And the thought of a sexual encounter never occurred to me," he said defensively, but then added, "But now that you mention it . . ."

She put her hands on her hips in consternation and tapped her bare foot with impatience.

But then he noticed her attire. Flame red pants with a black camisole type top (sans bra), edged in red. Both in some kind of silky material, that moved when she did, delineating her buttocks and the curve of her breasts right down to the nipples. Her dark red hair was down, spilling over her shoulders in disarray. He didn't think he'd ever seen her in anything other than a sophisticated upswept hairdo. She must have been in bed, or getting ready for bed.

Oh. My. Dormant. Libido! Daniel thought, then immediately amended. *Not so damned dormant!*

"What are you grinning about?" she asked, pivoting as she motioned for him to sit in one of the chairs, while she dropped down into a low sofa.

Just to be contrary, he sat down next to her.

She frowned but said nothing.

"Was I grinning?" he said in answer to her question. "Maybe I'm just happy." *Good Lord, Jimmy Fallon must be rubbing off on me.*

"You? Happy? That would be a switch. Why?" she scoffed.

Ooh, she was going to pay for that insult. "To see you, Samantha darlin'." *Holy hell! Am I developing a Southern accent?* "In all your sexy clothes." *And, yeah, she does look damned sexy.* "Were you expecting to greet my brother like that? All decked out and ready for . . . whatever?" *Not if I can help it.* He waved a hand as if lost for words. "Sexy lady."

"Holy shit!" a male voice said from one of the other rooms.

"Another visitor?"

"No, it's Clarence. A bird. Another rescue I can't get rid of. Mainly because that's the only thing it can say, and people won't adopt him because of the bad language around kids." But then she addressed his observation. "Are you crazy? This is not sexy. It's a sleep outfit, for heaven's sake," she said, glancing downward. Then, "I am not sexy."

"Believe me, Samantha, you are sexy."

Her face bloomed with color matching her attire, which,

incidentally, hugged her body as she sat. Pulling taut over her breasts. Outlining her belly and thighs.

He ran a fingertip over her bare skin from her shoulder to her wrist, and grinned some more. Just to tease her. Or was it to test if her skin was as soft as it looked.

She shrugged his hand off before it could make a return foray and made a tsk-ing sound, which he found seductive in a contradictory sort of way. Prim and proper on the outside, wild and wanton inside.

Well, he could hope. Not that he really wanted a relationship with Samantha. On the other hand, there were those arousing wet dreams he'd been having of her. But then an unwelcome thought hit him. "You haven't been having sex dreams about my brother, have you?"

"Holy shit!" Clarence said.

"Get real!" Samantha said.

"Does that mean you don't have the hots for Aaron?"

"Get real," she said again. Then, "Speaking of your brother, why isn't he here? I called him, not you."

"Aaron is otherwise occupied," he said enigmatically, but then explained about his missing brother and the lost phone. "But I could be available." A generous offer, if he did say so himself. "So, what's the dangerous situation you needed Aaron for? Won't I do?"

She gave him a narrow-eyed glance to see if he'd meant that as a double entendre.

He had.

"Aaron is a pilot, and I need transport out of the country."

His eyes went wide. "Whaaat?" Not at all what he'd expected! With as much patience as he could muster, he told her, "You need air transportation? Louis Armstrong International Airport is only ten miles away. Can you say 1–800-DeltaAir?"

"It's not for me, but . . ." She shrugged and proceeded

to tell him the most amazing story about Angus, her step-brother by marriage . . . the son of one of her father's numerous wives by a previous husband, or some such thing . . . and a young pregnant woman. It was a convoluted tale about gambling debts and the Dixie Mafia and Samantha's ex-husband who was selling babies. Bottom line was, Angus and the girl wanted to go to Costa Rica to hide out for a while.

"Is that all?"

"Isn't it enough?" she asked, failing to hear his sarcasm.

"The mafia, a baby selling operation, pit bulls, gambling debts, an advanced pregnancy. Seriously?"

"I know it sounds unbelievable."

"You think?" When she didn't back down from her story, he homed in on something else. "Where are Angus and the girl right now?"

She raised her eyes upward. "Upstairs. Sleeping."

"Of course they are," he said.

"They were exhausted and, frankly, I'm worried about Lily Beth. Her ankles and hands are really swollen. I don't suppose, since you're here . . ."

"Samantha! I'm not an obstetrician."

"You're a doctor," she said, as if he needed a reminder. "How swollen?"

"Very."

"She better see an OB-GYN asap."

"She claims that Nick, who happens to conveniently be an OB-GYN, by the way, has been giving her regular exams. And she's on prenatal vitamins."

"And you think that's enough? You trust your ex?"

"Of course not."

"Then she needs to get checked by another physician. No, not me. A baby doctor."

"Not gonna happen. At least not right away." Samantha shook her head adamantly. "I already told them that, as well as suggesting they go to the police, or John LeDeux, or Luc LeDeux for help. They refused all of those. They're really scared. In fact, I'm beginning to get scared myself."

"All the more reason to get help."

"That's exactly why I called you . . . I mean, Aaron."

"Yeah, Aaron knows a lot about pregnant women."

"I need Aaron for something else. But since you're here, and you're a doctor . . ." She pulled at her own hair with frustration. "Jeesh! I'm not asking you to do brain surgery, Daniel, or even deliver a baby. Can't you stop being so selfish and come out of your self-imposed pity party exile for a medical crisis? All I meant was . . ."

"Pity party exile? Why don't you tell me what you really think? Makes me really want to help you."

"Sorry. My nerves are shot. I hate that I've been pulled into this mess. And I hate asking anyone else to help."

"It's hell losing control, isn't it?"

"You would know, wouldn't you? Isn't that why you quit medicine?"

That was a low blow. And way too close to the truth. He put up his hands in surrender. "Give me a break. I'll look at her."

She nodded reluctantly. "Sorry. I have this thing about doctors."

No kidding! "That's okay. I have a thing about spoiled rich girls."

She was about to argue with him, he could tell, but clamped her mouth shut.

"I still can't wrap my mind around . . . do you believe all this stuff about mafias and baby selling?"

"I have to. Angus is pretty convincing. Plus, I've already had an alarming voice mail from Nick."

"I don't suppose . . . that car parked out on the street," he mused aloud. "Could it be your ex?"

"No, he'd come right in."

"What then? Oh, no! Surely it's not some gangsters watching your house."

"I wondered the same thing."

"Samantha! You need to call the police! Right now!"

Chapter Twelve

When the mob knocks, don't answer . . .

"I can't call the police," Samantha told him. "They'll arrest Angus, and Lily Beth might be in danger from Nick. It's time that we need, time to figure out a solution."

"What's with this 'we' business?" He already felt the walls closing in on him. He was being pulled into something that should have him running for the hills.

"Can't you locate your brother?"

As if Aaron is the answer! "I wish! He goes somewhere almost every night, and comes back just before dawn."

"A married woman," she surmised.

He shook his head. "I don't think so."

"Well, if it is a married woman, Tante Lulu will have a bird. Believe me, she eventually hears about everything on the bayou."

"That's for sure. She'd be signing him up for a novena at Our Lady of the Bayou." He shrugged then. "I would have guessed he had something going on with our neighbor, Delilah, the alligator farmer, but he only met her recently, and this affair, or whatever it is, has been going on for more than a year. Well, it's his business." He shrugged again.

"Can you bring him here when he gets back?"

"You ask a lot," he remarked.

"I know," she said.

And yet you still ask.

Me! Your least favorite person in the world! Probably holding your nose as you do.

There has to be a way to capitalize on that.

No, no, no. I do not want to capitalize, or anything else, with her.

"I don't know why you think Aaron is the answer to your problem. Aaron doesn't own a plane. He'd have to go to Remy LeDeux and borrow one, which would take more time, and would bring another person into this so-called secret. And not just him. Tante Lulu would no doubt hear about it and be poking her nose into the whole affair."

"You're not helping," she said, but she wasn't really being critical. She wrung her hands nervously.

He took one of her hands in his and straightened out the fingers before linking her hand with his and laying the joined hands on his thigh. Why he did it, he had no idea.

Guess I'm still a sucker for a person in distress. Kids with cancer, parents on drugs, broken families.

Why Samantha allowed it was an even bigger question.

Maybe she just needs a hug.

Now there's a thought that could merit me a slap. Hand holding, okay. Hugs, not okay.

Back to the subject at hand. "Here's what I think you should do. Short term. We should somehow whisk them from here out to Bayou Rose Plantation. God knows, there's plenty of room there. And no neighbors within viewing distance. I know, I know, it's not a permanent solution, but like you said, they need time to decide what to do."

"You would do that for them?" she asked, teary-eyed.

He was still holding her hand, and still kind of liking it. Who knew hand holding could be so . . . sensual? It was certainly zapping out every good sense particle in his rusty brain. "I wouldn't do it. *We* would," he emphasized . . . a bit distractedly as her thumb caressed his thumb. Holy frickin' hell! Now he was *really* liking it!

"But . . . but . . . I can't leave here. All these animals." She blinked the tears welling in her green eyes from seeping out, followed by more seemingly innocent thumb sex.

Tears? Somehow, he didn't see Samantha as the weepy type.

Or had he just fallen into a trap? Had she planned this all along? A rich girl like her could probably hire her own airline and a dozen bodyguards besides.

He guessed he would have to give her the benefit of the doubt. With a sigh, he conceded, "You'll have to bring the animals with you. A dog, a cat, and a bird shouldn't be too much trouble."

"Holy shit!" Clarence said again.

"And five puppies," she added. "And a pig. And two other cats."

He dropped her hand like a hot lead sinker.

She blinked away more tears, like sparkling emeralds, stunned at the idea of his generosity, no doubt, or stunned that he was so gullible. "I can't believe you would be willing to go out on a limb like that for people you don't know. For me."

He was surprised she hadn't said "For little ol' me." That would have proved his suspicion of a trap. Poor (*rather rich*), fragile (*Hah!*), Southern belle in need of a strong shoulder (*like, say, mine*) to lean on. *Bull-shit!* And, hey, he should be offended by that remark about him not going out of his way to help people, but he supposed his loner attitude and his snarkiness toward her gave the impression of callousness. *Whatever. I already committed myself, and I'll be damned if I back down now. If she'd let me.* "Darlin'," he said with a deliberate drawl . . . *I can play Rhett to your Scarlett any day.* "You have no idea what I'm going to ask in return."

Frankly, he had no idea, either.

But the possibilities were tantalizing.

She blushed. Obviously entertaining some of the same ideas.

It was not surprising that Clarence piped in with, "Holy shit! Holy shit! Holy shit!"

"Let's go into the kitchen and have a cup of coffee while we make plans," she suggested, hopping up off the sofa suddenly, which caused the dog, which had been lying flat out on the floor in front of the fire like a hearth rug, to yelp with surprise. No stirring from the exotic cat, though. It was sprawled across one of the chairs . . . probably a priceless antique . . . didn't even bother to raise its head off the one arm. Its tail lay over the other arm, hanging practically to the floor. The pig had jumped off its perch on the stool and was lying next to the dog.

What a madhouse!

"Don't you have anything stronger?" he asked.

"Are you kidding? I told you I'm of Scottish descent. There's always Scotch on the premises."

She smiled at him as he stood to follow her. There were no longer any tears in her eyes. Forget about sparkling emeralds, he decided then. Her eyes were murky green pools designed to lure a guy in and make him do things he didn't even know he wanted to do. And he was the dumb trout who'd taken her bait. Hooked, lined and hot damn sinkered!

It was probably some Southern voodoo kind of crap. Maybe he should ask Tante Lulu for a spell to ward off Samantha's allure. He could only imagine the old bat's reaction. She'd be calling for a *fais do do*, a party down on the bayou, and the theme would be, "Daniel LeDeux Ain't Gay, hallelejuah!"

But then he watched Samantha's buttocks move in the red silky pants as she walked out of the room. Was there anything prettier than a heart-shaped ass on a woman? And he decided, *maybe not*. And those long limbs . . . man, what a creative male could do with those!

Hot damn hell! He decided he could live with the spell or whatever the hell it was, thank you very much!

Any lewd thoughts he might have been entertaining were interrupted abruptly by a loud pounding on the front door. They looked at each other in question.

He arched his brows.

She shrugged.

The dog halted in its tracks toward the kitchen.

The cougar cat stopped mid stretch.

The pig raised its head and sniffed the air.

Then they all erupted with their respective sounds of alert. Barking, growling, meowing, and oinking. A female squeak of dismay, as in, "Oh, Rhett, the Yankees are comin'!" A male grunt of disgust, as in "What next?" All of which alerted the bird to voice its opinion, and the puppies and other cats to join in the chorus.

More pounding on the door.

"Let's just ignore it," she whispered.

The German Shepherd let loose with a wild howl that could probably be heard a block away, definitely through a measly door. Then the old dog lay down on the floor, its muzzle between its front paws, all tired out from the effort.

"I doubt whoever is there will just go away. Let me handle it," he offered, also in a whisper. *I gotta get my Rhett on once in a while*, he joked with himself. Then, he added, "Do you have a gun?"

"No. Damn, I knew I should have bought a gun. Just this evening I decided to ask Tante Lulu if she had an extra one. But I didn't have a chance to call her yet."

He gave her a glance of surprise; he hadn't been serious. That's all he . . . she . . . needed. Southern belle with a pistol. She'd probably shoot her eye out. At the least, everyone up and down the bayou would know about it, thanks to the Mouth of the South.

Daniel was beginning to feel like Alice in Wonderland . . . or rather, Alex in Wonderland . . . and he'd fallen down some crazy-ass Southern rabbit hole. Forget Scarlett O'Hara. His Alice would be wearing some silky red short shorts. And high heels. And nothing on top. And "Pretty Woman" would be playing in the background.

He could hear Aaron laughing in his head. Twins were like that sometimes. They shared long-distance thoughts and feelings. In fact, some scientists claimed that even during sex . . . well, never mind! Suffice it to say, it gave new meaning to multiple orgasms.

To the Aaron in his head, Daniel said, *Hey, it's my fantasy. If I want bimbo Alice, I get bimbo Alice.*

More Aaron laughter.

Daniel and Samantha walked softly toward the front door where Samantha peeked through the security hole and declared in a whisper, "I think it's the mafia."

"How can you tell?"

"Well, it's not Nick. And there are two of them. And they look . . . mafia-ish."

He pushed her aside to look for himself. What he saw was two men, their faces distorted through the fisheye lens in the peephole. They were scowling with impatience at their knocking not being answered. Definitely not Welcome Wagon, or Jehovah's Witnesses, or a passing traveler in need of directions. No *Gone with the Wind* Yankees, either. The short one wore a tight "Sleep With the Fishes, Motherfucker" T-shirt over a muscular chest and bulging biceps; there were tattoos on his neck and forearms. The other dude . . . taller, but equally muscular . . . wore a T-shirt with the logo "Pit Bulls Rule" under an open denim shirt. There was a livid scar on his cheek that lifted one side of his mouth in a perpetual grin. The Mutt and Jeff of creeps!

Daniel could swear he saw the shine of a pistol under the denim shirt. He amended his assessment to "the Mutt and Jeff of dangerous creeps."

Okay, definitely mafia-ish.

"Samantha Starr! You in dere, *chère*. We doan want no trouble here. Jist open the door, yes." This from Mutt, the short one.

Okay, definitely *Dixie* Mafia-ish.

"Call 911," Daniel advised Samantha.

She shook her head.

Daniel wasn't convinced that her way was the best way, but there was no time to argue. He kicked off his shoes, toed off his socks, and used both hands to mess up his hair. He tugged out his T-shirt that had been tucked inside the waistband of his jeans. As an added touch, he undid the button on the fly of his pants and zipped down halfway.

"*What* are you doing?" she asked in an undertone.

"Pretending I was in bed."

"Why would you be . . . oh!" Her cheeks bloomed with color.

He put a forefinger to his lips, signaling silence, then put the security chain on the door and opened it several inches. "Yeah? What do you guys want?" he snarled at the two figures on the doorstep.

Surprised, they backed up a step. They had to have seen him enter a short time ago, but apparently they hadn't been expecting a man to answer the door, or him in particular, as evidenced by Mutt's remark, "You ain't Angus Starr."

"No shit, Dick Tracy," Daniel countered, starting to close the door.

But the taller, scar-faced dude, Jeff, stuck his booted foot into the opening. "Wait a fuckin' minute. Where's Samantha Starr? Bet she knows where that stupid-ass brother of hers is, guar-an-teed."

"Angus isn't her brother, exactly," Daniel commented, as if that mattered. "He's actually the son of one of her father's—"

Scar face made a growling noise.

"Why do you want Angus anyway?"

"None of yer damn bizness, you!" Mutt said, putting his hand inside his pants pocket, as if reaching for a weapon.

"Hold on. I'll go get her," Daniel said.

Stepping behind the door, he acted quickly. Messing Samantha's hair into a sexy mess, he pressed her up against the wall and, before she could yell or kick him in the nuts, he leaned down to kiss her, hard and deep, even nipping at her bottom lip so that she would open for him.

Then he forgot why he'd made a move on her.

He kissed her and kissed her and kissed her, open and searching.

She made a low moan that encouraged him to do more.

Not that he needed any encouragement. With hair-trigger speed, he was in full-throttle sex machine mode. James Brown would be so proud.

She put her hands on his shoulders and drew him even closer.

He put his hands on her butt and ground his hips against her.

Those thoughts Daniel had entertained earlier today, about her height and his being a match-up in the sex department, turned out to be true. Breast to chest, belly to gut, thigh to thigh, cock to. . . .

Yeah, there was something to be said for similar physiques mating. An anthropologist could write a book on the subject.

Forget all the analysis. Daniel had never been turned on so hard and so fast in all his sorry life. He might have been a bit of a hermit these past few years, but he hadn't been celibate, not totally, until recently. Sex was nothing new to him; he'd had his first two-person encounter when he was fifteen. He wasn't in the same league as his brother when it came to the fairer sex, and didn't want to be, but there had been more women for him than he could count on both hands since then. Not many long-term relationships, but that was unimportant. What was important was that he couldn't quite remember the last time he'd gotten laid. More than a year, at least. Still . . .

But this . . . *this* was beyond imagination. In fact, his heart was thumping so hard, he feared he might have a heart attack, and didn't even care.

Thump, thump, thump.

She licked his neck when he came up for a breath.

Thump, thump, thump.

He could actually feel her hardened nipples against his chest . . . or imagined he could.

Thump, thump, thump.

She raised one leg and rubbed her inner knee against his outer thigh.

Thump, thump, thump.

"Open this door, or, sure as skunks shit, I'm gonna shoot a hole in it big as that Angus's fool head."

"The fool head what's gonna be gator bait by mornin'."

Both Daniel's and Samantha's heads shot up. Apparently, the thumping hadn't been Daniel's heart after all, but the continued pounding on the door by the Dixie Mob duo.

"Ooops," he said, stepping back.

Samantha looked dazed. Her mouth was wet and kiss-swollen. The one strap of her silk top had slipped off a shoulder. He could swear there was a hickey on her neck, though he didn't recall doing that. Maybe it was just whisker burn.

"Just the right effect," he murmured.

She flinched as if he'd slapped her.

He hadn't meant that exactly how it sounded, but he had no time to explain. Grabbing her by the waist, he yanked her to the opening in the door, molding her tightly to his side.

"*Mon Dieu*! Angus dint tell us he had a hoochie mama sister," Jeff remarked on first seeing Samantha. "You an uptown hooker or sumpin', *ma jolie fille*?"

Mutt chuckled and said, "No question what you been doin', babe!" He emphasized his words with a lewd thrust of his hips.

Daniel squeezed Samantha tighter in a silent message not to let them rile her into saying something she shouldn't.

She apparently got his message. "What do you guys want? It's almost eleven o'clock, and I need my . . ." She gave Daniel a fake sultry look. ". . . sleep."

"Yeah, right." Mutt chuckled some more.

Then Jeff's jaw dropped open as he stared at something over Samantha's shoulder.

Oh, crap! Daniel hoped Angus hadn't awakened and

come downstairs. But nope, it was someone . . . *something* . . . else.

"Son of a fucking pig! Didjya know there's an oinker in yer house?" Jeff asked Samantha.

"Yes, she's a pet," Samantha replied. "Don't say anything insulting. Emily is already depressed."

The two jerks were no longer looking at Samantha like she was hot stuff. More like batshit crazy.

Shaking his head to clear it, Jeff then demanded, "Let us in. We jist need ta talk ta Angus, and we'll be on our way."

There was no question in any of their minds what he meant by "talk."

"Angus isn't here," Samantha lied. "I haven't seen him in ages, and I have no idea why you'd think he's here now."

"So, it's been nice, but scram," Daniel added and tried once again to close the door, to no avail.

Just then a siren could be heard in the distance.

Mutt and Jeff stiffened and looked in that direction.

The sirens had no connection to their situation, unless one of the neighbors had called, but these goofballs didn't know that. "Samantha called 911 when she saw your car parked on the street," Daniel lied. "Guess the police are finally getting around to investigating."

"This isn't over," Jeff said with a scowl as he stepped back.

"Tell that brother of yours that The Boss wants his money, or he's pit bull kibble." With that warning, Mutt drew his booted foot out of the doorway.

And the two ran off to their car.

With the door now closed and locked, Daniel looked at Samantha, who appeared dazed. "That went well."

Samantha blinked away her daze and pushed away from him, walking back into the living room, heading toward the kitchen. "Where *is* that Scotch?"

Chapter Thirteen

T *here are road trips, and then there are ROAD TRIPS!* . . .

Samantha was thankful for Daniel's help. She really was. But her life since his arrival had turned into one madcap debacle after another. *Can anyone say mafia? Or the killer kiss?* Hard to believe that her seemingly normal life could have become so bizarre.

Who was she kidding? Angus was the one who'd brought on this disaster, but he walked around with such a hangdog expression on his face that it was hard to snark at him. Better she should snipe at Daniel who was doing plenty of complaining of his own, most of it muttered under his breath, as they packed up the vehicles to go to the plantation.

"Does she have to buy pet food in fifty-pound bags?"

"But, man, she does have a nice ass."

"If that dog pees on my car tires one more time . . . !"

"She's gonna owe me big-time. BIG-time!"

"How hard can it be to carry a Savannah cat, whatever the hell that is? Ouch, ouch, ouch!"

"I can't remember when I had my last tetanus shot. That is just great! I've probably got rabies."

"What do you mean, your pig is depressed? I'm the only one allowed to be depressed around here."

"This is a bad idea, a really bad idea."

"I think I'll go back to pediatric oncology. A lot less stress!"

"No, no, no! Not there, Emily."

"Maybe I'll wake up, and this is all a nightmare."

It was after midnight before they got all the animals, their various crates and food and toys, into her car and Daniel's SUV, which was now parked in the alley behind her garage. Thus far, there had been no further signs of what Daniel had come to call the Mutt and Jeff of the mafia. Thank God. There was no doubt in her mind, though, that they would return, possibly as soon as this morning.

And, hey, the way things were going for her, Nick could show up any minute with his gun collection and extreme athlete cohort. In that case, she wondered idly if Daniel would pull another sex-against-the-wall stunt. Or perhaps not so idly.

Lily Beth was curled up on her side in the cargo area of Daniel's vehicle, covered with some doggie blankets. Situated between the back of her bent knees and her rump was Clarence in his cage. Needless to say, they were all getting sick of his "Holy shits." Daniel was threatening masking tape. And Lily Beth came in a close second to Daniel in the complaint department. "If we doan leave soon, I'm gonna hafta pee again." Or "I'm hungry. Kin we stop at Claudine's fer some beignets?" Or "I have enough gas ta fire up a barbecue."

Angus had managed to fit himself in the trunk of Samantha's BMW. Probably glad to be away from Lily Beth's constant grumblings. Daniel's complaints, on the other hand, seemed to amuse Angus. Men!

Axel was lying, half on, half off of the front passenger seat of Samantha's car, his rump on the floor. Maddie, who was hissing mad, had been forced to sit on half of the backseat. The other side of the seat held a crate with two cats, Felix and Garfield. She and Daniel both had scratch marks up and down their arms from their efforts to carry the reluctant Maddie out of the house. There was no way they could have stuffed the big, angry cat into a crate.

"Are you sure this isn't an actual cougar?" Daniel kept asking Samantha. "Maybe we could drop it off at the zoo."

Daniel also carried a crate of puppies on his backseat, and sitting demurely beside him in the front was a pig. He still didn't think the pig was depressed, as Samantha kept telling him. It was a pig scam, in his opinion. Whatever that was!

"If I get stopped for speeding, how am I going to explain this pig to the cops?" he asked, once Maddie was locked into an animal seat belt.

"I'd be more worried about the pregnant woman in the cargo area if I were you. Or the cursing bird," she countered. Then she added, because she couldn't resist, "Don't speed."

Daniel was not amused. He'd lost his sense of humor somewhere between stepping in goose poop and her cautions not to hurt Emily's feelings by calling her fat. "Ditto to you, sweetheart," he said. "How you going to explain a cougar in your backseat?"

"I keep telling you, Maddie isn't a cougar. She's a Savannah cat."

"Same thing," Daniel grumbled.

Finally, the cars were loaded, she'd secured the house, and they were off to Bayou Rose Plantation. She followed Daniel's SUV. There didn't appear to be anyone following them; so, they were safe. For now.

The trip was mostly uneventful. In her car anyway. She could imagine what was happening in Daniel's vehicle, though. Between Lily Beth's moans and Clarence's "Holy shits!" Daniel would be spitting nails by the time they arrived.

It was after one a.m. when they drove up the alleé to the plantation house. In the misty light cast by a full bayou moon, their headlights, and the exterior lamps on the mansion, the property looked dreamlike. Almost beautiful. All its imperfections muted. The landscaping work that had been done the previous afternoon had paid off. *Oh, Lord! Had all this happened in less than one day?* The grassy areas were neatly mowed. Massive shrubs and bougainvillea vines had been trimmed. Even the Spanish moss hanging from the live oak trees appeared sparkly with dew, rather than their usual ghostly gray. The mansion itself, in bad need of a paint job, looked shabbily elegant, if that was possible.

She sighed deeply as she came to a stop behind Daniel's stopped SUV. But when he didn't immediately emerge, she noticed something else. Aaron LeDeux had just come home and pulled his pickup truck around Samantha's BMW and then around and in front of Daniel's vehicle.

Samantha got out of her car and approached the SUV just as Aaron was approaching from the other side. All they could hear, aside from the nighttime bayou sounds of crickets and frogs and hooty owls, was "Holy shit! Holy shit! Holy shit!" coming from the end of the vehicle. The puppies were barking in their backseat crate. Through the rear window could be seen a pregnant woman, attempting to sit up.

Samantha looked at Aaron, who was clearly stunned, and he looked back at her, in question. Daniel had his forehead pressed to the steering wheel, probably swearing a blue streak.

When Daniel finally opened the electric window and looked up, he snarled at his brother, "Don't say anything. Not a word. Or I swear, I can't predict what I'll do."

"Um. I was just going to say, bro," Aaron said, scrooching down so he was eye level with Daniel, "do you know you have a pig in the catbird seat?"

Then, there was no stopping Aaron's laughter. Eventually, Daniel joined in, emerging from his SUV and laughing so hard he finally had to sit down on the steps leading up to the verandah.

Samantha took that as a good sign.

On the other hand, she was clearly in the middle of a walking nervous breakdown.

His brother was his keeper only when he wanted to be . . .

You could say that his brother overreacted a bit to Daniel's suggestion that Aaron remain in the big house with Angus, Lily Beth, Samantha, and the animals while Daniel retired to his *garconniére* apartment. That was Daniel's opinion anyhow. After all, Daniel would be within shouting distance, practically, if there were a problem, which no one expected anymore tonight. But, no, Aaron was being unreasonable . . . when he wasn't laughing his ass off.

"No!"

"Are you frickin' kidding me?"

"Absolutely not!"

"Not a chance!"

"You're the expert on depression, not me. Besides, I like my bacon on a plate, not on my lap. Whoever heard of a lap pig anyhow?"

"And I thought Delilah was weird with her gators!"

"Do you realize that's a cougar over there? A Savannah cat? Yeah, right! And Delilah raises lizards."

"I only have one bedroom furnished. Are you suggesting that I sleep with Samantha? Jeesh! You don't have to yell. I was only teasing. I have a bunch of air mattresses."

"No, I am not going to tell you where I was all night. Oh, all right. I've been taking nocturnal dance lessons. No, I didn't say nocturnal emissions, you pervert. Lessons. Dance lessons. No, not in the French Quarter, gutter-brain. Down the bayou. Swamp dancing. You never heard of that? Man, you have a dirty mind."

"Speaking of dirty, who's going to clean up after all these animals? They're house-trained? I find that hard to believe. A house-trained pig! No, I am not going to shush. The pig can't hear me, and even if it could, would it understand? Better yet, do I care?"

Samantha was currently downstairs setting up accommodations for all her pets in the second salon, which was as yet empty of any furniture. Hell, hardly any of the rooms in the fifteen-room house had furniture yet. Luckily, there were a lot of paint drop cloths around.

Angus and Lily Beth had inflated a couple of air mattresses that Aaron had on hand (something about manufacturer's samples that doubled as rafts in small aircrafts in case of crashes) and were presumably fast asleep on the floor of the front parlor. The pocket doors had been closed for privacy more than an hour ago. The young couple had to be exhausted. Or maybe they just wanted to escape Aaron's blistering interrogation.

In his defense, Aaron had been brutally honest with them after he'd been told their sorry story. A lot of the concerns were ones Daniel hadn't even thought of. For example, Aaron said that Costa Rica was not even a remote possibility. Not only were there flight plans to be filed, but also required were pre-planned itineraries, passports, round-trip tickets, and plane parking permits. The biggest deterrent, though, especially with a pregnant woman, was that there had been several cases of the Zika virus in Costa Rica. A slight risk. Still . . . End of that plan!

Until better alternatives could be found, Daniel decided, hiding out at Bayou Rose represented a holding pattern for the couple. A temporary solution. And for Samantha, as well, since she was the linchpin on this whole Rube Goldberg-esque plan.

Which shouldn't be such a big problem for Daniel, but he kept thinking about The Kiss. Yeah, he had put the moves on Samantha as a ploy to make her look bed-mussed, but he was the one who'd ended up a muss . . . uh, mess. Talk about hair-trigger arousals and sex images now imprinted on his fool brain for life! Or at least until he replaced those images with some even more graphic ones. He could hope!

Bottom line: he wanted to do it again. And more.

And he couldn't . . . wouldn't . . . shouldn't.

What a muss-mess!

Muss-mess? Good Lord! I'm starting to think like Tante Lulu.

All these thoughts were going through Daniel's mind while he was upstairs in the only furnished bedroom. Well, it had an IKEA king-size bed and a tall, two-door chest for storing clothing (there being no closets in these old homes . . . due to taxes in historic times being based on number of closets). A matching, smaller-sized bedroom set was in the *garconniére*, which was a BOGO, Aaron had told him at the time of purchase. Buy one, get another one free. The things he learned in this renovation project!

Daniel was watching Aaron pack a duffel bag with a change of clothes and Dopp Kit with personal products. You'd think he was going on a trip, and not just across the yard.

"Listen, Dan, this is your problem, not mine. You brought her . . . them . . . here. Deal with it."

"Yeah, but she called you. You were her first choice for rescuer."

"Oh, no, no, no. First responders take precedence."

"Who told you that?"

"It's a man thing."

"Bullshit!"

"You stepped up to the plate, Mickey Mantle. That means you save the day. And by the way, if you're planning on hitting a home run, change the sheets."

"You're disgusting."

"I know." Aaron grinned, as if Daniel had paid him a compliment. "Where's my phone, by the way?"

"Out in my car. In the console." He waved a hand toward the window fronting the driveway. "If the pig didn't eat it."

Aaron grinned.

Daniel had to grin then, too. It *was* a ludicrous situation.

He walked over to his apartment with Aaron and gathered a few items himself . . . shaving kit, underwear, clean T-shirt, and shorts . . . then sat down wearily on the sofa.

"You know, Dan, this could be dangerous," his brother said, sinking down to the sofa beside him.

Daniel nodded. "Tell me about it. You didn't see the two gun-wielding mob dimwits."

"Death by stupidity is still death," Aaron remarked.

"I'm calling Lucien LeDeux this morning. I don't care what Angus says. Luc can advise us on whether to involve the police. And, dammit, as a doctor I have an obligation to report the kind of shenanigans that Coltrane is involved in."

"Shenanigans? Been hangin' around Tante Lulu much?"

"Way too much!"

"You still have that pistol?" Aaron asked him then.

"Yes, but I've never shot at a human before. Just targets. And snakes." Even though Tante Lulu recommended killing the snakes with a shovel, he just couldn't see himself getting that close. And bullets made for a cleaner kill.

Aaron enjoyed hunting and had several rifles and firearms. Back in Alaska, he'd often bagged a caribou and brought back enough venison to fill the freezer of their mother and Aunt Mel. Daniel, on the other hand, had never had the time or inclination. He had bought a pistol, though, and trained himself in its use, when there had been a string of drug-related armed robberies at the medical center where he'd worked.

"I have a couple jobs today, taking some Japanese bigshots out to the oil rigs," Aaron said then. "I wish I could stick around and help you."

"Sure you do," Daniel said. "I'll tell you one thing. You need to get some more furniture for the house. Not just because of the gang I brought here tonight, but if Aunt Mel decides to come, you can't have her sleeping on an air mattress."

"You're right. Well, you've got a plantation credit card. Go out today and buy some stuff."

"Buy some stuff," he muttered. "Me? Furniture shopping?"

"You went with me when I picked out paint colors."

"And had a headache for three days afterward. Who knew there were fifty colors of white? Honey Milk, Lily of the Valley, White Wisp, Summer Fog. And then you getting it on against the paint can shaking machine with the sales clerk."

"I did not 'get it on.' I was just talking to Melinda. Her brother is a pilot in the Air Force Reserve," Aaron contended. Then, "You can do it, Dan. Just a little shopping."

"Would that be before or after I meet with the LeDeuxs? Before or after I give Lily Beth the prenatal exam Samantha insists on? Before or after I check to see if this dump has any kind of security system? Before or after I put the brakes on Tante Lulu's plans to set up a medical practice for me on the bayou?" *When did I turn into such a whiner*? Daniel thought with disgust.

"Is that all?" Aaron was clearly amused.

"Another thing." *If I'm going to be a whiner, I'm going to do it big-time.* "Do you have any food in this place? Real food? I saw a bunch of mouse traps when I went into the kitchen to get a glass of water, but I didn't check the cupboards. There is a fridge, isn't there?"

"There's an old fridge, but they have new spiffy models with ice water dispensers and wine chilling racks. I heard about one that has a beer tap in it. Of course, it costs about ten thou, but hey!"

"That renovation budget of yours isn't worth crap. How much have you spent so far?"

"You only live once, bro," Aaron answered, clearly avoiding a disclosure of expenditures. "And while you're at it, bro, I wouldn't mind a party crisping drawer, the kind you can put a whole tray of hors d'oeuvres in."

"Planning a lot of parties, are you, *bro*?"

"I might. Hell, every time the LeDeuxs stop by, it's a party. Besides, if Aunt Mel does come, we probably should have a welcome party. Wonder if she'll be bringing her Barry Manilow CDs?"

Daniel groaned.

"Anyhow, I don't know about groceries. I don't do much cooking."

"No kidding."

"But there is a ton of Tante Lulu's leftovers from her impromptu lawn party here earlier today . . . rather yesterday. Peachy Praline Cobbler Cake, beignets, boudin sausage, mini muffulettas, crawfish po-boys, a couple salads, Cajun pickles . . . in fact, there's no room left in that icebox to hold even one bottle of beer."

"So, cake and pickles for breakfast?"

"There you go," Aaron said.

"That should please Lily Beth," Daniel remarked. "Please don't tell me that you expect me to shop for furniture, *and* a fridge."

"Well . . ." Aaron grinned some more, then added. "You might want to buy a small freezer, too. If one of Delilah's gators trespasses on this property, I plan to shoot it. They say gator meat tastes just like chicken."

"Don't you dare shoot any gators. We don't want to draw attention to this place. Plus, it's probably against the law."

"The Swamp People do it."

"And now you're one of the Swamp People?"

"I'm just sayin'." Aaron yawned loudly and stood, stretching. "It's two a.m. I'm gonna hit the sack for a couple hours. Wake me when you decide what to do."

"About what?"

"Anything. Everything. I'll help in any way I can."

"While you're flying over the Gulf?"

"Yeah, but before and after that."

Daniel headed back to the big house, knowing the majority of the problems had landed in his lap. It was his fault for answering Aaron's phone, but still . . .

There were times like this when he wished he was still hibernating in the fishing camp on the bayou. No one had bothered him there. He'd been alone, like he wanted to be.

Or had wanted to be.

Or should want to be.

Whatever!

Chapter Fourteen

In the still of the bayou night . . .

Although he didn't expect any bad company anymore tonight, he found himself scanning the perimeter of the property, and he checked the door locks after he entered the house. Not that any goons with ill intent couldn't enter by smashing one of the ten-foot-tall windows fronting the house! Hopefully, the dogs, cats, or pig would ward them off.

A flash of summer lightning cracked overhead, and in the distance, he could hear the rumble of thunder. The humidity level was at about a hundred and fifty percent. They'd have a rainstorm soon. The funny thing about the bayou was that the storms came sudden and often, but usually only lasted a short time, then dried up with a full blistering blast of heat or sunshine, all in a matter of minutes. It was the hurricanes that posed the biggest threat here near the coast, but this wasn't hurricane season.

Feeling grungy, he decided to take advantage of Aaron's high-tech shower. Which reminded him of the high-tech fridge Aaron had mentioned. He had to smile. As if they needed a keg on tap at all times! Or some hoity-toity party drawer!

The shower with its 360-degree, rain forest attachment did feel good. He was almost a new man after he dried off and put on a pair of running shorts and flip-flops. He didn't own any PJs.

He was about to go back downstairs and make a cup of coffee. No sense trying to sleep now. It was two-thirty a.m. and dawn would be here in a few hours. Not that Daniel couldn't sleep on demand, no regard for the clock, a habit required when he'd been a practicing doctor on call. Navy SEALs thought they'd invented standing REM sleep, where a soldier could catch a bit of sleep, standing up, eyes open, maybe only five minutes at a time. They had nothing on physicians who had to be mentally and physically alert, even after a few days on their feet. Many a time, he'd worked two-day shifts, then crashed for a full twenty-four hours.

When he was about to pass Aaron's bedroom, he noticed the door was half open; so, he decided to check on Samantha. Just to make sure she was all right. (*Don't laugh.*)

The wind was up, another indicator of the impending storm, causing the open French doors to bang against the wall. All of the bedrooms on this level opened onto a balcony that wrapped around all sides of the mansion. So far, the banging doors hadn't awakened Samantha, but just to make sure, he walked softly across the bare cypress floors and closed the doors. That was another on the long list of needed improvements for the property: latches to secure the French doors when open.

The room was dark, but he could make out basic shapes, including Samantha, who was hugging one edge of the king-size bed.

As he was about to leave, she murmured, "Is that you, Daniel?"

He stopped and looked at the bed. She was still lying down, but propped up on both elbows.

"Yeah. Sorry if I woke you."

"I was only half asleep. Too much on my mind. What time is it?"

He pressed the light button on his watch. "Two thirty-five."

"Oh, Lord! I don't know how I'm going to make it through another day, with so little sleep."

"You'll manage. You're a strong woman."

"You think?" she asked. Then, "Are you being sarcastic?"

"A little."

"I can't believe how much has happened in the past twenty-four hours."

"*Sweetheart*, twenty-four hours ago, we were having hot sex, in our dreams," he reminded her.

"Don't remind me," she said on a groan.

In the dark, like this, the groan sounded kind of sexy. He still had muss-mess on the brain.

"I've been making a list. In my head. Of all the things I . . . we . . . need to do tomorrow . . . rather, today."

He groaned then, too, and not at all in a sexy manner. A list maker! He should have known she would be one of those anal retentive list makers. He had things going on in his head, too, but not lists. Unless they were lists of things he wanted to do to Miss Muss.

"Sit down," she invited.

At first, he thought she'd said "lie down," and every sensible thought in his head dissolved and dropped with a thud to a spot between his legs.

There were no chairs in the room. But then, in another flash of lightning, she waved toward the bottom edge of the bed, catty corner from her mile-away spot at the opposite corner.

Ah! So, it wasn't an invitation to act out one of their sex dreams.

As if! a voice in his head said. Or maybe it had been her, sensing his rising libido.

Maybe I should take another rain forest shower. A cold one.

Or maybe I should invite her to join me. And not so cold.

No, no, no!

Down, libido, down!

Lowering his butt to the bed, he exhaled loudly. "Maybe I should give you my list first. It's probably way shorter." *And has only one word on it. Sex.*

"You have a list?"

"Don't sound so surprised. I do have a brain," *although it's in sleep mode at the moment*, "even if you think I haven't been using it since I gave up medicine."

"I never said—"

"I need to examine Lily Beth," he interrupted, before she started backtracking and tried to be nice, which would be a real stretch. He knew what she thought of him. "Not an internal exam. Just a check of her heart rate and blood pressure. If there's nothing apparent causing her swelling, at the very least I'll have to get a urine sample and draw blood for testing."

"You could draw blood here?"

"Probably lose my license, if I had one, a Louisiana one, that is . . . a real one, not a Tante Lulu quickie-stamped one . . . but, yeah, I can draw blood and Lily Beth can surely pee in a sterile cup. My medical bag is up to date with basic supplies."

"You couldn't test the blood and urine here, though. Could you?"

"No, I'd have to take them into Houma. The director of a cancer center there would do it for me. He owes me."

He could tell she wanted to question him about that connection, but she restrained herself and asked, instead, "Do you think there might be a problem?"

"I have no idea. Edema is normal during pregnancy, especially the later months. The usual swelling of hands, face, legs, or ankles. Like Lily Beth exhibits. But edema can also be a precursor to preeclampsia, blood clots, and even cellulitis. Another cause of swelling could be anaemia, but that can be cured with better food choices and iron tablets. I can almost rule anaemia out because your ex would have caught that if he's been checking her regularly."

"Blood clots? Preeclampsia?" Samantha groaned and pressed the fingertips of both hands to her mouth.

"Those are extreme cases," he was quick to add. "This is probably just normal edema, aggravated by the stress of their situation and all the running around during the past twenty-four. But it's best to be safe."

"Agreed. But, Daniel, you have to know how sorry I am for dragging you into this mess."

Oh, please! More attempts at niceness! It was enough to make him barf. He liked her better when she was being snarky. "Don't worry. You'll pay. Later." *Oh, God, I sound like a bad romance novel. (Not a good one, a bad one.) Rhett says to Scarlett, "You'll pay later, Scarlett, my dear."*

"What do you mean?" she snapped.

"Never mind." *Face it, I'm no Rhett.*

"You better not be thinking about that kiss."

On the other hand, she must be thinking about the kiss, too, if she brought it up. Hmmm. "Who? Me? What kiss?"

"Just because I let you kiss me—"

"No revisionist history here, sweet pea. You kissed me back. Don't you dare deny it."

"It was all part of the act."

"Uh-huh."

"And there won't be a repeat."

"Unless Mutt and Jeff show up again."

"Whatever."

"You must admit it was a really good kiss."

She said nothing.

"Anyhow, I'm calling Luc LeDeux this morning. We need his legal advice. This situation is beyond my expertise."

"Mine, too."

At least she was no longer arguing about involving an outside person. Not that Daniel was an inside person, to her! Although there were times when he wouldn't mind being inside her.

Oh, shit! Did I really think such a thing? Crude, crude, crude! Rhett would never think something like that. Would he?

It must be those outrageous sex dreams.

Wipe your mind clean, boy.

I don't even like her.

What does like have to do with sex?

A lot.

I wonder if she's wearing that fuck-me red-and-black silk sleep outfit.

Another point for the crude gods!

"Depending on what Luc suggests, we may or may not have to involve the authorities," Daniel advised, surprised that his voice didn't sound raw and sex-deprived. "The police, ATF, FBI . . . hell, I don't even know which agency."

"*That* is a last resort," she said emphatically. "Let's see what Luc says first before we involve anyone else."

"So, what's on your list?"

"I have to go to work today. I have a conference call scheduled at the foundation office at ten, and a lunch meeting of the Starr Foods board of directors."

"Oh, no! Uh-uh! Unless you're planning on taking all these animals with you, along with Angus and Lily Beth, you're not leaving me here alone."

"But—"

"No buts. You can call in sick."

"It would only be for a few hours."

"No."

"The animals pretty much take care of themselves, except for Emily who is very needy. Oh, I forgot, Emily has an appointment at the Pet Psychiatric Clinic in Lafayette. Her depression is getting better, but she still has periodic episodes of crying."

Has she lost her freakin' mind? A pig crying?

Good thing I didn't hit the sack with Samantha. Assuming she would be willing. Which she probably wouldn't be. Like in a million years. I do not need a nutcase relationship. I have enough nuttiness in my life.

I wonder if Rhett ever felt like this.

Still, there is that thing she did with her tongue in our last dream.

"I don't suppose you'd take her?"

"Who?" His brain was still back in sex la-la land.

"Emily."

"The pig?" he asked, just to be clear.

"Yes. To the clinic."

"No."

"I think Emily likes you."

"Nice try." *If Aaron were here, he'd be making jokes about my sorry love life, that the only female I can get is a pig.*

"Oh, all right. I'll notify my office that I won't be in today."

If she expected his thanks, she had another think coming.

"I'm supposed to deliver three of the puppies to new homes today, though. That, I can't cancel."

"I'll go with you," he offered. Just to make sure she didn't disappear on him and stick him with her menagerie. And it would be three less creatures in this zoo. Plus, maybe they could stop along the way and buy a bedroom set for one of the guest rooms (Aunt Mel's, if she came) and a new fridge.

Stop along the way?

Yeah, right.

Maybe I should stop along the way and get a brain transplant.

"Another thing, no new rescues while you're staying here," he said.

"Meanie," she grumbled.

"I think I'm being damn generous."

"You're right. Sorry." Then, out of the blue, she said, "You better go now."

Huh? "Why?"

There was a long pause before Samantha revealed, "I haven't had sex in over a year."

Oh, boy!

Oh, boy oh boy oh boy!

He blinked at her, not because he was trying to see in the dark, but his brain appeared to have shorted out. A definite possibility, he decided, when he told her, "Neither have I."

The silence could be heard like a gong.

"Why did you tell me that? Was it an invitation?"

"No! Just a statement of fact. Maybe a reason why it would be better if I were not staying here."

Another ploy to shuffle all her problems off on him.

Well, two could play that game. "Or a reason to stay,"

he suggested. Now, *that* was a Rhett-type remark, he decided with a smile, which she luckily could not see.

Daniel left before he said or did something he would later regret, any more than he already did. He took another shower. Forget rain forests. This time he dialed a blithering Arctic blast.

It didn't help a bit.

Tara was never like this . . .

Samantha thought she'd never be able to sleep, but then she zonked out so soundly that she didn't wake until seven a.m. Usually, she was up and about at dawn.

One reason for her late awakening was lack of her animals calling for business, the animals all being downstairs and behind closed doors. Plus, she'd been exhausted, mentally and physically.

And she wasn't going to think about the effect Daniel's kiss had on her last night, or her revelation about her nonexistent sex life, not to mention his own words about his equally celibate lifestyle. It gave a girl way too much to think about it. Luckily, she'd had no more of the annoying sex dream fantasies about him. Maybe they were gone for good now that she was in such close proximity to the Alaskan bad boy.

Jeesh! When did I start thinking of Daniel as a bad boy? And why Alaskan since he seems to have settled on the bayou?

When he began to star in my dreams, that's when. Alaskan or otherwise.

But he's a nerd.

A sexy nerd.

She made a quick trip to the bathroom . . . no time for a shower . . . and grabbed a pair of cropped sleep pants to go with her sleep shirt, and a pair of thongs for her bare feet. Then she rushed down the wide stairway toward the second parlor where the only sound she heard was "Holy shit!" Opening the pocket door, she discovered all the animals, except for Clarence, were missing. The cover had been taken off his cage, and she noticed that there was clean water and birdseed. For once, the bird was quiet and seemed to be staring out the window near his cage, almost with a yearning expression on its face. If birds even had expressions! Maybe it wanted to be free, to fly outside. Yeah, right. She should be so lucky!

A quick peek showed that Angus and Lily Beth were still asleep in the front parlor, curled up on their respective air mattresses. Daniel had suggested that the pregnant girl would be more comfortable in Aaron's bed upstairs, but Lily Beth said she was too tired to trek up all those steps, and Angus was sticking to Lily Beth like glue.

Angus was wearing only a pair of Star Wars boxer shorts, and Lily Beth wore boxers, too, hers imprinted with pink stars on a white background. Both of them were loaners from Daniel, even the pink ones. Samantha had been too tired last night to ask where he'd gotten them. On top, Lily Beth had a white sports bra that left her big belly free of restriction.

Samantha's heart went out to the two of them. Yes, they'd brought a lot of trouble into her life, but at this moment, they seemed so darned innocent, even Angus with all his silly piercings and tattoos. They'd been sucked in by Nick's on-again/off-again charm, just as she had at the same age and level of naiveté.

For a brief blip of a second, she entertained an outlandish idea. *Maybe I could adopt Lily Beth's baby.*

Immediately, she discarded that notion. She should be

thinking of ways to help the girl keep her baby, not ways to take it away.

She closed the door quietly and made her way down the hallway to the back staircase that led to the first floor kitchen. Looking down, she saw the imprint of her flip flops in the dust-covered floors and steps. In fact, the entire house was covered with a film of dirt, which was to be expected in a structure under renovation, but some of this dirt and grime was decades old. Good thing they didn't have any furniture yet. The whole place would need a thorough cleaning first. It was the kind of thing a bachelor, or bachelors, like Aaron and Daniel, would hardly notice. And she certainly hoped they would furnish the rest of the house from someplace other than IKEA, hardly historically appropriate for this old house.

There was an upscale coffeemaker sitting on the counter, the only thing less than fifty years old in the empty kitchen, as far as she could tell. The fridge, for example, was a putrid avocado color that had been retired back in the 1970s. A matching green Kelvinator electric range was missing two burners, and its oven door was hanging on one hinge.

The kitchen was huge with a gray flagstone floor, cracked in some places. A massive, walk-in, brick fireplace, now inoperable, had been used for cooking in the mansion's early days, although there was also a separate building, known as a summer kitchen, for cooking to avoid the intense heat.

Samantha poured herself a mug of surprisingly good coffee, and stepped out the back door to a wide, roofed verandah, where slaves would at one time have done house chores. There would have been benches here, and perhaps a rocking chair or two. Even a table for folding air-dried laundry, or preparing vegetables for dinner, like snap beans or peas. There might even have been dried herbs hanging from the rafters.

Old houses like this held a genetic memory, in Samantha's opinion. If you sat and listened, with eyes closed, you could almost see and hear and feel the people who'd passed through this place.

She stepped off the porch onto the hard-packed dirt yard, and relished the sun which was already up but pleasant this early in the day. That's when she noticed two unusual things:

> — The rare, white tupelo tree standing back about twenty yards from the house. It had to be at least fifty feet tall with a gray, furrowed bark on its old trunk-like alligator hide, and green fruit hanging from its branches, sometimes known as swamp limes. In fact, the tupelo was also called river lime, Ogeechee lime, sour gum, or swamp gum. But it wasn't its size or distinctive features that made this tree rare. It was because tupelos usually grew only in swampy areas, or along riverbanks. This specimen, which had to be hundreds of years old, was a testament to the fact that this property had once been under water.
> — The other thing she noticed was what sat under the tree. Daniel. And all her animals. Like a harem, they were. Daniel could be the pasha, sitting in the shade, on a large, circular, wrought iron bench with chipped white paint that surrounded the base of the tupelo, leaning back, his long legs extended and crossed at the ankles. Sitting next to Daniel on one side was an empty mug. On the other was Emily, whose snout was propped on Daniel's thigh. One of Daniel's hands rested lightly on Emily's head, as if he'd been patting her.

Axel was snoozing on the ground, or just plain exhausted from traveling from the parlor through the house, down the stairs to the kitchen, and then outdoors. His old German Shepherd bones tired easily these days. Then there was Madeline, who was frozen mid-crouch, about to attack some bees. The other two cats, Garfield and Felix, were nowhere to be seen, probably off munching on field mice. The puppies were gamboling in a patch of grass.

Samantha's chest tightened with sudden emotion. A man who was this comfortable with animals had to be amazing with children, or at least he would have been during his pediatric oncology career. A true doctor, unlike Nick and his pals.

Further adding to Daniel's allure were his heavily lashed lids that were half mast as he dozed, a testament to his having stayed up all night. He sported morning whiskers, and wore black running shorts, a pristine white T-shirt, and a pair of old, once-white athletic shoes without socks that highlighted the light brown furring of hair on his arms and long legs. In other words, sexy, sexy, sexy.

Her traitorous thoughts (traitorous to the shield she usually had up around Daniel) were broken by the too-sexy-to-live man who hadn't been asleep after all. "I liked your other sleep outfit better."

"What?" she said, looking down. "What's wrong with this?" She wore mid-calf, green-and-white polka dot cotton pants, and the long white sleep shirt with its I-Heart-Dogs logo, an animal rescue fundraising purchase from last year.

"Nothing. It's just not the same as your screw-me-silly, red silk harem pants and the touch-me-you-idiot, see-through top."

She gasped, feeling both outraged and pleased at the

same time. Despite her best efforts, she blushed and claimed, "They were not harem pants." And recalled her likening him to a pasha out here with his harem.

He shrugged, as if it were mere semantics.

"And how would you know harem pants anyhow?"

"I dated a belly dancer at one time."

Now, that surprised her. "And you could not see through the top."

"You could if you had a good imagination, and mine is really good." His eyes danced with mischief as he spoke. In the meantime, their voices had awakened the animals. He picked Emily up and placed her on the ground.

Samantha sat down on the bench next to him, but not too close.

He eyed her mug and said, "You could have brought me another cup of coffee."

"I didn't know you were out here." She handed him her mug and let him take a long drink of coffee, an oddly intimate gesture that came out of nowhere. To cut the alarming connection between them, she added, "I thought maybe you were out at the St. Jude birdbath, praying for deliverance from me and my brood."

"Wish I'd thought of that." He was looking at her in a way that made her really uncomfortable, and it had nothing to do with prayer.

"You know this tree we're sitting under is a real treasure," she said.

"A treasure, huh?" he gazed upward, clearly skeptical. "Aaron mentioned something about having the tree removed and putting a swimming pool here, instead. Not right away, but later."

She stared at him, aghast. "This is a white tupelo, for heaven's sake, a rarity. This species almost never grows this far inland. In fact, they flourish in swamps. You ought to contact the state horticulture society to have them come take a look at it. You'd probably get this plantation written up in some journals."

"That's what we need. Publicity."

"You don't have to be so sarcastic."

"Sorry. The only benefit I can see for publicity would be if we were going to flip this house after the renovations."

That idea dismayed her, for some reason. It wasn't her property. She shouldn't care. But she did.

"Tell me more about my too-puh-loh tree." He grinned at her.

She ignored his teasing. "Have you ever heard of tupelo honey?"

"Sure. Van Morrison."

She was taken aback that he'd be familiar with that old song. Somehow, his personality and demeanor were more in line with classical music, or maybe highbrow jazz.

"As sweet as tupelo honey," he crooned.

"You are full of surprises today, Daniel."

"Why? Because I've heard of tupelo honey, or Van Morrison?"

"Both," she said. "Of course, you'll get no honey from the blossoms of this tree unless you plan on starting some beehives nearby." She tilted her head. "Now that I think about it—"

"Don't you dare suggest beekeeping. I've got enough to do dissuading Tante Lulu and Aaron *and you* from dog kennels and animal rescue."

She blushed because she had, in fact, discussed the possibility with Tante Lulu. And she had, in fact, deliberately not discussed it with Daniel because she'd known how he would react.

"Is this fruit edible?" Daniel asked.

She looked at the dark green, oval object in his palm, about an inch or two long.

"Not really. It will eventually turn red, and can be used as a substitute for limes, in a pinch, but they're too sour and bitter by themselves. Some people use them for preserves, though. The Native Americans were the first to make use of the tree. In fact, the name tupelo comes from the Creek word for swamp tree."

"You are just a font of information."

She couldn't tell if he was being serious or mocking. She shrugged. "You can't live in the South and not glean all this information."

"I'm just teasing, Samantha. I like learning about Louisiana and the bayous. Have you ever read *Odd Leaves from the Life of a Louisiana Swamp Doctor*?"

"I don't think so."

"It's about this pre-Civil War dude, a young doctor, and his misadventures practicing medicine in the bayou. Very funny in parts, especially the dialect." He shrugged, rather embarrassed to have revealed so much. "Anyhow, even though I didn't grow up here, I feel a connection."

"Really?"

He nodded. "I wouldn't have stayed out in that damp, mosquito-infested fishing camp for so long if I didn't like the bayou. Must be in the genes, God help me! I understand one of my grandfathers was a swamp guide, and another one trapped muskrats, whatever they are. A great-grandmother gathered swaths of moss from live oak trees to sell for mattress stuffing. Lots of outrageous characters in my family tree, according to Tante Lulu, not the least of which is that father of mine, Valcour LeDeux. The less said about him the better."

"My great-grandfather many times removed was arrested twelve times for cattle *reaving* in Scotland, and his wife was a noted witch. Rumors are, my great-aunt Jez, as in Jezebel, was a French Quarter stripper. My mother is a career seducer of young men, and my father can't help but marry any woman who wiggles her butt his way. If you think Tante Lulu is crazy, you ought to meet my Aunt Maire who has an obsession with the color pink. Pink house, pink furniture, pink clothing, pink car. She only eats things that are pink. Salmon, lemonade, beet pasta, cotton candy, strawberry smoothies, grapefruit, Pink Lady cocktails, medium rare steak. I'd say you come out the winner in this pool of gene outrageousness."

He smiled at her. A real, genuine smile that included his dark brown, expressive eyes. How had she not noticed them before? They were beautiful. Her heart did another somersault. *First, he shows an empathy for animals, now he appreciates the humor of my family. I must be in some kind of hormone meltdown. Or he's another devil doctor out to get something.*

"Did your aunt have cancer?" he asked.

"No. She was doing this long before pink became the color for breast cancer awareness. Of course, the local cancer society has adopted her now. She's great for raising funds. They're always asking for the use of her house for events, or her pink Cadillac convertible for parades."

He nodded in understanding. "You can't blame them. There's never enough money, especially in the competition for charity dollars. I've been asked to donate plenty of times myself."

She imagined that he knew this firsthand, having been a cancer doctor himself and seeing the constant need for research funds until a cure was discovered.

But then, she thought, *oh, no! A sympathetic doctor?* She could practically hear another brick in the wall of her defenses crumbling.

"Are you playing me?" she asked suddenly.

"Huh?"

"Your remark about cancer charities, all caring and

noble. That is the kind of thing Nick would do. I can't count the number of charity events I've attended at his urging when his motives were to ingratiate himself with the movers and shakers of the Crescent City." She tossed the hair back off her face in a haughty gesture of disdain. Then mimicked Nick, "Darlin', we gotta go to the charity ball at the country club. Everyone will be there. How would it look if we didn't attend and make a big donation? Wear the green gown that covers more of your ugly freckles and makes your butt look smaller. And your grandmother's emeralds. They make you look so rich . . . I mean, elegant."

Daniel just stared at her for a long moment. "You have one helluva suspicious mind, Samantha. That dickhead you married did a real job on you, didn't he?" he said, with his own shake of the head.

Any further conversation was forestalled by the noise they heard coming from the kitchen. They looked at each other and gathered the animals to come inside . . . those that were so inclined. Cats had a tendency to be contrary, and Madeline looked at the two of them as if to say, "Later. Maybe." She was munching on something that looked like a mouse, but was probably . . . hopefully . . . a stick.

He made one further comment, though, as they crossed the verandah. "I don't think your freckles are ugly. At all. And your butt? Nick must be blind, as well as stupid." He patted one buttock as he passed in front of her into the kitchen.

She clicked her gaping mouth shut and followed after him.

Lily Beth was sitting at the table that could easily seat twelve people . . . a massive single block of wood on thick, heavy legs that was probably a primitive antique worth a fortune. Samantha would enjoy working on it with a hot mix of turpentine and linseed oil, applied with fine steel wool, to see what character emerged from the wood grains. There were long benches on both sides and straight-back chairs on either end.

Angus had put paper plates and cutlery on the table and was now pulling foil wrapped packages and plastic containers from the green fridge. Mostly these were Tante Lulu leftovers, which Lily Beth began to devour hungrily the second they were placed in front of her. Angus sniffed a carton of milk, then set it aside in the old, chipped enamel, cast iron farm sink. He also discarded some takeout containers that she could smell even from the doorway.

"Good morning," Samantha greeted them.

"Morning," they both said, without looking up from their breakfast feast.

"How are you feeling today, Lily Beth?" Daniel asked.

"Okay," she said around a mouthful of Cajun potato salad. Chewing rapidly, she swallowed, then told him, "Mah ankles and fingers aren't as swollen, and it didn't hurt when I peed this mornin'."

Samantha and Daniel exchanged glances. That was the first they'd heard of urinary discomfort.

"You're going to need an examination. I can do a basic exam. Not an internal," he was quick to emphasize. "But, if I detect any problems, I'll insist you see an obstetrician right away."

"I doan know," Lily Beth said. "Dr. Coltrane checked me over every week, and I didn't have this swellin' issue 'til this past week. I'm prob'ly okay."

Nick must have really frightened her about the dangers of seeing another doctor, who would in turn report back to Nick. Lily Beth thought that all doctors were in cahoots. As Samantha had herself, on occasion, she had to admit.

"I *do* know. Either you agree, or you're out of here, on your own," Daniel insisted, taking a much-needed hard line.

Clearly reluctant, Lily Beth nodded.

Angus seemed about to argue, but then said, "Whatever!"

Daniel put his hand on Lily Beth's shoulder and squeezed. "I'm going over to my apartment to get my medical bag. Stay off your feet as much as possible today. There's some folding lawn furniture in that storage room down the hall that Tante Lulu brought yesterday, including a chaise, I think. Angus can set it up for you outside, if you want, or on one of the galleries."

Lily Beth and Angus both nodded, then resumed eating. Food was their top priority at the moment. They were also guzzling back bottles of Grapico, that Southern carbonated grape beverage that rotted the teeth of more than one overindulged Dixie child.

"Samantha, can you give Lucien LeDeux a call?" Daniel asked. "Maybe at home since it's still pretty early for him to be in his office."

She got the message in the serious tone of voice he'd used with Lily Beth and Angus, and now her. No more procrastinating. No more excuses. They needed outside help.

"Now wait a minute, dude," Angus said. "A doctor is one thing, but we can't risk involving anyone else."

"You want our help, you're going to do it our way." Samantha spoke up before Daniel—clearly annoyed, as indicated by the clenching of his jaw—kicked them all out the door.

"But—" Angus started to say.

"I would suggest you sit down with a paper and pen, or that blasted computer of yours, and tabulate just how much money you owe whom," Samantha said sternly.

"Did you ever sign any documents listing an interest rate or repayment terms? No? I guess the mafia doesn't work that way."

"It's thirty-three percent," Angus revealed with a reddened face.

"WHAT?" Samantha and Daniel exclaimed at the same time.

"No offense, but are you two idiots?" Daniel asked.

To soften the blow of his insult, Samantha intervened. "You may find this hard to believe, Daniel, but Lily Beth is a physicist, almost has her doctoral degree. And Angus probably has enough college credits to equal a dozen degrees."

Daniel just arched his brows, probably questioning what they teach in college these days. Not common sense, for sure. And Lily Beth's strong Southern accent sometimes came across as rather illiterate, bless her heart.

"I was desperate," Angus said defensively. "I *am* desperate."

"I was desperate, too," Lily Beth added. "I needed the cash for tuition."

I'm becoming desperate myself.

Samantha tamped down her panic and added, "Both of you should take some notes on the money Nick has given you and any threats he's made. Also, anything you know about other pregnant girls he's worked with."

Daniel left, and Samantha poured herself another mug of coffee and grabbed a beignet. "I'm going upstairs to get dressed and make my phone call. In the meantime, clean up this kitchen when you're done," she told them both.

"Is this some tough love crap?" Angus snarked.

"If you don't like it," she replied, considering a raised middle finger in his direction, something she'd never done, "tough!"

Chapter Fifteen

Her eyes were opened . . .

Samantha made the bed and put on a pair of Chanel, faded blue, cotton shorts with a matching halter top centered with a big bow of the same color and fabric. For comfort, she put plain white, flat-heeled slides on her feet. She usually didn't like to leave so much of her freckled skin exposed, but it was going to be especially hot today, even for Southern Louisiana, and there was no AC here. Her attire had nothing to do with Daniel's remarks about her freckles not being ugly. Nothing at all. Really.

Okay, a little.

How pathetic was that?

She pulled her hair off her face into a ponytail. By the time she applied a little makeup and spritzed herself with some Jessica McClintock, it was eight-fifteen. So, she went out of the bedroom French doors onto the gallery and punched in Luc's home number on her cell phone.

"Hello," a woman answered on the third ring.

"Sylvie?" Samantha asked.

"Yes. Is that you, Samantha? How've you been?"

She'd been better, she thought, but didn't want to get into all the details with Sylvie, then have to repeat the story to Luc. "I'm okay. How about you?"

"I'm thinking about going back to work since the girls no longer need me to chauffeur them around." Sylvie was a chemist who'd gained some notoriety a while back when she discovered a love potion that could be embedded in jelly beans. It had been the impetus for her and Luc getting together. Their girls . . . three of them . . . must be teenagers by now. "By the way, we're having a pool party on Saturday to celebrate Tante Lulu's birthday, although she won't tell us exactly how old she is. Can you come?"

"I'm not sure." Who knew where she'd be five days from now? "Can I let you know later?"

"Absolutely."

"Anyhow, I'm sorry to call so early. Is Luc around?"

"Yes. He's having breakfast with the girls. I'll go get him."

After a few moments, a male voice said, "What's the prick done now?"

She laughed. "It's not about Nick this time. Well, not totally."

He listened without interruption while she gave a brief summary of the situation at Bayou Rose. When she finished, he used one of Clarence's favorite sayings, "Holy shit!" Then he asked a few questions. "You say Angus is involved with the Dixie Mob?"

"Yes. At thirty-three percent."

"Holy shit!" he said again. "And Nick is actually into

the baby black market? He must really be desperate for cash."

Desperation being the key word for us all. "Nick is always desperate for cash, as you well know."

"Especially after you cut off his access to the money tree."

The money tree being me. "What should we do?"

"Well, first off, I need to meet with Angus and Lily Beth. How about if I come out to the plantation at two? And I'll bring Tee-John with me, if he's available. He knows more about the mob than I do."

"I appreciate it."

"Don't let those two go anywhere until we make sure the plantation is secure. In fact, I'll bring Angel Sabato with me. He knows a lot about security systems. On the other hand, maybe I'll wait to see what Tee-John recommends."

"I'll tell Daniel."

"Speaking of the gloomy one . . . how's Daniel taking this invasion into his private life?"

"Pretty well, actually. And his medical background should help in assessing Lily Beth's condition."

"What a mess! This is the kind of nonsense my aunt usually brews up."

"Oh, Lord! Whatever you do, don't let Tante Lulu know what's going on. She'll show up with a shotgun and a satchel full of swamp prenatal herbs."

Luc laughed.

After she ended the call, she went down to the kitchen. Lily Beth lay on the sheet-covered table, which had been cleared, and Daniel was palpating her stomach and listening to the baby's heartbeat with a stethoscope.

"Sounds good. That little one has got a strong heartbeat."

Lily Beth released a breath of relief. "Thank God!"

Then he put a blood pressure cuff on her arm and studied a pocket meter. "Your bp is slightly elevated . . . one-thirty over eighty-three, but that could be usual gestational hypertension for the third trimester. Worth watching but no real concern."

"Does that rule out preeclampsia?" Lily Beth asked.

"For now," he answered.

"What is normal blood pressure?" Lily Beth wanted to know.

"One-twenty over eighty." He removed the cuff, then moved to the counter where there was a small closed plastic container with a yellow liquid. Urine, Samantha presumed. Also on the counter were a rubber tourniquet, a used syringe and antiseptic coated gauzes, and two test tubes of blood.

Angus was at the sink washing dishes, looking somewhat gray in the face. Probably a reaction to the needle. Some folks couldn't take the blood test procedure, even just watching it.

Daniel helped Lily Beth to sit up on the table, then to lower her legs over the side. "Your swelling is probably due to normal edema, but we'll know more after the test results. Considering all you've been through, you're in surprisingly good health, young lady."

Lily Beth put her hands on her belly and blinked away tears. "Thank you. I was worried," she whispered. Then, in a louder voice, "Does that mean I don't have to see an obstetrician?"

"Of course you'll have to see an obstetrician, but you should be okay for a few days. Providing the urine analysis and blood tests come back okay."

Lily Beth nodded and shimmied her rump off the table. "I'll dry those," she offered to Angus. The two of them hugged in apparent relief over Daniel's diagnosis.

Samantha moved out of the doorway and went over to

Daniel who was putting the vials and the urine container in a small insulated bag with blue ice. She told him, "Luc and John LeDeux will be here at two o'clock, if that's all right."

Daniel glanced up, then did a double take. He must not have realized she'd been back for the past five minutes or so. Scanning her body, and its scanty attire, he whistled softly and told her, "In the meantime, you and I are going for a ride."

At first, she felt a little thrill of excitement ripple over her, but then he added, "We're going shopping."

Her initial disappointment faded as she reminded herself, shopping could be exciting, too. "Shopping for what?"

"A fridge," he said. "And maybe a bed. And groceries. But first I have to drop off these blood vials and urine sample."

"All that in less than five hours? Remember, we have to be back here by two."

"How long could it take to buy a fridge and a bed? Don't they sell them both in the same place?"

"Are you kidding? When I shop, I usually have to hit at least three stores, to compare styles. For a fridge alone. For a bedroom set? Goodness! Maybe five stores."

"Five stores! What's to compare? A fridge is a fridge, and a bed is a bed."

"That is man thinking."

A short time later, they had been about to enter Daniel's SUV when Daniel said, "Oh, I forgot. Wait here a minute. I need to get something from Aaron's office." She enjoyed the sun while she waited, basking in its warmth and the smell of the myriad flowers that abounded here. Magnolia, bougainvillea, even the fecund scent of the bayou which was more than two hundred yards away, beyond the wide lawn, across a narrow one-lane road. At one time, flatboats would have docked here to pick up the sugar cane for market.

When Daniel returned, he shoved a binder into her hands. "Check this out. It's a list of furniture and stuff left in storage by the previous owner. There's not a lot, but some of it looks valuable."

"What? How could you have forgotten something so important? Men!"

He shrugged.

Once they were inside Daniel's SUV and were on their way, the AC a welcome pleasure, she opened the binder. There were lists, as well as photographs of furniture and accessories, like mirrors and a few paintings. Even some sepia-toned photographs of the original house and how it had looked back in the 1800s.

"Daniel! This is amazing. Wonderful! How could you . . . or Aaron . . . have bought that modern bedroom set when you have such treasures. This mansion is better suited to antiques, not IKEA assembly line stuff."

"We needed some furniture right away. I have a matching, smaller bedroom set in my apartment. What do we know about antiques? As far as I'm concerned, a Chippendale is a dancer."

She smiled. "I can help you, or you could hire a designer to come in and give you advice."

"All of that costs big bucks, and this renovation is a money pit, as it is."

"It doesn't have to be done all at once. You have years to furnish the place, but it's best to use the historically accurate pieces you have, or buy antiques, one at a time."

"You're assuming I . . . we . . . are going to keep this place that long."

"You aren't?"

"I have no idea what I'll be doing next week, let alone next year. And Aaron's not much better."

"I thought you said that you like the bayou, that you feel at home here."

"That's not exactly what I said. But, yeah, I suspect we'll stay in this region. I'm just not sure that we'll keep this plantation, though. It was a looney tunes idea of Aaron's, to begin with. And, honestly, I can't see myself involved in an animal enterprise, nor Tante Lulu's push for me to become a country GP. And spending my time antiquing doesn't appeal, either. I know, I know, you're thinking I have lots of free time since I gave up medicine. Still . . ." He shrugged.

"Here's what I suggest for today. Buy the fridge, if you need it, and a full-size mattress and box spring to fit this bedroom set." She pointed to a picture of an ornately carved, rice post bed frame, an armoire, a dresser, and a dry sink. "You can have someone deliver the items you want now out of your storage space. And while they're there, they could also bring these two mirrors. Everything else . . . pictures, parlor and dining room furniture . . . leave in storage until the sanding and painting is completed."

"Sounds like a plan."

"We can buy both the mattress set and fridge at Costco, unless you want to go to separate furniture and appliance stores. And we can get the groceries at Costco, too."

"I could kiss you for that," he said.

When she glanced over at him with surprise, he smiled. "It was just an expression." But the wink he added belied his words.

That kiss! That blasted kiss they'd shared stood between them like a big white sizzling elephant. Neither of them was forgetting it.

"The closest Costco is in Metairie, which is about fifty miles from here. We'd be cutting it short, getting back here by two."

"I'm a quick shopper."

"If you say so. Where's Aaron, by the way?"

"Working. He'll be back this afternoon. Hopefully."

They had just hit Houma and Daniel pulled off the road and into the parking lot of Terrebonne Oncology Center. "I want to drop off these blood vials and the urine sample," he told her before she had a chance to ask why they were stopping. "Stay in the car where it's cool. I'll be right out."

When he hadn't returned in fifteen minutes, Samantha got curious. Entering the automatic doors into the reception area, she asked an attendant at the desk. "I'm looking for Daniel LeDeux. He came in here a little while ago."

"You mean Doctor LeDeux?"

"Yes."

"He went up to the third floor, pediatrics, to do a consult for Doctor Laroche. Do you want me to page them?"

Samantha knew George Laroche, or rather, she'd heard of him from her attendance at charity events. He was founder and director of this medical clinic, and a well-regarded cancer specialist.

"No, I'll go up myself, if that's all right," Samantha said.

The attendant just shrugged.

Samantha entered a nearby elevator and hit the number three button. Immediately, she had reservations.

I should have stayed in the car.

I should mind my own business.

But how is it that he can just drop off blood vials for testing, without having a Louisiana medical license?

And what's his connection to Doctor Laroche?

And pediatrics? Wasn't that Daniel's specialty?

Hmmm.

When the elevator pinged and she exited onto the pediatric ward, she could hear the excited voices of children coming from the various rooms, along with some crying, one youthful scream, followed by a youthful exclamation of, "Ouch, ouch, ouch!" Then, "You're a poop head!" The colors here were brighter than the usual sterile hospital corridors. Here and there on the walls hung children's crayon drawings. From one room, she could hear Pharrell Williams's "Happy" song blaring out, probably a video playing on someone's TV.

She was about to go over to the nurse's station and ask for Daniel's whereabouts when she noticed what looked like a children's playroom up ahead and a man in blue scrubs and a surgical cap standing inside. He looked like . . . yes, he was George Laroche.

She moved in that direction, then stopped just outside the door, transfixed by what she saw. It was here that the TV was playing. Scattered about the room were child-size tables and chairs, beanbags, and a toy chest overflowing with stuffed animals and games. There was even a tricycle.

Doctor Laroche was watching Daniel who was down on his haunches speaking softly to a little girl wearing a ballerina outfit in hot pink and a knitted cap on her head. Ruffled anklet socks were on her feet, inside red, sparkly Dorothy shoes, as in *The Wizard of Oz*. The girl was sobbing.

"I doan want no more needles, Doctor Dan," she cried.

"I know, princess, but they make you better."

"Doan care! Where's Daddy?"

"He had to go home to work."

That caused another bout of sobbing.

"Will you let me give you the shot, Molly, if I promise it won't hurt?"

"Promise?"

"Cross my heart and never lie. Stick a noodle in my eye," he said, giving a cockeyed version of that old children's rhyme.

Molly, who had to be about five years old, smiled through her tears, revealing two empty spaces in front. "Okay, Doctor Dan," she said.

Doctor Laroche motioned toward a nurse who had come up behind Samantha, and she brought in a tray with an alcohol swab, syringe, and a Cinderella Band-Aid.

Sinking down to a cross-legged position on the floor, Daniel tugged the little girl onto his lap, adjusting her tutu to fit. Then, surreptitiously, the nurse handed him the swab and needle. The whole time, Daniel kept talking. "Now you know the drill, princess. Who are you today? Ariel or Belle?"

"Silly! I'm Jasmine," Molly said.

"Here we go," Daniel said, swabbing the skin of her thin upper arm. "Do you want to start?"

She nodded. "Eenie meenie miney moe."

"Catch a princess by the toe," Daniel said, pretending to grab for her foot, but then slipping the needle into her arm.

"If she hollers—" the little girl giggled and let out an exaggerated howl.

"Let her go." Daniel put a Band-Aid on the arm and raised both hands to show he was done.

Then they both said in a singsong voice, "Eenie meenie miney mo!"

"You were terrific, princess."

"Am I done?"

"Yep."

"Kiss, kiss, Doctor Dan." She threw herself at him, gave him two wet kisses, one on each cheek, then wrapped her thin arms around his neck and hugged him tightly.

Daniel hugged her back, his eyes closed with emotion. Just then, he glanced up and noticed Samantha standing in the doorway.

Their gazes held for a long moment.

Love.

The word hit her suddenly, not with a wallop to the heart, but a softening of all that had become hard in her the past few years.

Love.

When was the last time she'd felt this way and for whom?

It had been for Nick, of course, *before* they'd married.

And this scene, of a caring doctor and his desperately needy patient, it was exactly how she'd imagined Nick, *before* her eyes had been opened and *before* her heart had shut down.

Love?

For Daniel?

It was unbelievable. Unacceptable. Unwise. Untimely. Unreal.

Tears filled Samantha's eyes, and she turned, not wanting Daniel to see her emotion, but also not wanting to intrude further on his private moment. She went back to the car where she sat frozen with disbelief for about fifteen more minutes.

Me? In love with Daniel? Could I have been so blind? Sure, there's a fine line between love and hate, but the sniping between the two of us the dozens of times we've met was surely a sign of dislike, not like. Or love, bless my foolish heart.

The Great God of Irony must be doing the Snoopy dance over my falling for another doctor.

But maybe it's all my imagination. A blip of madness in the midst of the madness that has become my life.

When Daniel got in the driver's seat, he just sat, staring ahead for a long moment, his fingers clenched on the steering wheel. Then he turned to her. "Well, aren't you going to say something?"

There were so many things she wanted to say.

Like, "Why would you give up medicine when it clearly touches you so?"

Or, "So, you're a familiar face at a cancer medical center? Does that mean you have a Louisiana medical license after all?"

Or, "I think I'm falling a little bit in love with you."

But all she could come up with was a most innocuous, "Doctor Dan?"

Chapter Sixteen

Some people say shopping is a form of foreplay . . .

An hour later, Daniel wasn't surprised that they'd accomplished all their errands in record time, but Samantha was.

"No fuss, no bother. In and out," he told Samantha after pulling out of the parking lot for the Designer Overstock Home Warehouse. It was at his insistence that they'd stopped here, instead of going all the way to Metairie to the big box store. "Women could learn a lot about shopping from men."

She rolled her eyes.

After leaving the medical center and heading out of Houma, Daniel had noticed a billboard for the warehouse, which in smaller print had mentioned "appliances, furniture, fine accessories, everything for the home." Forget the

Costco that was almost an hour away, this could be a better alternative, he'd told her.

"But it's a scratch-and-dent kind of place," she'd protested.

"Who cares about a little wear and tear? Bayou Rose Plantation is a homage to wear and tear."

"That doesn't mean—"

Her words had been cut off as he'd abruptly pulled over to the side of the road and made a U-turn.

"Are you crazy? That pickup truck almost T-boned us."

"You mean the one with the cowboy who gave me the finger? Or the one with the bumper sticker that read, 'Keep Honking, I'm Reloading'?"

She'd just ignored his question and braced her feet on the floorboard, as if they were going to crash. Silly girl . . . rather, woman! He was a careful driver, having served a residency in trauma where the effects of lead-footed driving were often accompanied by massive amounts of blood.

Within an hour, he'd picked out a pillow-top mattress set for the antique double bed frame, which would go in a second floor bedroom, but also two single mattress sets, which would be placed temporarily in the front parlor for Angus and Lily Beth, and later moved upstairs to a guest room. Then he bought a whopping big, thirty-six-cubic-foot stainless steel fridge with a bunch of bells and whistles, and hardly a dent or scratch in evidence. Water and ice dispenser, of course. French doors. And, to appease Samantha's call for historical integrity, a special kit that would allow for wood panels to cover the fridge at a later date to match whatever cabinets were installed. Apparently, preservationists called for modern conveniences to be hidden. You weren't supposed to know there was a fridge, or a television, or dishwasher, or even, God forbid, a toilet. And, no, he didn't buy a fridge with a built-in keg, as Aaron had suggested, but this one did have a "blast chiller" that turned warm beer cold within minutes.

Samantha couldn't stop tsk-ing. "Are you sure that huge fridge is going to fit into the kitchen?"

"I'll make it fit."

She rolled her eyes again. "If you would've stopped flirting with that sales clerk, Deb-bie, I could have shown you a refrigerator model more fitting for your mansion. She was so short, she almost seemed like a teenager. She even giggled like one. Especially when you told that dumb story about Eskimo iceboxes. Your very own Little Debbie!"

He grinned. "Hah! You were the one attracting attention in that hoochie-mama outfit. I swear, half the male clerks in the store were watching your behind in those shorts, and the other half was aching to untie the bow in front of your top."

She put a hand to said bow, and blushed.

It was a kick that he could make her blush.

"You don't like this outfit."

"I love your outfit."

More blushing.

"Here's a deal for you. I'll let you take over renovation of *my* mansion . . ."

"You'll *let* me?"

". . . in return for all the favors I'm doing for you. Admit it, you know you'd sell your soul to get involved in renovating the old place. Go for it! Give Rose a historical facelift."

"Rose is it now? A female?"

"Aren't all these Southern mansions supposed to be grand old ladies?"

"Hmpfh!" she said, which was as good as saying, "I wouldn't sell my soul, but maybe a few family heirlooms, to be involved, dammit."

He'd been continuing to drive down the road when he suddenly put on the turn signal. "Oh, look. There's one of your stores." It was a Starr Foods Superstore. "And it's only noon. We can get the groceries here."

"Okay, but not too much cold stuff until the new fridge is delivered and has time to cool down."

"Do I get a Starr discount?"

"No."

"Aaah," he moaned in exaggeration. "I'd give you a discount if I owned a gazillion supermarkets."

"There aren't a gazillion Starr stores. Only a hundred and thirteen."

"*Only* a hundred and thirteen?"

"That's small . . . well, average . . . for a grocery chain. And I don't own the stores. I'm just a shareholder."

"Uh-huh," he said, disbelieving.

Actually, all this banter and inconsequential conversation was a concerted effort on Daniel's part to avoid the sudden, overpowering attraction that had exploded between them this morning. Well, not so sudden on his part. If he were truthful, he would have to admit that Samantha's appeal to him had been growing for some time now, even when she'd clearly been repulsed by him, mainly because he was a doctor, partly because of his taunting her about every little thing, a habit which gave him an inordinate, immature pleasure.

She clearly wasn't repulsed anymore. And, ironically, that was partly due to her seeing him as a doctor, the very thing that had put her off to begin with. Go figure. He'd be a fool not to notice that her attitude toward him had changed. Had it begun to change this morning when she'd seen him outside with her animals? Or maybe even last night when he'd offered to bring her and her motley crew back to the plantation? Or when she'd succumbed to their killer kiss. Or even later when she'd announced that she had been celibate for more than a year?

If he hadn't been convinced before that she was melting for him (*Man, I like the sound of that!*), he was for sure when he'd spotted her standing in the doorway of the children's playroom at the cancer medical center. The look in her eyes had been one of pure, unadulterated bone-melting, heart-melting, whatever-melting. Which wasn't a surprise to him. Women throughout the world considered doctors to be prime dating/marriage material. Little did they know or care about the high divorce rate for physicians. Not Samantha, though. Until today, he would have bet his balls that she would eat worms before she would willingly lay with another doctor. But now? Whoo-boy!

And, yes, he meant lay as in laid, or get naked, and do the deed.

So, now, the two of them were making a concerted effort to avoid the big frickin' elephant that sat between them, at the moment its big rump resting on the console, its trunk swinging back and forth like a pendulum. In his case, the pendulum seemed to be an argument of good sense against good sex.

Will we?

Won't we?

Make a move.

Run for the hills . . . or the bayou.

Maybe she'd like to have an affair.

I'd like to be a fly on the wall when that suggestion is made.

I'm going testosterone crazy.

It's lust. Pure unadulterated lust.

Let's give three cheers for pure unadulterated lust.

The pendulum probably had a different message for Samantha:

He's helping me with Angus and Lily Beth. Maybe he's not so bad.

But he's a doctor.

Doctor, doctor, give me the news . . .

Sometimes sex is the best prescription for what ails you. I must be going hormone crazy.

But, really, a doctor who can hunker down with a little girl and make her stop crying? Doctor Dan?

On the other hand, he was such a hermit, hiding in the bayou for two years, avoiding work. Lazy, selfish, just like all doctors, thinking of his own interests. The fact that he'd come out of hiding is probably just a ruse.

But he's so sexy he makes my bones melt.

That last was pure fantasy on Daniel's part, or perhaps wishful thinking. But he'd seen the way she looked at him. He was no fool. They were going to have sex. And soon.

"What are you smiling about?" she asked, breaking into his reverie.

They were in the middle of the produce department of the supermarket, he driving the shopping cart, she with a bunch of bananas in her hands. Not to be daunted, he was about to tell her, explicitly, when his cell phone rang. Taking it out of his pocket, he checked the caller ID.

"It's George Laroche. I better take this," he told Samantha. "They must have the test results already."

She nodded and continued to gather various produce items and place them in the cart. Two bunches of seedless grapes, green and red. Peaches. Cherries. Apples. Lemons and limes. Then, she added onions, celery, and bell pepper, muttering something about the Holy Trinity of Southern cooking. She added mushrooms, garlic, and a few ripe tomatoes. Was she planning on cooking in that pathetic excuse for a kitchen at Bayou Rose?

Hey, who was he to argue? As long as it didn't involve okra, he was game to try anything, even her cooking.

"All the tests have come back negative," George told him.

"That's good news," Daniel remarked.

Samantha stopped and looked at him.

He gave a thumbs-up and listened.

"No preeclampsia and only mild anaemia. Get her some iron pills," George said.

Daniel put his hand over the phone and asked Samantha, "Do they have a pharmacy section in this store where we can get some iron pills?"

She nodded.

Back to George, who continued, "The elevated blood pressure is still a concern, as you know. Make an appointment for her with an obstetrician asap. In the meantime, keep her off her feet as much as possible."

"Will do. Thanks so much, George. This was above and beyond."

"Totally self-serving, my boy. You know I want you to join our group. Anything to push you in that direction."

"I'm thinking about it, George. I'll give you an answer soon. How was Molly after I left?" Molly was the little girl he'd helped at the medical center.

"Devastated. Turns out her father couldn't come after all. No place to stay. Yes, yes, I know, you offered to pay for a motel room for him, but it's unfair to ask any one person to make that kind of donation, especially when there are so many other needy cases." He sighed deeply.

Molly's family situation was different than others served by programs like Ronald McDonald Houses, which were intended as temporary relief only. Her father had no long-term job and no permanent address, due to constant absences following hospitalization and travel for his youngest child. He and the other three siblings were spread among various family members. The mother had skipped town after Molly's initial diagnosis. Some parents just weren't able to handle sick children.

It was nothing new. And more of the kind of heartache Daniel had chosen to escape when he'd left medicine. Still, he said, "I wish I could do more."

"I know. We all do. Anyhow, take care and keep in touch."

"Likewise."

Daniel clicked off and turned back to Samantha.

"Good news about Lily Beth?" she asked.

"So far." He pushed the cart out of the produce section and asked, "Where next?"

"Butcher shop." Where she picked up some boneless chicken breasts and andouille sausage.

"Planning on doing some cooking?"

"Just a big pot of gumbo. That, with some rice and good bread should feed our small crowd, and the leftovers, if there are any, won't take up much room in the old fridge."

"So, you're a cook, as well as accountant, fund-raiser, and animal rescuer?"

"I don't do all that much cooking, but every Southern girl knows how to make her grandmother's gumbo."

"And Southern boys?"

"Their job is . . . always has been . . . to provide the meat or fish for the pot. The providers."

"Even if it was just possum from the bayou."

She nodded. "Or crawfish. We do love our crawfish."

"I got pretty good at catching crawfish while I lived in that bayou fishing camp."

She hitched a hip and tilted her head at him. "Is that an offer to become my . . . provider?"

He laughed. "Hardly. A few crawfish does not a provider make."

"Holy jambalaya!" she exclaimed suddenly. "I just noticed. You have a dimple. Where have you been hiding that?"

Daniel pressed his lips together, trying to retract the dimple, to no avail. But then, when he noticed the way she licked her lips when she stared at said dimple, he let it go. He was no fool. If dimples were one more step in her lust parade, he would be the drum major. "I have only one," he told her, as if that were important. "On my right side only. Aaron has one on his left side. Twins and all that."

She grinned and reached up a fingertip to touch his dimple.

Which felt a whole lot like she was touching him somewhere else.

Before he said or did something even more stupid than he already had, Daniel decided to move on and get them out of this supermarket and back to the plantation and sanity. Or something even better.

To Daniel's surprise, there was an aisle devoted to small household appliances. "In a supermarket?"

"It's not your mama's old-time grocery store," Samantha remarked with a proud smile. She suggested he get another cart, and they loaded up with an electric can opener, a toaster, a small microwave, and a big Crock-Pot.

At the bakery, she picked out two long baguettes and a sliced sourdough bread loaf for sandwiches. She also insisted that she had to get a large fruit tart . . . one of Lily Beth's favorites, apparently . . . that resembled a pizza covered with a cream cheese mixture, then strawberries, blueberries, pineapple, grapes, and kiwi. Forget Lily Beth; it looked good to him, too.

He grabbed a jar of tupelo honey and arched his eyebrows at her.

At the deli, she picked up some sliced lunch meat. Then, she moved on to get a small sack of flour, Cajun seasonings, a bag of rice, eggs, butter, milk, and orange juice. Also, mustard, mayonnaise, and Tabasco sauce, also known as Cajun lightning.

"Good Lord! I thought you said we should buy only a few things that would fit in that small fridge."

She shrugged. "Most of these items need no refrigeration. Besides, your very accommodating sales clerk promised to have the fridge and mattress set delivered this afternoon. By tonight, we should hopefully have a fridge big enough to hold a side of beef. If it fits!"

"It'll fit," he assured her, having no idea if it would or not. More important, he liked the way she said "we." And he liked the way she seemed to be jealous of the flirty sales clerk. And when he said, "It'll fit," he was thinking about something else entirely. That's how pathetic he was becoming in his lust for her.

When they got to the checkout, she shoved him aside with a hip and handed the clerk a card with the Starr logo on it. Apparently, she got her groceries for free, not just a discount.

"You didn't have to do that," he said.

"Consider it payback for all the favors you've been doing for me."

"I prefer another method of payback," he said before he could bite his fool tongue.

She stopped pushing her cart in the middle of the parking lot. He stopped his cart, too. "You keep making insinuations like that, Daniel. Why is that?"

"Not insinuations. Fact," he told her. "I've just come to a decision . . . no, not a decision . . . a realization . . . of inevitability. You and I are going to have sex."

To his surprise, instead of slapping his face, or making a snarky remark, she paused for a moment, thinking, then leaned up to kiss his cheek. "You're on, Doctor Dreamy."

Oh. My. God! Hoisted on my own doctorly petard.

Chapter Seventeen

Moving along, or was it, moves abound? . . .

Once they were back at the plantation, Daniel kept touching her. Oh, not in any overt, noticeable way. Subtle. In passing.

And that blasted dimple, which had been invisible to her this morning, was now like a blinking neon light. Was he smiling more? Or was it just her overactive libido that was seeing things of a lustful nature in everything he did.

Not that dimples were lustful, exactly.

Who was she kidding? His single dimple had amped her horniness meter more than a few points. *Forget shorts and a halter top. I should have worn armor.*

And it wasn't just the touching that disconcerted Samantha. The looks were just as bad. Smoldering. She'd only ever associated that word with romance novel heroes. Now she knew what it meant. *Whew! Where is air-conditioning when it's needed?*

And "horniness meter"? Where had that crude word come from? *Real classy, Samantha! If I'm not careful, I'll be kicked out of the Sweet Southern Belle society, if there is such a society.*

Before she did anything else, she checked on her animals while Daniel carried in the groceries. Even before she opened the sliding pocket door, she heard an angry bird, which just kept chirping nonstop, "Holy shit! Holy shit! Holy shit!"

"I'll second that," she replied, blowing the bird an air kiss.

The animals had already been fed and watered this morning, but they needed fresh water in this heat. The puppies were still in their crate, and two of the cats, Garfield and Felix, lay on their personal mats, content to stay put. All the other animals must be downstairs on the first level, or out back. Luckily, there was a small, as-yet-unrenovated half bath on this floor which had running water and little else.

With everything else on her agenda, she had to remember to deliver three of the puppies later this afternoon. She'd already notified her office that she wouldn't be in today and cancelled her noontime meeting, but she should call for a report.

When she got downstairs, she found Daniel helping Angus to hose off the extra lawn furniture, old wrought iron pieces, he'd found in storage and arranged outside, under the tupelo tree, just in case they wanted to meet outside. Lily Beth was already reclining on the chaise, and the chairs were arranged around her. Samantha, Daniel, Angus, and Lily Beth would all participate in the meeting with Luc and John, who should be arriving shortly.

Daniel was updating Angus and Lily Beth on the medical test results as he hosed. Every couple seconds, he gave Emily a misty shower, without pausing from his conversation. The pig gazed up at him with adoration.

That was another thing Samantha needed to put on her list: cancelling Em's psych appointment.

Maddie was outside, too, reclining in the sun. She gave Daniel a look that pretty much said, Spray Me and You Are Dead Cat Meat. Axel was there, too. Knowing of the Shepherd's bad hip, she figured Angus must have helped the dog down the steps. A plastic Tupperware bowl of water sat next to Axel's muzzle. Bless the boy!

When Daniel passed Samantha in the kitchen on the way to grabbing some old towels to wipe off the furniture, he just happened to brush against her butt as she was bent over attempting to plug in the Crock-Pot to an ancient baseboard electrical outlet.

She shot up to glare at him.

He just grinned, a big ol' dimpled grin, and murmured, "Excuse me."

Samantha put away the groceries and started the gumbo in the Crock-Pot, while Daniel found a power strip and hooked up the small appliances, including the Crock-Pot.

When he reached forward, she thought he was grabbing for her breasts, but, instead, he tsk-tsked at her assumption, and adjusted the bow on her halter top. "You were a bit lopsided," he explained.

She narrowed her eyes at him. "Are you putting the moves on me?"

"Moi?" he said with mock innocence. But then he grimaced in a self-deprecating way. "Any moves I might have once had have surely rusted from disuse."

"Maybe it's like riding a bike. You never really forget."

"You think?"

It was fun bantering with the usually dour Daniel, who was surprising her with his flirtatious actions. She liked it. Of course, he would probably zap her with a sarcastic remark any minute now, if she didn't snark him first. Their mutual bickering had become a hard-to-break habit.

Just then, they both glanced upward at the sound of someone walking on the first floor of the mansion.

"Luc or John?" she guessed.

"Maybe, but they would have probably knocked." He grabbed a broom, as if that would provide protection against the mob or Nick. Once again, she thought she should get a weapon. Add that to her list.

As Daniel began to walk up the back stairs, she got an enticing view of his very fine behind in the black running shorts. How did he keep in such good shape?

"Do you run, Daniel?" she called after him with what was an out-of-place question in the midst of possible danger.

He answered with the same disregard for timing, "Only when I have to. Were you thinking about chasing me?"

Or being chased, she thought, but didn't dare say out loud.

A short time later, he returned with Aaron, the two of them laughing about something to do with animals. They would have passed the second parlor on their way to the back stairs.

"Hey, Sam," Aaron greeted her with the nickname she disliked so much, second only to the hated "Sammie" that Nick taunted her with. She'd been haunted by the "Sam" nickname in childhood. "Sam the Yam," they'd called her because her hair had been the color of the root vegetable back then. Thank God for modern hair products! It wasn't worth correcting him, though. And at least he wasn't calling her "Beanpole," her other nickname.

She'd been taller than all her classmates until high school, and even then, taller than most of the girls. Later she became comfortable with her "model thin" height, but back then, not so much.

"Aaron," she returned his greeting. "You done working for the day?"

"Nah! I need to go back later this afternoon. A swamp tour by some real estate investors."

"I appreciate your letting us stay here until we resolve . . . well, you know the situation."

"No problem. Is there anything to eat?"

Angus and Lily Beth joined them for lunch, and soon the kitchen table was spread with bread, sliced ham, Cajun chicken breast, bologna, and all the condiments, along with Tante Lulu's leftover salads and Lily Beth's fruit tart. Daniel gave his brother a brief update while they ate.

Aaron's grin kept getting wider and wider as he listened, especially when Daniel, who was sitting on the bench across from him, next to Samantha, kept finding excuses to touch Samantha. Once he even blew against her forehead to push back a strand of hair that had come loose from her ponytail. That gesture was so outrageously personal it caused everyone at the table to stop and stare.

"Idiot!" Aaron remarked.

"Moron!" Daniel countered.

Samantha couldn't help but notice the closeness between the two brothers as they ate and chatted, even the exchange of insults. They were twins, of course, and there was a strong resemblance, even though they dressed differently. Daniel was more the khakis and loafers type, even though he wore running shorts and Nikes this morning, while Aaron was more cowboy, right down to his Levi's and boots. And his hair was longish, pulled back with a rubber band at the back of his head into a knot or small bun . . . a mun, some people called those popular ponytails which weren't really big enough to be tails.

Aaron caught her looking him over and winked at her.

Daniel caught the wink and reached across the table to jab his brother with a serving spoon.

"What?" Aaron pretended his chest hurt where Daniel had jabbed him. "Private property? Already? Whoo-hoo! Everybody, raise the flag and do a drum roll. My brother has his mojo back. The doctor is back in the game!"

Samantha arched her brows at Daniel. So much for his rusty moves!

"That'll be enough, Aaron," Daniel said. "You're embarrassing Samantha."

"Me? Why would I be embarrassed? I haven't done anything."

"Yet," Daniel said, and squeezed her thigh, under the table.

She pretended not to notice.

Aaron looked from her to Daniel and back again, then did a fist bump in the air.

Was her attraction to Daniel so apparent? Or his to her? She . . . *they* would have to be more careful. She could only imagine what their expressions would reveal if they'd actually done anything.

Luc and John LeDeux joined them then, having parked out front and walked around the house to the kitchen entrance. Apparently, they'd rung the doorbell and got no response except, according to John, "some dude inside saying 'Holy shit!' over and over."

Luc wore a gray business suit that brought out the threads of gray in his dark hair and black-and-gray striped tie that he explained was needed for his appearance in court that morning. He was representing a restaurant being sued for serving gator meat out of season.

John, who was known in Cajun land as Tee-John, or little John, from a young age, though he was now over six feet tall, was in jeans, pale blue dress shirt, unbuttoned at the neck with no tie, and a navy blazer, suitable for his job as a police detective in Lafayette. Luc was close to fifty, and John somewhere in his thirties, but they were both good-looking men. All the LeDeuxs were, men and women alike.

As they walked inside, they were complaining to each other about two of their children, John's thirteen-year-old son Etienne, and Luc's youngest, Jeanette, who was a high school senior.

"That boy, he gonna put me in the crazy house, guar-an-teed," John declared in a slow Southern accent that probably had women swooning, despite his marriage and children. "How ya punish a boy who buys a shirt in the French Quarter that says, 'I Shaved My Balls For This?' and wore it ta Sunday mass at Our Lady of the Bayou Church?"

"Tante Lulu would say ya reap what ya sow," Luc commented with a laugh.

"What the hell does that mean?"

"It's only fittin' that the baddest boy in the bayou should get a boy with his own bad habits."

"I wasn't the baddest," John protested with a grin.

Clearly, he had been. Even Samantha had heard about some of Tee-John LeDeux's antics, all the way to New Orleans. Of course, that was before he'd married Celine, a newspaper reporter who trimmed his tail feathers.

"Anyways, wait 'til he get older. The problems, they get bigger. Jeanette wants a fluorescent tattoo on her butt that says 'No . . . No' on each buttock but in the dark, her ass says, 'Yes . . . Yes.' Can you imagine?"

John's mouth dropped open, and he actually appeared to be interested. "Wish they had those when I was her age."

"You would!" Luc said.

The two of them realized that all those in the kitchen were listening intently to their conversation.

"Sorry for airin' our private shit," John said.

"So, you called," Luc said to Samantha. "What's the problem?"

Instead of going outside where the heat was becoming brutal, they decided to talk around the table in the kitchen, where there was at least a ceiling fan. Aaron went upstairs to shower and change before his work assignment. Samantha and Daniel cleared the table while Angus told the story of his gambling debts and the mob loan, and of his and Lily Beth's involvement with Dr. Nicholas Coltrane. Lily Beth inserted a comment here and there, but mostly she remained silent, yawning occasionally. She probably needed to lie down and take a nap.

Samantha and Daniel sat down then. Daniel told about the visit last night from the two Dixie Mob dimwits, and Samantha related her threatening phone calls from Nick, including two more voice mails this morning, which she hadn't told Daniel about yet. He gave her a questioning look, and she just shrugged. Too much had been happening.

Daniel wasn't putting the moves on her in front of Luc and John, but sitting next to her, thigh to thigh on a bench, felt intimate . . . and promising.

"*Mon Dieu!* Y'all are in a mess of trouble," John concluded.

"No shit!" Angus muttered.

"This is way beyond the scope of local police, although ya do need ta contact them," John went on. "I'll put ya in touch with the police chief in Houma. Beyond that, I suspect the feds'll have ta be involved, both for the mob and the baby sellin' crimes. Not just 'cause of the

RICO Act, but crossin' state lines, and all that. The chief kin handle the details."

"That's pretty much what we've already told them," Samantha said, "but they're afraid to get the law involved. Not just for their own legal liabilities, but if the mob or Nick hear that they've contacted the police, they'll surely come after them."

"That's where I come in," Luc interjected. "As your lawyer, I'll try to get you a deal where you both avoid prosecution in return for testifying against them."

Lily Beth groaned and clutched her stomach protectively.

"Is she all right?" Luc asked Daniel. Samantha had informed Luc earlier about Daniel's plans to examine the pregnant girl.

Daniel nodded. "The stress can't be good, though."

"Darlin', yer job is ta take care of yerself and yer baby. Ya need ta trust us ta take care of all this other crap," John said.

She nodded tearfully.

"Are we safe here?" Angus wanted to know.

John shrugged. "Seems ta me yer as safe here as anywhere. Long as ya doan go blabbin' yer whereabouts ta anyone."

"Including Tante Lulu," Luc added.

They all agreed to that.

"Well, I already notified the contractors not to send any men this week for the roof work and painting," Daniel informed them. "So, no strangers hanging around."

"If any strangers . . . even folks you know, like family members . . . come on the property, you two should stay out of sight," John advised.

"How long will this all take?" Samantha asked. She hated that they were imposing on Daniel and Aaron like this, especially for any length of time.

John exchanged a look with Luc before answering. "Hard to say. Maybe a week or so before any arrests take place. We'll want to act quickly, though, before word leaks out that they're in trouble. Otherwise, they'll hide evidence and skip town."

"From arrest to trial, though, could take months," Luc elaborated. "But if the perps are in jail, you won't need to stay in hiding."

"If the feds decide this location isn't secure enough, they'll find a safe house fer you," John told them.

"You did the right thing calling us. Take it easy for now, and I'll call you tomorrow with an update," Luc told Angus and Lily Beth, who was weeping softly now. Angus stood and said he would take Lily Beth to the front parlor bedroom so that she could rest.

When they were gone, Samantha asked, "Do Daniel and I need to stay hidden? I mean, can I go into my office, or to the stores in the area?"

"No, don't go to work, for the time being," Luc advised. "The fact that Nick is calling you to ask about Angus's whereabouts is alarming. He's probably calling Angus's father and friends, as well, casting a wide net. But I wouldn't take any chances . . . yet."

"Oh, geez. I went to a Houma medical center, a furniture warehouse, and the grocery store today with Daniel," Samantha said, cringing. "And I'm supposed to deliver some rescue puppies to homes outside Nawleans today."

John waved a hand airily. "I think you're okay with short, local trips like that. Occasionally. I mean, Nick has no reason to connect you with Bayou Rose Plantation, does he? But don't take any chances, like delivering the animals."

Daniel pretended to groan. "Damn, I thought I was going to be rid of some of the creatures."

She turned to glare at him.

And he winked at her, at the same time flashing his dimple.

"Hey, if your other felines are like that monster cat I saw out back, they would scare any intruders away. Guard cat, ya could say." This from John, who also glanced meaningfully at Emily who was parked outside the green fridge, which was a little cooler than the rest of the room. "Or a guard pig!"

"Very funny!" Samantha remarked, becoming used to all the comments about her animals.

Luc and John said their good-byes and left, but before they could relish the blessed silence, Aaron appeared in the ground floor hallway that led to the front of the mansion. Having changed into black jeans and a Bayou Aviation shirt, he looked cool and clean.

"Oh, brother," he cooed, leaning against the door frame, grinning at Daniel. "Congratulations are in order."

"Huh?" Daniel said.

"You are now the proud papa to seven new babies. And you know that favorite Barry Manilow sweatshirt of yours? You might want to ditch it."

"What the hell are you talking about, Aaron?"

"I went over to the *garconniére* to get some papers, and guess what? Your cat just popped out a bunch of kittens . . ."

"*What*?" Daniel exclaimed.

". . . right on Barry's pretty face."

"You know damn well Mom gave both of us those stupid shirts. I couldn't care less about that. But more cats! I'm getting a rash already."

Aaron flashed his dimple at his brother, the one on the opposite side of the face. It wasn't nearly as nice as Daniel's.

Daniel turned on Samantha. "You knew about this when you gave me that damn cat, didn't you?"

"Well . . . um . . . uh," she stammered.

"Your markers are piling up, sweetheart."

"Okay, so I owe you."

"Damn straight you do. You got me involved with three live-in guests, one of whom is very pregnant, and—"

"You invited us," she pointed out.

". . . then there is the cougar—"

"I keep telling you, it's not a cougar. It's a Savannah cat."

". . . and two other cats—"

". . . who are no trouble at all. You hardly know that Felix and Garfield are here."

". . . and a dog the size of a pony that can barely walk . . ."

"Now, that's cruel. Axel is sweet, you have to admit that."

". . . and five puppies . . ."

". . . three of whom are going to be gone soon . . ."

". . . and a foul-mouthed bird . . ."

"You got me with that one."

". . . not to mention, the Dixie Mob, a whacko doctor, the police, the FBI, and now a pregnant cat and seven freakin' kittens. God only knows what else you'll pull out of your witchy hat."

She cringed. It didn't sound good when he listed all his favors and the impositions on him like that. In fact, very bad. "Don't worry. I'll make it up to you."

"Hah! I'd like to know how."

"I could pay you—"

"If I wanted money, I'd get a job."

He had a point there. "I'll take care of the new kittens and find homes for them, along with the other two, Felix and Garfield."

"That's a given."

"While I'm here, I'll help clean up the place and do the cooking, and—"

"I could just as easily call Bayou Maids 'r Us and get takeout like I have been the last few years. Big deal!"

"Don't you mean 'Happy Meal'?" she tried to tease.

He didn't crack even a tiny smile.

"I'll make up a plan for restoring this mansion. And give you a list of experts to help with some of the more complicated work."

"Blah, blah, blah." He was unimpressed.

"I'll think of something."

Meanwhile, Aaron was getting an earful. He followed their exchange by glancing first at one of them, then the other, back and forth. Finally, he leaned in to Daniel's ear and whispered, loud enough for her to overhear, "I have an idea." He paused for dramatic effect. "Someone could get laid tonight."

Samantha was pretty sure he wasn't talking about himself.

And Daniel looked interested.

Who was she kidding? She was interested, too.

Chapter Eighteen

If love was a merry-go-round, he was on the Tilt-a-Whirl . . .

"We need to exchange vehicles for the day," Daniel told Aaron after Samantha went off to care for the mommy cat and her new brood. The prospect of these latest additions horrified him, but he couldn't think about that now. Especially with that scary cougar cat spread out in a predatory fashion on the bottom step of the mansion, eying a hummingbird in a nearby bougainvillea bush, and with the potbellied pig already sitting on the passenger seat of Aaron's truck, waiting for Daniel. "I'm gonna use your frickin' truck to get some frickin' things from the frickin' storage facility."

"No problem," Aaron said. "And the *frickin'* pig?"

It was a sign of Daniel's deteriorating mood that he

didn't even smile at his brother's obvious teasing. "I'm taking Emily to the Pet Psychiatric Clinic in Lafayette. She's depressed. And stop with the constant grinning. You look like an idiot."

"Whoa! Talk about an overreaction. Are you annoyed with me?"

"Hell, yes. Do you have to be so crude? In front of a woman?"

"What? What did I do?"

"Someone could get laid." Daniel repeated Aaron's recent words back to him, words said in the presence of Samantha.

"Oh. That." Aaron paused to stare at him. "I take it you haven't done the deed with Sam yet."

"No, I haven't, not that it's any of your business."

"How can you be a brother of mine? Are you an alien or something? You and Sam practically sizzle when you're in the same room. I should know. I'm your twin. I can feel your burn."

Great! Shared lust. "I've discussed it with her," he said defensively. "Sort of."

"Discussed? You don't discuss having sex. You just do it." Aaron put his face in his hands, then raised his head. "Sort of? This oughta be good."

"I implied, and she concurred." *That sounds dumb, even to me.*

"And still you haven't done anything?" Aaron threw his hands in the air.

"Give me time."

Aaron rolled his eyes. "She's not really that attractive, you know. All those freckles. Eew!"

"Are you nuts? She's so hot, she makes my blood steam. As for the freckles, can you imagine licking them? One at a time. Everywhere."

Aaron grinned, having gotten the reaction he wanted.

More grinning! Daniel fake-punched his brother in the chest.

Aaron left then, but he was shaking his head at Daniel's hopelessness.

It was true. Daniel did think a lot about things. It was probably the doctor in him. You could take the man out of medicine, but you couldn't take the medicine out of the man, or some such thing. That wasn't hopelessness. It was smart. So what if he didn't act impulsively! Well, except for his impulsive invitation for Samantha, Angus, Lily Beth, and the animals to come to Rose Plantation. And look where that had gotten him? Drowning in animals . . . and lust quicksand.

As a doctor, a student of science, Daniel knew that sexual arousal had four stages: excitement, plateau, orgasm, and resolution. It began in the brain as an erotic thought (*Boy, do I have a few, or twenty, of those.*), or image (*Can anyone say nudity?*), or touch (*I wanna hold your haaaaand, or another body part.*), or feelings of affection for a particular partner (*Not so much that one, except . . .*), each or all of which triggered signals to all the erogenous zones on the body, especially the genitals Easily explained by dopamine D4 receptors in the brain, as well as biological chemicals, like hormones and testosterone.

Forget the doctor perspective. As a man, Daniel recognized the overwhelming desire to engage in sexual activity, i.e. fucking, simply for what it was. Lust, libido, horniness, the itch that couldn't be scratched. When he was being nice, or trying to worm his way into a woman's bed, a man might use less graphic words, like passion, or desire, or even love, if he were particularly desperate, or emotional. Sexual deprivation did tend to make a man desperate. Whatever the word or the cause, sexual arousal to a man was an overwhelming drive for satisfaction that only a woman could provide. Like being caught on a fast train with no brakes. Okay, a man could do the job himself, but that wasn't nearly as satisfying.

Daniel wanted Samantha, pure and simple. And he wanted her bad. It was all he could think about. Like a seed planted in his brain, it kept growing, and nothing was going to make it go away. (Except for the obvious.) The seed . . . the idea of sex with Samantha . . . had grown into a big honkin' plant, a vine with tendrils extending to all parts of his body. Like kudzu, it was, and everyone knew kudzu was "the vine that ate the South." If the South couldn't overcome the assault, how could he?

Holy crap! Now I'm making jokes with myself about kudzu. And all these stupid analogies: trains, seeds, vines. What next? Rockets?

So, he and Emily went to the storage facility where he hired a couple of high school kids to help him load the double size bed frame and dresser, along with a couple of antique mirrors that weighed a ton. He would come back tomorrow for the rest of the bedroom set . . . an armoire and a dry sink . . . as well as two single bed frames that were lodged in the back of the unit.

And the mental assaults continued. The whole time he was lugging furniture, including the antique rice bed frame (*Whatever the hell a rice bed was!*), his fool brain kept picturing a bed sitting arranged before open French doors with a soft white down comforter. On it reclined Samantha, reddish hair spread all over the pillow, miles of creamy skin, and freckles. Her arms were raised above her head, and one knee was raised. She was nude, of course, wearing nothing but an old-fashioned ankle bracelet, which in this case was just a thin chain of fine gold. Her nails were unpainted, but her lips were cherry red.

Yes, he fantasized in detail.

And, yes, now he was having sex dreams in the day-time, while he was awake. Walking sex dreams.

Why did ankle bracelets go out of style, anyway? They were sexy as hell, in his opinion. In fact, he and Aaron had talked about it one time. Aaron considered seamed stockings and a garter belt on a woman to be a lost female attraction. Whereas Daniel thought seamed stockings and garter belts were just sort of silly, right up there with padded bras and waist cinchers. Well, some-times waist cinchers held an appeal, depending on the circumstance . . . or fantasy. But honestly, an eighteen-inch waist and fifty-two-inch hips?

You could tell he'd thought about this a lot. Now *that* was hopeless!

Emily looked at him, as if to say "I know just how you feel."

He put a leash on Emily when they got to the Pet Psy-chiatric Clinic, which was probably unnecessary since she couldn't trot more than ten feet a minute and stopped to take a dainty dump every other step. While at the clinic, an overweight psychologist with halitosis oohed and cooed over the pig, pretending to communicate in pig language (Pig latin, maybe. Ha, ha, ha!), and pro-claimed that Emily was getting better. And handed her a pig treat for being such "a good piggy."

"That will be fifty dollars," the receptionist told him. "And bring Emily back in two weeks."

Yeah, right.

He stopped once at a park where he gave the pig a chance to do its job again. The grass was lush and green here, thanks to the tropical heat and rains, and of course he pictured himself and Samantha lying, naked, on a similar lawn. No, it was a pasture filled with clover. The crushed clover smelled like fresh-cut grass with a hint of basil. When he rolled over, on top of her—

"Oink, oink," Emily said, ready to return to the truck.

"We need to get you a boyfriend, Emily," he told the pig, as he adjusted the seat belt around its fat belly.

The pig gave him such a soulful look, you'd think she understood.

When he got back to the mansion, he took the pig to the second parlor with the other animals, then looked for Angus to help him unload the truck. He found him in the first parlor with Lily Beth, slow dancing to some John Legend song playing on his laptop. Which was kind of sweet and comical at the same time, with her pregnancy bump, which was more like a mountain, impeding any real closeness.

Dancing? In the midst of all the danger they faced? He could hardly believe it!

But then, he got a sudden image in his brain (Surprise, surprise!) of him slow dancing with Samantha. Except this time the music was something more intensely sexual, and even more cornball, like Marvin Gaye's "Let's Get It On." He was wearing jeans and nothing else, not even shoes. She was bare-footed, too, wearing that hot sleep outfit, red silky pants and silky black camisole top edged in red. No underwear, he could tell, because he could see her nipples and the curve of her buttocks. She looped her arms around his neck. His hands held her hips, just above her butt cheeks. He wasn't all that interested in dancing, but they were just swaying, feeling the rhythm of the music. *Oh, man! Man oh man oh man!*

Just then, a horn honked outside, jarring him from his reverie and Angus and Lily Beth from their dancing. It was the delivery truck from the furniture warehouse. Daniel told Angus and Lily Beth to stay out of sight, just in case.

Samantha came to see what was going on.

"How's Max?"

"Just great, and the kittens are so cute."

"I'll bet." He was being sarcastic, but at the same time, he was picturing her petting the big cat. Her long tapered finger caressed the feline from nape to tail, softly, like butterfly wings on the skin . . . uh, fur. The cat arched its back with sheer pleasure and—

"Why are you looking at me like that?" she asked.

He blinked several times and looked at her. She still wore that blue shorts outfit with the bare shoulders and halter top with a bow tied right between heaven and hell. The things a guy imagined he could do with a bow!

"Earth to Daniel! Why are you looking at me like that?" she repeated.

Busted! "Like what?" He pretended to be confused. Then, "I was just noticing the cat hair on your shoulders." *And all that creamy, freckled skin.* He reached over and pretended to flick some stray hairs off the bare skin, which caused goose bumps to rise all over her arms. He took that as a good sign.

She narrowed her eyes at him suspiciously.

He winked at her. *When all else fails, try the wink*, he told himself. *Lust is turning my brain to mush.*

She was still eyeing him suspiciously, or maybe like he'd lost a few marbles. Enough of this madness! They had work to do. She oversaw the installation of the new fridge (which did fit, hallelujah!) and the removal of the old, while he directed the two delivery men. Afterward, while Samantha put the food from the old fridge into the new, he prepared to go outside with Angus and unload the furniture from the truck.

"Just put those twin mattresses in the front parlor for now," Samantha suggested. "I don't like the idea of Lily Beth having to get up and down from that air mattress on the floor. Did you bring any twin bed frames?"

"No. They're in the back of the unit. I'll get them to-morrow."

"Well, then, maybe you should set up the double bed in there, for now, since you have a frame for it."

The infamous rice bed. He thought about asking what a rice bed was, but decided he didn't really care. "Okay," he said, his mind elsewhere. Again! He was looking at the freezer on the bigass fridge and thinking about buying some ice cream. Not because the cold ice cream would be welcome on this hot day, but because of the kinds of thing a creative man could do with ice cream. And they wouldn't even have to leave the kitchen. There was that table, and—

"You're looking at me like that again," she pointed out.

"Like what?"

"Like I'm a cold drink on a sizzling Louisiana day, and you'd like to suck me up."

He laughed. "You got that right, babe." Then, he went back outside with Angus. It was best he got out of her sight before he acted on his fantasies. Not that he didn't intend to act on them at some point. Just waiting for the right time. On second thought, he went back inside, pressed her up against the fridge and kissed her, open-mouthed and hungry, with his hard-on obvious and hard against her belly. She was so surprised, she still held a carton of orange juice in one hand, and a package of cheese in the other. Then, without saying a word, he turned again and left.

Yep, drowning! Either in lust, or stupidity, or both.

It was a hundred degrees in the shade today, and he was feeling every bit of the heat. And, yes, he meant that as a double entendre.

No mission was impossible for this old lady . . .

Louise awakened from an afternoon nap to the sound of thunder clapping in her head. She imagined that St. Jude

was tapping her on the shoulder, not to come to the Pearly Gates, but to start on a new heavenly mission. "Tante Lulu, thou art needed!" the heavenly voice said in her head.

Yes, even St. Jude called her Tante Lulu.

She tried to go back to sleep, but the thunder kept a-clappin'. She checked the bedside clock and saw that it was four o'clock. Time to get up and work on some of her herbs before dinner. Leftover gumbo. The best kind!

She didn't get up yet. It was so comfy in her small bed.

Her family always acted worried when they walked in on her sleeping during the daytime, like the next step would be her napping in a coffin. Holy crawfish! Young folks didn't understand that naps energized a person . . . persons of any age. You didn't need any of that Red Bull stuff when you took a daily nap.

"It's a power nap, fer heaven's sake, not one of those old age, fuddy duddy naps," she told the naysayers, repeatedly. "Doan be puttin' me in no grave yet. Age is what ya want it ta be, and I ain't old yet. I still got giddyup in my heart and juice in my lady parts."

That always caught their attention and they tsk-tsked at her for speaking her mind. "Who else'll speak iffen I don't?" Not a bit of humor in the whole lot, 'cept for Tee-John and Charmaine.

Her knees creaked as she eased her way off the bed. Not from old age, mind. Just a little cramp from sleeping in one position.

But back to the thunderbolt that had awakened her. The sky was clear blue, no storm in sight. She grinned then and did a little Snoopy dance around her bedroom. *I cain't be old iffen I kin still dance.* To prove her point, to herself, she added a little spin to her dance, and almost fell on her hiney.

She knew exactly what the thunderbolt meant. The thunderbolt of love was hitting someone she knew, and

they needed her help to recognize it for what it was . . .
a heavenly gift. And she knew exactly who it had hit,
too. That stubborn, grouchy, too-sensitive-to-live Daniel
LeDeux.

She already had his hope chest made. She made hope
chests for all the men in her family, and the men who
were close to her family. She would have to check and
see if she had enough embroidered pillowcases, and doilies, and St. Jude place mats for Daniel's. Maybe she
should start on a bride quilt for Samantha, who was no
doubt being hit by the thunderbolt, too.

The phone rang, and she picked it up right away.

"Tante Lulu?" her nephew Luc asked.

"Who else would it be? Richard Simmons? Not that I
would mind if he were here takin' a nap with me."

Luc groaned. "I'm calling ta remind you about your
birthday party here on Saturday."

"How could I forget? Ya keep callin' me every day ta
remind me. Do ya think I got de-men-chah jist cause I'm
approachin' eighty."

Luc made a snorting sound at that number. Louise
never disclosed her true age. It was nobody's bizness. But
Luc was a lawyer. He could count.

"Anyways, I was jist about to call you. I'm thinkin'
about goin' over ta Bayou Rose Plantation t'morrow ta
help Daniel with his . . . uh, problem. And I was
wonderin'—"

"*Mon Dieu!* Who told you? You weren't supposed ta
know."

Huh? Red flags went up in her head. Her family was
always trying to hide important things from her. "Doan
matter how I know," she said carefully. "Daniel and Samantha need my help, and that's that."

"No, it's not *that* that. No one needs your help. The
FBI will be there, and police. Stay home and give yourself a perm or somethin' fer your party."

The FBI? *And* the police. "So, Tee-John is involved, too?" She was going to smack that boy up one side and down the other. He was her favorite nephew, and he usually understood her need to be involved.

"Of course, Tee-John is involved. He and I were the first ones ta learn about this mess."

"I could bring over a mess of greens and a crawfish casserole. Mebbe I should bake a pie. I got blueberries big as marbles."

"No! Samantha can do any cooking that needs done. Or Lily Beth. Unless the girl decides to pop out her baby in the middle of the chaos."

A pregnant girl? He cain't mean Samantha. I jist saw her on Sunday. And chaos? My favorite thing. But they're shuttin' me out? We'll see about that! "I doan think I know Lily Beth. How far along do ya suppose she is?" Tante Lulu asked.

"Supposedly seven months, but she looks more than that."

She did a mental inventory of the closet in her second bedroom where she stored all the knitted and crocheted items she made in her spare time for "just in case" situations. Yep, she recalled a little green jacket and cap she'd made a few years back. She could take that for a gift.

"Are you still there?" Luc asked.

"'Course I am. Where ya think I am? In mah bayou stream doin' laps?"

"Don't you dare go near that water. I don't trust that pet gator you keep around there. We oughta call Pet Control ta relocate that beast."

"Useless is harmless," she said.

"Anyhow, stay home tomorrow. Rest. Don't even think about goin' ta Bayou Rose."

"How could I go even if I wanted to? Ya took mah keys ta Lillian." Lillian was the name of her vintage lavender convertible.

"Fer your own good, darlin'."

Bull puckies! "I know, sweetie. Well, I gotta go pee."

"Okay, I'll pick ya up at five on Saturday. Love ya!"

"Love ya back," she said.

Wonder where I hid that second set of car keys?

Chapter Nineteen

It always comes back to sex . . .

Samantha's cell phone kept ringing all day. Some of the callers left voice messages, some didn't, but she saw their caller IDs.

There were seven voice messages from Nick that went from polite to not-so-polite. Everything from, "Hey Samantha. Nick here. Just touching base. Give me a call when you can" to "You didn't call me back. I stopped by your house, and no one was there. Where are you, darlin'?" to "I'm really getting pissed" to "This is important, dammit. Don't push me too far, I'm warning you" to a bunch of swear words that included something about a "stupid bitch."

Her father Bruce called, too. He was still at a conference in Los Angeles where Nick apparently had him pulled from a meeting to ask about Angus's whereabouts. "Nick has been calling me. What's Angus done now?" Her father was clearly beyond annoyed. "I swear, I'm done bailing that boy out of one scrape after another. I also got a call from someone named Jimmy Guenot. Do you know who that is? Florie claims he's the head of the Dixie Mob in Southern Loo-zee-anna, but I can hardly credit that." Florie would be Florence, Bruce's fifth and current wife, the one who had been a superintendent of women's prisons. She ought to know.

There were also a number of calls from the Starr Foods headquarters (Nick had probably been bugging them there, too.), the foundation office, two of her neighbors, and the rescue farm that wanted to know if she could foster two more pets . . . a pet python "that is really cute," and a bunch of gerbils "that are no trouble at all." Even under normal circumstances, she wouldn't have taken either of those.

Her Aunt Maire, the one with the pink obsession, said on her voice mail, "That cute ex-husband of yours stopped by. I gave him one of Larry's old pink ties." Larry was Maire's long deceased husband, the one who'd given her a pink diamond engagement ring that started this whole craze more than fifty years ago. "Did you know that Nickie loves pink as much as I do?"

Um, I don't think so. Nick would only love pink if money suddenly turned that color.

Aunt Dot, the butch lesbian, was blunt. "I kicked Nick Coltrane's slimy ass out of my office today. What did you ever see in that loser?"

I wish I knew!

Her grandfather called, too, on another subject. He apparently hadn't been contacted by Nick. Yet. "Samantha, honey, I'm plannin' on takin' Louise Rivard ta that Le-Deux pool party on Saturday. It's her birthday. Will you be there? Luc is your lawyer, isn't he? Haven't seen you in ages, honey." Her grandfather Stanley Starr, founder of Starr Foods, was a good friend of Tante Lulu's. How good, she did not want to know.

Samantha was putting some linens on the new bed when she heard a ruckus coming from the second parlor. Lots of "Holy shits," puppies barking, cats screeching. Samantha finished straightening the bed and went out to see what was going on.

Lily Beth, sitting in a lawn chair in the hall, supervised while Angus and Daniel were putting all five puppies in wire travel crates, along with two of the cats, Garfield and Felix. Madeline watched the proceedings from the window seat, her posture daring anyone to try and put her in a cage. Axel, secure in his place with Samantha, bored with the proceedings, gnawed on a rawhide bone. Clarence was squawking so much his expletives ran together in one long scream, "HolyshitHolyshitHolyshit!" Emily emitted several distressed oinks as she kept following after her new best friend, Daniel. Apparently, they'd bonded on the trip to the pet shrink.

"*What* are you doing?" she asked Daniel.

He didn't even stop. Instead, he and Angus continued carrying the crate with five puppies out into the hall, through the front door, across the gallery, and down the steps to the waiting pickup truck with the open tailgate. He did explain over his shoulder, though, as she followed after him, "I'm taking matters into my own hands. Decreasing the pet population."

"How?" She put her hands on her hips and glared at him. "You better not be thinking about putting them down."

After arranging the one cage in the truck bed, Daniel turned on her, wiping perspiration from his forehead with a forearm. "Oh, you of little faith!" He chucked her under the chin and walked back up the stairs. "Do you really think I'm that heartless?"

"No, but . . ."

"I'm taking the three puppies to those people who already agreed to adopt them. The other two puppies and the two cats will go to folks I know who are in need of a pet."

"Like who?"

"Let's just say I'm pulling in some chits."

"Daniel! You can't just push pets on people."

"Wanna bet."

"Do you want me to go with you?"

"No. It's best that you stay out of sight. Just give me the addresses. I'll go myself. On the way back, I might stop at the cancer center."

What need did he have to stop at the medical center? Did it have something to do with that little girl? Or some work he's doing there? Or maybe one of the nurses is a girlfriend.

"On the other hand, I'm pretty scruffy. Maybe tomorrow. In any case, if I'm not back by eight, don't worry."

"But . . . but I made dinner."

"Go ahead and eat . . . you and Lily Beth and Angus. Save some for me." He seemed to think of something else, which caused him to smile. For a man who had been prone to frowning most of the time, he sure was smiling a lot now. "Maybe I'll bring some ice cream back with me."

"Uh . . . okay." She didn't see why ice cream would make him smile in such a mischievous way. Maybe he had a sweet tooth.

"Peach ice cream," he elaborated. "Tongue licking good!"

Whatever that meant. "Well, if we're picking favorites, I choose Ben & Jerry's Salty Caramel."

"That'll do, too." He waggled his eyebrows at her and licked his lips. More mischief!

Men! Honestly. They put innuendoes on the oddest things.

After a quick shower, she changed into classic black cotton, Calvin Klein boxers and an old, gray silk Alexander Wang tee that she'd had for ages. She would have to wash clothes soon; she hadn't packed much last night. Oh, God! Had it only been one day that she'd been here, since this whole escapade began? It seemed like a week.

She shook her head to clear it of these reminders of the mess she was in. It was still hot and muggy, which caused her hair to frizz up; so, she pulled it off her face and scrunched the mass into a knot on top of her head, leaving her face and neck blessedly cool, or relatively so.

Samantha ate with Lily Beth and Angus at about six. The gumbo turned out delicious, especially with a frozen baguette she put in the oven (She'd kept the door shut with some duct tape), cold sweet tea (thanks to the new, glorious fridge), and the last of Tante Lulu's beignets for dessert.

While they cleared the table and washed the dishes, they talked. Lily Beth was worried about Nick finding her, about how big and clumsy she was becoming, about her constant heartburn, about the approaching birth, and about what she would do with the baby once it was born. She still hadn't decided whether she would keep the baby, which she would like to do but would be difficult if she resumed her education, or give the baby up for adoption. Angus wasn't worried at all, which was a worry in itself; he trusted that she and Daniel would handle everything.

Lordy, Lordy! as her grandmother used to say. "We should know more tomorrow after Luc and John LeDeux have spoken with the authorities. Why don't you go rest, Lily Beth," she suggested. "The new bed is guaranteed to be more comfortable than the air mattresses. I'll finish up here."

Lily Beth accepted the offer, gladly, and waddled off.

To Angus, Samantha said, "Be careful what you say or do on that damned computer of yours. Maybe the mob could put a trace or something on it. I saw them do that on *NCIS* one time."

Angus poo-poohed the idea. "My laptop is secure, believe me. As for Jimmy Guenot and his mob, they don't know a computer cache from money cash. I once told Jimmy that I had five gigabytes on my flash, and he asked me how the hell I got pig bites on my ass."

"Still, be careful."

It was nine o'clock before Daniel returned, and he didn't have any ice cream. Darn it! He didn't have any animals with him, either, which she supposed was a good thing. She would ask him for details later.

He looked beyond exhausted. The white T-shirt he'd donned this morning was plastered to his chest and back with sweat and covered with animal hair. He had scratch marks on his forearms. A nighttime stubble covered his face.

She met him in the front hallway, where she noticed that everyone, people and animals, seemed to have settled down for the night. The pocket doors to the front parlor were closed, but the low sound of a movie streamed from Angus's laptop. She thought she could hear Lily Beth snoring.

From the second parlor, where the pocket doors were also closed, Clarence was calling out his usual expletives, but the other animals must be sleeping. Someone needed to teach the bird something new. It was amazing to her that the animals who had insisted on sleeping with her at home were content together here behind closed doors.

Aaron had returned a few hours ago, ate, and went back out again, no explanation for where he was going, or when he'd be back. Not that she'd asked.

"You found homes for all the animals?" she asked Daniel.

He nodded.

"Everything okay at the cancer center."

"I decided to wait until tomorrow."

"Do you want to shower before you eat dinner?"

"Oh, God! Yes, please."

He trudged tiredly up the steps, and she went back to the kitchen to reheat the gumbo and rice. Everything was set out on the table when he came down fifteen minutes later.

"Feel better?" she asked.

He hadn't shaved, but he'd put on a clean white T-shirt, a pair of cargo shorts and rubber thongs. He smelled like Irish Spring. "A thousand times better," he said, sitting down on the bench at the table.

She sat down on the opposing bench and poured them both iced sweet tea in large Solo cups.

He ate ravenously, a big bowl of gumbo and rice, with four slices of the baguette, then asked for a second helping. "My mother prided herself on her gumbo. Even though she lived most of her life in Alaska, she remembered her Cajun roots," he told her conversationally. "This is almost as good."

Daniel had never talked about his mother, or his notoriously lecherous father, Valcour LeDeux, but now was not the time for questions. "Almost?"

"Equal, maybe," he said with a smile.

Increasingly today, she'd realized that his smile was a killer. The kind that made a woman think of things she probably shouldn't. Maybe she'd always known, but didn't want to admit her attraction.

"Anything new here?"

"Not much." She told him about all her unanswered phone calls. "I think Nick is starting to connect my sudden inaccessibility with Angus's disappearance."

"As long as he doesn't make a connection with me, or this plantation, you should be safe."

"I feel really guilty about getting you involved in all this."

"I can take it. My shoulders are wide."

"I noticed," she said, before she could bite her tongue.

He smiled again, and this time the impossibly sexy dimple emerged.

"I never thought that my initial offer to help Angus would spiral out of control like this." She was circling the rim of her cup with a forefinger, nervous for some reason. Maybe because of the way Daniel was staring at her so intently.

"Would you have refused to help him if you knew?"

She barely hesitated before answering, "No. I couldn't have turned him, or Lily Beth, away."

"So, you deal with it."

"'If life gives you lemons, make lemonade'?"

"Something like that. Or 'if life gives you lemons, add some salt and tequila'?"

They both smiled at each other then.

"Oh, I forgot," he said suddenly. "I talked to Luc on the way back. He'll be coming here tomorrow, about nine. He's bringing a couple FBI agents with him. John will come, too, with the local sheriff. They might want to post some officers around the property, or at the least have officers pass here often on rounds. The other alternative is a safe house."

She groaned. "It's going to be chaos here. Even more so than it is now."

He couldn't argue with that. He was staring at her again in that strange way.

"We should probably go to bed . . . I mean, you look totally beat. Did you sleep at all last night? Sleep is what you need. Me, too, though I don't know if I can sleep with all this stuff running around in my head."

"I have a solution," he said, taking her hand in his, the one whose forefinger had been nervously stroking the Solo cup.

A zing of apprehension raised all the fine hairs on her body. Or was it pleasure at that mere tactile feel of skin on skin?

Still holding her gaze, with her one hand in his, joined in the middle of the table, the thumb caressing her wrist, he suggested, "Let's go to bed together."

"What . . . what do you mean?" She tried to yank her hand away, but he held it tighter. In fact, he tugged her forward so that they both leaned into the table.

"You know exactly what I mean."

The heat that filled her cheeks betrayed her. "You mean, you want sex."

"Oh, yeah."

"Daniel, you're clearly exhausted. You are not up for this. Not tonight."

"Oh, I'm up all right. I've been up all day," he said, deliberately misreading her.

I stepped into that one. "So, any woman will do."

"No. I want *you*."

"Why?"

He shrugged. "Why not?"

"You don't even like me. You've made that more than obvious ever since I met you."

"I like you now."

A thrum of something began to beat in her breasts and low in her belly. An erotic pulse. "What is it, exactly, that you're suggesting?"

"Anything. And everything." He used his free hand to wipe across his face. "Listen, don't make a big thing about this. I want you. I'm pretty sure you want me. We're not talking about forever. You want a big family, I don't want even one child. But we can still enjoy each other."

No children reminded her of Nick. "Have you had a vasectomy?"

"Hell, no! But that doesn't mean I ever want to bring a child into this world. *Ever.*"

"A one-night stand then, that's what you're suggesting?"

A grin twitched at his lips. "I wouldn't put it exactly like that. I doubt this whole situation, with you and your gang trapped here, will be over in one day or night. It could be a week, or more."

"So, a one-week stand?"

"Semantics."

"An affair? For the duration of my stay?"

"A mutually agreeable affair, until one of us calls a halt. No hard feelings. Not even a break-up because there would be no real relationship to begin with."

Men! They thought women could turn sex on and off with no emotional involvement. It was out of the question, of course. She had her pride.

Sensing her hesitation, he told her, "I've been thinking about you. Fantasizing. All day. Last night, too. It's driving me crazy. I . . . want . . . you."

"Like those sex dreams we shared?"

"Worse. No, better." He went on then to describe in graphic detail the sex fantasies he'd been entertaining throughout the day, all of which starred her. One of them involved ice cream, warm fudge topping, and sprinkles. And bananas!

She tried to hide the fact that she was shocked . . . and, yes, turned on . . . by remarking as calmly as she could, "Sounds messy."

"Doesn't it!" he said, as if messy sex were a good thing.

Then he elaborated on an outdoor sex fantasy. No way to hide her body secrets in the bright sunshine, he told her, because he was looking at her. Everywhere! They were lying on a grassy field, or a meadow. And the things he did to tickle her with petals of wildflowers! But then she'd been showing him how to weave a flower chain around his favorite body part.

Samantha couldn't help but blush. "You certainly are creative."

"I've had years to practice. Nothing else to do when you're retired with nothing else to pass the time."

"Uh-huh," she said.

Then he told her about his other sex fantasies involving animal furs (fake ones, of course), nude dancing, and ankle bracelets. He seemed to have a thing about the sleep outfit she'd had on yesterday evening . . . the silk pants and camisole top; they featured in lots of his scenarios. The most interesting to her was the one where she was stretched out on a bed, her freckled nude body a pure temptation against the white background of the sheets. Cascades of auburn hair (he said red, but she knew it was auburn, aka Mahogany Fire by Charles Max) were spread around her and on her. Her lips were cherry red. In essence, she looked like a sex goddess. His words, not hers.

Imagine that! Me, a sex goddess!

"So, what do you say? Wanna play?"

She was stunned speechless. Of course, she was interested. But should she? Could she?

"Just think about it," he said, standing. "I need to go over to the *garconniére* to check on the cats and lock up. Aaron won't be back tonight."

And just like that, he was gone. Leaving her stunned and so turned on she squirmed on the bench.

But then, she narrowed her eyes. The teaser! The cool manner with which he'd made such a hot suggestion.

He'd probably done it on purpose to rattle her. Probably thought she was such a prude that she'd go hide under a sheet somewhere.

It was a challenge.

And she'd never backed down from a challenge before, even though she'd never had one quite like this.

Did she have the nerve?

Would she be making a fool of herself?

Who cared!

Boy, did Daniel have a surprise coming!

Chapter Twenty

S *he showed him! . . .*

Daniel made sure the house was secure and did a final check on Samantha's animals. He even kissed the pig. No, not on the lips, but on top of its adorable head.

I can just hear Aaron mocking me. So, sue me! I've developed an affection for Porky Pig's needy, mini cousin.

No way would he attempt to kiss Maddie, though; the cougar cat would probably scratch his eyes out. Nor Axel who needed a bath after rolling around outside in something that smelled like chicken shit. The pig smelled better than the dog did. But then, Daniel was beginning to think pigs got a bad rep. Small, potbellied ones, anyhow.

And, yes, he knew what chicken shit smelled like because Aunt Mel had once had the bright idea of a chicken coop in their backyard. A *heated* chicken coop since the birds would have frozen their feathery asses off in an Alaska winter. They had lots of poultry to eat that year when his mother discovered that the electric bill had sky-rocketed, that chickens made a lot of noise, especially when she was trying to sleep, and that Daniel and Aaron made piss-poor chicken shit shovelers.

Those were the days! he thought, with a sigh. It was at odd moments like this that he missed his mother most.

Would Aunt Mel want to have chickens here, if she came? He decided that he didn't really care, one way or the other. Hell, he'd become used to a foul-mouthed cockatoo, barking dogs, narcissistic cats, and a depressed pig. What did one more species matter? Look what he'd conceded for Samantha's sake. *Whatever Samantha wants, Samantha gets.* Too bad she didn't want him. At least, he didn't think she wanted him.

Thank God he'd been able to get rid of . . . find good homes for . . . the five animals today. Aside from the three adoptees Samantha had lined up, one of the nurses at the cancer center that he'd helped move one day from an apartment to a cottage with her toddler son (a leukemia survivor) now had a "cute" little puppy. Remy LeDeux and his big adopted family had a puppy *and* a cat named Garfield. Remy hadn't been home, but his wife Rachel had, and several of their kids. Daniel would probably be hearing from Remy later. And then there was the fisherman who'd sold them several truckloads of crushed shells for the driveway; Henri now had a new boat cat named Felix.

As he climbed the front staircase, he chuckled to himself as he recalled the shocked expression on Samantha's face when he'd made his sexual proposition. She was no doubt hiding in one of the six bedrooms on the second floor where Lily Beth's air mattress had been moved. Aaron's bed was his tonight, he'd called dibs on it earlier today.

He'd been teasing about the friends-with-benefits, one-week-stand sex, of course. Sort of.

No, he'd been serious.

Semi-serious.

Testing the waters, so to speak.

Samantha's waters.

That is crude, even for me. Blame it on sexual deprivation syndrome.

He still had the half hard-on he'd been carrying around all day when he thought about her, which had been a lot. He might have to take care of business himself if he wanted to get any sleep.

With a jaw-cracking yawn, he opened the door to Aaron's bedroom and went stone still.

The room was illuminated not with the overhead light or the bedside lamp, but instead by a dozen different candles of all shapes and sizes. Aaron must have kept a stash for emergencies . . . or seduction purposes. Tonight they were clearly for seduction.

Samantha lay on the white sheets of the bed, her arms extended over her head, one knee raised. Her red hair, which had been in a knot atop her head a short time ago, was now spread over the pillows and on her shoulders. She'd even got the lips right. Cherry red.

Did he mention she was nude? Skin-baring, freckles-glaring, eyes-beckoning. And, man, was she beckoning, with that little Mona Lisa smile! But she was also embarrassed, he could tell by the way she blushed. Or was that a sexual flush heating her face and neck?

He'd thought to shock her with his sexual fantasies, but she'd hoisted him on his own . . . well, you know what. And he was glad of it!

His half hard-on went instantly hair-trigger, full tilt boogie hard and aching. He put a hand to himself. *Slow down, Trigger*, he told himself. He might have even said it out loud, so disoriented was he by this wonderful surprise. He had enough sense, though, to begin to pull his T-shirt over his head and toss it to the floor. He toed off his bath thongs and kicked them aside. One of them shot out the open French doors onto the balcony.

He was still frozen in place, just inside the doorway.

"Did I get it right?" she asked in a voice husky with what he hoped was arousal. Her nipples were erect if that was any indication. Delicious pink nubs atop mounds the size of grapefruit halves. Just right.

The red curls between her thighs seemed to glisten with moisture. But that might be due to the flickering candlelight, or wishful thinking on his part.

"Perfect," he said in an equally husky voice, and no doubt at all that his was due to arousal, which became apparent when he shoved down his shorts and briefs together to puddle at his feet. If she had any doubts, she could tell by the erection that sprang forth. Full-blown, vein-popping, bead-showing arousal.

He stepped further into the room and slammed the door shut with a bare foot. They probably heard the sound all the way to Lafayette. The sound of a man crossing the line.

"If you keep gawking at me, I'm going to die of embarrassment." She groaned. "This is a bad idea."

"No, it's the best idea I've heard in a long time." He took several more steps 'til he was almost at the foot of the bed. He studied her body with fascination. Truly, Samantha had a body like no other woman. Maybe it was the freckles against the creamy skin. Maybe it was her long legs and small waist. Maybe it was the good parts . . . her perfect breasts, her nest of red curls, her full red lips, or her green eyes that sparked resistance even as she surrendered to him.

She closed her eyes and said, "Turn around so I can crawl out of bed and go hide in a closet."

He laughed. "Not a chance. Besides, there are no closets here."

"If you dare to laugh or make fun of me, I'm out of
here."

"Why would I mock you when I've just been handed
my number one fantasy?" With that, he knelt on the bottom edge of the bed and began to crawl up and over her,
like her cougar cat when on the hunt, except he had no
claws, just fingers that itched to explore.

Her eyes shot open as she felt his weight on the mattress and his movement on the bed.

He used his knees to separate her legs and arranged
himself between her open thighs. Chest to breast, belly to
belly, divining rod to the mother lode. Braced on his elbows, he looked down at her. "Cherry lips," he observed
and grazed his mouth over hers, a teasing whisper of a
kiss. He was trying his damnedest not to move too fast or
this fantasy would be over before it began.

"'Cherries in the Snow' by Revlon," she informed him
with a breathy nervousness. "A classic color. Supposed to
be kissproof."

"Ah, we should test that, shouldn't we?" And he did.
Thoroughly. He kissed her with soft, sweeping motions,
shaping her lips to a perfect fit with his. He kissed her
hard, demanding an equal response. He pressed his
tongue into her mouth and began a slow thrusting rhythm.
He encouraged her to explore his mouth as well by sucking on the tip of her tongue.

Once, he raised his head to study her already kiss-
swollen lips. "Yep. Kissproof."

"Good thing. I wasn't looking forward to returning
the lipstick to the beauty counter at Nordstrom's. Imagine
trying to explain your experiment. 'But he's a doctor,' I
would say. 'If he says the product is defective, then it
must—'"

He nipped her bottom lip to stop her nervous ramble. Then he resumed his kisses, and he didn't care if they were experimental or any other bloody thing. He liked kissing Samantha.

The whole time, he tried to keep the rest of his body still, but even so, he instinctively brushed his chest hairs back and forth across her breasts, teasing the nipples into rigid sentinels of aching pleasure. He knew they were aching because she moaned into his open mouth and arched her back to give him better access.

"Do that again," she said huskily.

He did.

Her cherry lips parted, and her green eyes glazed over.

Down below, he did not dare move. His throbbing penis rested along her female channel, on the outside, but hot damn wanted to be inside. He tried not to think about the primal yearning for intercourse so he could concentrate on other "matters" first. Like her ears, which appeared to be especially sensitive, and her breasts, of course, which were driving them both crazy, and the neat little inverted belly button he'd noticed before covering her with his body, along with the silk-like red curls that begged to be touched, along with the treasures they hid. He even wanted to explore the back of her knees and the arch of her narrow feet. Not that he had a knee or foot fetish. It was just that he'd discovered in his not-so-vast (compared to his brother) sexual experience, these were often-missed erotic zones on some women's bodies.

He raised himself so that he was kneeling between her legs, then leaned down to swipe his tongue between her breasts. He smiled and said, "I knew they would taste like this."

"What?"

"Your freckles."

"Oh, God!" She tried to cover herself with her hands,

which was impossible. She had freckles everywhere. "My ugly freckles!"

"No, no, no!" he chided. "No lowering your arms." He put them back where they had been before, the hands wrapped around the spindles in the headboard. Then he told her, "Your freckles are not ugly." It was amazing to him that a woman with so much business self-confidence could be so insecure about her body.

"Furthermore," he went on, "they're delicious." It was a sign of his melting brain that he could actually use the word *furthermore*. He continued, "Your freckles taste like honey with a ginger zing. I can't wait to taste them all."

"Fool!" she said, but he could tell that she was pleased. "That's my Honey Love Triple Milled Soap."

"Well, then it must be your freckles that add the ginger tones."

"Ginger, huh? You better watch out. Ginger has a bite to it. You could get ginger brush burns on your tongue."

"I'll risk it," he said, and began his tasty exploration.

Sometimes she giggled, sometimes she gasped, sometimes she admired his expertise, sometimes she expounded on his daring, but all the time he had her attention.

He kneaded her breasts and flicked the nipples with his thumbs before he put his mouth to one and sucked and licked then sucked again. By then she was flailing from side to side with one continuous, "Oh . . . oh . . . oh . . . oh . . ."

In response he moved to the other breast for equal ministration. He felt like saying, "Oh . . . oh . . . oh . . . oh!" himself.

And all the while, he kept having to return her hands to the headboard spindles, forcing her to be more vulnerable to his lovemaking.

When he kissed his way down the center of her body, he skipped over the place he most wanted to be. Instead, he stroked and caressed her from thigh to knees to toes and back up again.

At each spot along the way, he asked, "Do you like that?"

"How about that?"

"And this?" He tickled the back of her knees with his fingertips.

"Does this hurt?"

"Harder?"

"Enough!" she said finally, taking hold of his most precious body part and pulling him toward her.

"Careful, careful, careful," he gasped out.

"You can torture me more later. Or I'll torture you. But for now . . . DO IT!"

He tried to laugh but it came out as a choking gurgle because she was guiding him with precision into her body where the inner muscles were already convulsing around him into orgasm. She was tight and hot and he felt so good. In fact, he might have murmured, "So good! So good!" Or it might have been her.

But that was not the end of it. Not by a long stretch. They got down to the serious business of fucking then . . . or lovemaking, if he were capable of politeness.

With his outstretched arms braced on the mattress he thrust into her, then made a slow, slow exit, relishing the way her channel tightened on him, as if it didn't want to let go. In again, and out. Over and over.

She had her hands on his butt. Her feet were flat on the mattress with her knees raised high, bracketing him. She kept giving him directions, as if he was capable of following anything but reflex at the moment.

"Go slower."

"Faster."

"Stay. Stay, stay, stay."

"What was that you just did. Do it again!"

At one point, he rolled over on his back and she sat atop him like the redheaded goddess she was. Her lips were still cherry red, but he was incapable of telling her at the moment that the lipstick was in fact kissproof.

Then he was on top again.

Good thing it was a king-size bed. Otherwise, they would probably be on the floor by now.

But then he was the one to give orders when he said, "Now!" and slammed into her one last time. She cried out in a long affirmation of her orgasm while he arched his neck back and roared out his ejaculation.

He lay heavily atop her while they both attempted to bring their breathing back to normal. When he raised his head to look at her, he saw that she was as stunned as he was by the intensity of their lovemaking.

"Ain't lust grand? We might want to renegotiate our one-night . . . rather one-week . . . stand," he said. "I'm thinking I won't be satisfied for at least a month."

For some reason, what he'd considered a compliment displeased her. "Sorry, but just until this caper is over. That's all. It ends when I leave here," she said, but she wouldn't look at him as she spoke.

Trying to ameliorate what offense he must have committed, he leaned down to kiss her lightly on her face which was turned to the side and asked, "How do you feel about making love in a rain forest?"

Thankfully, she looked back at him and smiled. "As long as there are no animals in the trees. I draw the line at monkeys."

It wasn't the Amazon, exactly, but there was a snake . . .

For a brief moment, Samantha felt a twinge of hurt at Daniel's dismissal of their lovemaking. His remark pretty much said that she . . . they . . . could enjoy each other in casual encounters, but their "relationship" would be of short duration.

The only problem was, what had happened with him . . . the best sex of her life . . . hadn't felt casual to her.

Her pride was dinged, but, honestly, she wasn't sure she wanted more than that, either. In fact, she'd told him a short time ago that she didn't. He wasn't the forever kind of man she was looking for. One who would cherish her *and* a family.

Yeah, she'd thought this afternoon that she might be falling in love with Daniel, but she hadn't fallen so far yet that her heart could be broken. At least she didn't think so.

If men could separate lust from love, surely women could, too. *Cosmo*, and Hollywood, and the Internet certainly thought so.

Her reverie was broken by Daniel speaking. "Are you really balking about getting in a shower with me after what we just did?" He was leaning against the open doorjamb, arms folded over his chest. Nude.

She, on the other hand, was still in bed with a sheet drawn up to cover her intimate parts. He was probably laughing at her sudden modesty after the show she'd just put on.

"Of course not," she said, still clutching her linen protector. "I'm not sure I want to get my hair wet."

"Your hair is already damp from all this humidity . . . and our hot sex."

"What if someone sees us?"

"Who? Angus and Lily Beth have a bathroom downstairs. I doubt whether they're going to want to shower or take a bath in the middle of the night."

Did he have to be so logical?

"All right then. Stay in bed, and you can play out my second best fantasy."

"I've already heard all your fantasies."

"Not this one. I was saving it for another time and a more adventurous partner. Anyhow, there's this guy standing in doorway, very nonchalant, even though he's just had mind-blowing sex."

"Is he nude?"

"Oh, yeah."

"Horny?"

"As a bull during mating season."

She made a prissy tsk-ing noise.

"So, this guy is just standing there, watching this red-haired lady who is sitting in his bed. She doesn't know he's there. So, she drops the sheet she's been clutching like a virginal shroud and begins to pleasure herself."

"Whaaat?"

"First, she touches her own breasts. Lifts them up from underneath. Then she fondles her nipples, even tweaks them a little. Her breathing gets heavier."

"You're crazy."

"Thank you. She drops back onto the pillows and spreads her legs. Ever so slowly, her one hand moves lower and lower. Her hips rise and fall as she imitates the rhythm of sex."

"I'm not listening."

"She's panting now as she raises her knees and spreads wider. Her fingertips brush over the curly pelt between her legs. There's already a moistness there that—"

Samantha jumped out of the bed and stomped over to him. "All right. A shower sounds good."

"I thought you'd agree," he said, pinching her butt as she passed by, then taking her hand to lead her to the bathroom. Like she needed him to find the bathroom! He was probably holding on to her so she wouldn't run away.

"How many of those fantasies do you have tucked up your sleeve?" She looked pointedly at his bare arms, sans shirtsleeve, and she amended, "Rather, filed away in your wicked brain?"

"Hundreds."

"What?"

"Aaron and I used to memorize passages from *Penthouse Magazine*."

"How old were you?"

"Twelve."

"And you still remember?"

"Honey, there are some things a guy never forgets."

They were in the bathroom by now, and Daniel said, "Wait here."

The bathroom was one of those large ones like they didn't build today; there was so much wasted space. Because there was no closet, a white, two-door, tall chest held linens and bath accessories. The bathroom's size also accommodated a clawfoot tub, a pedestal sink, a dressing table and stool, and a man's shaving stand. And, of course, the ultra-deluxe shower that Aaron had installed. Totally out of sync with the historical nature of the mansion, but deliciously enticing on a hot Louisiana night. Any night, actually.

Daniel returned, carrying a bunch of lit candles from the bedroom. "That fluorescent overhead light isn't moody enough," he said, placing the candles at various spots around the bathroom.

"Moody? That's how everyone describes you. Doctor Moody."

"This is another kind of moody." He waggled his eyebrows at her.

Really, she'd never witnessed this playful side of Daniel, but then she'd never seen his sexy side either, except in her dreams. She liked them both.

"C'mon," he encouraged, drawing her into the large shower stall with him. "Welcome to my Amazon paradise." He pressed a button which caused a hazy green light to fill the space and highlight the tropical flowers and trees etched into the glass.

"Very nice. Do you have luscious fruits growing in your rain forest?"

"Only passion fruit," he said, glancing at her breasts, then downward, adding, "and bushes with lacy red foliage."

"And a snake," she pointed out, glancing at his penis which was erect again.

He laughed and asked, "Do you want hot or cold water?"

"Lukewarm at first, then cool."

"Whatever the lady wants."

There was a huge rainfall showerhead on top of the stall, at least two feet in diameter, and a number of wall-mounted showerheads designed to jet spray, pulse, wave, mist, and massage. There was even one called an aeration or champagne setting that was extra soft. Daniel demonstrated all of them on her. And then she reciprocated.

They laughed and shivered and moaned, with ecstasy, not pain.

He shampooed her hair, she shampooed his hair. They soaped each other down, and up.

Then he pulled out the *coup de gras* from under a bench seat on the far side of the shower stall, where some waterproof sex toys were hidden, including what appeared to be suction cup handcuffs. Who knew? Daniel bypassed those and other weird looking objects and took a sponge from its plastic wrapper. Holding her gaze, he inserted a bar of soap inside the sponge, then turned on a switch, which caused the sponge to vibrate. God bless technology!

"Are you game?" he asked, a mischievous twinkle in his eyes.

"Are you?" she countered with equal mischief.

By the time they finished and had to shower again, Samantha had come to orgasm three times, and Daniel roared to a climax so fierce he dropped to his knees afterward. Peering up at her as he fought for breath, he said, "You are a goddess."

And she felt like one.

Maybe he wasn't offering her everlasting love. But goddess? She'd take that. For now.

Chapter Twenty-One

And then the big gun arrived . . . in a lavender convertible? . . .

Long after Samantha fell asleep, Daniel lay awake. Thinking, thinking, thinking.

The lovemaking between them had been good. Spectacular, even. But the playful, teasing nature of the sex couldn't hide the intense feelings boiling under the surface, despite his best efforts to keep it light.

He almost wished he could be the kind of man Samantha yearned to settle with. One who could give her children and a secure home life. He couldn't see himself being that man. Best not to go down that road. Not just because the prospect of fatherhood, knowing all the medical catastrophes that hit the young, was anathema to him.

Samantha's life was here in Louisiana. All her family and friends were here. Whereas Daniel, until recently, had been living like a hermit, and he still wasn't settled. Maybe he would end up here at Bayou Rose Plantation, or somewhere else in the South, or maybe he would end up in Timbuktu. He was coming to the realization that it didn't matter where he lived, it was the people who made it home. Surprise, surprise. The rest of the world knew this, he'd just been slow to catch on. At first, he just went where Aaron did, but individuals here on the bayou were beginning to wear his defenses down.

And people weren't far off base when they referred to him as a grouch or Mister Moody. He had only recently begun to shake the depression that overwhelmed him.

A wuss, that's what he felt like. A big, fat pussy! Real men didn't obsess over the stones life threw in their path (i.e. a few kids dying of cancer, or rather, a lot of kids dying of cancer). Real men didn't hide out in a bayou fishing camp. Real men didn't get depressed.

What a load of bullshit, he told himself. Depression was a malady, same as any physical illness. As a doctor he should know better. As a dumb man, not so much.

For now, all he could offer Samantha was good sex, and plenty of it, with a dash of caring thrown in. Maybe that would be enough.

He finally fell asleep, and when he awakened, she was gone. Checking his wristwatch, he saw that it was only seven a.m. He'd slept like the dead for five straight hours, which was something he hadn't done in years. Too bad he couldn't write a prescription for that on his trusty Rx pad. "300 mg good sex." But then, someone would find out about it. He could see it now. He'd make the tabloid headlines for sure. Doctor self-medicating with sex! Then the bayou grapevine, aka Tante Lulu, would hear the news. She'd have him buried in St. Jude statues.

Once downstairs, he saw that the animals had been fed and watered, probably exercised, too, by the contented look of them all. He assumed that Samantha had also checked on Max and the new kittens, as well.

Emily immediately attached herself to him, rubbing against his pant leg. When she followed him to the back staircase leading to the kitchen, she oinked a few times, indicating that she didn't do stairs well. So, he picked up the pig and carried her down to the kitchen and set her on her short legs. She immediately waddled over to the table where she could beg for scraps.

Samantha was preparing scrambled eggs and toast for Angus and Lily Beth, who were already dressed for the day. Angus in clean cutoff jeans and a T-shirt that looked familiar. Yep, it was a Juneau "Beat Cancer" marathon shirt he'd gotten a few years back. And Lily Beth, looking better than she had since he'd met her, wore a blue Hawaiian print, tent-like sundress, what Aunt Mel used to call a muumuu. He had no idea where she'd come up with the thing since he hadn't seen her with a suitcase or anything last night. Maybe it was something Samantha owned, for the odd occasion when she was feeling bloated or something. Lily Beth's hair was pulled off her face into a single braid. Her skin carried that characteristic pregnancy glow, and her eyes were clear and sharp. The edema seemed to have disappeared. A day of rest had done wonders for her.

Samantha was looking bright-eyed and bushy-tailed, too, if he did say so himself. She wore tight black cropped jeans and a short-sleeved, white tailored blouse. It was the first thing he'd seen on her that didn't look like it came off a designer rack.

He caught her gaze and winked at her.

She blushed.

Man, oh, man! Women were so predictable. They could

rake a man's coals, screw him upside down and sideways, then be embarrassed at a mere wink. He loved it!

"I'm making a grocery list," she said, putting a plate of eggs and toast in front of him when he sat down. "I don't know how much longer we'll be here, but we're short on everything."

Daniel felt a foreboding at her mention of the duration of their stay. Was she already looking forward to the end of their "affair," if you could call it that? "We'll know more after Luc and the feds arrive. But, yeah, I can go to the grocery store later. I imagine you guys will be here for at least a few more days, unless the authorities insist you go into safe houses."

"I doan care what they say. I am not goin' inta a safe house. They'd probably put me in some godawful place lak Chic-ag-o," Lily Beth said in her Southern accent, which, frankly, made her sound rather dumb, not at all like the doctoral physics candidate she was. She must have guessed his thoughts because she added, "And someone needs to get the mail from mah office at the university. Mah teaching schedule fer the fall should be there by now. If I doan show up soon with lesson plans and evidence of research fer mah thesis, they'll cancel mah assistantship, permanently. And I gotta buy text-books fer two courses I'm takin'."

Daniel and Samantha exchanged glances. Had Lily Beth decided to give up her baby so she could continue her education, or did she have some plan that allowed her to do both?

"I could probably sneak in and out at night when there aren't many students around," Angus offered.

"No!" Daniel and Samantha said at the same time.

Aaron strolled in then, clearly just coming in from a night spent who-knows-where. He looked longingly at the food, and Samantha began to whip up more eggs and put bread in the toaster.

For a moment, Aaron stood in place, a frown furrowing his forehead as he studied Daniel, then Samantha. Then he grinned. "Hallelujah! The boy has fallen off the celibacy wagon!"

"Aaron," Daniel cautioned his brother. He and Aaron could sense certain things about each other that might not be apparent to others. Aaron knew what his twin had been doing all night, might have even shared some of the sensations. Too bad Daniel couldn't use the same twin detecting talent to find out what Aaron was doing every night.

Instead of teasing, Aaron addressed Samantha, "You better not hurt my brother, or you'll have me to answer to."

"Aaron!" Daniel said, louder this time.

And Samantha seemed puzzled. "How could I possibly hurt Daniel?"

"I'm just sayin'." Aaron smiled from ear to ear at Daniel before plopping down onto the bench next to Angus, and saying, "Great tats! I hear you're a computer genius. Can you help me get a virus off my laptop?"

"Sure," Angus said.

"You were probably watching too much porn," Daniel sniped.

"Could be," Aaron said agreeably, refusing to be baited. Daniel should take pointers from that lesson.

Aaron said he had to get ready for work, even as he wolfed down his eggs and toast.

"Don't you need to sleep first?" Daniel asked, which he should have known would be a mistake.

"I already slept," Aaron said, standing to stretch with a wide yawn, "although sleep is overrated, as you well know, bro."

"How come I'm bro only when you're leaving a mess for me to clean up?"

"That's because I'm your older brother."

"By two minutes."

Aaron shrugged. "Besides, this is your mess, not mine."

After Aaron left, Lily Beth remarked, "It's nice to see two brothers so close."

Which was true, despite their constant ragging on each other.

"My two brothers fought all the time."

They all turned as one to stare at Lily Beth. This was the first time they'd heard she had any family. Her parents died in a car accident last year and Daniel assumed . . . they all assumed . . .

Even Angus looked surprised.

"Lily Beth, you didn't tell us you have brothers," Daniel said.

"Didn't I? I have two. Paul and Vic."

"Do they know what's going on? What's happening with you and Angus? Why didn't you go to them for help?" Samantha asked, apparently not caring how insensitive that sounded at this point.

Daniel could see that the stress was getting to Samantha.

"Vic is in I-raq. Too far away ta help. And Paul is a minister in a really conservative church in Alabama. He would never approve of mah having a baby out of wedlock, or giving up mah baby ta Dr. Coltrane fer adoption."

Well, big fucking deal! Daniel thought. *It's okay that strangers get involved in your problem, but don't bother blood relatives.*

Lily Beth started to cry, realizing . . . a bit late, if you asked him . . . how her secret impacted all of them.

Softening at the tears, Samantha patted Lily Beth's shoulder and said, "That's all right, honey. You might have to contact them, though, depending on how things pan out."

"The authorities might insist on notifying them," Daniel guessed.

"No, I'd rather go ta jail or get beat up by Dr. Coltrane than go ta Paul."

Beat up? Is that what Nick threatened her with? Beat a pregnant woman? I've heard that Nick is a loser, but that is low, even for him.

"And I jist caint tell Vic, not when he's in such a dangerous place. Last time he got bad news, when his wife left him fer her gynecologist, he went out and got himself wounded, bless his heart." Lily Beth sobbed loudly now.

That is just great. A gynecologist screwing his patient, who in turn was screwing her husband while he was away at war! Women did that all the time. Otherwise, Dear John letters would have never been invented. But this is another doctor to add to Samantha's list of sleazeball physicians.

In fact, he saw Samantha's lip curl with disgust.

Angus gave Samantha and Daniel dirty looks for making Lily Beth cry and helped the heavily pregnant girl get up and walk outside with him. He was trying to reassure her with remarks like, "Don't worry. They can't make you call your brothers." Or "They're just old farts who don't know what it's like to be young." Or "We can always run away, except I don't have a car anymore."

Lily Beth sobbed louder.

Which left Daniel alone with Samantha in the kitchen, facing a bunch of dirty dishes, and an old-fashioned Philco radio on the counter suddenly playing some twangy Cajun version of "Jolie Blon." The radio only worked intermittently.

"Well, that went well," Samantha said.

"Did he really call us old farts?" Daniel said. "We're not that old."

"To them, we are."

"Bet he wouldn't call Aaron an old fart. It's probably because I'm so stodgy. Folks are always saying that about me," Daniel mused.

"I don't think you're stodgy," she said.

"That's because I gave you five and a half orgasms."

"You were counting?"

"Damn right."

"A half orgasm?"

"That time when I used my tongue to—"

"Never mind!"

They smiled at each other then, and his heart did a little flip-flop. Yeah, he knew how corny that sounded, especially for a doctor. But he did feel something. Suddenly, he knew that no matter how short-lived their affair turned out to be, it wouldn't be enough.

But there was plenty of time to think about that later. Instead, he said, "Wanna go back to bed and fool around?"

"That's the best offer I've had today."

Unfortunately, their window of opportunity closed before they had a chance to make it up the stairs. The hordes swooped down on Bayou Rose in the form of Luc and John LeDeux, a police chief and several deputies, the FBI, a bunch of muscle men in ATF T-shirts who looked like they could bench-press a bayou barge, and a "person-of-interest" whom one agent referred to as "a crazy old lady in a lavender convertible."

And then the posse arrived . . .

There were five FBI agents, several ATF operatives, the local sheriff and his deputy, a state trooper, and several men who didn't identify themselves. None of them wore uniforms. They sat around the kitchen table and on folding lawn chairs that had been brought inside, or they stood against the walls or in the doorways.

Samantha had never been involved with anything illegal before, and the scene, heavy on testosterone and legal power, was rather daunting. She wouldn't want to have any one of these guys after her.

Lily Beth and Angus had just finished telling their stories, again, and answering numerous questions along the way. Samantha had heard the tale so many times, she felt as if she could recite it herself, verbatim.

One of the agents was operating a tape recorder, and another was taking voluminous notes on a high-tech laptop that had Angus practically drooling with envy. Several times the men exchanged meaningful glances . . . meaningful to them, not to Daniel, Samantha, Angus, Lily Beth, or Tante Lulu.

Tante Lulu, no longer a "person of interest," was puttering around the kitchen counter making drinks and snacks while listening intently to every word being spoken, having interrupted only twice. The first time, to exclaim, "Holy Sac-au-lait! If Jimmy Guenot's brains was dynamite, there wouldn't be enough ta blow his fool nose. I know Jimmy's mama, bless her heart. Let me tell her what her boy's been up to, and she'll tie a knot in his tail lickedy split."

"Shhh!" her nephew John warned. "Let the experts handle it."

"Hmpfh! That ain't the bayou way."

The other time she interrupted, it was when Angus was telling them about Nick's baby-selling scheme. "I do declare, I never heard such nonsense! I got a pistol in mah handbag. I'm a good shot, too. Been practicin' on snakes in mah shower. Mebbe I should jist go shoot the rat. Bam, bam, bam!"

Everyone turned in shock to the senior citizen hit

woman, then turned to stare at her handbag sitting on the floor. It was big enough to hold a machine gun. John and Luc put their faces in their hands.

"Some men jist need killin'. Thass a legal defense in Loozeeanna, ain't it, Luc? Thass what Tee-John always sez."

Luc cautioned his aunt to keep her mouth shut or go home, in much gentler terms. After that, the old busybody remained silent, but her thoughts were clear on her expressive face. It didn't help matters that today she sported a Farrah Fawcett wig, white pedal pushers, orthopedic shoes with pink ruffled anklet socks, and a black shell top with the neon colored words *Hot to Trot* emblazoned across her little chest.

Samatha had known Tante Lulu for a long time and was no longer surprised by anything she said or did. Not so much others. At first sight of the bayou yenta, Brad Dillon, the head honcho from the FBI . . . a good-looking, crew-cutted guy from D.C., wearing a gray suit, blue and gray tie, and white dress shirt . . . had gone wide-eyed with surprise. But then he'd chuckled and said, "Now I've seen it all."

That was before he'd seen Maddie.

"There's a frickin' cougar in your parlor!"

Or the pig that followed Daniel around like a lovesick swain, or whatever you called a female admirer.

"I've heard of guys who date pigs, but come on!"

Of course, Clarence didn't help matters with his constant refrain of "Holy shit!"

Which did not amuse the FBI agent, at all. "I'm a crack shot with clay pigeons, you know? One bird or another, makes no difference to me," he told Clarence up close and personal, nose to beak. And he was serious.

Brad was a no-nonsense kind of guy, barely cracking a smile, except with Samantha with whom he was a little bit flirty. To Samantha's delight, Daniel acted jealous, making sniping remarks about Brad under his breath, such as, "Probably sucks up steroids like lollipops." Or "Didn't anyone tell him the fifties are over with that haircut." Or "If he winks at you one more time, I'm gonna puke."

"There are two separate cases here, the only link between them being Angus, as a gambler with loan sharking issues to the Dixie Mob, and Angus working with Dr. Coltrane in illegal baby trafficking."

Angus cringed, but Luc pressed his arm in assurance.

"Despite their differences," Brad went on, "we've got to act quickly on both cases. Normally, I would put you two in safe houses until all the legal proceedings are completed." He was looking pointedly at Lily Beth and Angus. Ignoring their obvious displeasure, he added, "But there's no time for that."

Uh-oh! Why is there no time? Samantha wondered.

"Instead, we'll post guards here 24/7. One inside and one outside."

More unwanted guests for Daniel! That was proven truc when Daniel complained, "But there are no more beds here for . . . guests." He was probably picturing more trips to the furniture warehouse.

Brad glared at Daniel for interrupting, but explained. "The agents will rotate shifts. It won't be the same person all the time. And none of them will sleep here, or they'll know why they call me the buzz saw." That last was probably a joke, FBI humor, but no one laughed.

Daniel nodded, uncaring that Brad could do what he wanted, with or without Daniel's approval. Samantha was about to warn Daniel to be careful but Brad had already moved on.

"Okay, two cases, two separate but overlapping crimes. The Dixie Mob first. Fred Olsen from our Baton

Rouge office is already heading up that investigation. Fred, you want to explain the situation to these folks?"

Fred, about fifty years old, with steel gray hair, wearing a lime green polo shirt and khakis, looked like he would be perfectly at home on a country club golf course.

Scotsmen were avid golfers and the men, and women, of the Starr family were scratch golfers, except for Samantha who couldn't see the sport in spending half a day hitting a little ball with a stick. Nick was a good golfer, too, more for the networking possibilities. Not that golf had anything to do with the current situation.

"We're already well into an investigation of the Guenot branch of the Dixie Mob," Fred told them. "In fact, we expect to make the arrests later today or tomorrow morning. We have enough evidence to put the bunch of them away for decades. That's confidential information, by the way."

"Does that mean, you don't need me?" Angus asked hopefully.

"As you know, Mister Starr, your lawyer negotiated a deal for you," Fred said, clearly not a happy camper about the deal or Angus's question.

At first, Samantha didn't realize that the FBI agent was referring to Angus when he said, "Mister Starr."

Angus glanced over at Luc with surprise.

Luc shrugged. "I didn't have a chance to tell you yet."

"We'll take all your testimony, Mister Starr, but we won't use it in open court filings. A grand jury presence might be required, but that remains to be seen . . . and negotiated," Fred explained. "However, we will require you to give us detailed intel on the Guenot compound, and you'll come into my office this afternoon to look over some mug shots. We consider your information to be corroborating evidence."

Angus did a little fist pump in the air, then asked in a

way too aggressive voice, "And what do I get from this deal? Will I still have to pay Jimmy back the money he loaned me, with interest?"

Fred bristled at Angus's tone, and Luc stepped in to elaborate. "Criminals, even those in prison, have long arms. If Guenot and his gang know you have anything to do with their conviction, they might have hit men on the outside come after you. You'd be looking over your shoulder for life."

Angus's Adam's apple bobbed a few times at that prospect, and he wasn't looking quite so aggressive.

"So, your benefit, young man, is anonymity," Fred said sternly, "or as far as we can keep it anonymous."

Angus nodded his acceptance.

"That doesn't mean that you won't have to testify against Dr. Coltrane, however. Same goes for you, Ms. Starr, and you, Ms. Fontenot," Brad interjected. "Besides, Mister Starr, you could still be arrested for your involvement in the baby-selling scheme. Your hotshot lawyer hasn't negotiated you out of that one."

"Yet," Luc mouthed to Angus.

"As for the money to be repaid, no, you would not be handing over any money to the mob, but you might be handed a sizeable fine by the courts."

Angus appeared duly chastised.

"Does anyone have any questions about the mob case before we move on?"

No one did.

Samantha wasn't sure what she would have to add to the baby-selling case against Nick, but she certainly could testify about his sleazy character. Lily Beth, on the other hand, was dismayed. "Mah brothers will find out," she wailed.

Brad was unmoved, probably figured it was her fault for getting involved with Nick to begin with. "It might be advisable for you to contact them yourself, rather than hearing your name on the news."

"Easy fer y'all ta say!" Lily Beth whined. "If this gets in the newspaper or on TV, everyone will know at the college. Mah career will be over."

Ninety-nine percent of the people in the room wondered why a girl with her seeming intelligence didn't think of that before.

"Don't worry, honey. We can figure that all out later," Samantha soothed Lily Beth. But she had no idea how.

Chapter Twenty-Two

Trouble always comes in threes . . . in their case, fours, or fives . . .

The meeting was far from over, Samantha soon realized.

Brad had introduced everyone in the room initially. Now, he reintroduced one of them. "Theodore 'Sonny' Sonnier, also from our Baton Rouge field office, is in charge of the Coltrane case. I'll let Sonny give you a status report."

Sonny was young, under thirty, long-haired, and built like a bodybuilder in a tight black wicking shirt tucked into belted jeans. He wore wire-rimmed glasses, and a cell phone was clipped to his belt. He was the one who'd been pounding away expertly on a laptop. Rambo meets Steve Jobs.

"This baby sellin' scheme, she is news ta us," Sonny

said in a deep Cajun accent, "but the minute Luc contacted us, we began investigatin'. Bank records. Births. Adoptions. Background checks. With the evidence you two have given us t'day," Sonny looked pointedly at Angus and Lily Beth, "it's still not enough ta put the bastard away. We'll need your assistance, Ms. Starr."

What? Me?

Seeing her confusion, Sonny went on, "We'd lak ya ta contact yer ex-husband and set up a meetin', soon as possible. We'll wire ya up, and help ya rehearse what ta say. If we kin get Mr. Coltrane on record, admittin' his crimes, then his arrest is a done deal."

Samantha was stunned. "But why me? Wouldn't Angus or Lily Beth be the better persons to get him to incriminate himself." She took one look at Lily Beth's horrified face as she clutched her belly, and immediately amended, "I mean, shouldn't Angus be the one to confront Nick?"

Sonny shook his head. "That's just what Dr. Coltrane wants. To get his hands on Mister Starr. We cain't take that chance."

But they could take a chance with me? "I wouldn't know what to say."

"Not ta worry. We'll prep ya, good and proper."

"I'm not that good an actress."

"Do ya wanna see Coltrane behind bars?"

"More than you can imagine."

"Well, then, *chère*, yer ship cain't come in if ya doan send out any boats."

"And I'm the ship?"

"*Mais, oui!* Do ya agree ta participate?"

"Yes," she said.

"Hell, no!" Daniel said at her side. He'd been stunned speechless apparently on first hearing the proposal that she be the bait. Now, he was more angry than stunned. "Samantha's been a spectator at best in this whole mess.

It would be too dangerous to put her in close proximity to her slimeball loser of an ex-husband."

Even Samantha was surprised at the vehemence of Daniel's reaction.

"I assure you, we will have her back every step of the way," Sonny assured Daniel.

Who was not assured. "If she goes, I go with her," Daniel insisted.

"Out of the question," Sonny insisted right back. "And, furthermore, if Ms. Starr is unable ta get the needed evidence in her meeting with Mr. Coltrane, we might need Mr. Starr ta set up his own meetin', pretend ta be comin' back ta work fer the good doctor."

Angus groaned, no more an actor than she was an actress.

The calmer voice of Luc intervened. "Let's set this aside for now. We can discuss Samantha's involvement later. Or Angus's. Go on, Sonny."

"There's a reason why we have ta act quickly with Dr. Coltrane," Sonny said, still pursuing the same subject. "Under other circumstances, we could take our time investigatin' and interviewin' witnesses. But perps like Dr. Coltrane skip town the minute they get a whiff of the law on their tails. Doctors, no matter their backgrounds, are able ta relocate easily ta other countries that bar extradition. Besides, desperation makes even the sanest criminal do bad things, and Dr. Coltrane is desperate, and worried. We already know that."

Sonny seemed to have an opinion of doctors similar to Samantha's. But more important, what did he mean about Nick being desperate? That sounded ominous. What did he know that she didn't?

"All the more reason not to involve Samantha," Daniel persisted. "Or Angus, who has the brain of a computer and the common sense of a duck."

"Hey!" Angus protested.

"I appreciate your concern, but I can speak for myself, Daniel." Samantha patted Daniel on the arm to ameliorate her words.

He shrugged her arm away and glared at her.

"We haven't had a chance to inform you yet, Ms. Starr," the state trooper spoke up for the first time, "but Nawleans police reported a break-in at your house last night."

Samantha gasped at that news.

"Not a lot of damage, but someone was clearly looking for something other than valuables. Broken window. Drawers pulled out. Pages ripped out of an address book. PC computer hard drive missing. Desk overturned. That kind of thing." The trooper was reading from a small pocket notebook. Then, he looked up. "No fingerprints. The perp knew enough to wear gloves."

Samantha frowned. It was probably Nick trying to figure out where she might be and whether she was hiding Angus. That theory proved true when the trooper added, "The only thing that seems to be missing is a picture that must have been hanging in your bedroom. Nothing but an empty hook on the wall."

Daniel gave her a "See, I was right!" look.

"Definitely Nick," she said. "The painting that hung there was a rather valuable, antique miniature by a Southern artist. A wedding gift from my mother that Nick wanted, but didn't get in our divorce settlement."

"Ya have photographs of the picture, yes?" Sonny asked.

She nodded. "For insurance purposes."

"Well, if we find it in his possession, or discover evidence of its sale on the open or black market, we kin nail him fer that, too, guaranteed," Sonny said. "And that's another issue ya could discuss with him durin' yer meetin' . . . the break-in."

Daniel made a sound under his breath that sounded like a growl.

For more than an hour, they continued to discuss the case, while Tante Lulu handed out cups of sweet tea and beignets she'd made early this morning, probably at the crack of dawn. She was in her element! Feeding the masses.

"These beignets, they are almos' as good as the ones from Café du Monde, yes," Sonny complimented her.

"Bite yer tongue, boy. I was making beignets before that restaurant opened."

Which was highly unlikely . . . in fact, impossible . . . since that famous New Orleans restaurant had opened during the Civil War.

Lily Beth went up to take a nap, still distraught over the prospect of her brothers discovering the trouble she was in. And Angus went off with police officers in a van with blackened windows to check out some mug shots and give more details as he could remember on the Guenot compound. Luc insisted on going along with his client, which made Samantha anxious. Angus must not be safe from the law, yet.

Before he left, Luc took Samantha aside and said, "The Fibbies will try to talk you into meeting with Nick. Don't agree to anything without me present. I'm not saying you shouldn't do it. Just don't feel coerced. They need you more than you need them."

She nodded, feeling a little shaky without him being there. But then, Angus must be feeling even worse, going to a police station.

John went out to show the police and several agents the property so they could set up a plan for surveillance.

Brad and Sonny stayed behind, presumably to discuss Samantha's possible meeting with Nick. And Daniel wasn't moving anywhere while that was still a possibility.

This whole debacle wasn't as over as she'd thought it would be when the feds rode in on their white chargers.

One of the officers came back shortly to report, "There's a freakin' alligator farm next door. If the mob gets in here and breaks down that fence, we're gonna be overrun with about two hundred of those gators."

Samantha didn't bother to tell them that gators wouldn't travel that far over land, away from the bayou, or their water habitat on the neighboring property. Whatever! Let them squirm a little.

"Two . . . two . . . hundred?" Brad sputtered.

"The owner of the farm, a woman, cussed us out and raised a rifle, warning us not to trespass. Flashed us a license to carry and told us to get the hell away from her property."

"That would be Delilah Dugas. Ain't she sumpin'?" Tante Lulu commented to no one in particular. "Sometimes she enters alligator wrestlin' contests. I wish I could wrestle alligators. Well, I could wrestle mah pet alligator, Useless, but he ain't vicious or nothin'. At least his breath doan smell lak dead animals. All Useless eats is Cheez Doodles."

Samantha noticed that the old lady, as she talked, had been adding things to the grocery list Samantha had started this morning. Wait until Daniel saw the size of the thing! It looked like there were two more pages.

Brad's jaw dropped open at Tante Lulu's words, but Sonny just chuckled, knowing that anything could happen in the bayou. And he was no more worried than she was that they'd have gators knocking at their door.

Daniel's cell phone rang then. When he checked the caller ID, he stood and apologized, "Sorry. I've got to take this call." He went over to the other side of the long kitchen. While Brad and Sonny compared notes, and Tante Lulu stood before the open fridge taking inventory, Samantha could overhear one side of the conversation.

"George," he said. "What's up?"

"Oh, no!"

"And her father can't get here in time?"

"I told you I'd pay for his motel."

"Dammit!"

"What can I do?"

"Yeah, I'll be there as soon as possible." He glanced at his wristwatch. "Is an hour too long?"

"I'll make it in a half hour."

"Okay. Listen, tell Molly to hold on. Tell her I have a special present for her."

"You don't want to know."

Daniel clicked off and stared grimly off into space before coming over to tell her, "I have to go to the cancer center right away. Come out in the hall a minute so we can talk in private."

Brad looked up with interest but didn't stop them from leaving the kitchen. Tante Lulu was sitting at the table with a mug of coffee, entertaining Sonny with a story about the Bayou Black Sonniers, his distant cousins, who used to trap muskrats and squirrels in the nude. "One time Yancy Sonnier almos' got his wienie caught in a trap. Hoo-boy! Scared the livin' daylights outta the boy! Took ta wearin' a pie tin in his jockeys."

Out in the hallway, which led to the storage rooms and out to the ground floor, front verandah, Daniel took her in his arms and kissed her. Just what she needed after a harrowing morning! And a good reminder of the night they'd just shared.

The kiss was short and sweet, unfortunately.

"What's happening at the cancer center?" she asked.

"There's a bit of a crisis with the little girl you saw there."

"And they need you?"

He shrugged. "Need is too strong a word. I can help. I'm going to take some cell phone pictures of the kittens to show Molly and tell her she gets her pick when she gets better."

"Will she? Get better?"

"It's fifty-fifty."

"What's that about her father?"

"He lives in Savannah and has no place to stay when he gets here."

"I thought there were accommodations. Temporary housing solutions for parents of sick kids."

"Her father is a convicted felon, armed robbery, out on probation. These places are overcrowded anyhow, and when push comes to shove, they'll take the person with a clean record first."

"And her mother?"

"Gone. Left with a boyfriend when Molly first got sick. A grandmother helps, but . . ." His words trailed off.

"Go. I'll make your excuses to Brad and Sonny. And, oh, wait a minute." She went back into the kitchen and got the grocery list.

When she came back and handed it to Daniel, he asked, "What's this?"

"I know you have other things on your mind, and you might not be in the mood after you leave the center, but just in case things go okay, would you mind? This is a little list of things you could get on your way back."

"Holy crap! I should have asked Aaron to leave the truck again."

"It's not that bad."

"Are you kidding? Ten pounds of rice? A half bushel of shrimp?"

"I think Tante Lulu is planning on making shrimp étouffée for dinner."

"For who? An army?"

"She means well."

"So did Attila the Hun. And how long is the old bat staying?"

"Now, be nice."

"I wish we could go back to bed and hide under the covers. I haven't had nearly enough of you." He nuzzled her neck.

"Likewise." She arched her neck to the side so he could nuzzle some more.

"A rain check?"

"For sure. Maybe you could dream up a couple more of your fantasies by then."

He grinned. "Or you could tell me some of yours."

They smiled at each other and wished they could be alone for a while.

"Later," she said.

"I'll hold you to that."

He left then, but not before extracting a promise from her. "Promise you won't go to meet Nick the Prick. Wait till I get back. We'll talk about it then."

She didn't exactly promise, but she leaned up to kiss him one more time, which he might have taken as a promise.

As soon as she was sure he was gone, she went back into the kitchen and addressed Brad and Sonny. "What do you want me to do?" She should probably wait until Luc, her lawyer, was with her, or until Daniel returned, but she just wanted this whole nightmare to be over.

After a half hour of rehearsals, Brad suggested that she call Nick to set up a meeting. They practiced lots of different scenarios. "If he says this, you say that." Or "If he says that, you say this." Sonny even wrote some notes for her to read on his computer while she was on the phone.

"When should I suggest that we meet?"

"Today. As soon as possible."

Panic began to set in. She was not ready for this. "Won't that seem strange to Nick, that I'm so anxious to meet with him? After all, we've been enemies for years now."

"Time is our enemy. The longer we wait, the more suspicious he will get," Brad told her.

"And a suspicious perp is a running perp," Sonny added to emphasize Brad's point.

Samantha insisted on calling Luc to get his advice before she committed. She put the call on speakerphone. After the agents made their case for an early meeting, Luc agreed to the plan, provided the agents contact him when they had a time and place set up so that he could be there, too. Once the police set up Angus in a viewing room, Luc said he could leave and come back to pick him up later. Or else, John could come and take Luc's place.

So, she hit Nick's number on her cell phone's list of contacts and left it on open speaker.

"Nick?"

"Samantha? Where the hell have you been? I've left a dozen messages on your voice mail."

"I know. I just got back in town. My cell phone was out of range until this morning."

"Where are you now?"

"At the airport."

"Well, come to my office right away."

"Why should I do anything for you?"

"C'mon, Sammie, don't you think it's time we call a truce?"

Calling me by a hated nickname doesn't sound like a truce to me. "A bit late for that, don't you think?"

"Better late than never."

"I'm not going to kiss and make up, if that's what you have in mind."

He laughed. "Far from it."

"We don't have to meet in person to make peace with each other. Do it over the phone."

"Uh-uh! Believe me, you'll want to know what I have to tell you, and it's got to be face to face."

She exchanged glances with Brad and Sonny. Could it be as easy as this? Did Nick want to confess all to her? Sounded too good to be true.

Tante Lulu murmured under her breath, "Dumb as dirt!"

Brad and Sonny glared her way and Tante Lulu made a zipping motion across her lips.

"I need to go home and shower first," Samantha told Nick.

"No, come here first."

He probably didn't want her to see the mess at her house, the mess he had made. "Is it really that important?"

"Yes."

"Nick, if this is about more of your frivolous lawsuits, forget about it. I'm not reinstating your alimony."

"It's not about that. This is something about . . . um . . . your family."

"*What?* Did something happen to my father? Or my mother?"

"No, no, no! Nothing like that. By the way, do you know where Angus is?"

"Angus? How do you know Angus?"

"Never mind. Just come. It's eleven-thirty now. When can you get here?"

"I don't know. Two? Three? I need to stop by Starr Foods headquarters first."

The FBI agents had warned her to allow at least two hours for them to wire her up and prepare her, but not to wait too long or nervousness would set in, and she'd blow the whole meeting. She probably would, anyhow. But they'd assured her that they would be a short distance away. Why was she not assured?

"See you then," Nick said.

When she clicked off, Sonny told her, "Ya did great, darlin'."

Brad was already on his cell phone advising the other agents or cops where they would be at "fourteen hundred hours" and to make sure there was plenty of backup.

Luc called her almost immediately when he got wind of the final plan. "Are you sure you're up for this?" he asked.

"I have no idea."

"You don't have to do it. Legally, they have no grounds for forcing you to do anything."

"No one is forcing me, I swear."

"Okay. I'll try to get over to Nick's office once I'm done here with Angus."

After she ended the call, Tante Lulu told them all, "I'll stay here and hold down the fort. If any bad guys show up, I'll shoot 'em first and ask questions later."

"Someone needs to lock up that woman," Brad told Samantha in a loud whisper.

"Better men than you have tried," John LeDeux remarked, on overhearing. He'd come back to try and convince his aunt to go home. Fat chance of that happening now.

"Cain't anyone take a joke?" Tante Lulu asked.

"Some joke!" Brad muttered.

"C'mon, auntie. I'll drive you home and pick up your car later."

"Not yet," Tante Lulu said. "I jist started the roux fer the étouffée. Besides, someone needs ta look after the animals."

"Well, I'll come back fer ya later then," John said, "but do not . . . I repeat, do not drive home yerself. The police are threatenin' to put a boot on your vehicle ta prevent it from movin'."

"Yer the police, Tee-John."

He rolled his eyes. "The other police."

"Whatever ya say, sweetie."

"Yeah, right," John said, rolling his eyes at the others in the room.

Brad and Sonny went out to the front driveway to get the wiring equipment from their vehicle, and John went with them. Which left Samantha alone with Tante Lulu.

Tante Lulu set two glasses of iced sweet tea on the table, along with two slices of her Peachy Praline Cobbler Cake that she'd thawed from her freezer. She motioned for Samantha to sit down across from her. You'd think this was her home, the way she took over.

"Now, let's talk about the thunderbolt," she said.

Chapter Twenty-Three

Love makes fools of men . . . and women, too . . .

Daniel was reclining beside Molly on her hospital bed, his one arm around her little shoulders, the other arm holding his iPhone in front of them both. Her face was pressed against his chest, and he could feel the heat of her fever even through the cloth of his shirt. He'd been shocked by the blueish shadows under her eyes and her labored breathing when he'd first arrived. What a change from yesterday!

He kissed the fuzz on her bald head, which she usually kept covered, and it was like the down of a dandelion. People, like Samantha, couldn't understand his aversion to having children of his own. It wasn't that he didn't like children. Obviously, or he wouldn't have specialized in pediatrics. But the attachment to them was just too strong, too devastating when it was broken. Molly was a case in point. He hardly knew her, and yet . . . and yet!

Molly hadn't let him shut down his phone since he'd first shown her the present she would get when she got better. It was the picture of the seven kittens, and Molly couldn't make up her mind between the pure white or the yellow-and-black striped one. Of course, their colors might be entirely different when they lost their birth hair, but she didn't seem to care about that.

It was presumptuous of him to promise a pet to a child without the parents' approval, but he would worry about that later. Somehow, he would make it happen.

"That one!" she decided conclusively, pointing her finger at the white one. "Snowball."

"Are you sure? Bumble is cute, too." Molly had given each of the kittens names. The yellow-and-black one was named after . . . what else . . . ? A bumblebee.

"No. Snowball is smaller, like me. And you told me she's a girl. Bumble is a boy. Maybe you could find a boy to adopt Bumble."

Somebody is going to take all seven of these cats, that's for sure. Maybe even eight, if Maxine can be thrown into the mix.

Molly had acute myeloid leukemia and while she had responded well to the initial high dosage of chemo, today she had relapsed, and her white cell count had skyrocketed. A stem cell transplant was her only hope, but she had to be in remission for that to take place.

Ideally, one of her siblings would be a good donor match, but both parents had to agree to the procedure, and thus far, Molly's mother couldn't be reached. Her father was a match, thankfully, and although parent to child bone marrow transplants weren't common, they could be done. But that meant getting Molly back into remission and getting her father here from Savannah.

"I want my daddy," Molly said, suddenly losing interest in the kittens.

"I know, sweetheart. He's on his way." He glanced up to see a nurse approaching with a syringe. "Why don't you take a nap, and maybe your daddy will be here when you wake up?"

"I don't wanna sleep," Molly whined, even as she cuddled even closer into his embrace.

To distract her, he began to describe the situation at his home. He'd told her about the plantation before. Now, he said, "Did I tell you about the animals who have come to visit me this week? There's a biiiiig dog, who has a sore hip, and can only move around slowly. Then, there's a biiiiig cat that looks like a cougar. Do you know what a cougar is? Yes, the wild animals with the stripes. And get this . . . a little pig called Emily who follows me around like a shadow."

Molly giggled at that. A wonderful sound, especially considering how bad she must feel. She didn't even notice the needle entering her upper arm.

"And did I tell you about the bird . . . a cockatoo . . . that can only say one thing, and it's a bad word? Maybe if you came to visit one day, you could teach Clarence some new words."

"Betcha I could," Molly said.

Within minutes, she was fast asleep, and he was able to slip off the bed. The nurse arranged the child more comfortably in the bed, and checked her temperature once again. "No change," she remarked shortly.

George came in then and motioned for him to come out into the hall. "Did you get her father on the line?" George asked him.

"I did. He should be en route, as we speak."

"How did you manage that?"

"Threats. Bribery."

George laughed, halfheartedly. "When I talked to him earlier, he had a half dozen excuses. Couldn't get off work; he just got a new job working construction. No money for gas. His car needs repairs. No place to stay when he gets here. All legitimate excuses, of course, but . . ."

"I offered him a job and a place to stay until Molly gets better."

"What?" George blinked at him with surprise. "Doing what? Staying where?"

It had been a spur of the moment decision, but one that could work out well. "Aaron and I can never get enough help renovating that damn plantation house. If Molly's dad can wield a paintbrush or hammer a nail, he can work for us. For a while, anyway. And I figure one of those old slave cottages is better than the run-down motels where he's been staying, even without indoor plumbing. Hell, he can put plumbing in, if he has the expertise."

George was smiling at him. He didn't have to say the words. He knew that Daniel was being pulled back into medicine, whether he wanted it or not. Fact is, he was ready.

After he left the medical center, with a promise to George that he would check in later, Daniel sat in his car and looked over the ridiculous grocery list Samantha and Tante Lulu had put together. He tapped his fingertips on the steering wheel. Thinking, thinking, thinking. Something had been niggling at the back of his brain ever since he'd left the plantation.

He thought about his last words with Samantha, and suddenly he knew what the problem was. Samantha was going to meet with her ex-husband, despite his asking . . . rather, telling . . . her not to.

Fear shot through him. Nick was a desperate man, as

the FBI agent had told them, and desperate men were unpredictable. There was no knowing what Nick might do to Samantha to get what he wanted.

Then the fear was replaced with anger. How dare she take such chances? If she didn't care about herself, why didn't she care about his feelings?

But then, how did she know what his feelings were? He didn't know himself.

He called Samantha's cell phone, and was not surprised to get no answer. Then he tried Luc and John LeDeux's respective cell phone numbers. No answers there, either. Finally, he tried the last resort. Tante Lulu.

She answered on the first ring.

"Tante Lulu, is Samantha there?"

"No. Do ya know where the Tabasco sauce is? I cain't find it nowhere."

"What do you mean, no? Where is she?"

"Who?"

"Samantha."

"Oh, I ain't supposed ta say."

That was answer enough for Daniel. He clicked off and put his car in gear, heading toward New Orleans. He had a rough idea where Nick's new medical building was located.

He saw enough evidence of the harm that came to people, without trying. He'd be damned if he'd let her put herself in harm's way, willingly.

As a result, he drove like a maniac north on 90 toward New Orleans, and had no trouble finding Nick's three-story Southern Women's Maternity Center, which looked like a mini Taj Mahal. No wonder he was in financial trouble. All black onyx, marble, and glass. It even had a dome and finial on top like the Indian architectural wonder. Obviously, the clientele served here had to be of the wealthy class (except for Nick's black market baby mothers). No way would regular insurance pay for the kind of luxury this place exuded.

He assumed there were already unmarked police and FBI vehicles parked around the perimeter of the building. At least, he could hope so, for the benefit of Samantha's safety.

He picked a spot near the front entrance and hesitated, not sure if Samantha and her "posse" had arrived yet. He could go in and case out the place, maybe ask a receptionist if they'd seen Dr. Coltrane's ex-wife, but then the question was taken out of his hands as he saw Samantha's BMW pull into the far end of the lot.

"I knew it!" he muttered to himself as he realized he'd been half hoping that he'd been wrong. That she really wouldn't be coming to meet Nick the Prick as he went looney-bird, batshit crazy.

Her BMW was immediately followed by several other vehicles that were probably the FBI and/or local police, although they were innocuous enough. A Comcast van. A beat-up pickup truck. A private mini-bus for handicapped folks. And, holy crap! Was that an ice cream wagon? The vehicles pulled in on either side of Samantha's BMW and one just across the lane from her. The ice cream trunk was parked off to one side of the parking lot, near the building, though he noticed its bell wasn't ringing. There was also a black guy with expensive sunglasses trimming the bushes, and a female jogger, with the biceps of a linebacker, who'd made two laps around the parking lot so far.

And Samantha was dead center, like a bull's-eye, in the middle of this goat rodeo. He exited his car with a foul expletive that caused the lady getting out of the next car with a toddler to flinch. "Sorry."

After riding in his air-conditioned car, the hot Louisiana sun hit him like a blow. *Hotheaded* came immediately to mind, in more ways than one. He stomped quickly to the back of the parking lot so he would be out of range of any security cameras in case Coltrane was watching. Though the good doctor wouldn't have any reason to be suspicious of him. As far as Daniel knew, Coltrane wasn't even aware of his existence.

The FBI saw him almost immediately. In fact, there were probably other agents planted around the lot and even inside the building, prepared to record Samantha's wired meeting. And they expected Samantha to suddenly become some kind of Jennifer Garner/Sydney Bristow CIA agent from the old TV series, *Alias*. Insanity!

Brad Dillon stepped out of one side of a cable company van, and Sonny Sonnier stepped out of the other. The fire in their eyes turned the temperature about ten degrees higher. And that fire was aimed at him.

Brad held a map in one hand and pretended to be asking Daniel for direction but, instead, he hissed, even as he took hold of his upper arm, "What the hell are you doing here, LeDeux?"

Sonnier came around his other side, also grabbing an arm. "I shoulda known. Ya cain't tell a LeDeux ta do nothin'." The agents and law enforcement officers in the other vehicles were probably shaking their heads at the crazy ass doctor who was going to ruin the show.

Almost magically, the sliding door on the side of the van opened and he was shoved inside, and Samantha was shoved into the other side, rather stunned.

"I give you five minutes to send this asshole home or we abort this mission," Dillon told Samantha.

"Let me jist shoot 'im with a stun gun. Quicker and more fun," Sonnier said.

"No, give me the stun gun. I'll take care of him." Samantha shot him a look that would curdle milk.

He sank down onto the bench seat facing hers, and

the sliding doors slammed shut. There was even a click of the lock. What did they think he was going to do? Pick her up in his arms and run from the vehicle. Even if he made it out, in this heat, he wouldn't make it ten feet. Hell, even without this heat, he wouldn't make it that far.

He made a quick survey of her appearance and felt a little sick. Yeah, she was wearing the same clothes she'd had on this morning, but she'd amped up the sex factor with makeup, hooker high heels, and a scarf around her waist that pulled her blouse tighter against her breasts. A wave of unwarranted possessiveness swept over him as he realized she'd done all of this to impress her ex-husband. That was unreasonable, he knew, but what place had reason in a jealous mind?

Jealous? Me? Aaarrgh!

"You were supposed to be gone for hours," she said.

The wrong, wrong, wrong thing to say! "With that grocery list you gave me, I would have been."

"And?"

"I went to the medical center and spent some time with Molly, who is not in good shape, thanks for asking."

She made a clucking sound of disgust at his sarcasm.

"I suspected all along that you would agree to this lamebrain wiring, putting yourself in the hands of a madman, but it was after I left the hospital that it hit me. Here were all these people, mostly kids, who, through no fault of their own, are living with a dangerous disease, or dying from it. And then, there you were, perfectly healthy, taking on danger. Why not just smoke a pack of cigarettes a day to give yourself cancer?"

"It's not the same thing."

"It felt like it to me at the time. Still does."

"Daniel, Nick has to be stopped. What he's doing is evil."

"Let someone else stop him."

"You don't really mean that."

"Yeah, I do. Let me go with you."

"Why?"

"Because . . . because I . . . care."

He could tell she was touched, maybe even reciprocated the . . . caring, but she stiffened and said, "Well, you can't come with me. Nick will never open up with a third party there. If he's going to reveal anything, it will only be if he thinks I'm there alone."

"Shouldn't your lawyer be here with you? Does Luc approve of this madness?"

"Luc should be here any minute. He was at the police station with Angus. And, yes, he agrees, sort of."

"What the hell does 'sort of' mean?"

"He says the FBI and police will step in at the first sign of danger. But in the end it's my decision whether to participate. And, Daniel . . ." She paused to make sure she had his attention. ". . . I have decided to get this whole mess over with. Me. Not you, or anyone else, will make that decision."

"I thought . . ." He wasn't sure what he'd thought. He wasn't her husband. He wasn't even her boyfriend, or lover. Just a one-night stand . . . or one-week stand . . . or whatever. A good fuck. Who'd fucked up. "Forget I ever showed up," he said and pounded on the window for the Fibbies to open the door.

"Daniel, wait," she said, even as the door slid open and he stepped out. "I didn't mean that the way it sounded."

"You meant it exactly how it sounded, but that's all right. I crossed the line. I won't do it again."

"Daniel . . ."

He heard the pity in her voice. So, he left before he made even more of an ass of himself.

Luc arrived then and gave him a passing, questioning glance as he went into the van, presumably to give his client some last-minute instructions. He hoped one of them was, "Be careful!" Because she sure as hell wasn't listening to him.

Chapter Twenty-Four

There was a pot of gold, but no rainbow . . .

Samantha entered Nick's empty, third-floor, corner office. The receptionist had told her that Dr. Coltrane would be with her shortly. Despite her fear and anxiety over the situation, she couldn't help but stop her mental hand-wringing and admire her surroundings.

If Nick's building was something out of *Architectural Digest*, his office was a cover for *Luxury* magazine. Very modern and elegantly appointed. It reeked of money. Money which . . . *Hello!* . . . Nick did not have.

Massive windows on two adjoining sides gave an arresting view of the Mississippi River and the Port of New Orleans, several ships on the horizon. Another wall, containing floor-to-ceiling bookcases, displayed medical books and *objets d' art*, such as a bronze sculpture of two alligators fighting, some rare Newcomb pottery, and a sterling vase of her grandmother's that she hadn't realized was missing all these years. He must have taken it from an attic chest when they'd first separated. The floor was polished golden cypress with a jewel-toned oriental carpet in its center. The desk, in the vee of the two show-case windows, was large and sleek, probably specially designed for the space.

But it was the massive sideboard on the fourth wall that drew the attention most. A fifteen-foot-wide and ten-foot-high masterpiece, with beveled glass mirrors and gold-plated knobs, had to have resided in some European castle at one time. She couldn't even guess what it had cost.

Just then, the door opened and Nick strolled in, as cool and handsome as ever. He wore blue scrubs and a surgeon's cap, which he tossed into a tall, sterile-looking wastebasket with a swinging lid by the door. His blond hair was neatly cut with not a strand out of place. He must have just completed an operation in the surgical suite Angus had described to her. Maybe he'd even delivered a baby, which he was about to sell.

"Samantha! So good of you to come!"

Like I had a choice. Well, I had a choice, as Daniel so aptly pointed out. But to me, there was no choice. "Nick," she acknowledged his greeting. "I didn't mean to take you away from work. We could have met another time."

He glanced down at his scrubs, which did, in fact, have several dark stains, which could only be blood. He pulled that off, as well, the pants and shirt, exposing a white, oxford collared dress shirt with sterling cuff links and a designer tie, tucked into gray, pleated slacks. "No, no, just a routine birth."

He walked closer and appeared about to give her a hug, but she stepped back. No way was she letting him put his hands on her. Already his Bleu de Chanel cologne was making her queasy, but maybe that was just nervousness.

He raised his eyebrows at her silent rebuff, though why he should be surprised, considering their past history, was a marvel of male cluelessness. Instead, he went to sit behind his desk. He motioned for her to sit on one of the two leather chairs before his desk.

"What do you want, Nick? What was so important that I had to rush here?"

"There's no need for hostility, Sammie."

Her upper lip curled with distaste.

Before Nick could catch himself, he grinned. He knew full well how she loathed the nickname. But then he clearly forced himself to be serious. "It's been a bitch trying to connect with you." He pretended to wince as if he hadn't meant to use "bitch" in connection with her. Hah! She'd be bitch to his bastard any day. "Where were you?" he demanded to know.

"The South of France," she lied. *Or South of New Orleans, anyhow.* "A little vacation." *In a run-down plantation house with a horde of people and animals . . . including one very sexy doctor.* "You could say it was a working vacation." *Now, there's a truth!* "Although I did visit with my mother while I was there, of course."

"How is the old broad? Still shagging teenagers?"

She didn't bother to respond, and she could hardly be insulted at the truth. Although teenagers might be a stretch. Her mother, Colette, homed in on twenty-somethings these days. Or, horror of horrors, an aged thirty-five-year-old a few years back, but Enrique only lasted a few months, couldn't keep up with her mother, or so Colette had said.

"You know she put the moves on me one time?"

"So you said."

He gave her body and attire a quick, disdainful survey, probably comparing it to a memory of her always elegantly dressed mother. It was not the way Nick would have insisted that Samantha dress while traveling when they were married. Images to keep up and all that nonsense.

She was still wearing the black skinny jeans and white tailored blouse she'd had on this morning, but she'd added a bright silk scarf at her waist as a belt and a pair of high heels that Tante Lulu found in the backseat of her car, which Charmaine had left behind following a party or something. Samantha had arranged her unruly hair into a neat French braid and expertly applied makeup, including foundation to mute her freckles, mascara, eye liner, and lip gloss. She even wore diamond stud earrings that had been in the jewelry pouch she brought with her to Bayou Rose, for safety.

She'd thought she looked pretty good.

Apparently not.

He did take note of her earrings and get the familiar cha-ching gleam in his larcenous eyes. "Why France? Don't tell me, dear old grandpa is opening some stores there?" The snide note in his voice was not going to gain him points with her, if he only knew. But then, Nick had an over-inflated view of what he could say or do and still appear charming.

"No new stores in France," she declared, setting her handbag, which held a secondary wiring device, on the floor at her feet. "I have to get home and take care of my animals. What's up, Nick?"

His eyes went wide, and she realized her mistake. If he was the one who broke into her house, he would know there were no animals there presently.

"A neighbor offered to care for my pets while I was gone. I have to pick them up and bring them home before

I even unpack. And, frankly, I'm dog tired, ha ha ha, from my trip. You know how jet lag affects me." *Oh, Lord! I'm rambling. Slow down, Samantha. Let Nick do the talking.*

"Actually, I do remember. You slept for twenty-four hours straight after we returned from our honeymoon trip to Paris. But then, you might have been tired out for other reasons." He grinned knowingly at her.

She felt like hurling the contents of her stomach. Tante Lulu's beignets and dark chicory coffee suddenly felt like hockey pucks and tar in her stomach.

She stared at him stonily.

"Where's Angus?" he asked.

"Huh?" She'd been prepared for that question, but she needed to feign ignorance.

"Your brother Angus . . . where the hell is Angus?"

"Angus isn't really my brother. He—"

"I know what he is," he snapped. No more Mr. Nice Guy, apparently. "I need to talk to Angus, and I need him *now.*"

"Why?"

"He stole something from me."

Oh, so that's how he was going to play this. "Money?"

"Not specifically. Something a lot more valuable than mere cash."

Mere cash? Bite your tongue, Nick. Cash has never been mere to you. Ever. "How do you know Angus anyhow?"

"He is . . . was . . . working for me."

She tilted her head to the side. "In what capacity? Angus has no medical training, as far as I know."

"Computers."

"Oh. Well, I don't know where he is. Why would I?"

"I've checked everywhere else? And he disappeared the same time you did. I sense a connection."

She tried her best, but she felt a blush coloring her cheeks. And Nick saw it, too.

"You do know where he is! What a goat fuck this is turning out to be! The time for games is over, sweetheart. I want Angus, and I want him now. Either you bring him to me, or I go to the police."

"The police?" She frowned in confusion. "What would you tell the police?"

"Well," he eyed his bookcase unit, "several valuable items of mine seem to have gone missing. A Samuel Remington bronze sculpture, two Newcomb vases worth ten thousand dollars, and an antique silver vase that once belonged to Robert E. Lee."

She barely stifled a scoff at that last. Her grandmother had been from Scotland, not the South. More important, Samantha realized that Nick was going to fabricate thefts by hiding the objects himself. But this was just a ploy, it had to be. Nick wouldn't take any chance of Angus being in police custody and spilling the beans about his illegal activities.

What then did Nick hope to accomplish with Angus now? Surely he didn't think he could continue with his baby selling gig. The answer came to her immediately and ominously. Nick was going to kill Angus. He had to. How else would he ensure that Angus would forever remain silent?

But Nick a murderer? Was that possible?

Desperate men did desperate things, she reminded herself of the FBI agent's words. And Nick had too much to lose now. Money. His medical license. His reputation. Prison. Oh, yeah, those were reasons to turn an already immoral man to evil.

"Where's that brother of yours hiding? And, by the way, I don't suppose he has a pregnant girl with him. Lily Beth Fontenot ring any bells?" Nick stood and was coming around the desk, hands fisted with fury, convinced now that she knew something.

She stood, too, not wanting to be sitting while he hovered over her. "Don't be ridiculous, Nick. First, Angus is not my brother, not even my stepbrother. And why would he have a pregnant girl with him? Oh, my! Is that what this is about? Angus getting some girl pregnant? Well, that's not the end of the world, is it?"

"I'll tell you what's the end of the world. You. If you don't stop these games and tell me where those two idiots are. They owe me! They owe me big-time."

She shoved her chair to the side and was backing up with each slow, threatening step Nick took toward her. "You want to stop playing games? I do, too. Tell me exactly what the problem is. What is so urgent that I had to come here today?"

Just then, the door swung open and Angus rushed in, followed closely by the receptionist who was yelling, "Hey, you can't go in there."

"No? Watch me," Angus yelled back, shoving the receptionist back out and slamming the door in her face.

Both she and Nick stared at Angus with amazement. His blond hair was standing on end, half in and half out of a ponytail. One of his athletic shoes was unlaced. And he was out of breath, as if he'd run up all three flights of stairs, instead of using the elevator. Did the FBI and police know he was here? Had they chased him, and that's why he was so disheveled? What the hell next?

"Angus! What are you doing here?"

"I couldn't let you do this for me. Nick, let Samantha leave."

"What? Are you crazy, Angus? Nick isn't holding me here," Samantha said.

"C'mon, Nick, you and I can handle this. I won't tell anyone about the baby selling scheme. I can't give you Lily Beth, but I won't rat on you about the past stuff."

Oh, good Lord! He was going to spoil it all.

Nick looked from Angus to Samantha with sudden understanding. "You told her," he accused Angus. "You friggin' fool!" He began to back up slightly, and tripped over her handbag, which spilled onto the floor, disclosing a wallet, a hairbrush, her cell phone . . . and the wiring device.

Nick picked it up, narrowed his eyes at her and Angus, then swung around back behind the desk, pulling out a drawer and a pistol, which he aimed at Angus. "Who's on the other end of this wire?" he asked.

"No one," Angus lied. "It's just hooked up to my computer. I had a plan to get you on tape. Not to go to the police."

"It would have been used as leverage so you would let Angus and Lily Beth go," Samantha elaborated. "Honestly, Nick, can you see Nick and Lily Beth going to the police when they might be arrested themselves?"

Nick seemed unsure whether to believe them or not. He raised his weapon while he considered the situation.

Taking no chances, Samantha picked up an amber paperweight off the desk and threw it at Nick, which missed his fool head and hit his shoulder, but it caused the pistol to discharge. The bullet hit Angus, causing him to fall backward.

"Oh, my God! You killed him," she shouted, rushing to Angus who lay prone on the floor, unconscious.

"He's not dead. I just nicked his scalp."

"How do you know that? Are you crazy? You're a doctor, for heaven's sake. Hippocratic Oath and all that crap! Come over here, dammit, and check him."

Nick ignored her and picked up her handbag and its contents off the floor. He stomped on the wiring device, then walked over to her with the pistol still raised. "I told you. It's just a scalp wound. A bleeder. He'll live."

She stood and glared at him. "What kind of doctor are you?"

He shrugged. "Give me the other device," he snarled, holding out his free hand. "I know Angus would have put a wire on you, too."

At least he was buying the story of Angus, not the FBI, setting up the sting. And hopefully, the feds and police would be descending on them shortly, having heard the gun shot.

She yanked the device out of her bra and handed it to him. He stomped on that one, too. Then, while she attempted to kneel and help Angus, noticing the flutter of his eyelids, Nick looped the shoulder strap of her handbag over her head and grabbed her by the upper arm, keeping her upright.

Angus made a surreptitious flicker of his fingers, signaling that he was, in fact, not dead, although there was a huge amount of blood, which would surely stain the precious carpet. Luckily, Nick didn't notice. With the weapon pressed against the back of her head, he steered her toward the bookcase unit. And just like in the movies, he pushed a secret lever, and a part of the unit opened onto a dark stairway. The bookcase closed behind them.

"Holy freakin' Alfred Hitchcock! Why would a doctor need a secret entrance to his offices?"

"Not a secret entrance. Just a quick way to go down to my private surgery suite. That way I don't have to go through the halls in soiled scrubs, like I just did. It puts the patients off to see all that blood." She couldn't see his face in the dark stairway, but she suspected he was grinning at his ingenuity. "But you know why I really wanted this private entrance or exit. Angus must have told you. Because of my extra-curricular activity. But it also leads to the parking garage, which is next door, connected to my first floor by a corridor."

Uh-oh! He plans to leave the building. With me. Are the cops watching the parking garage? Or just the ground floor entrances and exits of this building? Oh, crap! I am in over my head! "Where are we going?" she asked as he pushed her down the steps.

"To the bank, where we're going to empty out your safety deposit box. You're going to pay, and pay big for what you cost me today, bitch."

What I cost him? How about what he cost himself? Did the jerk ever take responsibility for his own actions? Why was it always someone else's fault that he was: a) born poor, b) had a professor who had it in for him just because he skipped five classes, c) messed up that one operation during his residency and had to repeat the whole year, d) had an overactive libido, e) couldn't help but cheat with a dog of a wife like Samantha, f) drank too much at the hospital Christmas party and hustled the director's daughter, g) etc., etc., etc.

But now she understood where they were going. Nick was still fixated on the gold bullion in her bank deposit box. Did he really think he could get away with that? "Nick, that gold has to weigh more than a hundred pounds. How in hell are you going to remove it without sticking out like the thief that you are?"

He pressed the revolver harder against her back, causing her to trip and almost go forward, flat on her face. Which would probably be a good thing, if he fell forward, too, except she might very well break her neck in the process.

"You'll be with me, Sammie dear. All the bank employees will see is my lovely ex-wife who has reunited with me. And I have a small, wheeled luggage I keep in my trunk for spontaneous, weekend trips. A Louis Vuitton."

"Spontaneous, as in getting lucky with some young bimbo?"

This time, he pinched her arm, hard.

She yelped.

They had gone down three flights of stairs by now, and Nick opened a door, shoving her into the tunnel-like corridor, where the overhead lighting, after all that darkness, blinded her, at first. Nick frog-marched her the short distance to the lower level of the parking garage. She fully expected . . . no, hoped . . . to have a SWAT team waiting for them with weapons raised. But, no, there weren't even any people around. Just a couple dozen vehicles.

"Where does Angus have the computer that was receiving your transmissions?" he asked suddenly.

"Uh," she hesitated. She couldn't say her house because he had already been there. Or Angus's apartment, which he'd probably also ransacked.

He pinched her arm again.

She was going to be black and blue . . . and purple. "At my office at Starr Foods," she lied.

"Shit!" he said. "No way we're going there. Well, there's nothing to be done about the laptop then. Just need to get the gold and leave the country." He was talking to himself, not her.

He steered her toward his Mercedes, opened the passenger door, then forced her to slide over the gearshift and onto the driver's seat, then he followed after her. Apparently, she was going to be driving the getaway car. He clicked the lock lever on a remote he held in one hand. The other hand still held the pistol, aimed at her. He shoved the remote into his pocket and pulled out a cell phone which he manipulated with one thumb, calling someone.

"Misty, where are you?"

"Good. Don't go near the medical building. Pack a bag for both of us."

"Yeah, a major fuck-up, caused by my ex-wife."

She said something that made him laugh. "I agree.

Listen, call Jerry at the airfield and tell him to have the plane ready in—" he glanced at his Rolex"—an hour. I'll meet you there. It might take me a little longer than that, but we'll leave immediately once I hit the tarmac."

How could Nick think he had an hour to get the gold out of the bank and get to an airfield without the cops picking him up? But wait. Nick didn't know the FBI and law enforcement were already on-site. He must think it would take a while for the receptionist to go into the office and discover Angus's body. He would speculate that the receptionist's first reaction would be to call an ambulance and then the police to whom she would report that her boss was missing.

She felt somewhat relieved to know what Nick didn't. The good guys were probably already tailing them. She hoped.

"Love you, too, babe," Nick said into his phone.

When he clicked off and shoved the phone back in his pocket, she asked, "Is that your muscle-bound marathoner girlfriend?"

"Angus talks too much," Nick said and motioned for her to start the car. It had a keyless ignition, and he had the key remote on his person; so, it was easy to start. The Mercedes motor purred like Maddie after a tasty meal of Starr Foods albacore tuna. Why wouldn't it? The vehicle had to cost a hundred thousand dollars. But it was probably leased. Otherwise, Nick wouldn't leave it behind. He'd find some way to stow it on an airplane or arrange its transport.

"Where to now? The bank?"

He grinned evilly at her. "No, darlin'. We're going to visit dear ol' Aunt Maire."

"What?"

"The pink lady is going to be the grease on the wheels of my escape. Pink grease. Ha, ha, ha."

"What are you up to, Nick?"

"Your sweet aunt is going to sit in her pink Cadillac in her pink garage with the motor running. I figure it will take forty-five minutes for her to die from the carbon monoxide poisoning. A little added incentive for you to help me get the gold out fast and return to rescue your aunt. Ingenious, huh? And I just thought it up now."

Samantha was becoming very, very afraid. This was not one of the possible scenarios that the feds had sketched out for her. Not even close.

And suddenly Samantha wished she'd listened to Daniel and let him come with her. How much more dangerous could it have been? Would she ever have the chance to tell him, "You were right, honey."

In fact, would she ever see Daniel again?

Because, sure as sin, Nick was never going to leave her alive as a witness to his crimes.

Chapter Twenty-Five

Storms come, and storms go . . .

When Daniel stomped off, he was so blindingly angry that he stomped in the wrong direction. Instead of heading for his car, he ended up by the ice cream truck, which was, in fact, an ice cream truck and not a tricked-out FBI surveillance vehicle. He'd been watching too many *Die Hard* movies with Aaron.

"Whatcha want, bud?" some old codger at the window asked him. He wore a Polly's Pralines cap and a T-shirt advertising his ice cream, Sweet Scoops. He had little or no teeth. Too much of his own product, Daniel assumed.

He ordered a vanilla waffle cone. Yes, boring vanilla for a boring ex-doctor who'd made a boring effort to rescue his woman, who wasn't his woman, at all. Dumb, dumb, dumb. Boring, boring, boring.

"Dontcha want sprinkles on that?"

"No, I don't want sprinkles," Daniel said, barely restraining himself from saying something rude. It wasn't the old guy's fault that Daniel was in a foul mood.

Fuming, he leaned against the wagon. He watched as Samantha exited the Comcast van and headed toward the building, unaware that he was still hanging around like a . . . *boring* . . . stalker. For once, he wasn't ogling her ass as she walked in those high heels, not even thinking of Aaron's theory of women and high heels. Well, hardly at all.

Instead, he watched as the landscaper moved closer to the building, and the jogger entered one of the side doors. All was quiet in the parking lot then with normal activity. People coming to and leaving doctor appointments. A few coming up to the ice cream truck.

Vacillating between extreme anger and extreme worry over Samantha, he stood there for fifteen minutes before he gave it up and tossed the remainder of his dripping cone in a waste bin and wiped his hand on a napkin, discarding that, too. He considered heading to the fishing camp, hiding out, till this whole fiasco with Samantha blew over. But, no, he needed to return to the plantation and see what he could do about fixing one of the slave cabins for Molly's father.

Just then, he heard a popping noise. He wasn't sure where it came from, but all hell was breaking loose in the parking lot. Brad and Sonny and cops with SWAT T-shirts, and the landscaper, were running toward the building, all with weapons visible. Daniel saw Luc following on the melee and yelled in a panic, "What's up?"

"A gunshot from inside the building," Luc said as he ran past.

So, Daniel ran, too. *Oh, God, oh, God, oh, God! I should have stopped her from getting involved in this de-*

*bacle. I should have tied her down, if I had to. If she's
dead, I'm going to kill someone. Nick, and then the FBI
agents who conned her into this mess. But she's not
dead. She can't be dead. Why think the worst? Oh, God,
oh, God, oh, God!*

Daniel made it inside just before the cops began pulling out the crime scene tape and barring people from entering or exiting the building. He swerved away from the
elevators where a bunch of cops were filing in, and instead followed those going up the stairway. One of them
with earbuds, reported to the others. "The kid's been
shot. Head wound. Non-fatal. The perp has the sting out
in the parking garage."

The kid . . . that would be Angus. And the sting . . . son
of a bitch! Coltrane had Samantha. In the parking garage.

As he assimilated those words, Daniel swiveled on his
heels and headed back down to the first floor and the
door leading to the parking garage. He was at a full-out
sprint through the connecting corridor, but was unprepared for the sound of gunfire that he heard ahead of
him. He might have cried out in dismay. Too late! He was
too late!

Some cops tried to hold him back, but he struggled
against their restraining arms and hollered, "I'm a doctor. Let me through."

He was unprepared for the sight that met his eyes. A
cop with an apparent thigh wound was being helped upright by his fellow cops. Daniel started to go to the cop,
but he was waved over to the other wounded, instead.
The other wounded being Nick Coltrane, who lay on the
stone floor of the garage, blood pouring from his face, his
chest, and one thigh. Maybe even more places. Samantha
was standing off to the side, sobbing with shock, her face
pressed against John LeDeux's flak vest, his arms around
her heaving shoulders. She appeared unharmed.

Daniel dropped to his knees beside Nick, and someone handed him a pair of disposable gloves which he
pulled on with expert speed. He checked for a pulse.
None. Heartbeat. None. Then he pulled Coltrane's eyelids back. Pupils constricted. With a weary exhale, he
glanced at his wristwatch and declared, "T.O.D. Three
twenty-seven." He stood up, tossed his gloves aside, then
looked toward Samantha, who was still plastered against
LeDeux's chest as he murmured some words of comfort
to her. She hadn't even noticed Daniel's presence. Without a word, he left the building.

Once outside, he saw Angus being helped toward an
ambulance. He appeared to be arguing with an EMT
about getting into a wheelchair. A bunch of gauze ban-
dages circled his scalp, but he was ambulatory. So, that
was good. He waved at Angus, and the boy waved back.
The cops were rushing Angus and the EMT's to avoid the
news vans that were already barreling into the parking
lot. They would want to keep Angus's . . . and Samantha's
names out of the press until the mob bosses were no longer a threat. And on the remote possibility that Coltrane
might have associates involved with him, other than the
Misty person.

Daniel was probably in shock as he drove back to
Bayou Rose. Death was traumatizing, even when the
victim was a bad guy. He was too upset to think beyond
the moment. Driving his car. Watching the highway,
that's all he was capable of. He did think about what
would happen next in terms of the FBI and the cops.
With Coltrane's death, the baby trafficking case was
over as far as Angus and Lily Beth and Samantha having
to be in hiding, although the feds would be working to
arrest his overseas connections, those people facilitating
the sale of the babies. But, more than that, there was still
the Dixie Mob situation that required Angus to remain

hidden, and by association, Samantha and Lily Beth would stay, too.

Well, Daniel couldn't stay himself. He just couldn't be around Samantha and pretend there was nothing between them. There wasn't, apparently, from her end. Other than the one-night/one-week stand business. But he was a fool for love, as the old song went, and if he ever said that out loud, he was going to surgically remove his own tongue.

On the other hand, he had things to do at Bayou Rose.

When he got back to the plantation, Lily Beth and Tante Lulu were the only ones there. Emily, at least, was glad to see him. She oinked and oinked and oinked until he picked her up and gave her a kiss. No, not on her mouth, but on the top of her snout. And, really, it was only a sort of air kiss. Axel and Maddie barely gave him a glance, considering him of no importance. Clarence, on the other hand, greeted him with the usual, "Holy shit!" But then the bird let loose with a whole string of new words, "I'm a Ragin' Cajun!"

Daniel glanced at Tante Lulu who shrugged. "I dint have nothin' ta do whilst y'all were gone."

He set Emily down with an admonition to stay put. Ignoring her woeful eyes, he left the room and went down the back stairs with Tante Lulu and Lily Beth.

"Don't you want to know what happened?" he asked.

"We already know," Lily Beth said. "Angus called us from the hospital."

"Samantha is at the hospital, too. Jist ta be checked over," Tante Lulu added.

"You should be relieved that there is no more threat from Dr. Coltrane," Daniel said to Lilly Beth. "Now you can do whatever you want about the baby."

Which caused Lily Beth to burst into tears and leave the kitchen.

"What did I do?" Daniel asked Tante Lulu.

"Nuthin'. The girl is jist confused, and her hormones is hummin', givin' her the blue moodies."

"Did Angus say when they'd be back?"

"In an hour or two," Tante Lulu answered. "Where's all mah groceries, by the way. I knew I shoulda gone ta the store myself."

"Just hold your horses. Aaron is bringing them."

Daniel went into an anteroom where he grabbed a broom, dustpan, some rags, and cleaning products. "I have a little job to do," he explained to Tante Lulu, whose eyebrows were raised with curiosity.

Which, of course, was like raising a Cheez Doodle before her pet gator, because Tante Lulu immediately followed after him as he went out the back door. "Whatcha gotta do?"

"I need to see if one of the slave cabins is liveable for a few days . . . or weeks."

"Why? Ya gonna turn it inta a honeymoon cottage?"

"What? No! Geez, where do you get these ideas?"

Tante raised her eyes heavenward.

Great! She has connections to the Great Beyond! He tried to explain, "The father of one of the kids at the cancer center in Houma needs a place to stay. I volunteered one of these cabins. The guy has construction experience; so, he might be able to fix the electricity and plumbing, if there is any."

Tante Lulu asked some questions and he found himself telling her about Molly and the lack of housing for men like Molly's father, Edgar Gillotte, who had less than a pristine rap sheet.

"So, yer bringin' ex-cons here now."

"He's not an ex-con. He's just a guy who made some mistakes, minor mistakes, and needs a break. It's as much for his kid, as for him."

"Ah," Tante Lulu said.

"What does 'Ah' mean?"

"Jist that life has a way of workin' things out."

"That doesn't make any sense at all."

"Sometimes we doan know why things happen the way they do. Like you and Aaron buying this ol' plantation. Ya thought it was ta open an animal rescue mission."

"That was never *my* intention."

Tante Lulu waved his contradiction away. "But God . . . and St. Jude . . . had other plans in mind fer you."

"I swear, following your mind is like traveling down a Louisiana bayou. So many twists and turns, you get lost."

"Huh?"

He should know better than to encourage her with questions, but he had to ask, "What do God and St. Jude have to do with me and Aaron buying this plantation?"

"It's obvious, ain't it? I kin see it all clear now. Yer supposed ta open a refuge fer sick kids and their families, lak Ronald McDonald House, 'cept yers will be Rose House, or sumpin' lak that."

"Whoa, whoa, whoa! You are way ahead of me here. All I'm doing is fixing up one cabin. One. And it's only for a short period."

"Uh-huh!" Tante Lulu said, not convinced.

Even she was a bit taken aback at their first sight of the interior of the first cabin. Dogs had run free rein here at one time, both inside the cottage and in the fenced yard, but that had been thirty or so years ago when the former owner was raising Redbone Coonhounds, according to Tante Lulu. Whatever feces or urine stains there might have been were all dried up now, but the whole place would need a good scrubbing and a bleach disinfecting. Even so, Tante Lulu declared it had possibilities. No wonder she was a fan of St. Jude, the patron saint of hopeless causes.

In fact, Tante Lulu told him she was going to call her

niece, who was at her Houma beauty shop today. She apparently had other salons or spas, as well, including one at the ranch where she lived with her husband Raoul Lanier, better known as Rusty. And another which did everything for a woman's body except plastic surgery . . . waxing, massaging, exfoliating, manicuring, pedicuring, hairstyling, braiding, corn rows, eyebrow shaping. He knew all this because Tante Lulu told him so, in enough detail that his eyes started to roll back in his head.

She pulled a cell phone out of her apron pocket.

"Charmaine, honey, kin ya do me a favor?"

"Yes, I know yer allus willin' ta help me. Kin ya go ta that used furniture store down the street from yer salon. See if they have enough stuff ta furnish a small cottage." She turned to Daniel and asked, "How much ya willin' ta spend?"

He waved a hand as if it didn't matter but then he immediately amended, worrying that giving a woman like Tante Lulu an open checkbook would be like leaving an open door on an alligator farm, insanity, in other words. "Two thousand, maybe three." Tante Lulu repeated the amount to Charmaine.

"I doan s'pose Rusty is in town and he could bring the stuff over in his pickup truck?"

"He is? Oh, good!"

Oh, crap! He never intended for Tante Lulu to impose on someone like that for his benefit. In fact, he never intended to involve her at all. But there was no stopping the living bulldozer. Several times, he tried to interrupt her call, but she just ignored him.

When her call was over, she told Daniel, "You'll have stuff here by this evenin'."

"Thank you," he said, for more reasons than one. He hadn't thought about his disastrous relationship with Samantha for, oh, fifteen minutes, with all the old lady's chatter.

Lily Beth waddled up and helped as much as she could. And when Aaron returned, complaining about the amount of groceries he'd been forced to buy, Tante Lulu went back to the kitchen to start dinner, but not before she pulled a framed St. Jude picture from her handbag and hung it on the wall. To no one's surprise, she also had a hammer and nails in the blasted bag.

Lily Beth went back to the house with her. And Aaron stayed to help Daniel pull out the rusted metal fence.

"I think there's some white picket fencing stored in one of the sheds. Used to encircle these cottages at one time," Aaron told him. "Of course, it hasn't been white for a lot of years, but nothing a little paint won't handle."

"Let's not go overboard. This is just for one guy, for a short time."

"Uh-huh," Aaron said, just as disbelieving as Tante Lulu had been.

"By the way, do you still have the key to Remy's houseboat?" Until they bought this plantation, Aaron had been living on Remy LeDeux's old houseboat while Daniel lived in the bayou fishing camp.

Aaron stopped what he was doing, stacking the dismantled wire fencing, to stare at him. "Trouble in paradise already?"

"Aaron," he cautioned.

"Yeah, I have the key. It's in my bedroom dresser. Why do you need to stay there?"

Daniel declined to answer.

"Ah, Dan," his brother said. "I knew she would hurt you, but I didn't expect it so soon."

"It's not her fault, and don't you dare say anything to her. It's my fault for assuming too much."

"Uh-huh. So, this whole safe house business here still goes on?"

Daniel shrugged. "I expect so. The Dixie Mob arrests still haven't taken place, as far as I know. And I'm not

sure when the news will break on Nick Coltrane's death
and crimes, and whether Samantha and Angus's names
will come up. At the very least, they'll want to avoid the
news media, at first."

Aaron continued to study him, the way only twins
could, and did. Seeing more. "Why don't you go back to
your *garconniére* apartment, and I'll stay in the houseboat?"

Daniel shook his head. "I'd rather not be here when
they all come back."

"Bok, bok! A little chicken-ish, dontcha think?"

"I'm not afraid to be around Samantha, but it could be
a little awkward today with so many people around. Besides, Tante Lulu will probably still be there, and you
know damn well she'll be harping at me about thunderbolts."

Just then, there was a crack of thunder in the distance.
It was probably just a portend of a typical Louisiana summer storm to come.

But, holy crap! Maybe not.

They looked at each other and burst out laughing.

When the dust settled, she was alone . . . again . . .

Much to Samantha's disappointment, Daniel wasn't at the
plantation when Samantha returned with Angus and
John LeDeux around six o'clock. Two cops came, too, to
provide continued security for them until all the danger
was gone, but they became invisible almost immediately.

Tante Lulu explained that Daniel and Aaron had gone
off somewhere and hadn't said when they would return.
Couldn't Daniel have waited for her to come back first?

And Tante Lulu had also relayed some crazy story
about Daniel renovating one of the slave cabins so the

father of some kid with cancer could live there. Well, that part she could sort of understand, but Tante Lulu went on some rambling discourse about life and fate and things meant to be, and this was why Daniel and Aaron had bought this plantation in the first place, though they didn't know it yet. All of this was accentuated by the arrival of that too-hot-to-believe cowboy husband of Charmaine's, Rusty Lanier. Whoo-boy! He gave a new twist to Cajun and cowboy in one neat package. Rusty, without Daniel being there to direct him, just emptied his pickup truck of a load of furniture that supposedly Daniel, via Tante Lulu and Charmaine, had ordered that afternoon. He left it all on the cabin porch for Daniel to sort out tomorrow, or whenever.

Daniel had apparently been a busy bee while she'd been off at the hospital being checked over this afternoon, after the incident with Nick.

She didn't like the way their meeting had ended earlier today, when he'd tried to convince her not to meet with Nick. For the first time, she began to wonder if he was still upset. She'd been thinking how happy Daniel would be to see her safe and Nick out of the picture, though none of them had wished Nick dead. How naïve of her!

Maybe he wasn't as happy as she'd imagined.

But then, maybe she was overthinking everything.

They ate dinner . . . a sumptuous feast of shrimp étouffée that Tante Lulu had whipped up, along with fluffy rice, accompanied by fresh bread that Aaron had bought in the bakery of the Starr store where he'd shopped. He'd also picked up another fruit tart, much to Lily Beth's delight, and Angus's and Samantha's, too, not having eaten since this morning. John also said it was wonderful, almost as good as Tante Lulu's Peachy Praline Cobbler Cake, which had made the old lady beam.

Throughout the meal, Samantha and Angus regaled the others with a retelling of the day's events. They were both still in a state of shock, or at the very least, on an adrenaline rush.

"I almost shit my pants when I walked into that office and saw Nick with a gun aimed at Samantha's head," Angus said with a laugh.

"Hush yer mouth, boy!" Tante Lulu said, flicking Angus with a dish towel. "That kind of language ain't proper."

"Ya shoulda said poop, instead of shit," John advised with a grin, probably having been flicked many a time in his life by his beloved aunt. Everyone, even as far as New Orleans, had heard of Tee-John LeDeux, the baddest Cajun to ever cross a bayou. He must have given Tante Lulu every one of the gray hairs she hid . . . under her Farrah Fawcett wig, which was incidentally lopsided at the moment. In fact, John leaned up and adjusted it for her.

"Or mebbe ya shouldn't say no bad words at all," the old lady said with a harrumphing sound.

"Anyhow, I don't even remember bein' shot," Angus went on. "It only hurt when I woke up."

"Ah, yer mah hero," Lily Beth drawled out, patting Angus on the shoulder. They were sitting side by side on one of the benches. It was a wonder the bench didn't tip over like a seesaw with the disproportionate weight. Really, Samantha could swear the girl had gained five pounds just since yesterday.

"Weren't ya scared?" Tante Lulu asked Samantha.

"Shaking in my high heels. Don't forget to give them back to Charmaine, by the way. The funny thing is, when you're in the middle of something dramatic like that, you don't stop to think, 'Boy, am I scared!' You're too caught up in the frenzy of your wildly beating heart, your light-headedness, and what's happening around you. Almost like you're hovering above the scene, and it's happening to someone else."

"I know what ya mean," Tante Lulu said. "I felt lak that when I first heard that mah fiancée, Phillipe, had died in the war." Everyone knew that long ago Tante Lulu had been engaged to Phillipe Prudhomme, a frogman, one of the original Navy SEALs, and that he'd died on Omaha Beach during World War II. "In fact, I felt lak that fer a long, long time. Fergit about that *Walkin' Dead* show on the TV. I was lak a true, blue, walkin', talkin' zombie. Fer years! I drank too much, smoked lak a chimney, and slept with more sailors than a French Quarter pros-tee-toot."

Whoa! TMI! I do not want to picture this old lady as a hooker.

"What made ya stop?" Lily Beth asked, in awe, hearing this story for the first time. Well, part of it was a first for Samantha, too.

"St. Jude, bless his heart. He come ta me right on Jackson Square before St. Louis Cathedral in Nawleans." Tante Lulu sighed and swiped at her teary eyes. "But thass another story."

John pulled his aunt down onto the bench beside him and kissed the top of her wig. "Now, doan be gettin' the moody blues."

"I won't," she said, "but sometimes it jist hits me, of a sudden, what I lost." She turned to Samantha. "Yer situation is different. You'll be feelin' better by t'morrow."

Samantha nodded. "Funny thing, though. Much as I had grown to detest Nick, and loathed the baby selling scheme of his, I never wished him dead. It saddens me."

"Course it does." Tante Lulu was back to her usual opinionated self. No longer weepy with memories. "It's cause we allus hope that bad folks will see the light before they go ta their Maker, and be saved. Lak I was by St. Jude."

Samantha wasn't sure about that. Not about Tante Lulu and St. Jude. But about everyone hoping that everyone would "see the light."

"It dint hafta end lak it did," John said. "If Coltrane hadn't shot at a cop and been aimin' his gun at Samantha, he wouldn't have been gunned down. 'Suicide by cop' probably hadn't been his intention, but that's how it worked out."

"Did he die right away? Before he could see the light?" Tante Lulu asked, making the sign of the cross.

"I don't know 'bout the light," John said, with a wink at Samantha, "but Daniel pronounced him dead at the scene, almost immediately after he was shot."

"Daniel was there?" Samantha tilted her head to the side. This was the first time she'd heard that. "In the parking garage?"

"*Mais oui,*" John answered. "Dint ya see him, *chère*?"

She shook her head, guessing that she'd been even more out of it than she'd recalled. But the idea that he'd been there, and left, gave her a foreboding of things not so right between them, more so than she'd thought.

John was telling Angus and Lily Beth what the situation would be from now on. "There will probably be a day or two before the paperwork is done for the Coltrane case. The accomplice, Misty Beauville, was arrested at a private airport outside the city, and she'll be spillin' the beans all night long, is mah guess. We doan think there'll be other arrests, too difficult to investigate perps outside the country, and it looks lak Coltrane was using some Nigerian middle men ta sell his product . . . i.e., babies."

Lily Beth groaned at that image. Her baby being shipped outside the country.

Once again, Angus hugged her in comfort.

And Samantha wondered if something might be developing between the two of them.

"Shouldn't I go back home to see what damage might have been done at my house?"

John shook his head. "Not yet. The house is secure. Give it another day or two. Let the Fibbies give you the all-safe signal before you leave here."

She nodded.

"The biggest concern now is Jimmy Guenot and his branch of the Dixie Mob," John went on. "Until those arrests are made, y'all have gotta lay low. Not you so much, Samantha, but by association, yer still in danger. As evidenced by those lowlifes that visited you before you left Nawleans."

"I keep tellin' y'all. Lemme call Jimmy's mama. If she knew what her boy was up to, she'd hogtie 'im and roast 'im over her bar-b-q." Truly, Tante Lulu was enjoying all the excitement, you could tell by the gleam in her eyes and the way she practically bounced on her seat as she talked.

"Yer not callin' anyone," John told his aunt. "Everything is still hush-hush."

"Right," Tante Lulu agreed, zipping her lips, but grinning mischievously. The bayou grapevine would be singing as soon as the old lady got the go-ahead, or maybe even beforehand.

After more discussion about the day's events, John said he was going to drive his aunt home, promising to pick up Tante Lulu's car the next day.

"I gotta come back mah self t'morrow to help with the cabin," she protested.

"Not tomorrow. You're having lunch with Charmaine, Sylvie, Rachel, and Valerie. A planning session for yer birthday party, remember?" Rachel and Valerie were the wives of Remy and René LeDeux. Tante Lulu's big pool party bash was planned for Saturday, only four days from now.

"Hmpfh! I doan see why I hafta plan mah own party? It should be a surprise."

"How could it be a surprise when it was yer idea ta begin with?"

She was still arguing with her nephew while they walked off. But almost immediately, she came back and told Samantha, "Tell Daniel I'll be puttin' the finishin' touches on his hope chest."

Then she was off again.

Samantha had to smile as she explained to Lily Beth and Angus how Tante Lulu made hope chests for all the men in her family. Quilts, monogrammed pillowcases, doilies, and lots of St. Jude imprinted items, like place mats, napkins, and wind chimes.

Aaron and Lily Beth went to their room where they planned to watch a *Big Bang Theory* marathon. The double bed they'd put in the front parlor for Lily Beth to use, temporarily . . . the one with the rice frame . . . had been moved up to the guest bedroom, aka Aunt Mel's room for when or if she ever came to visit, along with the rest of the matching bedroom furniture that had been delivered by some high school boys that day . . . an armoire and a dry sink. The boys had also brought two single bed frames that had been unreachable in the back of the storage unit, but for which Daniel and Samantha had already bought mattress sets.

Apparently, Daniel and Aaron had not only set up the guest bedroom, but they'd put together the two twin beds in the front parlor for Lily Beth and Angus to use. A lot of work for a temporary situation. Something more for which she had to thank Daniel. And Aaron, of course.

Samantha took care of all her animals, delighting in Clarence's new vocabulary. Maybe she should have spent more time teaching him. But then, maybe his ability to be taught would make him more adoptable.

It was almost ten o'clock before Samantha heard a vehicle in the front driveway. She'd taken a shower and put on clean clothes . . . well, relatively clean, considering her dwindling supply . . . and was running a comb through her damp hair. She rushed downstairs, anxious to see Daniel. She heard a vehicle shut down, and voices raised in discussion, then another motor turning over and a vehicle departing. She figured it was probably Aaron, off for his nightly trips to no one knew where.

By the time got to the front gallery and was going down the steps, though, all she could see by the exterior lights was Aaron. It was Daniel who had taken off.

"Where's Daniel?" she asked Aaron.

"Um . . . he decided to sleep on Remy LeDeux's houseboat tonight, to allow more room for you all here at Bayou Rose. It's just temporary." Aaron didn't quite meet her eyes as he relayed this news.

The message being: *temporary, as in, after I leave.*

Maybe it was better that she was alone tonight. So much had happened in such a short time. She wasn't thinking clearly.

Even so, the first thing she did when she got back in the house was hunt out a bottle of good Scotch whiskey. This was a night that warranted booze. Even Southern Belles, especially Scottish ones, appreciated the medicinal value on occasion of a good binge.

Chapter Twenty-Six

Who needs soap operas with a life like his? . . .

Daniel was not in a good mood when he arrived at Bayou Rose at nine o'clock the next morning. He'd barely slept all night, and then he had to go to the bus station in Houma at seven-thirty to pick up Edgar (call me Ed) Gillotte and take him for a quick visit to the cancer center before bringing him to the plantation.

Luckily, Molly was having a good day, and if she could keep her numbers steady for a week, a bone marrow transplant would be scheduled soon. Her daddy's presence proved to be the best medicine available. As the potential donor, Edgar would begin testing tomorrow, but that would only take a few hours every day until the surgery. In the meantime, he would work on the slave cabin and live there. Hopefully. Everything was based on hope.

Edgar was about thirty years old and overly thin, but with wide shoulders and impressive biceps. A receding reddish blond hairline led to long hair, clubbed at the neck into a ponytail. One of his incisors was missing. Probably no money to replace it once it had been pulled. Despite all that, he wasn't a bad-looking guy, and his clothes were well-worn, but clean.

But wait till Tante Lulu got a look at his tattoos, though. Up one arm and down the other, like a colorful billboard, and presumably on other body parts, as well. Daniel hadn't looked too close. He hoped they weren't pornographic. Oh, hell, no, he didn't care. And Tante Lulu probably wouldn't either. Except . . . oh, crap! . . . was that a horned devil peeking out of a bush? *Tante Lulu will have a screaming Cajun fit.*

Daniel skirted the mansion and went past the struggling rose garden with the St. Jude birdbath.

"Whoa! Who is that dude?"

"St. Jude. Patron saint of hopeless people."

"Like me?" Edgar asked with a laugh.

"Or me."

"You do seem kinda down," Edgar observed.

"You could say that."

"Woman troubles?"

"You could say that."

"I can give you advice. I've been married three times. My first wife got a bun in the oven when we were in college. Never did take to the baby. She ran off with an ROTC guy on campus 'cause she liked his uniform. I was in my sophomore year. Football scholarship. Had to drop out, of course.

"My second wife decided she'd rather be a lesbian, and don't think that doesn't kick a man in the nuts. She left me with two more kids.

"My third, and present wife, went to do the laundry

one day and never came back. That marriage resulted in one more kid, Molly. I'd get a divorce if I could find her, or if I had the money.

"Thank God for my mama, the world's number one babysitter, but she's getting up in years, and my cousins Erline and Dorsey, who help out sometimes, are a little bit sluttish and tend to wander off at the most inappropriate times, and . . . well, you get the picture."

In 3-D, high definition, color! Under normal circumstances, Daniel would have told himself he should count his blessings, but he wasn't in the mood for counting blessings. He'd rather count all the ways Samantha was driving him batshit crazy.

"This is a great property," Edgar remarked, looking around, "and the house has good bones. I know because I worked on a mansion down in Savannah's historic district that was filled with termite holes, practically fell down on itself, like Swiss cheese. 'Course I'm only seein' your place from the outside."

"It's about the same inside. A lifetime of work to be done."

"Well, that's why I'm here. To help. While I can."

"But just with the slave cabin, at first."

Edgar nodded. He understood that this was a trial. "You won't be disappointed."

After his initial inspection of the cabin, which was really just a square space, roughly twenty by twenty with a small fireplace, and an extra room hardly bigger than a closet for sleeping. Edgar declared it "a piece of cake." He went on to explain that the rudiments of electricity were there. A trip to the hardware store for some parts and tools, and "there would be light," he proclaimed. Plumbing was a bigger deal; it would require some digging to connect to the main line of the house. Still, something he could do with some rental equipment.

"I'm thinking a little kitchenette over there with a sink under the window, an apartment-size fridge, and a little two-burner stove. It would be like an efficiency. Living room and kitchen combined, all in one space, no divider. They must have used that fireplace over there for cooking and heating in the winter. I would just shove a portable heater in there.

"The biggest problem I see is no bathroom. They didn't have indoor bathrooms back in the day. If you want a bathroom, you'll have to give up that little bedroom. It could barely hold a bed, anyhow. That couch out there on the porch looks like a sleeper sofa. Works for me. What do you think?"

"Works for me, too, but in the meantime?"

"I'll get this main room cleaned up and the furniture inside. That will be enough for me, as long as I can use your shower and bathroom for a few days."

"You can use the facilities in the *garconniére* apartment. No one is there during the day most times, anyhow." At least while Aaron was sleeping there.

Edgar nodded. "I'll make my first priority the plumbing so I can get a bathroom up and going. Nothing fancy. One of those surplus warehouses should have everything I need."

Daniel knew all about warehouses. In fact, he felt like an expert on the subject, after the visit he and Samantha had made to the furniture warehouse . . . was it only two days ago?

Samantha! There he went again! Samantha on his mind!

"Yo, Dan!" It was Aaron coming up the walkway.

Daniel motioned for Edgar to join them. "This is Edgar Gillotte, the man I told you about last night. Ed, this is my brother Aaron, who fancies himself a hotshot flyboy."

"A pilot," Aaron corrected, as he shook Edgar's hand. "A *hotshot* pilot." He looked freshly showered and shaved, must be going to work. After a five-minute tour of the premises, Aaron patted him on the back. "I'm impressed, bro. Looks like you have everything under control."

Hardly. My life is out of control.

"Luc called this morning. He and the feds will be here this afternoon. Are you going to be around, or should I tell Luc you're hiding out like a wimp?"

"I'll be here," Daniel said. He probably would have made some excuse if Aaron hadn't pre-empted him with the wimp accusation. Daniel wanted to ask about Samantha, and Aaron knew he wanted to ask, if his smirk was any indication, but Daniel would be damned if he would give in first.

"Do you happen to have a crowbar? I could pull up . . ." Edgar stopped midsentence as he came out onto the porch. His jaw dropped as he was staring over Daniel's shoulder. "I think I'm in love," Edgar said, and he appeared to be serious. "She is absolutely gorgeous."

Damn! Samantha must have decided to join the crowd. But when Daniel turned, it wasn't Samantha he saw. It was Lily Beth waddling toward them, and Emily was waddling right behind her, oinking joyously, no doubt in anticipation of a kiss from her best bud, Daniel.

Daniel glanced back at Edgar to see if he'd been teasing. But no, Edgar stood gaping, not at Emily, of course, but at Lily Beth, like a poleaxed teenager at first sight of his first nude woman. And Lily Beth stopped at the broken gate, staring at Edgar with equal appreciation.

Daniel and Aaron exchanged glances and raised eyebrows.

Emily trotted forward and Daniel picked her up like a baby with her snout on his shoulder.

Aaron gave him a look of disgust.

"Tante Lulu keeps harping about some thunderbolt of love, but maybe she meant Edgar, not me," Daniel said, even as he stroked Emily's bristly back. But then he set the pig down so she could do some exploring in the yard.

"Or not me, either," Aaron added. "She's been after me with her matchmaking wand, too."

But the contrast! A very pregnant almost-doctor of physics and a college dropout, blue collar, unemployed worker?

Did wonders never cease?

Apparently not, because Angus came running out of the back door and along the path to the cabin. He was singing that Pharrell Williams "Happy" song and every couple steps, he stopped to do a few hip hop dance moves. When he got closer, out of breath, but smiling, he announced, "It's over. Jimmy Guenot and his gang got arrested last night. Just saw it on *Huffington Post*. It's hotdamnohmygodyippee over!"

"It's over?" Lily Beth asked. "Really?"

"Yep. I pulled up the *Times-Picayune* page on the Internet to double-check, and the raid involved three mob bosses, including Jimmy Guenot, twelve other 'soldiers' and some sleazy lawyer/accountant. In all, they brought in ten million in loan sharking notes, fifty pounds of cocaine, a truckload of marijuana, and a warehouse full of stolen property. They also closed down a strip joint that was a front for prostitution."

They all began to clap and then join Angus in an impromptu "Happy" dance. Not Daniel, who wasn't much of a dancer, though he was dancing on the inside. Aaron, on the other hand, could be one of those Chippendale dancers with his sexy moves. Where did he learn that crap? And Lily Beth . . . oh, Lord! She looked like an elephant dirty dancing with Edgar whom she was calling

"Eddie" already. As skinny as Edgar was, you could call it "Elephant Pole Dancing."

That's how out of control Daniel was. He was making jokes with himself.

Just then, it occurred to Daniel that Samantha hadn't come outside to celebrate with them. That was odd.

"Where's Samantha?" Daniel asked Angus.

"She stayed inside to start packing her bags. She's pissed at you."

"Uh-oh! More trouble in paradise!" Aaron said as he hip-bumped him in the middle of his fool dancing.

"Huh? How dare she be pissed at me. I'm the one who's pissed. At her."

"Dontcha just love a good pissing contest?" Aaron said, out loud, and everyone laughed, even though they had no idea what pissing contest Aaron was talking about.

In the midst of all that gaiety, Daniel left the premises. He was not going to be here when she left.

The gig is up . . .

Samantha kept watching for Daniel to come see her all morning and then into the afternoon. When the two feds, along with Luc and John LeDeux, arrived at three and there was still no Daniel, she had to accept that he wasn't just avoiding her, he was saying good-bye. Sayonara. Adios. Every which way but in person.

"Where's the doctor?" Brad Dillon asked. He wasn't wearing a suit and tie today, but he *was* wearing a blue dress shirt . . . the collar unbuttoned and sleeves rolled up . . . tucked into black slacks.

"I think he went to the hardware store," John said. "Do you need him here for this meeting?"

"No, but I would have liked to thank him for his service at the scene."

"Send him a Hallmark card," Luc advised.

"Bite me," Brad countered. "Do you know the difference between a skunk and a lawyer? No? The answer: No one wants to hit a skunk."

"Ha, ha, that joke is as old as you are."

"Cajun douche bag!"

"D.C. dimwit!"

Luc and the FBI agent had been sniping at each other ever since they arrived, something about a promise being put in writing that hadn't been so far.

Samantha would have liked to escape, maybe go check out the progress on the cabin and to learn more about Daniel's plans. Was this a one-shot deal for one parent of a sick child, or a bigger deal, like a whole new mission for Bayou Rose? But she could be as stubborn as Daniel. Let him make the first move.

Brad told them what had happened with the Dixie Mob arrests and the implications for Angus. Also, he gave an update on the baby selling scheme.

"Does that mean we can go home now?" Samantha asked, with a sinking heart because she hated to leave with things unsettled between her and Daniel.

"I'd prefer that you wait a few days, maybe until after the weekend. There are a lot of loose ends to be tied up, and we need to cross our *I*'s and dot our *T*'s to make sure there aren't any stragglers out there who could pose a danger."

"Is that an official order?" Luc asked.

Brad sighed with exasperation. "No, it's not an order. It's a recommendation."

Luc turned to Samantha, Angus, and Lily Beth. "Then I suggest that you all stay here a few more days. It's not a hardship, is it? And y'all are invited to the pool party at

my house on Saturday to celebrate Tante Lulu's birthday.
Maybe you could plan on leaving Dodge on Sunday."

"That would work," Brad said.

"You're invited, too," Luc said with exaggerated generosity.

"That would be just great. I'm not your aunt's favorite
person. Tante Lulu told me to get the pole out of my ass
when I made an offhand remark about her hair."

"Did she use those exact words?" John wanted to
know.

"No. She used the word hiney."

They all laughed at that.

"I can't believe this all went down so quick and easy,"
Angus said.

Sonnier . . . "Sonny" . . . was the other agent at the
meeting, dressed like he was ready for the gym, again.
He addressed Angus's remark. "Not so quick . . . 'cept in
the case of Coltrane, and, believe me, that's not the way
we want an investigation ta end. But the Dixie Mob case,
we've been workin' on that fer two years now. Yer evidence was just icing on the cake."

"So, you could have done without me?" Angus said, a
little pee-ohed.

"Not at all," Sonny interjected. "Every bit of evidence . . . physical, oral, whatever . . . is a brick in the
wall of the cases we develop. One brick slips out, and the
whole wall kin collapse. Do ya get mah meanin', *cher*?"

"I do," Angus conceded grudgingly. Then, he bright-
ened and asked, "I don't suppose you could get back my
Jaguar that I sold to Jimmy for half its value to pay off
one of my early debts."

Sonny laughed. "Jimmy still has the Jag. We wondered
about that. Not his usual style. But, no, my friend, you are
not gettin' yer car back. It's government property now."

"Will it be sold?"

"Possibly. At public auction." It was Brad speaking now. "Why? You want to bid on it?"

Angus's face reddened. "Maybe my father would buy it back for me."

"Angus!" Samantha and Lily Beth both said at the same time.

"Okay, okay, I guess that was pushing it," Angus conceded.

"A bit of advice, son," a somber-faced Brad said then, "cut the gambling."

"I already have. I haven't even played online poker for two weeks."

They all rolled their eyes at that.

After this was over, Samantha was going to find out if Angus had a gambling addiction, and, if he did, he was going to land in a rehab center quicker than he could say, "Royal Flush!"

You'd think the chaos of their lives with its peculiar ups and downs these past few days would be over. Not a chance.

Just then, Fred Olsen, the other FBI agent, in country club attire again . . . i.e., slacks, golf shirt, and even an Augusta National cap . . . came into the doorway, the one leading through the hall to the ground floor verandah. "You won't believe who just arrived."

"Oh, no! Did Tante Lulu come back? How did she get here? Her car's still parked out front," John said.

Luc grimaced and replied, "Are you kiddin'? She could have hitchhiked if she wanted ta come bad enough."

"It's not Tante Lulu," Fred told them with a wide grin. "It's Braveheart and Florence 'Hatchet Face' Henessey."

And in walked her father in full Scottish dress, complete with kilt, tartan, and sporran, attire which didn't surprise her or Angus, but must be a bit of a shock to the rest of them in the room. And beside him walked a frowning Florence, his wife, who apparently was also known as "Hatchet Face."

"What the hell is going on here?" her father asked at the same time Brad asked, "How did you know these folks were here? It's supposed to be a friggin' secret."

Her father waved a hand airily. "I have a friend in the police department."

Brad shook his head with disgust, then put up his arms in surrender. "Well, our cover is blown here now. You all might as well go home."

So, it was over, Samantha thought. In more ways than one.

Turns out it had been a one-night stand, after all.

Chapter Twenty-Seven

S aved by Braveheart . . .

Daniel knew something was different at Bayou Rose when he returned from the hardware store. His first clue was that there were no vehicles parked in the front driveway. Not Aaron's truck, though he was probably still at work. Nor the FBI or police unmarked cars, which meant the meeting was over. Even Samantha's BMW was missing.

Daniel felt a sudden lurch of despair. For some reason, he'd thought Samantha and her gang would be staying another few days. Something must have happened.

He drove around the side of the house and parked as close as he could to the slave cabin, rather "the cottage," which he supposed was more politically correct. Edgar, who'd stayed behind, came out to help him unload all the plumbing and paint supplies he'd purchased. The celery green paint for the walls . . . not moss green, nor sage green . . . but celery green, as ordered by Tante Lulu before she'd left. As if she was some kind of bleepin' construction foreman for this project.

Even though he kept emphasizing that this was only a one cottage venture, Tante Lulu was making plans, he could tell. In fact, she'd called his cell phone this morning and without preamble declared that all the cottages should be painted a different color, like Sunshine Yellow for the first, and others could be such cornball colors as Bluebird Blue, Grassy Green, Pansy Purple, and so on. Apparently she'd had a dream about them. Samantha would have a fit about the historical inaccuracy of the colors, if she ever found out.

Edgar asked Daniel to come inside and see what he'd been doing while Daniel was out shopping for supplies. Edgar, his face flushed with pride, paused in the act of tossing some cushions onto the sofa.

Daniel glanced around at the used furniture arranged on a green-and-black area rug, and he had to admit that the room looked nice. The oak coffee table with matching end tables, brass lamps, even a bookcase. Once the walls were painted, a few pictures hung, and maybe some curtains put on the windows, it would be a cozy little retreat for the parent of a sick kid. Just what he'd envisioned, but more.

It occurred to Daniel that, if Samantha and Angus and Lily Beth were no longer here, he could call the workers to return for work on the mansion. Somehow, the thought wasn't heartening. More pounding and scraping and power tools!

"Where is everyone, by the way?" he asked with as casual a tone as he could manage.

"They all left after that meeting with the police and

FBI goons. Man, don't think I wasn't nervous with all those police cars around?"

"So, the FBI said it was safe to leave here now that the arrests were made."

"Well, not exactly. It was when Samantha's daddy showed up and raised hell."

"What?"

Edgar went on to tell a preposterous story, which had been related to him secondhand by Lily Beth, about this kilt-wearing Scotsman and a woman named "Hatchet Face" interrupting the FBI/police meeting. Afterward, Daniel said, "So, it's over."

"It's not over 'til the fat lady sings," Edgar opined.

Daniel didn't know any fat singers, but he did know a witchy Cajun matchmaker, who probably thought she had the final say in anything affecting any and all members of her extended LeDeux family.

Unfortunately, or fortunately, Daniel was a member of that family.

When all else fails, go to the expert . . .

Samantha was back in her New Orleans home, considerably lighter on animals, but heavier in the heart.

She now had only Axel, Maddie, and Emily . . . and Clarence, of course, who was going to be adopted soon. She hoped.

But she was a different woman now. A woman in love. Dammit! Unrequited love. Dammit. How had this wonderful/awful attachment happened so quickly and so powerfully?

Well, it wasn't so quickly, she was beginning to realize. Over the past few years, since she'd first met Daniel at John LeDeux's wedding, there had been a spark. She'd always considered it a spark of hostility, but now she was beginning to think there had been an attraction from the get-go, and she'd chosen to handle it with snarkiness. After all, he was a doctor and she'd been committed to lumping all doctors in one big dungpile of egotism, self-ishness, and greed.

Which made her think of Nick, of course. His funeral was tomorrow. How sad, that such a bright, handsome man could have gone down the path he had! She felt no regrets, except that she would have wished him in prison, rather than wherever he was now.

To add to her misery, every member of her family had been on the phone to her. Commiserating. Wanting details. Discussing past associations with Nick.

"So sad!" (*Yep!*)

"He always was a louse!" (*Well, yeah! Hindsight is 20/20.*)

"But he wore a pink tie when he visited me!" (*Well, duh! He was trying to con you.*)

"Do you think I'll ever get back the money I loaned him eight years ago?" (*When gators fly!*)

"Are you going to the funeral?" (*Hell, no!*)

"What will happen to his new building?" (*Sold to settle debts, I would think.*)

The news media was after her, too. She was tempted to go back to Bayou Rose to hide out till the scandal blew over, but her pride was too great. And Daniel hadn't invited her.

Her father and Florence had taken Angus to Costa Rica with them for a "little vacation," which meant that the law was being laid down, and strict rules set for Angus's future. He was going to return to college when they got back and/or get a job. And he was going to live at home until his finances were in better shape. The prospect of living with Florence would straighten him out, if nothing else would.

Samantha wasn't really alone, she had to remind herself. Lily Beth was staying with her until her brother Vic got home on leave in a few weeks. She hadn't told her preacher brother, Paul, about the pregnancy, but she had told the soldier brother in Afghanistan. Turned out Vic was delighted for her. He was engaged to marry a girl from Lafayette and he said he could buy a small house when he returned for them all to live together, including the baby. And she could continue her studies, if she wanted. Lily Beth had no intention of telling her brother about Nick, which was none of Samantha's business.

So, all's well that ends well, she thought. *For some people.*

It was Lily Beth in all her youthful wisdom who gave her the answer, after another day had passed and no word from Daniel. "What do ya really want, Samatha?"

"Daniel," she answered without hesitation. Yeah, she wanted him to want her. She wanted him to chase her. She wanted him to coax her into coming back. But bottom line? She repeated, "Daniel."

"Well, golly gee, Samantha, bless yer heart, why don't ya go get him then?"

Was it as simple as that?

No, Samantha was a list maker. She made plans and then acted them out. But how to do that? She had an idea. Could she? Should she? She picked up her cell phone.

"Hello. Tante Lulu?"

"Yes, is that you, Samantha?"

"Yes. I hate to impose, but . . ."

"But what, dearie?"

"I need help."

"Ta get Daniel?"

"How did you know?"

Tante Lulu laughed. "I may be old, but I ain't blind."

"Can I come over to tell you what I'm thinking?"

"I'll put the coffee on and the cake's already in the oven."

Nothing soothes a woman like shopping . . . at the local porn shop . . .

Charmaine was with Louise when Samantha's phone call came.

Louise explained the situation to Charmaine.

"I swear, that Daniel is two times a fool, worse even than Tee-John when he was fallin' in love with Celine," Charmaine said. "Do you think Samantha would mind if I stay? I have a few things to tell her that might help."

"Stay, and if she's uncomfortable, ya can leave."

They had just made a cake together . . . a new one for Louise. Orange Marmalade cake, according to a recipe Louise had found in a series of books about a preacher in some town called Mitford. With a few modifications, if the cake turned out as good as it smelled, Louise might very well have a new specialty, Cajun Orange Marmalade Cake, as good as her Peachy Praline Cobbler Cake. A woman was never too old to learn something new.

Samantha arrived an hour later, just as they were icing the four-tiered cake and decorating it with little mandarin oranges.

Louise reached up and gave Samantha a hug. And she really did need to reach because Samantha was tall for a woman. But then, Louise was small, compared to anyone.

Samantha greeted Charmaine warmly, too, and she only revealed with a sudden widening of her eyes how she felt about Charmaine's attire today. An off-the-shoulder blouse, Daisy Duke short shorts, and high-heeled wedgie sandals. Her hair was swept up on top of her head and she wore that new lipstick featured in her salons, "Rose Satin."

Louise asked, "Do ya mind if Charmaine stays? She might have an opinion or two ta help."

Samantha hesitated, but then she said, "Sure."

"I assume this is about that pighead, prideful Daniel?" Charmaine said right off. "All the LeDeux men are the same, bless their Cajun hearts."

Samantha laughed, then nodded.

"Tell us what the problem is, 'zackly," Louise encouraged.

She did, and Louise tried to bite her tongue about the sex outside of marriage. She wasn't a prude, but she still didn't like women offering themselves up without a ring. A little hanky panky would be fine, but the whole shebang? Uh-uh! She was of the old school about men. Why should they buy the cow when they got the milk for free? So to speak.

"Honey, ya need ta understand Daniel's history. It wasn't a woman that made him so walled up, though there have been plenty, I'm sure. Workin' with sick young'uns saps the life out of any doctor, but one as sensitive as Daniel . . . well, after his favorite patient died, a little boy, followed by his mother, he jist broke down. Not like a nervous breakdown, which shows on the outside. He kept his grief all inside."

Samantha's jaw dropped. "How do you know all that?"

"I bin talkin' ta his aunt Mel on the phone. An' I gotta tell ya, Daniel's sit-ye-ay-shun is jist lak my nephew Remy's, before he met his Rachel," Louise said. "Remy was burned in Desert Storm when he was flyin' planes fer the Air Force. 'Cause he was scarred all along one side of his body and 'cause he became sterile, he dint think any woman would ever want him. Kept himself shielded up, jist like Daniel."

Charmaine was nodding.

"Back ta Daniel. We gotta find a way ta shake the boy out of safety nets. How 'bout we stage one of the LeDeux Cajun Village People acts? Mebbe all the females in the family could be dressed in sexy nurse outfits, and you could shimmy out on ta the stage, and—"

"No, I don't think that would work. For me or for Daniel." Samantha blushed and said, "I have something else in mind." She went on to explain something about sexual fantasies. "I have an idea. It probably won't work. I might not have the nerve to even give it a try."

Louise, who had been bustling about the kitchen, cleaning up from the cake baking, plopped down on one of the chairs at her kitchen table. She and Charmaine stared at Samantha with interest.

"Go on," Charmaine encouraged.

"I might shock you," Samantha confessed.

"Girl, ya cain't shock me," Louise asserted.

"Me, neither," Charmaine said. "Wait 'til I tell ya 'bout the time I became a born again virgin. 'Bout ta gave Rusty a heart attack."

"My sexual fantasies allus centered on my crush, Richard Simmons. But before that, they starred Phillippe, of course," Louise told them.

"Mine were about Rusty, from the first time I met him. There's somethin' 'bout cowboys that get a girl's juices goin'," Charmaine disclosed.

"What about you, sweetie?" Tante Lulu asked.

"First of all, I need a harem girl outfit," Samantha revealed. "I have no idea where I would even look for one. The Internet, I suppose. But that would take too long to get here."

"Oooh, oooh, ooh. Wait jist a minute." Louise rushed out of the room and pulled out a box from under her bed.

When she returned she showed them the belly dancing outfit she'd bought in the old days, like ten years ago, when she and Charmaine had been entering belly dancing contests. She spread it out on the table in front of Samantha. All sheer fabric and sequins and little bells along the hem of the pants. "It might be a little small fer you, but it's supposed ta be one size fits all."

Charmaine said, "I'd lend you mine, but I wore it out from overuse."

Samantha said, "This is perfect. But I need some other things, besides. Tools of the trade." She was blushing redder than a June bride now.

"Tools?" Charmaine asked.

"Velvet handcuffs, that kind of thing." If her face got any redder, she was gonna explode.

"I allus wanted to get me a pair of velvet handcuffs."

"I already have a pair. Two pairs, actually. One set fer me, and one fer Rusty," Charmaine said.

Samantha looked at them both as if they were crazy.

"Well, there's only one answer to the dilemma. We gotta go shoppin'," Charmaine said.

"Shopping? Where?" Samantha asked.

"The Frisky Fun Boutique in Houma," Charmaine answered.

"Whoo-ee, I allus wanted ta go there," Louise said.

Thus it was that, three hours later, after another cup of strong chicory coffee and slices of the marmalade cake, which was, indeed, a big hit, Samantha was driving back to New Orleans with not just velvet handcuffs, but vibrating thingees, a strange whip made with feathers, some kind of balls, and nipple rings made of flexible brass, which didn't require piercing. Ouch!

Louise had also made some purchases for herself, but she wasn't telling. There might be crotchless panties involved.

Who says big boys don't cry? . . .

Friday night, and he was alone at Bayou Rose.

Daniel thought about moving all his stuff back to the *garconniére*, but he would do that tomorrow. He was, frankly, beat after a day of hard labor with Edgar. With shovels and a small rented backhoe manned by Edgar, they'd managed to trench plumbing lines from the mansion to the cabin. They would cover the pipes with dirt tomorrow, and then Edgar could begin the inside plumbing work, installing a bathroom sink, shower, and toilet, plus the kitchen sink.

The inside and exterior painting had been completed, and it did look nice and cheerful. Tante Lulu had sent over some extra curtains she just happened to have.

Daniel was thankful for all the help, and he was very impressed with Edgar's expertise and work ethic. Next week, the carpenters and painters would return to renovations on the mansion. Daniel had already decided to hire Edgar to work with them, perhaps oversee the whole project.

No matter what use the cabins were put to finally, they would have had to be updated anyhow. The mansion renovations, however, were on hold. He kept picturing Samantha, who got a dreamy look in her eyes every time she talked about this or that historical detail.

There he went again. Samantha on his mind. Wasn't there a song about that? No, that was Georgia. But it could have been Samantha. Aaarrgh!

Daniel had already decided that he was going to have to dump his pride and approach Samantha. Lay his feelings out before her. And see what happened. If he got shot down again, so be it. But at least he will have tried. Maybe he would see her at Tante Lulu's birthday party. Then he could appear sort of casual and not have to humble himself.

Who was he kidding? If he was in love, like he was ninety-nine percent sure he was, humble was the least of his problems. He should be crawling on his knees, begging her to . . . what? That was the question. What did he want?

He wanted Samantha, that's all he knew. And not just for a one night stand. Did he want to marry her? Hmmm He hadn't thought that far.

Enough thinking for tonight. He went over to the *garconniére* to check on the kittens. Amazingly, they seemed to have doubled in size since their birth a few days ago, especially the little white one. If all went well, Edgar had permission to take Molly out of the hospital for a few hours on Sunday. The one thing she was determined to do was see her kitty, Snowball.

While he was at the apartment, he noticed a UPS package addressed to him, sitting by the door. It had an Alaska postmark on it, but not one he recognized. Aaron must have forgotten to give it to him.

Opening it, he was surprised to see a pile of old superhero comic books. Superman. Spiderman. Captain America. Batman. And there was a letter.

Dear Dr. LeDeux:

Remember me? Jamie Lee Watson, Deke's dad. Bet you're surprised to hear from me. Thanks to you, I've been clean for two years now, and Bethany and me just had a little girl, which we named Danielle.

But that's not why I'm writing. We were cleaning Deke's old room to make a nursery for the new baby when we found a silly little "Last Will and Testment" he'd written before he went into hospice. In it, he willed you his comic book collection. Don't know what you're going to do with it, but, hey, I got his goldfish, which have long since gone to the Great Goldfish Beyond. Deke really liked you, Dr. LeDeux, and not just as his doctor.

I just wanted you to know that you made a difference in a little boy's life, and in mine and Bethany's, too.

Fondly,
Jamie Lee Watson

Daniel had tears in his eyes when he finished the letter. Maybe this was the closure he'd needed after all these years. Maybe this would be the impetus for his return to medicine.

After watching a little TV, he went back to the mansion, took a long shower, and went to bed. He was sure that tonight he'd be able to sleep.

On the other hand, maybe he would have one of those hot fantasy Samantha dreams. He fell asleep smiling.

Chapter Twenty-Eight

The things a girl will do for love! . . .

Samantha arrived at Bayou Rose about ten p.m., later than she had planned. Emily had been acting particularly depressed, missing her best bud, Daniel, no doubt, almost as much as Samantha did. It had taken Samantha an hour and several piggie treats before the animal would settle down.

Plus, Samantha had driven very carefully on the way here. How would she have explained to a state trooper why she was dressed like a harem girl/belly dancer, with removable nipple rings, no less? He would probably have thought she was a call girl on the way to meet a John. Or something equally distasteful.

The lights were out in the mansion, except for the outdoor security lamp, which meant Daniel was probably already in bed, maybe even asleep. That would be good. She wanted to surprise him.

She got out of her car and pulled a tote bag with her, a tote bag filled with the tools of her trade. And didn't that say something about how far gone she was? She was careful to not slam the door, and she crept slowly up the steps, not wanting her tiny ankle bells to jingle. Yet.

The key was in its usual place under an urn by the front door. Once inside, she closed and locked the door. Standing still for a moment, she listened. Silence. So far, so good.

Once she got to the second floor, she set her bag down in the hall and pulled out one of those disposable lighters. She was hoping the candles were still around the room that she'd set there earlier in the week, the night of her one-night stand. Well, now she was hoping to go for a two-night stand, and maybe more than that.

Daniel was asleep and he didn't awaken while she crept around the room, lighting candles. He didn't even awaken when she dragged her tote bag into the bedroom and closed the door.

He did awaken when she forgot to walk carefully and her bells tinkled softly, but still, in the silence of the room, they sounded like gongs.

Propping himself on both elbows, he blinked several times, then went wide-eyed. "Holy shit! Am I dreaming?"

"No, you're not dreaming. It's me. In the flesh. Ta da!" She gave a little pose to show off her outfit. Tante Lulu's belly dance costume fit her better than it ever did the old lady. Her breasts filled the cups of the upper sheer blouse, and the bottom pants hung low on her hips, showcasing her new (glued on) belly button ring. She was bare-footed, and there wasn't much of her body that wasn't exposed.

"Turn around," he said. When she did, he asked, "Are you jingling?"

"Like a bell choir." She lifted an ankle to show him the little bells sewn onto the bottom hem of the pants.

"Why are you doing this, Samantha? You wanna get laid, just ask."

She cringed. "Does there have to be a reason?"

"It's not like you."

"This is the new me."

"How is this going to play out?"

"You had your fantasy night. Now I'm going to have mine."

"Okaaay. But I have to tell you, I've decided I'm not into one-night stands anymore."

"How would you know what you're into? You've been blocked up for so long, a laxative wouldn't move you."

He laughed. "Sounds like you've been talking to Tante Lulu. Good Lord! This was her idea?"

"No, it was totally my idea."

Meanwhile, she had taken a small disc player out of her tote bag and set it on the dresser. It began to play some eastern belly dance music. She swayed her hips like she thought a belly dancer might.

"Oh, my God! Do that again."

She did, and she threw in a little hip thrust.

"Interesting, but not enough to change my stance on one-night stands."

Since when did he get to take a position on one-night stands? That was her right to make such a demand. Damn, she was getting confused. Must be the wine she'd drunk before leaving her house, to give her fortification.

"Okay, so you don't want a one-night stand. How about I give you a fantasy sex event every night, like that Arabian Nights story?" she offered.

"You've got my attention now, sweetheart. You do know that was a thousand and one nights?"

She shrugged. "Give or take."

He was sitting up straighter now, and the sheet which had been drawn to his chest slipped away, revealing a pair of boxer briefs, and nothing else.

Good.

"Would you like a glass of wine?"

He was clearly surprised by the offer. "Sure."

She reached down and took out a bottle of wine and two crystal glasses, set them on the dresser, and poured.

He laughed. "What else have you got in the bag?"

"You would be really, really surprised." She handed him his glass and took a sip from hers. The wine was no longer chilled, but it would do.

"Give me a hint." He took a sip of his wine and nodded his appreciation of its taste.

"Suffice it to say, I went to the Frisky Fun Boutique in Houma today to make a few purchases."

"A sex shop? You didn't!" he said, and took a really long sip this time.

"I did."

"By yourself?"

"Nope. Tante Lulu and Charmaine went with me."

He choked on his wine and set it on the bedside table. "I do not want to picture that scene. And I definitely do not want to know if they bought anything."

"They did," she told him anyway.

He groaned, then sat up on the side of the bed. "What did you buy?"

"Well, I don't want to disclose all my secrets at once."

"God forbid you should do that!"

"I will show you these, though." She lifted out a pair of velvet handcuffs and waved them in the air.

He laughed. "Are those for you or for me?"

"Me at first. I have this fantasy, see. You're the sheik, and I'm the slave girl you've just added to your harem. I'm fighting my captivity, so you cuff me to a tent pole, and—"

"You've really thought this fantasy through, haven't you?"

"Oh, yeah. Anyhow, the sheik . . . you . . . are torturing me with . . . things."

"What things?"

"Oh, some of the tools I have in my bag."

"Tools now?"

"Uh-huh."

"Samantha, this is all cool and everything, but I'm really pissed at you, and until I resolve—"

"Did I tell you I have nipple rings?" she interjected quickly, not wanting to have that particular talk. Later, after they made love a time or three. In case he hadn't heard her, she flashed him a nipple.

He stood so quickly he almost knocked over the glass of wine. "I thought I was good at fantasies, but I can see I'm way out of my league."

"Not really. If I stand here much longer, I'm going to lose my nerve."

He reached out and grabbed the cuffs from her. Before she knew it, she was backed up against one of the bedposts, her hands restrained behind her back on the other side of the tent pole/bedpost, her breasts thrust out, making her appear bigger than she was.

He noticed. "I think it's time I took over this fantasy . . . before you lose your nerve, or I lose . . ." He glanced down at the bulge in his boxers.

"Whatever you say, master."

"Isn't that a little demeaning for a woman?"

"Not if you refer to me as Mistress in later fantasies."

"*Later* fantasies? Better and better," he muttered. "And what is your name, slave girl?"

"Salome."

"Of course it is. Okay, Sal baby, let's see what you have in your magic bag."

She groaned. "We should probably be drunk before you do that."

"That good, huh?"

"Or bad." She groaned again. "I am going to be so embarrassed."

"Why should I be the only one embarrassed? I bared my soul with all my secret fantasies."

"You weren't embarrassed at all."

"You're right."

He was digging in her bag and took out the red vibrator thingee. He flicked on a button and it made a whirring sound in his palm. "Interesting. For later." He set it aside.

Next, he took out a little leather case.

"Don't you dare laugh."

Inside was a string of silver balls. "Ben wa balls. I'm not sure I know what to do with these. You'll have to show me."

"Like I know what to do! I didn't know whether to buy that one, or the Adam and Eve ones."

"What?" He looked at her, rather puzzled, and set those aside, too. "For later." Then he took out the last of her "tools." It was the long whip with the feather tails. "Now this one I know I can use." He came toward her and flicked the feathers across her breasts, causing the already turgid nipples encased in the nipple rings to grow even bigger and harder.

He noticed.

She moaned.

"Do you like that, slave girl?"

"Yes," she breathed.

He did it again, then ordered, "Dance for me, Salome."

"I can't, with my arms behind me."

"Yes, you can. Dance in place." He flicked the disc player on again. It had apparently turned off at its end. The eastern music filled the room again.

She began to sway from side to side, and realized that she actually had room to move a little, and so she undulated a bit, emulating the sex act.

Daniel muttered something under his breath, which she took for a good sign, and did some more undulating. "Am I a good slave girl?" she asked, glancing downward.

He knew she was teasing him for his own over-arousal and asked, bluntly, "Are you wet yet?"

"I don't know. Why don't you check?"

"Tsk-tsk-tsk! Didn't you ever hear that saying, 'Never challenge a Cajun!'?"

"I think that referred to something else."

He set the feather whip aside and unbuttoned her blouse, setting free her breasts with the gold clips on them. "Oh, my!" he said and touched each of them with his fingertips. "Don't stop dancing," he ordered.

What? She couldn't dance and concentrate on what he was doing at the same time. She tried, but it was difficult, especially when he'd taken up the whip again and was feathering across the nipples, back and forth, slowly, then rapidly.

She was panting, even as she continued to sway and undulate to the music. When he pinched each of the nipples, softly, she whispered, "More."

"Slave girls do not give orders. Spread your legs, but don't stop dancing. Now, are you wet yet?"

She was going to tell him to check himself, like she had before, but she knew better this time. Besides, his one hand was braced against the bedpost and the other hand was already sweeping down over her abdomen, across her belly where he paused to look at the ring she'd pasted there, then inside the elastic waistband of her low-slung harem pants until he reached her wetness. One, two, three strokes of his finger in her slickness where her clitoris felt the size of a marble and she swooned into an orgasm that had her knees buckling and her breasts arching outward.

Luckily, he was able to catch her with his hands at her waist. "Good girl," he said against her ear. "What would the slave girl like now? To be spanked, or fucked?"

"Both," she said.

"Good answer," he said, but he pinched her buttock for her sauciness. Then he undid her handcuffs.

She was about to take off her harem attire and follow him to the bed where he'd already shucked his briefs, but he said, "Oh, no, I have more plans for that outfit. Don't you dare take it off yet."

"Yes, master," she said.

And he grinned.

Why do fools fall in love? . . .

Daniel was in male fantasy heaven. There wasn't a man alive who wouldn't be tempted by what Samantha was offering.

He lay flat on his back, his head propped on the pillows, and arranged Samantha astride his hard-on so her channel rode his rod. A perfect fit, without an actual fit. Then he removed her shirt so she wore only the harem pants. "Tilt forward, sweetheart," he said.

When she did, he leaned up and took one breast into his mouth, nipple, nipple ring and areola. And then he sucked rhythmically. She tried to pull back, but when he wouldn't release her, she began to thrust her pussy forward and back on his cock. He didn't know who was in greatest danger of a premature climax, although she'd already had one of those.

"Slow down," he urged, even as he gave equal treatment to the other breast. He was supremely pleased to see that her nipples had turned a rosy color, whether from the clips or his suckling, he couldn't be sure, but what a pretty picture she made!

"Slow down?" she said with consternation. "How about you hurry up."

"Follow orders, slave. I can still spank you."

"Hah! Promises, promises."

He did, in fact, smack her behind, which surprised both of them. He'd never done that before, and apparently she hadn't ever had it done to her, either. He liked it, and so hotdamnhallelujah did she.

"Come here," he said, tugging her by the nape so her lips almost touched his. And then he kissed her. And she kissed him back. The kisses were hungry, hungry, hungry. Deep, wet, noisy. They'd gone too far for gentle and coaxing.

Daniel had never been so turned on in all his life. There wasn't any part of his body that didn't feel stimulated. But he wanted to prolong this delicious anticipation. He tugged the harem pants down so that the waistband was under her butt in back and on her thighs in front. "Now, touch yourself. Show me how you like to be touched."

Her green eyes were misty with arousal, almost like she was drugged . . . drugged with excitement . . . drugged with wanting him. Now that was a compliment! -

She lifted her breasts from underneath and used her thumbs to flick the nipples. She caressed her breasts in wide circles, the nipples being abraded by the palms. Then she flicked the nipples some more. Her lips were parted and she made a soft moan deep in her throat.

"Lower now," he entreated, "and keep looking at me. Don't close your eyes."

He could tell she was embarrassed, but she was here to please him, and she complied. Then, while he held her gaze, her hand dipped lower, between her legs. Glancing down, he could see her middle finger stroking the slick folds. In fact, he could even see her swollen clitoris rising out of the wetness, just waiting to be touched. He'd love to take it into his mouth, but that would have to wait for later. They were both too excited to wait that long.

"Do it," he said then. "I can't hold out much longer, babe."

She knew exactly what he meant and touched the oversensitive bud, once, twice, then arched her back, pressing herself forward on the ridge of his cock, trying to ride him.

"No! Don't stop. I want to see."

She screamed out her ecstasy as she exploded into what had to be a rocking hard climax.

He couldn't wait. Rolling her over onto her back, he yanked the pants off and thrust into her so hard and deep that he moved them both halfway across the bed. Her inner muscles were contracting wildly around him, but still he needed to move. He stroked in and out, long and slow, but he couldn't maintain that pace, and he plowed into her with shorter, harder strokes. And, God bless nature, Samantha began another rise to orgasm, almost as if her body were sucking at his cock, trying to keep it inside when he was on the out strokes. He couldn't hold back any longer. With a roar of the most intense pleasure, he surged into her, farther than he had ever been before, and he could swear his cock was convulsing with its own separate orgasm.

He might have passed out for a minute, he knew she did, and, no, that wasn't a medical diagnosis. When she opened her eyes to gaze up at him, she had tears.

"Did I hurt you?"

She shook her head.

"What then? Did I do something you didn't like?"

She shook her head again.

"You're regretting making love with me?"

"No, of course not." She wiped her eyes with the edge of a sheet that was under her. "It's just that . . . well, I missed you so much. And you didn't call, and you didn't come to see me. With everything that's happened and then being crushed by your rejection, the tension has been growing. Ever since that one night, you changed. I thought we were going to make love again, but then . . . we didn't."

He frowned. "I never rejected you. You're the one who rejected me. You deliberately put yourself in danger, and you talked about one-night stands, and limits on how long we would be together."

"What? I don't think I ever said that, not precisely anyhow."

He put a hand on either side of her face and said, "I love you, Samantha."

"You do?"

"Yes, and I'm in it for the long haul. Doesn't matter if you don't love me now. You will, eventually, because I'm going to keep on trying to convince you to reciprocate. Hell, I have a thousand and one nights of fantasies to go."

"I thought I was the one who had to come up with a thousand and one fantasies."

"That works, too."

He was still cupping her face with his hands. There was so much he wanted to say and wasn't sure how much to say or how to say it. They had a lot to resolve, like whether they might marry someday, or have children, or stay in Louisiana, but none of that mattered in the scheme of the bigger issue. Love.

"You fool! I already love you, too," she said.

"You do?" he repeated the same words she'd said to him.

When realization hit at how misguided they had both

been, they smiled at each other. And then they kissed, gently, to seal their words.

It was a good thing Daniel was still inside her then because she said, "But don't let that stop you from convincing me. For the rest of our lives."

And that part of him that was quiescent inside her knew exactly what she meant. There was more than one way to pledge love between a man and a woman, and, in his opinion, this was the best way. And lucky him! He got a thousand and one chances to do it right.

Chapter Twenty-Nine

L et the games go on . . . and on . . . and on . . .

They made love again two more times that night, and Samantha couldn't be happier. Of course, she wouldn't be able to walk when she arrived at Tante Lulu's birthday party later tomorrow . . . rather, since it was past two a.m . . . but it was a small price to pay for the happiness she felt now.

"Are you smiling again?" he asked, turning his face to the side beside her. He was splayed out on his stomach, as depleted as she was . . . for the moment anyhow.

"Yes. I'm happy."

"Me, too," he said, sitting up and settling a pile of pillows behind them before pulling her over to rest her face on his chest. "Samantha?"

"Hmmm?"

"I promised myself that I wouldn't rush you, but . . . oh, hell, will you marry me?"

"Yes."

He held her away so he could see her face. "Just like that, yes?"

"Why not? I'm not a kid. I know what I want. Why wait? I'm excited to begin my life with you."

"I feel the same way. Man oh man, I can't believe what a difference there is in my life since this morning. Depression to euphoria."

"Same here. Even Emily was getting sick of being around me, I was so sad."

"Will Em be our flower pig?"

She laughed. "Why not?"

"I feel like I have a whole life of firsts with you to look forward to. First marriage. First honeymoon. First home together. First . . ."

As his words trailed off, she realized why he hesitated. It was the big elephant still in the room with them. Children.

"If you want children, Samantha, we'll have them. Or at least one. I'm afraid, but I'll find a way to overcome that. I know I can."

She kissed him and said, "We can talk about that later. Truly, we've been handed a second chance here. We could have very well lost each other without ever confessing our love. Let's savor that. Problems can be solved in the future."

He kissed her, then asked, "Will you go to Tante Lulu's birthday bash with me?"

"Yes."

"Do you have to go back to your house to get clothes?"

"No, I packed an overnight bag. And Lily Beth is there to take care of the animals."

"You were that sure of me?"

"No. Only hopeful."

"Speaking of bags . . ." He jumped out of the bed and went over to the dresser where he dug into the bag she'd brought upstairs with her. "Aha!" he said, holding up two objects. "What'll it be, baby? Balls or vibes?"

"Aren't you tired? Aren't men supposed to be incapable of doing it more than once or twice a night?"

"It's amazing how a little nap can energize a fellow." He held up the balls, in fact jangled them in the air, then held out the object in his other hand which began to Bzzz.

She laughed and chose both.

Hail, hail, the gang's all here . . .

Even though it was only four p.m. they were late for Tante Lulu's birthday bash at Luc LeDeux's luxurious home outside of Houma. When he'd seen Samantha come down the stairs at Bayou Rose in that strapless, green, satiny sundress, wearing those fuck-me black high heels with the little straps around her ankles, highlighting an ankle bracelet, he just had to show her how good she looked. Afterward, she'd had to repair her makeup, but did she look like she cared? Hell, no, and thank God!

He glanced at her and smiled. Little did she know, there was a sex flush on her chest and neck, and her lips looked kiss-bruised. She smiled back at him in a knowing way. He figured he looked as if he'd had his coals raked, too.

God, how he loved this woman! Wonder filled him, that he had fallen so hard, so fast for her. And even greater wonder, she returned the sentiment.

He linked his fingers with hers as they walked side by side. They'd had to park more than a block away because there were so many cars. Even though this was supposed to be family only, and a few friends, Luc had told them, when they called to say they would be late, that he had expected seventy-five people, but at least a hundred had shown up so far.

It always amazed Daniel that he had lived more than thirty years in Alaska without knowing he had such a large family here in Louisiana. Not just Tante Lulu, who was a great-great aunt (or something) to them all, but there was Luc and his wife Sylvie and their three daughters, Blanche, Camille, and Jeanette; René and his wife Valerie and their kids, Jude and Louise; Remy and his wife Rachel and their six adopted children, Rashid, Maggie, Andy, Evan, Stephan, and Suzanne, plus their natural-born son, Michael; John LeDeux and his wife Celine and their sons Etienne and Rob, and daughter Annie; Charmaine and her husband Rusty and their daughter Mary Lou; and LaVerne, Amelie, and Simone, whom he'd never met. And those were just the ones he knew about!

Missing from today's party would be Valcour LeDeux, the father of them all. He and Tante Lulu were archenemies. If he came within twenty yards of the old lady, she would probably shoot him in the balls with one of her pistols.

"You look good today," Samantha remarked, pulling him out of his reverie.

He glanced down at himself. He wore a navy sport coat over jeans with a blue dress shirt and tie. Samantha had helped him pick out the tie, which had given him more ideas. He was probably overdressed for a pool party, but he'd wanted to please Samantha, who'd said he should be as dressy as she was. *Did he mention her sexy dress with the cleavage down to here, and those fuck-me black strappy shoes?* She was wearing the nipple rings underneath, at his request. He'd probably have a half hard-on all night just thinking about them. She had sworn that she would buy him a penile ring in retaliation, but he didn't know about that!

Once they walked up the driveway and skirted around the house to the backyard, they saw that half the people were dressed like they were, while the rest were casual, or in swim attire, especially the younger ones. The patio was converted into a dance floor for the music that was already being played by René LeDeux's band, The Swamp Rats. Right now, it was a raucous version of "Diggy Diggy Lou," a Cajun song about a man in the doghouse again. People were scattered around the huge lawn on folding chairs and chaises, or standing about in small groups.

A tent had been erected for food which smelled delicious, even from here. Another tent held an enormous cake, which Tante Lulu would have insisted on making. It appeared to hold only a few candles. The old lady had always been cagey about her age.

Even though she had insisted on a "no gifts" policy, there was a pile of gaily wrapped presents, just the same. Instead, Luc had asked people to send little memories they had of Tante Lulu, and the enormous album that held those notes sat beside the cake. In fact, there were two big albums.

Samantha's grandfather Stanley Starr, who was a friend of Tante Lulu, came up and kissed his grand-daughter, asking her if she was all right following the whole Nick Coltrane business. Stanley Starr was a character. Aside from being an astute businessman, he dressed in true Southern gentleman style (despite his Scotch heritage and other family members' proclivity to kilts), complete with white suit, white hair, mustache, and goatee, and a straw hat, a la Colonel Sanders. They talked to him for several moments before an older lady,

Fleur Robicheaux, Charmaine's mother, called Stanley over. Fleur was more outrageous in attire and mannerisms than Charmaine, Daniel had learned soon after moving to Louisiana. *Can anyone say aging stripper?*

Tante Lulu saw them and waved. She was in rare form today, too, wearing a sleeveless pink dress, pink wedgie shoes, and even pink highlights in her gray hair. Her makeup defied description. Suffice it to say, there was pink lipstick. And pink dangly earrings. Samantha's Aunt Maire would love her!

When she got closer, Tante Lulu looked at them suspiciously, as if she knew what they'd been doing, all night and all morning, even when Edgar arrived to work on the cabin. Then Tante Lulu smiled widely and said, "Thank you, St. Jude! The thunderbolt has done its work again."

Samantha blushed, but he gloated. Let the old lady have her fun. He had the prize, and for that he could put up with her taking all the credit.

"Daniel, come with me. I jist remembered somethin'," Tante Lulu said.

He glanced at Samantha who was now talking with Charmaine, who matched her aunt in a matching pink dress and pink wedgie shoes, but on her they were hubba hubba hot (Yes, he'd been hanging around Tante Lulu too much and picking up her expressions.) He squeezed Samantha's hand and said, "I'll be right back. I'll bring some drinks with me."

She nodded and blew him a kiss, just to tease.

He blew one back, just to tease.

Tante Lulu watched the byplay and smiled as if she'd invented love. She took his arm and walked with him toward the house, speaking to family and guests along the way. When they went through the sliding glass doors into a den, she went straight for her big carry bag and pulled out a small box. "I finally remembered where I put yer Grandma Dolly's gift."

Daniel had begun to think there was no bequest. He took the box and eyed her suspiciously. "You knew all along where it was, didn't you?"

She eyed him back and said, "And you knew all along that I knew but dint want ya ta know that I knew."

Talking with her was like going around in circles. You always forgot where you started.

"Dolly Doucet always regretted the way her family treated yer mother, but her husband was a mean man. It was hard fer a woman in those days ta defy her husband."

That made Daniel feel a little better about that side of his family, but not by much. Hell, Valcour LeDeux on the other side was no better. Past history!

"So why are you giving me this now?"

"It's the right time."

He opened the box and saw a sparkling diamond ring in a gold setting. He frowned in confusion.

"It belonged to yer Great-Grandma Doucet. I figgered ya might wanna give it ta Samantha fer an engagement ring. 'Course it might be too old-fashioned fer her and the diamond too small, but ya kin allus have it reset and add some other stones."

"If I got a ring, what does Aaron get?"

"He gets a ring, too, but not till the time is right. His is from the other Great Grandma. She was a Chaussin."

Touched more than he thought he could be for a gift from a side of his family he'd never connected with, nor wanted to, he merely nodded, and said, "Thank you, Tante Lulu. Thank you very much."

"Thass all right, honey." She tugged him down and kissed his cheek. When he put a hand to his face, he said, "Dontcha be worryin' 'bout no lip print. I'm usin' the kissproof lipstick Charmaine gave me."

He didn't dare ask why.

When he went outside, he bypassed the drinks table, for now, and went up to Samantha, who was talking with

Aaron, who was looking good tonight, but then he always did, no matter what he wore. Tonight he was in rare form with a crisp blue, tapered dress shirt (Like minds and all that!) worn outside navy blue shorts with his bare feet tucked into Docksiders. Daniel saw several women eyeing Aaron already. The boy was going to get lucky tonight. If he wanted to. One never knew with Aaron.

Surreptitiously, Daniel slid the ring onto Samantha's finger while she was talking to Aaron. She felt the movement and glanced down, and then did a double take. "Daniel!" She raised her hand and gasped. Tears immediately filled her eyes. "Daniel!" she repeated.

"If you don't like it, you can have it reset. I know it's small, but—"

"It's perfect!" She wrapped her arms around his shoulders and gave him a big kiss, right in front of everyone.

He wasn't even embarrassed.

After that, Aaron said, "Congratulations, little brother," and yanked him into a bear hug, from which he wouldn't let go. Holding on tight to him, Aaron whispered against his ear, "Be happy!"

When he drew back, he could swear Aaron had tears in his eyes.

"Where did you get this?" Samantha asked. "You had no time to go shopping today."

"I'll explain later," he promised, wrapping his arm around her shoulder and tugging her closer to his side.

They moved through the crowd then, ate heartily from the array of gumbos, jambalayas, étouffées, rices, and various desserts, and even danced to a slow version of "Jolie Blon." Once again, he marveled at how well he and Samantha fit together. Especially with the high heels, they were almost the same height.

Later, they listened to Tante Lulu give a little speech after blowing out the few candles on her birthday cake.

"I wish everyone was as happy as I am t'day. I have been blessed with a long life filled with love and family." She raised her champagne glass and said, "Ta love and family!"

"To love and family!" everyone shouted, and drank. And drank.

It was a wonderful party, everyone agreed, but the best part for Daniel and Samantha was when they went home. And, yes, Bayou Rose was beginning to feel like home, to them both.

Epilogue

In the end, life is just one big fantasy . . .

The wedding of Samantha Starr and Daniel LeDeux did not take place until October. Both the bride and groom wanted the Bayou Rose mansion to be renovated enough to show off to company, although there still wasn't much furniture, and years of work yet to do. That didn't matter because the ceremony and reception would be held mostly outdoors in the rose garden. And, yes, thanks to a landscaper and much, much money, Bayou Rose once again had a rose garden to be proud of.

Daniel was working again as a doctor at the cancer center in Houma. He told everyone he had to return to medicine to pay for all the work on Bayou Rose.

What started out as a small family wedding ended up being the Wedding of the Year. With all of the Starr family and all of the LeDeuxs, along with some friends, the number of attendees exceeded a hundred.

Samantha wore an antique lace cocktail dress that probably cost as much as the fancy new range they'd bought for the remodeled kitchen. The stove had cost almost ten thousand dollars and did everything but sing Dixie.

Daniel and his ushers wore tuxedos. Black, even though white was preferred in the Southern weather.

Bruce Starr, dressed in a formal kilt (Who knew there was an informal kilt?) gave his daughter away. His ex-wife Colette, Samantha's mother, wearing enough jewelry to sink a ship, came all the way from France with her latest boy toy, Armand.

Melanie Yutu . . . Aunt Mel . . . arrived a few days ago from Alaska and was playing the role of "mother" of the groom. She hadn't decided about moving to Louisiana yet, but she was staying with Tante Lulu in her little bayou cottage for a few weeks. That would either convince her to stay or run for the hills . . . uh, glaciers. Unlike Colette, the only jewelry Aunt Mel wore was half of a silver heart on a chain. The other half had been buried with Claire Doucet.

Molly Gillotte, who had recently been released from the hospital following a successful bone marrow transplant, was flower girl, bumping out Emily for the honor. Molly and her three siblings were living in an expanded cabin on the Bayou Rose estate with their devoted father, Edgar. They were babysitting Samantha's pets during the wedding. Five of the cabins had been renovated so far, all currently filled with families of children with cancer.

Aaron LeDeux was, of course, his brother's best man. There was much speculation during the reception about the rumored secret night life of his twin. One person said that she heard he was dating a stripper. Another person said that she heard he was stripping himself. Another said he was making nightly copter flights back and forth to the oil rigs, taking the roughnecks to the New Orleans French Quarter. Someone even conjectured that he was studying to be a priest.

Daniel's ushers were the rest of the LeDeux brothers: Luc, René, Remy, and John, and Angus Starr. Samantha's bridal party included Tante Lulu, Charmaine, Rachel, Celine, and Valerie, along with Lily Beth who'd recently delivered a beautiful little Southern belle, Marie Fontenot.

Rashid LeDeux, one of Remy's adopted sons, a music prodigy who was a student at Juilliard, played the wedding march on a piano which had been brought in for the occasion. The music for the reception came from The Swamp Rats, traditional Cajun classic, along with a few Barry Manilow ballads, in honor of Aunt Mel and Daniel's mother. Especially appropriate, some said, was the bridal dance song, "It's a Miracle."

The couple planned to honeymoon in Alaska, of all places, but they would make their home in the Bayou Rose mansion. Aaron had moved permanently into the *garconniére* apartment, or as permanently as anything Aaron did.

Later, Tante Lulu was heard to speculate over where the thunderbolt would hit next. Would it be Aaron LeDeux, who was doing a shocking dirty dance with Luc's oldest daughter? Well, not so shocking compared to what Tee-John was doing with his wife, Celine. That boy could dance!

Or maybe Simone LeDeux, who had flown in from Chicago for the wedding. A real Cajun beauty, that one was, but mysterious. With a rather haunted look in her dark eyes. There was a secret there that Tante Lulu vowed to uncover.

The party went on into the wee hours, but the bride and groom slipped off to spend their wedding night at a motel recommended by Charmaine Lanier and her blushing husband Rusty. Its best feature was the vibrating bed.

Later that night, Samantha told her new husband that she was gifting him the gold bullion.

"Isn't that a rather extravagant wedding gift?"

"It will do more good renovating Bayou Rose than sitting in a bank vault. Plus, we should set up a foundation to run the cancer housing operation."

Daniel rolled his eyes. He'd never intended his charitable giving to go beyond one cabin and one father. But he would do anything to please his wife.

His gift to her was much less valuable. A book. *A 1,001 Sexual Fantasies.* He figured they'd already tried out sixteen of them. He turned to one page and looked at her.

"Isn't that a bit . . . dangerous?" she asked.

"Trust me, I'm a doctor," he said with a wink.

"Hmmm. What do you say we try for Number Seventeen, too?"

"I thought you'd never ask."

Samantha was wearing an old time nurse's outfit, even though Daniel had never seen a nurse's uniform that was so short her thong underwear was exposed. Not that Daniel was complaining. Daniel was dressed as a cowboy.

"Yee-haw!" and "Whatever you say, Doctor!" could be heard at a motel down the bayou that night, accompanied by much laughter. Who knew a horse could vibrate? But that was going to be the best part of their marriage, they promised each other. Love and laughter.

Reader Letter

Dear Readers:

Finally, Daniel LeDeux has had a chance to tell his story. Doesn't it seem like forever since he first came on the scene? I like to think the burned-out pediatric oncolo gist is like a fine wine, he gets better with age.

Speaking of age, you will notice that I rarely mention ages in this book. For those who have read the other books in this Cajun series, if you go by the year of first publication, Daniel and his twin Aaron would have to be in their forties by now. Instead, I have said that they are an ambiguous thirty-something. For those who are a stickler for details, let's pretend this book came out before *So Into You* and *Snow on the Bayou*. Either way, *The Cajun Doctor* should stand on its own.

Another age issue . . . the ageless Tante Lulu. I have promised that the outrageous old lady will never die in any of my books, and that is still true. She has always been cagey about her age. So, maybe she'll just fool us all.

And, by the way, keep in mind that the very first book in the Cajun series is still available new (and updated and reissued with a new cover). *The Love Potion* is Lucien LeDeux's story and the very first place/time that Tante Lulu makes an appearance. She seemed well into senior citizenry, even back then. But again, only Tante Lulu knows her real age.

Of course, now that Daniel has told his story, his twin Aaron will get his chance. Then, too, I think the mysterious Simone LeDeux warrants a closer look. And Charmaine LeDeux's daughter, Mary Lou Lanier, has got to be special. Will she be as outrageous as her mother (Can anyone say born again virgin?) and Tante Lulu (still belly dancing after all these years), or as good-looking as her father, Cajun cowboy Raoul "Rusty" Lanier, so handsome women trip over themselves when he walks down the street? Then there are the grown-up children of the original Cajun brothers: football pro Andy LeDeux, music prodigy Rash LeDeux, that wild Etienne LeDeux, etc., etc.

And there are historicals and time travels and other genres of books to write yet. Surely, there have to be more Viking Navy SEALs, for example. Or how about the other sons of Tykir and Alinor? Or Alrek, the clumsy Viking? Or Jamie the Scots Viking? So many characters with stories yet to tell!

I love to hear from readers and can be reached on my website, www.sandrahill.net, by email at shill733@aol.com, or on my Facebook page at SandraHillAuthor. As always, I wish you smiles in your reading.

Sandra Hill

SHRIMP GUMBO

INGREDIENTS:

2 cups diced tomatoes with juice
4 cups water or broth (shrimp, crawfish, chicken,
   whatever)
1/2 cup chopped celery
1/2 cup chopped onion
1/2 cup chopped green pepper
2 cloves minced garlic
2 cups cooked, boneless chicken (see below)
1/2-3/4 cooked shrimp
1/2-3/4 cup andouille sausage (see below)
1 1/2–2 cups okra (sliced, crosswise)
1/2 cup bacon fat (or oil) plus two tsp.
1/2 cup flour
2 tsp. Cajun seasoning (or more, to taste)
Dash of tabasco (or more to taste)
Salt and pepper, to taste
2–4 cups of cooked white rice

DIRECTIONS:

Using the flour and 1/2 cup of fat, start making a dark
chocolate colored roux, a staple of much Cajun cooking.
It can take up to 45 minutes to get the rue just right. A

roux must be stirred and watched constantly so it doesn't burn. This can be set aside when done.

In the meantime, use the excess two tbsp. of grease to brown the boneless chicken breasts which have been cut into large chunks and the sausage, and to sauté the celery, onion, and green pepper (called the Holy Trinity of Cajun cooking). Toss in the garlic as well. After the chicken and sausage have been drained of fat, cut the sausage diagonally into ¹/₂–³/₄ inch slices.

Put this entire mixture into a large pot filled with the water and tomatoes. Add the okra, which has also been sliced diagonally. Season with salt, pepper, Cajun seasoning, and tabasco. Bring it to a boil, then reduce the heat and slowly stir in the roux, if it is ready. Now, simmer, covered, for at least two hours. Add the shrimp near the end (the last half hour). Otherwise, it can get rubbery.

Turn on some rowdy Cajun music, pour several glasses of sweet tea and serve the gumbo over white rice with some good bread. Serves six to eight people, and it's even better warmed up the next day, if you have any left. (Enjoy!)

NOTE:

Like all cooking, the measurements are subject to individual tastes. Add more, or less, shrimp, chicken, and sausage, if you prefer. Same goes for okra, which is not a huge favorite of many people, but it is quite palatable in this Cajun "stew."

Many recipes call for filé (sassafrass) to be added near the end as an additional thickener, but it can be tricky and go slimy if not handled properly. Also, it's not readily available in some markets.

If the bacon fat strikes you as odd, it's an old-fashioned practice to always save the excess fat when frying bacon. It can be used as a better substitute for oil or butter in many recipes.

Keep reading for a sneak peek at
Sandra Hill's next sizzling Cajun romance

CAJUN CRAZY

Coming December 2017

Chapter One

Between the cheats . . .

Simone LeDeux replayed the voicemail from her mother, Adelaide Daigle, for the second time as she stood at the kitchen counter of her Chicago apartment, eating a cheese sandwich on toast with a glass of cold sweet tea. She always kept homemade sweet tea in her fridge, like the good Cajun girl she no longer was. As for food, whatever!

It was midnight, and Simone had just ended her shift as a detective with the Chicago P.D. After her grueling night . . . images of a pre-teen girl overdosing came to mind . . . her mother's voice was soothing to her bruised senses. Hard to believe after the years of strife between the two of them, most of it ignited by Simone, who'd given "difficult child" new meaning.

She had to smile at the length of the message. Her mother had no concept of electronic devices. There had been a few times when her long messages . . . as much as five minutes . . . had caused her mailbox to shut down.

Simone also smiled at the familiarity of her mother's deep southern accent. She'd lost most of hers, except for an occasional lapse into a Cajunism, such as, "Holy Crawfish!" Or the traditional, *"Mon Dieu!"*

However, even as she welcomed her mother's call, she felt a shiver of alarm at the synchronicity of her words. The timing was, at the least, a coincidence. Was God, or the powers that be, conspiring to draw her back to the bayou . . . her worst nightmare? Or was it just Cajun mothers who had this instinct for sensing when their daughters were in need of help, even if only a hug?

> *"Hi, honey:*
>
> *I haven't heard from ya since las' week. Did ya kick that no-good Jack Daltry out on his cheatin' be-hind, lak I tol' ya to?"*

"Yes, Mama, Jack is history," Simone replied out loud to her cat, Scarlett, who was enjoying the remnants of the unpalatable sandwich. Talking to her cat was nothing new, but this time, it was an indication of her exhaustion and, yes, disgust, at once again being duped by a man she trusted. Honest to goodness! One year and thirteen days wasted!

> *"Heavens ta horseradish, girl, how ya manage ta attract so many losers is beyond me, and all of them from Loo-zee-anna? Even when ya move ta Chee-cah-go, ya gotta latch onto a slow-drawlin', southern man."*

She couldn't argue with that. There was something about a man who could say "darlin'" in a husky, slow croon that could make any girl melt. Especially her, with her southern roots. Face it, she was a magnet for a Louisiana man, even if he'd lived in Chicago for almost fifteen years, as Jack Daltry had. "World class architect, low class loser," she muttered.

Scarlett stretched with disinterest, expressing her boredom, as only a cat could, pretty much saying, "Man problems again! Yada, yada, yada. You oughta be fixed, like me." The cat went off to sleep on Simone's bed, which was forbidden. The cat had heard her man complaints before. Lots of times!

> *"Are ya Cajun crazy, or sumpin'? I remember the first time I called ya Cajun crazy. It was when ya were fourteen years old and ya fell head-over-hiney in love with that pimple-faced hell-raiser Mike Comeaux, jist 'cause he had that devilish Cajun grin . . . and a pirogue with a motor.*
>
> *I talked ta Tante Lulu yes'ti'day an' she said some wimmen jist got bayou mud in their eyes when it comes ta a Cajun man who's hotter'n a goat's behind in a pepper patch, 'specially when they're in the middle of a stretch of hormone hot-cha-chas. I tol' her ya were smarter'n that, bein' a po-lice detective an' all, but mebbe she's right.*
>
> *Me? I got a thing fer men with a mustache, as ya know. But thass another story. Ha, ha, ha!"*

Yep, a billy goat's butt. She'd have to remember that one when the hot-cha-cha hormones hit her next time. Which would be NEVER AGAIN.

Her mother was right, though. You'd think Simone would have learned her lesson by now. She'd been married and divorced three times (*well, one of them was an annulment after one week, don't ask!*), and she'd been jilted, robbed, humiliated, punked, and seduced by more men than one woman should have in her twenty-nine-and-a-half years. With a college degree and eight years in police work, she should have more sense.

> "*Anyways, I went ta the bone doctah t'day, and he said I gotta lose thirty pounds and I gotta have two new knees, lessen I wanna spend my las' years in a wheelchair.*"

What? This sounded serious.

> "*I ain't that old yet! I'm only fifty. I would lak ta have them new knees, though. But, nope, cain't do it, not 'cause I cain't lose the weight, please God, but the doctah sez I gotta have someone at home with me fer three months of out-patient rehab after I'm released from the hospital. My insurance won't cover no three months in a rehab hospital. Oh, well.*

> *I'm gonna buy the 'Skinny Girls' exercise video t'morrow or sign up fer the 'Prayers Fer Pounds' program at Our Lady of the Bayou Church.*"

Uh-oh! Was her mother pitching a guilt trip her way? Come home and help her, live with her once again in the Pearly Gates Heavenly Trailer Park on Bayou Black, best known as The Gates? *Me and Mom as roomies? Horror of horrors!*

Wait . . . wasn't it a timely coincidence that this all came up just when she'd ended another relationship?

But, no, even her mother wasn't devious enough to do that. The situation must be dire. Last time she'd been home, her mother had walked with a decided limp, and could only go short distances before sitting down, due to the bad knees and her excess weight. All of which hampered her duties, even back then, as a longtime waitress at Crawfish Daddy's restaurant.

And thirty pounds was a gross underestimation, in her opinion. Her mother had been plump as long as Simone could remember, but she hid it well, being so tall and big-boned. Like all the women in her family, including Simone, darn it, who were always fighting diets, and the genetic big butt bane. Thank the exercise gods for jogging and daily rounds of tush crunches!

> *"Thass 'bout all that's new here. I hear the pingin' noise. I think it mean it's time fer me ta shut up. Why doan ya get a bigger mailbox?*
>
> *Call me, sweetie, and doan be cryin' no more tears over that Jack Daltry. I'll be prayin' fer ya. Kiss, kiss!"*

Simone yawned widely. She would call her mother in the morning.

As for Jack Daltry, Chicago architect, but born and bred in Baton Rouge . . . Simone was done crying. In fact, from the moment she'd discovered his secret life, she'd been more embarrassed than hurt. Okay, she'd been hurt too. Badly. She'd been dumb enough to think Jack was "the one." Which was ridiculous for a twenty-nine-and-a-half-year-old woman. When would girls stop looking for "the one," and settle for the "not so bad"?

All Simone could do now was repeat an old joke that had become her motto, or should be. George Strait might wail about "All My Exes Come from Texas," but Simone would modify that to, "All My Losers Come from Loozee-anna."

She was thinking about having it tattooed on her butt, which was big enough.

From the mouths of babes . . .

Adam Lanier was driving his daughter Mary Sue, or "Maisie," to her kindergarten class at Our Lady of the Bayou School. Wending his Harley through the early morning traffic, with Maisie riding pillion behind him, he barely noticed the people who gave them double takes, not so much because of their mode of transportation, but him in a business suit with biker boots, and his little Mini-me with her arms wrapped around him, wearing a tee-shirt and skinny jeans tucked into her own tiny boots. (Yes, they made skinny jeans for five-year-olds! And teeny tiny bustiers for tykes who were a decade or so away from having any bust to speak of. But that was another story.)

After dropping off the kid, he would go to his Houma office, LeDeux & Lanier, Esquire, where he'd recently formed a partnership with Lucien LeDeux, the half-brother of his cousin Rusty Lanier's wife, Charmaine. A convoluted kinship by marriage that would have the average person crossing their eyes with confusion, but was typical of the bayou network of families.

He and Maisie had moved from New Orleans to Bayou Black six months ago, and it was the best decision Adam had ever made. At least, he hoped so. He'd made a name for himself in the Crescent City DA's office as a sometimes outrageous, almost always winning, prosecutor. The news media had loved him, and he played the image for his own purposes.

This was his first venture into private practice and a switch from indicting to defending. But it was a good match, working with Luc, who had an equal or more outrageous reputation for courtroom antics . . . uh, skills. Luc wasn't known as the "Swamp Solicitor" for nothing. Maybe Adam would become known as the Bayou Barrister. Or something.

Bottom line: the law was a game he'd learned to play, well. Didn't matter if it was in the city or in a Cajun courtroom.

Stopping for a red light with the cycle idling, he glanced over his shoulder and inquired with supposed casualness, "So, Maisie Daisy, ya settlin' in okay?"

"Oh, Daddy, stop worryin'," she advised in her too-old-for-her-five-years voice. "I'm fine. 'Specially since PawPaw came ta live with us. He makes better pancakes than you."

He laughed. His father made everything better than he did. Adam was one of the best lawyers in the state, hands down. And the best single parent he could be. But a cook, Adam was not. Nor a housekeeper. And reliable babysitters to hold down the fort while he worked were hard to find. Thus, his finally throwing in the towel and asking his widowed father, Jules Lanier, to move here from northern Louisiana.

Who would have imagined that a self-proclaimed legal (and personal, truth to tell) hell-raiser like himself, at the ripe old age of thirty-five, would be back to living with his father, who'd raised him pretty much alone after Adam's mother died in a car accident when he'd been only seven years old? But then, who would have imagined that Adam's wife Hannah would die of a brain tumor, diagnosed too late for treatment? She been only twenty-eight. That had been two years ago, and like the old cliché said, life went on.

"Thank you for taking off the ballerina tutu," he said. His dainty daughter, with her mass of black corkscrew curls, liked to pick her own attire, and if left to her own devices, it would have involved girly frills and ruffles, sometimes inappropriate-for-her-age choices. Like the tutu that showed her Snow White panties when she bent over.

He would be glad next year when Maisie moved into first grade where school uniforms were required. He didn't doubt for one minute that Maisie would find a way to glam up the staid plaid skirts and white blouses.

"Ya didn't give me any choice, Daddy," she pointed out, "but don't worry. I'm still wearin' my sparkle shirt."

She was, indeed, wearing a tiny red tee shirt that proclaimed in silver letters, "I'm Hot. Live With It." A gift from his brother Dave who was an Army captain serving in Afghanistan.

"Besides, you tol' me you would pick me up on the Harley after school if I changed. That way PawPaw kin get a haircut and a mustache trim soz he kin go ta the casino t'night with Tante Lulu and Addie Daigle."

The imp loved riding pillion on his classic motorcycle, and his father loved to gamble. The nickle slots or Poor Man Craps (a low minimum dice game). He guessed there were worse things than a bikeress-in-training and a senior citizen with a lust for the Big Payoff.

"Do you think Tante Lulu and Addie Daigle are Paw-Paw's girlfriends? Kin a man have more than one girl-friend? What's hanky panky? Thass what PawPaw said this mornin' . . . he has ta get his hanky panky on before his hanky gets rusted out. He was talkin' ta Uncle Dave. How can a hanky get rusty? Is your hanky rusty, Daddy?"

What could Adam say to that?

The light changed, thank God, and he went forward.